BY KATE SCHATZ

Rid of Me: A Story

Rad American Women A–Z

Rad Women Worldwide

My Rad Life: A Journal

Rad Girls Can

Rad American History A–Z

Do the Work!: An Antiracist Activity Book
(co-authored with W. Kamau Bell)

Where the Girls Were

Where the Girls Were

Where the Girls Were

A Novel

Kate Schatz

THE DIAL PRESS
New York

The Dial Press
An imprint of Random House
A division of Penguin Random House LLC
1745 Broadway, New York, NY 10019
randomhousebooks.com
penguinrandomhouse.com

Library of Congress Cataloging-in-Publication Data
Names: Schatz, Kate author
Title: Where the girls were: a novel / Kate Schatz.
Description: First edition. | New York, NY: The Dial Press, 2026.
Identifiers: LCCN 2025032771 (print) | LCCN 2025032772 (ebook) |
ISBN 9780593736975 hardcover acid-free paper |
ISBN 9780593736999 ebook
Subjects: LCGFT: Fiction | Social problem fiction | Novels
Classification: LCC PS3619.C3326 W47 2026 (print) |
LCC PS3619.C3326 (ebook)
LC record available at https://lccn.loc.gov/2025032771
LC ebook record available at https://lccn.loc.gov/2025032772

Printed in the United States of America

1st Printing

First Edition

BOOK TEAM: Production editor: Robert Siek • Managing editor:
Rebecca Berlant • Production manager: Sandra Sjursen • Copy editor:
Scott Heim • Proofreaders: Pam Rehm, JoAnna Kremer, and Tess Rossi

The authorized representative in the EU for product
safety and compliance is Penguin Random House Ireland,
Morrison Chambers, 32 Nassau Street, Dublin D02 YH68, Ireland.
https://eu-contact.penguin.ie

For my mother

I was supposed to be having the time of my life.
—SYLVIA PLATH, *The Bell Jar*

You're sad and you're sorry, but you're not ashamed
Little Green, have a happy ending
—JONI MITCHELL, "Little Green"

Whatever is unnamed, undepicted in images,
whatever is omitted from biography, censored in
collections of letters, whatever is misnamed as
something else, made difficult-to-come-by,
whatever is buried in the memory by the collapse
of meaning under an inadequate or lying
language—this will become, not merely
unspoken, but unspeakable.
—ADRIENNE RICH, *On Lies, Secrets, and Silence*

Where the Girls Were

Prologue

*B*aker never wanted the full-length mirror that hangs on the back of her bedroom door, but her mother feels that it's important. A young woman should know what she looks like.

One day she'd come home from school, hot and sweaty after sixth period gym class, and she'd closed her door, stripped off her clothes, and there it was. It startled her, seeing herself reflected like that.

She'd promptly covered the mirror, hanging her orange terry cloth robe from the hook above it. But every so often, when the robe was in the wash or on her body or in a damp heap on the floor, she'd catch a glimpse of herself. Mostly she'd look away quick, self-conscious. But a few times she'd smiled, given the girl in the mirror a little wave. Once she stuck out her tongue and laughed. Another time, she blew herself a kiss.

But that was all before. The robe's been hanging there, untouched, for over a month, blocking her view. Until now. She lifts it from the hook and drops it on the floor. There she is. She reaches under her blouse and runs her finger under the waistband of her navy blue skirt until she finds the silver safety pin that holds it all together, spanning the gap between the button and the buttonhole. As she unclasps the pin, her finger slips, and she pricks the soft slope of her waist. She gasps and pushes hard on the wound. The skirt falls to the floor, next to the robe. Then she pulls her shirt up over her head and adds it to the pile.

Her eyes drop down to the carpet beneath her feet. Multicolored horizontal stripes, jewel tones that blend together—it would be the perfect pattern for someone who really makes a mess, someone who spills their dinner, drops their drinks. That's not her. She vacuums frequently. Her room is tidy. And the only mess she's made is the one she's in.

She lets her eyes creep to the bottom of the mirror. There are the toes she just stared down at, reflected back to her. She wiggles them.

They look fine. Still ten. They all work.

It's okay. I look okay.

Past the toes, to the rest of the feet. She can't tell whether they look any different, but she knows how they felt all week. Swelling up around the thin strap on her shoes like rising dough. She went to slip on her Keds for gym class, and they no longer fit right. She had to untie them.

Then she looks at her ankles. She catches her breath.

This can't be me.

But it has to be. She looks at the room reflected behind her. She knows every inch of it, the little cracks along the baseboards and the chip in the upper-right corner of the windowpane. The wallpaper, floral, her mother's choice when she was a baby. Tender leaves, pink buds, thorny vines.

That's her bed, neatly made, sheets printed with little yellow daisies, two fat pillows tucked under the lavender chenille bedspread. The sky blue quilt that her Nana Anne sewed, folded at the foot of the bed. She's been rubbing its soft frayed border between her fingers since she was so little. *One day you'll rub right through it!* her mother would say. Above the bed is the canopy: white with a ruffle running around it, also her mother's choice, but she still loves to look up at it.

That's her nightstand stacked with books, novel upon novel and several slim volumes of poetry. That's the reading lamp with the bulb that gets too hot. That's her algebra textbook on the bed, and the copy of the most recent edition of *Twentieth Century Bookkeeping and Accounting* that her father gave her to review. That's her slide ruler. That's the pencil case she sewed in Home Ec last spring, the only class she ever got a B in. She still regrets that unfair assignment. Who *needs* to know how to make meringue? It's a waste of eggs.

That's her dresser, tall and painted white. On top is the piggy bank that must hold over a hundred dollars by now. The Eiffel Tower snow globe that her uncle brought back from France when he was stationed overseas.

That's her record player, *Blonde on Blonde* spinning and spinning, the needle at the end. She should turn it over.

That's her desk. Her calendar, her neat handwriting inside the tiny boxes of days. Her medals and awards—several from Girl Scouts, a plaque for her community service, the small trophy she won at the Speech and Debate regional competition last year. Her typewriter: a Smith Corona Sterling, pale yellow. A birthday present. A prized possession. Sitting in the carriage is a white piece of paper with a few lines typed, then struck. The last page of the abandoned draft of her editorial against the Vietnam War. She'd never missed a deadline before, but now it's just too late. And she's too tired.

That's a framed photograph of her mother when she was young, a glamorous dancer.

That's Wiley's bandanna, folded into a tiny square on the edge of her dresser. The one he gave her when they walked through Golden Gate Park. The one she kept under her pillow until that Valentine's party but still can't bring herself to throw away.

And that's her journal, the one she used to write in every day. She hasn't touched it for months.

Her eyes dart back to the mirror. She has her mother's legs now; that's what people tell her. She used to feel like a weird shorebird, a torso plopped on two too-long sticks. But these past few years, they've filled out just enough. She was fourteen when a man on the street called *Nice gams!* She asked what "gams" meant, and her mother just laughed.

So long and slim, says Aunt Stella with envy. *Dancer's legs.*

They're still her legs: those are her shins, a pale thin scar on the left one from a deep scrape during a tree climb long ago. And those are her knees—funny-looking, she's always thought—but really, all knees are funny-looking.

Her thighs, though. They've always been so twiggy, and now they're just a bit . . . fuller. And her hips. They exist now. They're not huge, not like *real* hips, but they're more than what's usually there.

Her stomach churns.

She left her underwear on—this is difficult enough; she would never just stand here *naked*—and she can see how the soft white cotton pulls across her low belly, the zone that's always been so flat it was nearly concave. Now she's soft. Now there's something.

Underneath the underwear. The dark mound peeks through the fabric, warm, a little itchy. She refuses to look.

Her hands fly to her middle on instinct, wanting to hide it from view. But just as quick as she lifts them, she lets them drop. She doesn't want to touch it. She's terrified of what she'll feel. So she lets her hands rest at her newly wide hips while her eyes make their way to her chest. It's undeniable. She looks like someone else. Her breasts used to just point out from her body, like little ice cream cones, but now they have a rounded, weighted bottom. She lifts her hands and cups each one. They're substantial. And *sore.* Her once-pale nipples are round and dark. Ripe fruit heavy on a tree.

A breeze comes in through the open window. It's 5:30 P.M. She takes a deep breath to try to stop the tears from coming, and she is overpowered by aroma. The jasmine blooming outside, the wisteria vining along the front of the house. She doesn't know how it's possible, but she can smell the shaving cream that sits on the counter next to the sink in her father's bathroom, his Old Spice cologne, the Ivory soap in the silver dish. The Mr. Clean under the sink, the talcum powder in the pink plastic container. Actually, she can smell the entire house, as if her nose has left her face and gone on a tour. The Palmolive suds in the plastic bin in the kitchen sink where the day's dishes sit soaking, waiting for her mother. The jar of bacon grease next to the stove, left over from breakfast; the ripe oranges in the bowl on the kitchen table; the half-drunk martini with three green olives. The cigarette smoke and the acrid ashtrays. The chlorine in the pool, the wet cement around it. Furniture polish, potpourri with dried roses, the geraniums out back and the laundry detergent and someone barbequing down the block.

She takes another deep breath and is struck by one more scent that she suspects might be her own. She lifts her left arm and peers down, flaring her nostrils and sniffing just the tiniest bit. She almost gags at her own odor, her musky, sour human smell.

It's a Thursday in April. It's 1968. She is seventeen years old. And it's been months since she last bled.

Baker, she says to herself. *You're—*

The word won't form. She tries again.

You're—

She hears the front door open, then close. Footsteps in the hall.

Stupid. You're so, so stupid.

Her mother is calling her name.

"Baker! The mail is here!"

You've ruined everything.

"You have a letter! Come quick!"

What the hell are you going to do?

Part I

*T*t's 7:00 P.M. on New Year's Eve when May calls Baker to tell her she'll pick her up in an hour. *Just make something up. Tell your mom we'll be hanging out at my place,* May coos with convincing confidence. *Trust me, you don't want to miss this concert. It's New Year's, cuz. Time to live a little!*

A new year, Baker tells herself. *Time to get out and grow up.*

The dealership calendar on the wall is already flipped to January. *1968* is printed in big block letters above a photo of a sleek baby blue Galaxie 500, two-door, hardtop, the exact same one sitting out front in the driveway, on loan to her father from the lot since its release in September. The neighbors love it. Baker's cousins keep plotting to steal the keys.

The party is in full swing on the patio out back and the sounds fill the house, muffled but familiar—men talking, women laughing, glasses clinking, record playing. *Nineteen sixty-eight.* The number feels sharp and bright, confident and decisive. Your mouth smiles when you say it. Full of potential and ready for change.

When the patio door slides open, the party rushes in like the tide: the smoke from the cigarettes, the sweet citronella from the burning tiki torches, the tinkling sounds of the Arthur Lyman Orchestra record. The soft shuffle of her mother's feet, size eight, narrow, scuffing across the low-pile carpet, never clomping. Baker bites her tongue. She should be rehearsing her story.

Rose Phillips looks great. She always does. Her green caftan spins out around her fit frame like a tropical flower. Her freshly styled hair frames her face in soft waves, just brushing her jaw. A long Winston in one hand, an empty champagne bucket in the other, a hostess's smile on her face. She looks at her daughter and leans in close.

"Well? Are you going to make an appearance, or is there something more exciting here on this kitchen wall?"

"I'm sorry, Mother, I was on the phone. May called."

"Oh, May. Delightful." Rose opens the refrigerator and pulls out a tray of hors d'oeuvres. She pops a salami roll into her mouth. "And what kind of psychedelic mess is your cousin getting into tonight?"

"It's not like that, at least not tonight." Baker places a hand on the Formica countertop, bracing herself. Her heart races as she gathers the courage to lie to her mother. "She's going to a concert. And I'd like to join her."

"Mm-hmm." Rose pulls a box of Ritz Crackers from the cupboard and begins fanning them out on the tray next to the cheese slices and meat roll-ups. "And where is this concert?"

"San Francisco." Baker shrugs, attempting casual. "It'll be . . . mellow."

Rose laughs her tinkly party-laugh. "Your cousin is anything *but* mellow."

"I think it's, like, folk music."

"Folk. Music." Rose delivers each word staccato. "On New Year's Eve. In San Francisco. With *May.*"

Baker pulls her shoulders back, lifts her chin, sucks her navel back toward her spine. Her bare feet on the kitchen floor, also size eight, also narrow. She's taller than her mother now, no longer gazing up at her face. Nearly an adult. Nearly a woman.

"It's a special occasion. And, besides, I graduate in six months."

"Don't remind me!" Rose puts her hands over her ears, as if she can't bear to hear it.

"And then I can do whatever I want!" Baker grins and Rose raises an eyebrow, then laughs.

"Oh, is that how it works, my clever child?" When Rose laughs,

Baker can see so clearly that they have the exact same teeth. Straight and white and just a little too crowded. Rose eats a Ritz and holds one out to Baker, who shakes her head and wrinkles her nose.

"May's on her way to pick me up. She'll be here in an hour." Rose raises an eyebrow, and that's all it takes for Baker to falter slightly, to remember who's in charge. "I mean, if it's okay with you."

Voices call out from the patio: *Where's the hostess? Who's got my drink?* Gerald's deep voice hollers *Rose, the natives are restless!* Rose sucks on her cigarette and gazes at her daughter. Baker feels her mother's eyes on her—assessing, judging—and crosses her arms, self-conscious of her lanky, changing body. Her taut breasts. Her once-chubby cheeks that now hang on sharp cheekbones.

"I do like your hair like this," Rose says. Baker's hand flies to her head, patting the straight shiny sheet that she brushes one hundred times each night. "It's nice to see your hair out of that same old ponytail. I wish you'd wear some lipstick, though, and a little rouge. Instead of all that smudgy eye junk." Baker blushes in spite of herself. "All those brains, and now beauty, too? You're really something else. We're so proud."

"Because I brushed my hair?"

"Because you're Elizabeth Baker Phillips! The best and the brightest! The valedictorian!"

"That's not official yet, Mother."

"Pish posh, what are they waiting for? You're exceptional, and everyone knows it! Now go get dressed. You can't go to a concert in the city on New Year's Eve wearing that. Put on that nice green dress that you refused to wear on Christmas. And bring the *good* coat."

"I can go?"

"Don't question me! I'm in a wonderful mood, and besides." Rose takes Baker's hand in hers and squeezes. Her long, slender fingers are cool and soft, identical to Baker's but with more lines, more texture, more years coursing through the blue-green veins. "Your father and I trust you."

The pit that has been hovering somewhere in Baker's abdomen drops hard and fast. It's a familiar feeling: the weight of expectation. The same pit she felt at age eleven, when they decided to have her skip sixth grade and go straight to junior high. The pit she's always felt when she hears her parents' late-night arguments and knows exactly why they're both so worried. When she does her own private mathematics: the sum of what she dreams of doing with her life, divided by what's expected of her. When she's not in control of her surroundings, when she feels the eyes of boys and men along her body and can't figure out why she hates and loves it at the same damn time.

"It's okay to put down the books and have a little fun!" Rose opens the icebox and pulls out two frosty glass bottles. Baker notes the labels, black and gold, the words all in French. She doesn't know exactly how much that champagne costs, but she knows it's more than they can afford. And all that sophisticated cheese, the cured meats from the fancy delicatessen in North Beach. And the olives— the imported Italian kind that come floating in glass jars with bay leaves and peppercorns, not the regular black ones in cans that the kids stick on their fingers. Those aren't cheap. Her mind immediately begins to calculate what Rose must have spent to put up a spread like this. She knows what's in the accounts right now—she did the books just last week, staying up past ten on a school night to finish.

She shoots her mother a look and folds her arms. "This party doesn't look 'little.'"

Rose's voice drops to a hiss. "I got the wine on sale, and Mr. Villa gave me a discount on the food in exchange for those dance lessons I did for his daughter." Baker relaxes a little. Always figuring out a fix—classic Rose. "There are nearly fifty people out there, including your father's colleagues. They expect nothing short of excellence. And that," Rose says, popping the cork, "is what we provide."

Rose places two of great-grandma Mary's crystal glasses onto the counter. She pours herself a glass, then a few inches of the pale yellow liquid for Baker, who wonders how on earth a bottle of fermented, fizzy grape juice could possibly be worth that much money.

"Now raise your glass and go get dressed. And have a good time, dammit."

Rose raises her glass, and Baker meets her mother's gaze. She knows she's Rose's precious pride and joy, a brilliant baby who stands there, growing, glaring, threatening to fly away and become some kind of *woman*. Part of her feels so ready to be done with it all: high school, this house, the smothering fog of parental love and high expectations. But that part is still overshadowed by the part that wants to make her mother happy. Making Rose proud is still irresistible. Baker lifts her glass.

"To living a little!"

"To living a little."

"To the valedictorian!"

"To the hostess."

"To the new year!"

"To 1968."

When the van finally pulls up, Baker has been waiting on the curb in the dark for forty-five minutes, her body cold and shivering, her heart racing as she wonders if May changed her mind and decided against picking up her square younger cousin. Baker is wearing the green dress and good coat that Rose suggested, and a macramé bag is slung over her shoulder. Her hair hangs on either side of her face, parted perfectly down the middle.

May climbs out and runs up to her, all decked out in a ridiculous velvet coat with brocade and fur trim. On her head is a little old-fashioned hat with a black net that hangs diagonal across her grinning face. Her wild hair is pinned up, and she's penciled a fake mole above her red lips.

It's such a sight that Baker forgets to scold her for being late. She grins at her cousin. "Is King Arthur mad that you stole his royal coat?"

"Not at all, milady," May says with a sweeping bow. "In fact, he gave it to me himself, and proclaimed, 'You must wear this fine coat on this most magical of nights!'" May looks Baker up and down. "And is Doris Day mad that you stole her dress?"

Baker holds up the macramé bag. "I'm gonna change."

May's face lights up and she does a little dance. "Oooh! Someone's breaking the rules!" She claps like a child as Baker backs herself into the overgrown bushes that frame the front yard and begins unzipping her dress.

"Whoa, right here?"

"What, should I do it in the car in front of all your groovy friends?"

"I'm impressed, kid. Lying to Queen Rose *and* wearing the forbidden fabrics? What gives?"

Baker sneers in the dark as she sheds the polite dress. "It's a new year. And maybe it's time for a new me! Or at least, I can try a few new things." She pulls on a floral halter top and a tan suede miniskirt with beaded fringe, then glances around, suddenly terrified that a neighbor might spot her. The leather barely grazes her thighs.

"Hey, it's that skirt we got last summer in Berkeley."

Baker steps out of the shadows, lets herself be lit by the headlights. "Is it too short?"

"Ain't no such thing, sister! Now let's split before your parents try to come say hi."

The van is packed with people, which isn't unusual for May, whose social scene has been ever-changing and impossible to keep up with ever since she moved out of her parents' place and into a flat in the Lower Haight last year. Always surrounded by free spirits, wanderers, and wayward kids who need a couch to crash on, a blanket to wrap up in, a pot of something warm cooking on May's funky old stove. Baker, her steadfast sister-cousin, is still May's one constant best friend (and Baker is a little embarrassed to admit that

May is really her *only* close friend), but their lives are so different these days. Baker busy finishing high school, setting goals, her eyes locked on a big future somewhere else. Baker has been to May's place a few times, and May comes out to Baker's house for the obligatory family visits, but they rarely make plans to *do things* together. This is new, and exciting for them both.

"Where should I sit?"

"Just squeeze in the back." May climbs onto the lap of the guy sitting in the front seat. "Next to the sleeping one."

Everyone in the van laughs, clearly amused that the guy is asleep, possibly also amused that May's uncool cousin is going to have to cram in next to him. Baker shimmies herself between the window and the sprawled body of a tall man in a plaid cowboy shirt with shiny pearl snaps. She ends up twisted onto her side, perched on her hip, one elbow awkwardly propped on the back of the seat. Her miniskirt is all pushed up above her thighs, but she worries that if she wiggles around and tries to pull it down, she might wake him up, so she stays still and waits for the guy in the driver's seat to start the engine.

She's never been up close to a man like this, like a *real* man, not a relative or a classmate. She can smell him. Unwashed hair, campfire smoke, the sun. His breath. Warm and fragrant, like peppermint. And dirt. Her heart skips, her stomach jumps. She feels hungry. Suddenly ravenous.

The van pulls away, and Baker catches a glimpse of her house in the small square window. The smallest house on the nicest block— you'd never know how run-down it actually is beneath the fresh blue paint on the front door, the nice white shutters, the exhilarating pink geraniums bursting out of planter boxes. Rose sewed the curtains that cover the drafty windows; she planted the wisteria that blooms over the missing shingles. One time her little patch of grass in the front yard died in the heat of summer, so she took herself to the hardware store, bought a can of aerosol paint, and woke up at 4:00 A.M. to spray it a perfect emerald green.

If Rose could see her daughter now, smushed against a sleeping hippie in this smoke-filled van. Baker smiles to herself in the dark.

"Can I put the music back on now or what?" The guy in the front seat finds the round radio knob, skips from station to station.

"Just leave it, man," a girl calls from the middle seat when he lands on "Respect."

"That shit's square," the station-changer mutters, and May nuzzles into his neck.

"You're square," she says, and giggles.

By the time they're on the Bay Bridge, Baker has finally stopped staring at the sleeping man and is gazing out the window instead. She's seen this view so many times, but something seems different tonight. The city lights are extra vivid, like someone wiped the dust from each individual bulb. Are the buildings *taller*? Is the sky farther away? The water below churns dark and the bridge arcs above it, lit up and anchored by massive concrete pillars, held up with those long thin wires that look like delicate filaments from a distance. Treasure Island sits in the middle, built from Depression dirt and boulders. Rose worked there once, at the World's Fair, back when she was a young dancer who came out West with starry-eyed dreams. Before the war, before Gerald, before motherhood and all the money troubles. As the van drives through the tunnel in the middle of the bridge, Baker imagines her mother dancing on the verge of it all, barefoot and modern, dazzled by sculptures and murals and bridges, the limitless possibilities.

She looks back at the man beside her and wants so badly to touch his face. To feel the stubble on his cheeks, the wiry hairs of his eyebrows, the soft-looking lobes of his ears. Her hip hurts, her arm is falling asleep, and she's certain that everyone in the van can hear the pounding of her heart.

As the van cruises into the city, he finally begins to stir. With his eyes still closed, he reaches his long arms above his head. Baker tries to duck out of his way, flattening herself against the side of the car, but his arms still brush her head, the side of her cheek. Camp-fire smoke, peppermint, dirt. She feels dizzy.

Without opening his eyes, he mumbles. "'Twas bryllyg, and thee slythy toves did gyre and gymble in the wabe . . ."

The girl in the middle stops singing along to the song on the radio and twists around. She wears an enormous fur hat, and her teeth glint like tiny white seashells. "What the hell'd he say?"

"It's a poem," Baker whispers. She drops her voice even lower. "All mimsy were ye borogroves . . ."

Then his eyes pop open, big and bright like a cartoon. "And the mome raths outgrabe!" He gives Baker a puzzled smile. "Who are you, and why are we whispering?" The peppermint dirt smell is so intense, she can taste it.

"I'm Baker. May's cousin."

"What?"

"Baker." The words pour nervous from her mouth. "It's a nickname—I mean, it's my middle name, it's not made up, I just like it better than my real name, so—"

"Right on, Miss Baker. Pleased to make your acquaintance. I'm Wiley."

"Like the coyote."

"Indeed."

The girl in the fur hat leans half her body out the window and hollers, one hand holding on to her hat and the other yanking her crocheted top up over her tan chest. Three men in suits and ties howl at her from a street corner. Fur Hat pulls her body back into the van and holds up a small glass dropper, like the ones Baker uses in chemistry class. "Hey, May's cousin, we're all about to turn on. Wanna join?"

Wiley pulls a joint from his shirt pocket and strikes a match on the sole of his boot. The orange flame hisses inches from Baker's body and lights up the dark of the van. There's his face, bright and close. "Or there's this option. Pick your poison."

Baker feels everyone's eyes on her, especially Wiley's. She examines Fur Hat's dropper and suddenly can't believe that she's really there, in this car with her cousin, and these people, in this city, next to this man who smells so damn good, when just a few hours ago she'd been at home, in the kitchen with her mother. It feels like she's passed through a portal. How quickly it can turn, she thinks. How fast we can shift. Like a science experiment: all you need to do is add one new element, and a substance can be transformed. Or destroyed.

"She doesn't get high, you guys," May intervenes from the front seat. "She's way too smart for that." Baker makes a face at her cousin that says *Thanks, but I can speak for myself.* The guy whose lap she's on has his hand tucked far inside her coat.

"I have to get her home in one piece, or my aunt will murder me! And if I'm murdered, who will make you all the most delicious of breakfasts?"

Fur Hat laughs and laughs. "Good point! No dropper for *you,* little cuz! I need my huevos rancheros!"

May gives Baker a look, bugging out her eyes and flicking them back and forth between Wiley and Baker. *What's going on back there?* They both burst into giggles. No words needed. Not between two girls who've grown up like sisters. May leans out of her seat, leaning back onto Fur Hat's lap. She opens her mouth and sticks out her tongue, and Baker watches as Fur Hat holds the dropper just above May's lips.

The van pulls into a parking spot on a dark San Francisco street, and they all tumble out. The freaks are out in full force, swarming the sidewalks and spilling out into the road. Baker follows May and the crew as they join the clumps of what seem like hundreds upon hundreds of bodies huddled together in the sloppy line that snakes its way to the door of a large nondescript building. So many shiny-eyed, smudge-faced, long-haired, loose-limbed humans.

Swirling skirts and beaded headbands, bangles stacked on wrists, chests dripping with crystals and gems and silver and gold. Dilated pupils and dirt under nails, floppy felt hats and scruffy beards and dangly earrings on gorgeous heads that swing back and forth calling to one another. Baker's eyes feel overwhelmed; her nostrils fill with sweat and smoke, patchouli and rose oil, musk and must and night air and bare feet and a stick of incense that someone waves too close to her face.

As they get closer to the entrance, the crowd gets intense, pushing from behind. She loses track of May, which doesn't surprise her—May is attentive when it's convenient, but her attention span is limited, and her head always turns for shiny new things. Especially handsome ones with confident hands. The crowd intensifies, and someone steps on Baker's foot. A woman with peacock feathers in her hair starts shrieking; a hand brushes Baker's thigh. Then an arm drapes over her shoulder and pulls her close.

She smells his body before she sees his face. Wiley.

"You been here before?"

"It's my first time."

"Hold tight, I got you. We're going in."

He wraps his fingers around hers, firm and warm and just a little rough. The crowd plows forward, funneling through a narrow door. Baker glimpses the back of May's coat, and then a huge bearded guy at the door shouts, "Slow down, dammit!" Wiley's grip tightens as he pulls her up dark stairs, into a jam-packed red hallway, then finally through a pair of double doors that swing open, revealing what seems like another world: smoke and sweat and swirling lights and the loudest music she's ever heard. An explosion of rock and roll, high grade, pure, totally intense. It shakes her like an earthquake, washes over like a riptide. Wiley pulls her into the deep dark sea of bodies where everyone looks like strange sea creatures, like paisleyed jellyfish. At the far end of the auditorium is a magnificent stage, and on the stage is a band, the players tiny beneath the towers of speakers and a giant screen onto which is projected what is maybe melting lava. Baker scans the crowd for May, for anyone from the bus, but they've all been sucked up into the fray. It's Baker and Wiley and a million gorgeous strangers.

She laughs to herself. *What on earth would my mother think?* This is *not* folk music.

He leans in and yells over the churning guitar.

"Welcome to the Fillmore, mama. Want a beer?"

At some point, she loses Wiley, or he loses her, or they both close their eyes and move their bodies until other people fill in the space between them. The people around them dance like kelp in the ocean or ribbons fluttering in the wind, and she tries it, bending her knees, relaxing her arms, suddenly aware of her hips and wrists and elbows. She has finished her beer, and her body feels so relaxed. It briefly occurs to her that maybe the beer was not just a beer—*do they put LSD in beers?*—but the paranoid thought dissipates quick, and she moves and moves until she's right up close to the front, dancing beneath the tower of speakers stacked high at the foot of the stage.

Baker shakes her hands in the air and feels the lyrics in each fingertip, even though she has no idea what the singer is saying. She can't believe that the sounds, the *feelings,* so powerful, are being made right there by the people on the stage. It's so different from just playing the records in your room. It's like a version of the feeling she gets when she's deep in a book, lost in a world of words, but this is *alive.* Sound and color and throbbing liquid light—she sways and moves with the music, with the people. The core of each song seems to shoot up from the floor, straight into her legs and bare thighs, into her hot crotch, her belly, her chest, into her veins.

A tap on her shoulder and she whirls around, expecting Wiley, but it's Fur Hat with a huge smile and pupils round and bright like pennies. She holds out her hand and points to a closed door on the other side of the speaker tower. Another big bearded guy stands in front of it, arms crossed, and two girls saunter up to him, giggling. He runs a tattooed hand over each of their curvy bodies, then smacks them on their asses and opens the door just enough for them to glide inside. Through the crack in the door, Baker gets a peek: giddy faces lit from a single overhead bulb, a flash of fringe from someone's Naugahyde jacket, a bottle of brown liquor in someone's hand. And then the door is closed again.

Fur Hat cups her hands around her mouth and shouts, but Baker can't hear. She can read her lips well enough, though. She knows what she's asking.

Wanna come?

Does she?

Baker marvels at the two young women who went through the door, at Fur Hat, even at May, wherever she is. How do they *do* it? How and when did they make the choice to just be so *out there*? She's always been the observer, the book-smart girl with the high test scores who watches, fiercely curious, from a safe distance. She watches the fast girls who run with the hoods, with their visible bra straps and midriff tops, teased out hair and snarled lips. Driving fast, breaking laws, being so bad it's cool. The college students on TV with their fists in the air, screaming in the faces of the National Guard. Even May's friends, with their unshaved legs and gauzy blouses, perpetually visible nipples. Fur Hat's loud laugh—how casually they all open their mouths and alter their minds. Do they worry about what people will think, about the opinions of their parents? About *consequences*?

She's here, alone in a crowd, miles from her parents' patio, Fur Hat's hand reaching out to her, each finger stacked with silver rings. The distance has collapsed, dissolved, and she isn't just watching this scene, she's *in* it. And she can do anything she wants. Dive into an adventure. Kick off the new year. Follow this person, go through the door.

The big bearded man at the door waves Fur Hat over, and Baker sees his bloodshot eyes. His teeth glow like bones under the black lights. He leans down and strokes her hat, then grabs her tan, bony shoulders. His thick fingers dig into her flesh as he puts his face next to Fur Hat's and whispers into her ear. Baker can't see his lips, but she can see Fur Hat's reaction. How she shakes her head and tries to pull away, how he doesn't let go, how she finally twists free and slaps him across the face. How she turns and runs, disappearing back into the teeming mass. *Bitch,* he yells, pointing his middle finger to the sky, then he turns toward Baker, and she runs, too.

Baker doesn't find Fur Hat, but she does find Wiley, standing in the back by the double doors. She spots the shining pearl buttons on his shirt and heads right toward him, barreling into his body without hesitation. His arms wrap around her, and she breathes him in. Mint. Dirt. Smoke. Body.

"Hey, lady," he yells over the music. "You're just in time!"

She has no idea how long she's been dancing, moving, running, how long she's been gone from him. Her blood is still pumping, adrenaline racing; she feels freaked out and afraid but so alive and curious.

"Time for the countdown!" Wiley is grinning, and the people around them are beginning to cheer. Up on stage, the band stops playing, and a voice on a mic booms loud.

"Are you ready for it?"

Everyone screams. *YES!*

"SEE YA LATER, SIXTY-SEVEN!"

TEN!

They face the stage.

NINE!

His body behind hers.

EIGHT!

She says it again to herself. *Eight.* The year she moves out! The year she goes to college!

Anything is possible.

SEVEN!

His hands now on her hips. She turns and looks up at him. She doesn't even *know* him, but that hardly seems to matter.

SIX!

She's so curious. So hungry. So light and powerful she might levitate off the floor.

FIVE!

She reaches up and touches his earlobes. Feels his scratchy beard. Traces his chapped lips with her finger.

FOUR!

She pulls his face down to hers, a surprisingly easy thing to do.

THREE!

He tastes like he smells. His tongue is incredible.

TWO!

Everyone screaming.

ONE . . .

"Happy New Year," Baker howls—wild, electric, full—when she finally comes up for air.

They leave the concert soon after midnight, holding hands and walking the dark streets in a charged kind of silence. She considers telling him that she's really just a high school girl who lied a little to her mother so she could go to her very first concert, that she's a virgin who's only had one kiss, and it was on a dare at summer camp, so it didn't really count. How she may *seem* a little square— but really, she's destined for greatness. For big things. She's got a plan: graduation, then college, then the real stuff. She's going to move to Paris and become a writer, like a *real* writer, novels and es- says but also journalism, the hard-hitting kind that reveals the truths of the world. Her parents won't like it, especially not at first, be- cause they're depending on her to get an accounting degree that will help them level up their business. A franchise! Ownership! *The big time,* as Gerald says. Would Wiley agree with her, tell her it's okay to disappoint them? She guesses he'll understand how the thought of abandoning her dreams just to help her parents get rich makes her want to cry. He seems like the kind of guy who doesn't care what people think. Which must be so nice.

But she says none of it. He also seems like the kind of guy who doesn't want to know too much. And if she talks and talks it might break the spell, tip them back into reality. She just wants to keep being this person, this woman, walking in the dark, holding the hand of this guy she barely even knows. She doesn't need to know him. She leans into his body, lets their footfall be the soundtrack.

When they finally get to the van, they laugh at the comically haphazard parking job. Wiley opens the unlocked door and grabs a blanket from the back seat. A small grassy hill rises up next to the sidewalk, a grove of trees just beyond. He spreads the blanket on the ground and gestures to her to sit; then, he rifles through his pack and pulls out a canteen. She chugs it, unable to get enough of the cool water.

He looks up at the sky and proudly points out Orion's Belt. "I love the stars, don't you?"

She lifts her finger, tracing it down from the Belt's last star.

"That's Sirius. The brightest star in the sky. Also known as the Dog Star. It's part of Canis Major. The big dog, following Orion the Hunter."

A low whistle leaves his chapped lips, and he rolls over onto his side. "Okay, I see. You're smart."

"I know."

"Oh, yeah?" He leans in close, kisses her. "What else do you know?"

She looks at the sky spread out above them, bigger and brighter than any city could ever be. Endless and boundless. Eternal mystery. "A whole lot. And hardly anything at all."

The wind is gentle in the branches above them, and in the distance, the fog rolls in off the bay. For the first time in hours, she thinks about her parents. Are they still awake? Is the party still going? Are they wondering where she is, if she's safe?

"Hey," he says. "What's your real name?"

"Elizabeth."

"Like the queen."

"It's my grandmother's name. My mother's mother. But my mom says she named me for Elizabeth Taylor. She just loves her. I think she hoped the name would make me . . . you know."

"What?"

"Beautiful."

"I guess it worked, beautiful Baker."

She blushes in the dark, and her eyes say *Yes. More, please.*

The next kiss is fiercer, harder. A deep human exchange that somehow satisfies the hunger and leaves her wanting more. He climbs on top of her; she wraps her arms around the back of his neck. It's like the feeling she had dancing next to the speakers, but even better. Aware of her hips and arms and hands, her breasts and thighs and *self.* The pulsing energy and electricity. The firm body with good hands that move from her back down her thighs, and then up under her skirt. She doesn't flinch or push away. The earth is cold and damp below her; he is heat and heart and muscle above her. She pulls him close, open. When he asks about her cycle, she tries to think but it's so hard to focus, to remember anything before this moment.

"A week ago?" She pants. "Maybe two?"

He unbuckles his belt. "Great. Plus there's no moon tonight. So we're good."

That doesn't make sense to her, but she doesn't stop to question it. She doesn't want anything to stop, and she also doesn't know how any of this works. Her body, or his. *A whole lot. Hardly anything at all.* She's such a smart girl, the smartest in her class, but no one ever taught her what happens to two bodies in a moment like this. She got A's in geometry, in physics, she aced biology, but nothing prepared her for the angle of his hipbones, the force of his hands between her legs, the velocity of her miniskirt pushed up, the heat of her mouth, his face, her eyes rolling back in her head, her mouth dropped wide open to the night. This is not a test she studied for, but somehow, she knows what to do.

Afterwards, looking up at the sky again, Wiley smokes a joint while Baker breathes hard next to him. She wants to tell him what it all means to her, how heart-pounding and vibrant and new she feels. But she still doesn't want to break the spell, and she isn't sure if she could even find the right words if she tried. And then she hears him snoring, soft like a cat's purr. She turns and looks and there he is, asleep like he'd been when she first encountered him, how many hours before? She laughs. How could anyone sleep after something like that?

Baker is wide awake in the night all alone. She might never sleep again. She could lie there and watch the city for hours, alive and tingling, until May and the others return. At some point, she will go back home; at some point, she'll be back in her bedroom, back in the hallways at school. Will she look different? Will anyone be able to tell? Will she get to see him again?

She hears a sound in the darkness, a scratching and rustling. Out of the corner of her eye she sees something, small and quick, soft and white, running fast beneath the bushes, then darting into the trees. She blinks and it's gone, but she could swear it was there. A little white rabbit. A disappearing act, a good luck charm. An omen, she thinks.

This is gonna be a big year.

*B*aker goes back to real life the next morning. Eyes puffy, head pounding, brain absolutely buzzing when the van, packed with sleeping snoring still-high bodies, chugs up to her house and drops her off. Wiley opens his eyes long enough to kiss her goodbye and mumble *Don't be a stranger*. Baker tiptoes to the front door, exhausted and ecstatic. The sun is just coming up.

All day long Baker is impressed with her ability to feign normalcy. She gets in the front door undetected, pulls back her covers, and slides into bed. When she gets up at nine and joins her parents for breakfast, she smiles cheerfully and tells them it was a great, mellow time. She cleans up the breakfast dishes, and the party debris on the patio. She stifles yawns and resists the urge to crawl back into bed and dream the day away. She goes with Gerald to the office, reviews the logs from the previous week, gets him set up for the month ahead. She completes the homework her teachers assigned over the winter break. She eats dinner, she does the dishes, she watches the evening news with Gerald.

She does a remarkable job of acting like she doesn't feel completely changed. That she doesn't feel giddy and wobbly and shaky and silly and awestruck. It's like a door has slid open inside of her mind revealing an entire world she hadn't even known was there. And she couldn't close it now if she wanted to. She's consumed with thoughts of Wiley's smell, his lips, his body on hers. The way he complimented her, the way he touched her, the way her body felt, how it shook and trembled and tensed and released. Her waist and hips and back and the inside of her thighs and the back of her neck and *there*.

No one had ever put their hands there. Not even her. She replays each moment and wonders: Is he thinking about her, too? How and when can she see him again? What if he doesn't *want* to see her? What if he calls her? What if he *doesn't* call her? Should she ask May what to do? And what will May say?

When May calls two days later, her words are perfect.

"I ran into Wiley, and he asked for your number. Says he can't stop thinking about you."

"Really?"

"I told him you'd get in trouble if he called your house. Wanna come hang out again next weekend?"

It is everything Baker wants to hear. They concoct a plan.

"May invited me to lunch on Saturday," Baker tells Rose. "At a nice little café near her house." Rose agrees. How lovely! She has to run a few errands in the city anyway, and she likes seeing her daughter get out of the house. She wants Baker to be social, to live in the world, and she is happy to drop her off, happy to imagine the two cousins drinking coffee and ordering lunch like sophisticated young women.

When they get there, May is standing out front of the café, just like they'd planned. Baker's heart is pounding as she kisses Rose on the cheek and waves goodbye, then stands with her cousin as they wait for the blue Galaxie to turn the corner. Then they turn and run up the block, to May's place.

Wiley is waiting for her in his car, a beat-up little Volkswagen Beetle. He holds out his arms, and Baker nearly screams. She has an essay to write this week, and a history test to study for. And up until New Year's Eve, she'd been focused on finishing the rough draft of the editorial for the school paper she's been wanting to submit. It's unlike anything she's written for the paper before: a full-throated endorsement of McCarthy's presidential candidacy and a scathing rebuke of Johnson. It's also very, very good, according to her advisor. *Truly impressive.* She's been getting up the courage to put her opinions out there like this, sharpening her arguments, trying to craft the perfect opening lines. But all of that falls away as Wiley's arms wrap around her. May invites them to come inside, but he suggests they go for a drive instead. Baker has already climbed into the passenger seat.

"Be back before three," May cautions Wiley. "Her old lady's never late." May catches Baker's eye. Her face says *Don't mess this up,* and Baker's says *I won't!* The VW backfires as Wiley drives away, headed toward Ocean Beach.

Each furtive, sweet, brief encounter with Wiley that follows consumes her, fills her up, stuffs her with enough sensation and excitement and desire to carry her through to the next one. It's only a handful of times, really, once a weekend for five radiant weeks. A series of little lies and concocted plans. Two bodies in the back seat of the car, on the floor of the extra room in May's apartment, on an itchy wool blanket in a thick grove of trees in Golden Gate Park. They make love and they walk and they talk, and then she goes home, savoring his scent on her body but also anxious to cover it up before Rose gets a whiff. She borrows May's scented oils, puts incense in her pockets, rubs her neck and the inside of her wrists with fresh eucalyptus pods that she finds on the ground.

When she isn't with Wiley, she is thinking about him, wondering about him, replaying his face and his hands and his body. She goes through the motions of her daily life: doing her homework, drying the dishes, skimming the leaves from the pool, checking the math in Gerald's ledgers. Getting dressed, brushing her teeth, walking to school, raising her hand, answering questions, gossiping and laughing. In the evenings, she sits in her spot on the couch next to Gerald in his leather recliner, and they watch the news as always, but she's barely there. Her eyes fixate just above the television screen, and while Bob Young drones about troop mobilizations, the DMZ, student demonstrations—phrases that normally make her sit up straight and listen close, that make Gerald huff and grunt with paternal indignation—she is deep in the soft pink curves of her imagination, making love to Wiley in hotel rooms in Paris, on blankets at beaches, backstage at concerts.

This is *a whirlwind romance,* she thinks, like something from the pages of the books she reads. She's an exuberant protagonist, on the brink of discovery, dancing on the edge of being a real woman. All the things she'd been for so long—careful, pragmatic, observant, protective—feel like dried pieces of a cocoon from which she's finally emerged. The things that felt so urgent—her college acceptance, the graduation, the homework and tests and journalism assignments, the state of the nation and the entire chaotic world— seem to fall away. It feels incredible to not have to care all the time. It feels *liberating.*

Anyone would describe her as a practical girl, *such a good head on her shoulders,* and those things are true and steady—but also true is the burning romantic inside of her, the dramatic soul who's lived vicariously through books until now.

And isn't it incredible.

Isn't he fascinating.

She yearns to know everything about him: the details of his childhood, his future plans, his food preferences and favorite animals and secret protected desires he harbors under his flannel shirts and tan skin.

For those dazzling precious weeks, he is the whole world. Life's fun this way, she realizes.

*M*ay is throwing a party the weekend after Valentine's Day—"a celebration of love in a time of war," she tells everyone—but it's also a going-away party for a few roommates who are going to live in a commune in the woods somewhere. Wiley will definitely be there, and Baker plans to be, too. It's been more than a week since their last rendezvous, and Baker feels she might actually explode with desire. Emboldened, she tells Rose something close to the truth, and Rose says she can go, because who doesn't love a Valentine's Day party? And who doesn't love a daughter who is finally blossoming into a social butterfly?

"It's nice to see you out and about," Rose exclaims. "We can bake cookies for you to take to the party. Gingerbread hearts!"

They spend an entire afternoon baking together, something they haven't done in a while. Baker always loved helping Rose in the kitchen, specifically with the sweets. She'd stand on a stool and help roll out the dough with Nana Anne's wooden rolling pin. They'd get flour on their faces and Baker would sneak nibbles of the raw dough. Baker feels a wave of aching nostalgia. She suddenly wants to hug her mother and tell her everything, to laugh and cry and just spill it all, ask *Is this what love always feels like?* But she could never do that. She can't be this new version of herself in front of her mother. It is not what Rose expects of her daughter.

They roll out the rest of the dough and slide the soft little hearts onto the baking sheets, set the timer on the oven, and begin to clean up. As Baker wipes the flour from the counter, she pictures him waiting for her. In the living room, in the kitchen, maybe on the stairs. Holding a cold beer, probably a joint. Holding a valentine that he's made just for her, grinning his grin, taking her hand. Tiny beads of sweat form on her forehead and the corners of her mouth, which twitches up in a lopsided, dreamy grin.

The drive to May's feels longer than usual, and Baker keeps the window rolled down even though it's cold out. She wears her red dress with the little white polka dots, but plans to change into something else at May's. One of her cousin's hand-me-down halter tops, and maybe a gauzy skirt. Rose is chatty, full of gossip about the difficult women in her various service clubs and organizations. Baker grips the platter of still-warm cookies in her lap. The scent wafts up, burrows deep into Baker's nose. All that butter, the cinnamon, the sharp punch of ground cloves. It's overwhelming. She feels her mouth water, but not in a good way. She rolls the window down more and sticks her head out, lets the cool air rush over her face. *It's just nerves,* she tells herself.

Rose drops her off right in front of the apartment. "Maybe someday I'll be invited in," she says, only half-teasing. Baker gets chills at the thought of her mother stepping foot inside the flat, how she would *tsk* at the funky busted furniture and dust and clutter, the incense smoke and the bodies lounging everywhere. "But I suppose today is not the day!" She kisses Baker on the cheek and drives off to run her errands. Baker feels the pit in her stomach again. Lying to Rose isn't that hard—but it's not easy, either. An unwelcome thought appears: *What am I doing? Who am I?* She shakes it off and climbs the worn wood steps.

The first thing Baker sees when she opens the front door is a homemade poster that someone has tacked to the wall in the foyer. In big bright letters, it reads:

ROSES ARE RED

THEIR HEARTS ARE BLACK

END THIS WAR NOW

SEND MY FRIENDS BACK

The words are surrounded by an elaborate border of tiny red hearts that are made to look like they're dripping blood. Baker is standing there, holding the platter of cookies, staring at the poster, when she hears his laugh.

She finds Wiley in the living room. And he does have a joint in one hand. But he doesn't have a valentine for her, and he isn't waiting for her. He's not even looking at her. He's looking at the woman standing next to him, her arm wrapped around his waist, her head thrown back laughing, as though she's just heard the most hilarious joke. And then he is bending down; he is whispering into her ear and kissing her neck, her cheek. Her lips. Her blond hair so long it brushes his hand that rests on her round hip. Then she turns her head, a huge stoned smile on her face. She isn't wearing the hat, but Baker recognizes her anyway.

"Heeeey, May's cousin," Fur Hat calls out, her voice like liquid. "What's shakin'!"

Wiley's bloodshot eyes find Baker's, and his mouth begins to open, but she's already spun around, headed for the door. He's calling her name as she runs down the stairs. She hears him but she doesn't stop. May is yelling, but Baker keeps going, as fast as she can in the platform sandals, still holding the platter of cookies. When her feet hurt too much, she takes the sandals off and runs barefoot until she gets to the park. She sits on a bench and cries and cries, and eats cookies until she vomits on the grass.

*F*or the next few weeks, Baker feels sick and exhausted and stupid and silly and guilty and mad. The glorious romantic scenes that played on repeat in her wild imagination are replaced with reliving Wiley in the living room with Fur Hat, Wiley in the living room with Fur Hat, over and over again on a deadening loop. Love is terrible. Love is humiliating. Love is exhausting.

She vacillates between heartsick and furious. Angry at Wiley, yes, but even more upset with herself. How she let herself go like that, so consumed and naïve. How she put her *self* aside just to waste her time lost in his gaze. She feels like such an idiot. An unserious idiot, the exact kind of girl she never wanted to be. The kind who doesn't care, who doesn't have bigger plans, the kind who just giggles and gets high and stares at the sky and thinks *that* is liberation. *Stupid.*

She skipped homework assignments for him! She didn't study for who knows how many tests. And she missed the deadline for her editorial. For *what.* She's mad at everything and everyone: at May for encouraging her, at herself for believing she could be someone else.

"Elizabeth, what is the matter with you?" Rose finally asks one evening as she watches Baker, eyelids drooping, barely touching her roast chicken.

"I'm just tired from school. I had a math test today, and I need to finish an article for the paper."

"I thought that article was due weeks ago," Gerald says. "I remember discussing it with you over Christmas. I don't agree with all your arguments, but I'm looking forward to reading it."

Baker shoves a bite of chicken in her mouth to stall for a moment. "Mr. Martin changed the deadline," she lies, her mouth still full.

Gerald frowns and glances at Rose. "That's unusual. He's a real stickler, isn't he?"

Baker spears a piece of broccoli and pops it in her mouth. She nearly gags, but she needs to get out of this conversation.

"Don't speak with your mouth full, dear." Rose puts her hand on Baker's forehead. Baker flinches, annoyed by the touch. "Tired but no fever," she says, decisive. "Are you on drugs?"

"Of course not."

Gerald rolls his eyes. "She doesn't do drugs, Rose."

"I know that. But she *has* been spending all this time with May lately. Which is lovely, but May is not exactly . . ."

"I'm not on drugs, Mother."

Rose narrows her eyes and looks closely at Baker, who feels panicked. The chicken and the broccoli feel lodged in her throat.

"Something is going on. Do you feel okay?" Rose's eyes seem to penetrate her skin. She's certain that her mother has x-ray vision, can see directly inside of her.

"I feel fine." *Can she tell that I had sex?* She knows that's entirely irrational, but her cheeks still flush and burn.

"You've been off lately." Rose stares at Baker in silence for several seconds. Baker's head begins to throb, right behind her eyes. She feels weak, and her vision blurs.

But then Rose sits up straight, jaw clenched, and passes the basket of buttered rolls to Gerald. She smiles and changes the subject. "The auxiliary is planning a luncheon for April. The theme will be 'Festive Florals.' Gerald, would you like some green beans?"

*   *   *

That night in the bathroom, Baker takes her temperature, the slim glass thermometer cold and hard against her tongue. 98.6. Normal. She puts the thermometer back in her mouth. She takes it several more times. She wills her body to produce a fever. An answer. A terrible, rare malady that could explain it all. Maybe Wiley has a contagious disease that he didn't tell her about because he's a liar who doesn't care about her.

She considers mono, remembering last year when Susan Brown had it. Susan missed months of school, and when she finally returned, she was so gaunt and weak she couldn't even swing the tennis racket in gym. Baker remembers Susan talking about the swollen glands in her throat, *like ping pong balls,* she'd whispered during a passing period. Baker rubs two fingers up and down her neck, palpating the soft flesh of her throat. No lumps. Just her pulse, fluttering like a panicked rabbit just below her jaw.

What else could explain how tired she feels? The exhaustion is deep: in her bones, primal and profound, like the center of the earth dragging her down. And also there's the issue of her breasts. How they suddenly ache, so swollen and tender, like when she was in seventh grade and they first appeared, taut and painful to the touch. They feel so different all the sudden. She can't even sleep on her stomach, her preferred position.

She cups a hand around the bottom of each one and lifts. They're still small, but they have a new weight to them. She remembers Wiley's hands slipping under her bra, his fingers fumbling, grasping at her nipples, and she feels repulsed. Ashamed. She lets go and then winces when they drop, heavy against her ribs. They've never been big enough to *drop.*

She looks at herself in the mirror and shakes her head. *No.*

Tomorrow after school, she'll go to the library and do some research and figure out the terrible mystery disease that causes fatigue, nausea, giant sore boobs.

And also: the other symptom. The one she can barely bring herself to think about. She's late. Baker hasn't bled.

*   *   *

Her last period came in January, when she returned to school from the break, a few days after the second time she slept with Wiley. When she'd seen the blood, she'd smiled, taking it as a sign that they'd gotten it right. And if it came right away, so quickly after they'd done it, that meant everything was fine. And surely it would come again. For the next few days, every time she went to the bathroom and unhooked her pad, glimpsed the deep red stains, she'd felt a satisfied rush of pleasure. Like her body was giving her permission to continue.

But lately she's been frequenting the bathroom, even when she doesn't have to pee, just to wipe, desperate to see that red streak again. Just a bit of pink, even. Every time she flushes the not-red toilet paper, she wants to cry, or throw up, or both. She can't bring herself to actually count the days on the calendar, but she can't deny that February has come and gone, that it is now March. That she should have bled again before Valentine's Day.

And she can't deny what happened this morning at school in Home Ec, when the class was cracking eggs into mixing bowls to make Bundt cakes. Mrs. Fletcher was reading from her recipe book, the one she wrote herself, and Baker had never been so repulsed by an egg. This *thing* that was once inside of a chicken, the yellow blob sliding into the bowl, the clear goo dripping down the inside of her wrist. The sound of all the other girls expertly tapping, cracking, mixing, stirring, and the sudden collective clashing of all their shampoos and perfumes—the patchouli and Youth-Dew and Lustre-Crème. Baker made it out of the classroom before the heaving started. She managed to get to a trash can before anything actually came up. And then she ran to the nurse's office.

She'd lain for a while on a cold vinyl cot. The pit in her stomach throbbed, and tingles spread out across the back of her neck, her shoulders, her throat, until everything felt tight and constricted. She rolled over to heave once again on the waxed shining floor, just missing the metal can. The nurse sighed and rolled her eyes, then pulled out her intake form. Baker looked up at her ruddy face and tried to sound confident. "I ate too much for breakfast. No need to call home."

The nurse pursed her lips.

"I'm really okay. I'll go back to class once it passes." Baker managed a smile, then dropped her voice to a whisper. "Please. Don't call." Then she closed her eyes and curled up in a ball. She heard the nurse's pencil scratching on the paper.

"Here's your hall pass. If you come back again, I'm calling your mother."

*I*t's a rainy Sunday afternoon when Baker finally calls May and asks if she can come by. She doesn't mention the fact that she hasn't returned to the flat since the party, well over a month ago. She's relieved when May says *Sure, come on over.* They go up to May's room and still say nothing, just lie beneath an open window in a nest of old quilts. It's cozy and familiar and Baker feels at ease for the first time in weeks. May puts on side one of the new Jefferson Airplane album and they go without words for a while, letting the music fill the space.

When the truth is found to beeeeeeee lies

"I love this album," Baker finally says.

"Me, too. I'm seeing them play next Friday, at the Carousel. You should come."

"Maybe."

"Cool." May waits another minute. She's not as patient as Baker, not as good at saying nothing. "I haven't seen you since the party, Baker. What gives?"

"I know. I'm sorry."

"Are you okay?"

Baker looks her cousin in the eyes. She wants to dissolve, to disappear. On instinct, she begins to answer *yes,* but May cuts her off.

"You're pregnant, aren't you?"

The word is a bird, released from a cage. A ball shot from a cannon. A punch to the face, to the gut. Where, Baker realizes with a nauseating shock, something might be growing.

Baker's hand flutters up to touch her midsection. "What?"

"Are you?"

"No!"

"You sure?"

May's eyes are wide. Welcoming. They don't judge, but they do know. The record spins around and around, the needle scratching quiet.

Baker's face is beginning to crumple. "I don't know."

"When did you bleed last?"

Baker bites her lip. Hard. "January."

"When in January?"

"I don't know. Maybe a week after New Year's."

May looks down at her hands and begins to count on her fingers. When she's finally done, she sighs and then flops back into the quilts. "And you feel sick?"

Baker's face looks pained.

"And this hurts?" May reaches over and pokes Baker's chest. She flinches. May tilts her head and purses her lips.

"May." Baker's voice is so faint. "No."

"I know, kid."

"*No.*"

"Baker . . ."

"NO!" Baker's scream is so loud that May jolts back, knocking into the bedside table. The record player crashes to the floor, and the black disc cracks in half. They both freeze, then May murmurs "Fuuuuck" and Baker puts her face in her hands.

"I can't. I *can't* be. I just can't."

"I know. But . . . you might be."

Baker stands and begins to pace the room, sidestepping the cracked shards of vinyl. "It could be something else, an infection, or a rare disease. I got a medical textbook from the library, and—"

"Baker." May speaks slow and careful, the way she does when she's talking down a friend on a bad trip.

"I *could* be sick." She looks at May with desperation.

"Would you rather have a *deadly disease*?"

"Yes. Then at least I could take medicine. I could get treatment, and I could get better."

"You're being dramatic, Baker."

"I'm being practical. And if there is no treatment, it would be really sad and I would die and that's that."

"Jesus." May shakes her head. "You really love a plan, don't you."

Baker stomps over to the window, her back to her cousin. She stares at the sky, as if the answers are just beyond May's cluttered room, somewhere up in the clouds. May sits quietly on the bed until Baker comes to sit next to her again.

"I just don't *understand* how this could have happened."

May cracks her knuckles, a sound that makes Baker cringe. "You don't *understand*?"

"What?"

"You had sex, Baker. More than once, right? Do you not understand how this all works?"

"Don't be a jerk, May."

"I'm sorry, kid. Don't worry, you don't *look* it yet."

"Then why are you so sure?"

"Because you're not the first person I know to have this happen. I've seen it before. Have you?"

Baker squints, as if that will help her see her memories better. She flips through women and girls she's known: a few neighbors have had babies over the years, sure, but they were older women, all married with families. Has she ever actually been up close and personal, has she *known* a pregnant woman? Her mother's cousin's daughter was pregnant at Christmas two years ago, but she and her handsome new husband only stopped by the house briefly, a holiday drop-in. So the answer is no. It's something that happens to other people.

"Plus, I know what you've been up to. You and Wiley going at it. But no one else would ever guess."

Baker's eyes get wide. "Are you sure?"

"Me? Sure, they'd expect it. But not you." She takes Baker's face in her hands. "You're *good*. And you're going to be okay."

Baker's not convinced. "I just didn't think that I was that kind of girl."

May can't help but laugh. "The kind of girl who what? Gets pregnant because she's so naïve she doesn't know how her own body works? Guess they don't teach the valedictorian everything, do they."

Baker says nothing. She lets May's words hang there, cruel but true. She feels defensive and scared, but also, somehow, comforted. She's never felt so unmoored, so afraid, so isolated. There's comfort in being with May, even if she feels like the stupidest idiot on earth. At least she's not alone.

"So what are we going to do?" May asks, finally.

"I don't *know*."

"Do your parents suspect anything?"

Baker thinks about Rose and Gerald. They're concerned, yes, but they still seem clueless. It would never occur to them. This was not in the plan. "No."

"What about Wiley?"

"I haven't said anything. To anyone. And besides, you remember what happened at your party. Wiley's got other women to worry about now."

May scrunches her face, then releases a loud breath. "Great. We'll call my friend Amber right now. She knows people who know a doctor. Just over the border, in Tijuana."

"What are you talking about?"

"It's fine; she's done it before, she knows how to get it all arranged."

"Get what arranged?"

"You said you wanted a solution. You don't have a disease, Baker, you have a situation. And there's . . . a treatment. Amber said it wasn't that bad. I mean it's no walk in the damn park, and it's *expensive,* but she's fine. And what's the alternative?"

Baker feels the floor below her, the crush of gravity pinning her to this very real moment. Time feels slowed down, warped. The air stings. Her lungs feel cold. Her stomach spins.

"I'm serious, Baker. What do you think is going to happen? Are you going to, like, *have a baby?* Wait—do you want to have a baby?"

No, Baker thinks, shaking her head. The answer is *no,* but she can't think of anything beyond that. She tries to focus, to go into her brilliant brain and access the information. She imagines a multiple-choice question on a test: *When a teenage girl gets pregnant, what are her options?* She tries to picture the answers.

A)

B)

C)

D)

Empty. Blank. She has no idea. How could she have felt so much, but know so little?

May carries on. "We'll say we're going to San Diego, like on a road trip."

Baker thinks about herself in a car, whooshing down the coast, crossing the border in search of what? A secret doctor? She's never even left California. She's never even been to Los Angeles.

"May," she manages. "I can't do that."

"Why not?"

"It's illegal. And . . . dangerous."

"Five minutes ago you were willing to die from some disease!"

Baker wraps her arms around her knees and buries her head. It's too much. It's all too much. She can't take it in.

May turns and goes over to her old-fashioned vanity. She digs through her piles of junk—magazines, seashells, foreign coins, a hairbrush, love beads, ostrich feathers, roach clips—until she finds a pamphlet. She hands it to Baker. "Look. I got this at a party a while back, some women's libber was handing them out."

Baker examines the narrow, three-fold pamphlet. *ARE YOU PREGNANT?* in big bold letters. Then, beneath it: *Is yours a wanted pregnancy? If not, why not see an abortionist?* The rest of the page is a long list of names and addresses—none of them, Baker notes, in the U.S.

Tijuana, Mexico.
Tokyo, Japan.
Stockholm, Sweden.
Poland.
Hungary.
. . . And other locales

"It's not 'legal,' but come on," May continues. "It should be. And who cares what's legal, anyway? How is this *war* legal? How is *poverty* legal? Laws are bullshit. This is your life, girl." May takes the pamphlet back and turns it over, points to a phone number and P.O. box. At the bottom of the paper, in print so small Baker has to squint, it reads: *By the Society for Humane Abortion (SHA).*

"The women's libber, she said you just call this number. They set you up with an appointment. And they don't ask a lot of questions."

Humane, legal, illegal. May is right, that none of it seems to matter anymore, but Baker still can't fathom what it all actually means. She can't comprehend how much there is that she doesn't know. Three months ago, it felt like a big deal that she'd stayed out all night in a miniskirt. Two months ago, she was daydreaming about the back seat of Wiley's car. And now she's here, trying to figure out which laws to break and wondering what, exactly, an abortion even *is*. How does it work? And what if something goes wrong?

She'd seen a picture, once, in a magazine. A terrifying article about a woman who died from an illegal procedure (it never used the word *abortion,* just "procedure"). The woman was on the floor, in a lifeless slump, her hair covering her face. It was grainy black and white, but you could tell that the puddle was blood.

Baker looks at the pamphlet again. It feels charged with some kind of intimate, mysterious energy. The name sounds so official. A secret society. An image pops into her head, unbidden: the witches from *Macbeth,* stirring their cauldron. *Toil and trouble . . .* Baker's stomach rumbles. Is it nerves? Or is it the . . . is there something inside of her?

Is this really happening?

"I can't look at this right now, May."

"Fine. But what are you going to do?"

"I don't know." And she doesn't. It's the worst feeling.

"Put it in your purse. Just in case, okay?"

Baker slips the slim piece of paper into her purse, a brown leather pouch with rainbow embroidery and smooth beads at the end of long fringe that clack when she walks.

May goes downstairs and returns with a cup of Constant Comment tea and a package of saltine crackers. Comfort food. Baker accepts both, allows herself to be taken care of. It's one of May's skills, part of why the wayward kids flock to her. She's good at helping with heartbreaks, nursing strung-out junk-sick kids.

Baker is sipping her second cup when they both hear Wiley's voice coming from outside. He's down below, talking to the kids on May's stoop.

"Hey," he's saying. "Anyone seen Baker? May's cousin?"

Baker's eyes go wide. She jumps up and rushes to May's closet, ducks inside.

"May," she pleads from behind a row of peasant dresses, "I can't see him. Please. Don't tell him I'm here." May narrows her eyes. "And *don't* get mad at him. Just act normal."

May clenches her fists. "Fine. Stay here. And it's going to be *very* hard not to punch his pretty face." Baker listens to the thump of May's clogs as she heads down the stairs. Once she's certain that

May is out front she creeps out of the closet and crawls over to the window. She crouches below the sill and listens.

"Hey, Wiley."

"May, what's happenin'? Your cousin around?"

Baker holds her breath.

"No. Why?" Baker exhales, imagines May leaning against the doorframe, arms crossed, head cocked.

"Bummer. Guess I won't see her before I take off."

"You leaving?"

"Draft board's breathing down my neck. I flipped a coin, and it came up tails, so I'm going south. Got a buddy down in Baja. Camping, surfing, watching the sunset, tacos and shit."

"Good luck down there." May's voice is icy cold.

"Baker doing okay? I feel bad, you know, with how things went down. She got real mad."

"She's fine, man. Actually, she's *great*. Busy. Really happy."

Baker smiles, grateful. It's quiet for a few moments, and Baker thinks that maybe he's left. But then he speaks again.

"She's a cool chick, you know?"

"Damn straight she is." Then the door slams shut, and Baker hears May coming back up the stairs.

Baker peers out the window. There he is, running one hand through his hair, blowing kisses to the kids on the porch with the other. The sun is all over his face and he's grinning.

He gets to walk away, just like that.

She opens her mouth and feels the shape of the words that might come out—*baby* and *father* and *future*—but she says nothing. What good would it do, she reasons. Would telling him change anything? Does he *want* to be a father? Does *she* want that? And what if he did—would they live together in his car? On the beach in Mexico? Would she sit on the sand while he surfs, a baby in her arms? Would he shave his face, get a job, learn how to change a diaper? Move into her bedroom at her parents' house, or come with her to her college dorm and watch the baby while she goes to class? Would he get down on one patched denim knee and ask her to marry him? She nearly cackles at the thought of it. Gasping and panting beneath his beautiful body is one thing. But becoming his wife? Becoming a *mother?*

So why say anything? *It takes two to tango,* she can imagine her mother telling her. *You didn't do this on your own.* But that implies some sort of equality. As if the reality of pregnancy sits equally with them both. As she watches him cruise up the street, giving a high five to an older guy leaning against a liquor store door, she wants to scream. But even if she ran down the stairs and grabbed his arm and told him everything, there's no way in hell that it would change his life the way it's about to change hers. He could still just go to Mexico. He could have beautiful women laughing into his neck all night. He could still just walk away. He might not, but the fact that he *could*—she knows this so clearly, and the wild unfairness roils her stomach, makes her chest tight. No, telling him won't change anything. It would only make a terrible situation worse. *Fuck you,* she thinks. She yanks the window open, and spits down onto the street.

She's still standing there when May comes back into the room.

"Well, that's that. Adios, Wiley."

"Thank you." Baker grabs her cousin, and they stand by the window in a tight embrace.

"Shit's unfair," May mutters into Baker's neck. "It's not exactly a dream vacation he's heading for, but still."

Through teary eyes, Baker looks back out the window once more, just as he turns the corner and disappears. Out of sight, out of the state, out of the country. Free as a gorgeous goddamned bird.

"*B*aker? Is everything okay in there? You have a letter!"

In the mirror, Baker watches herself scramble, as quietly as possible, to pull the blouse back over her head, to adjust the skirt and refasten the safety pin. She pricks herself again, this time on her finger. She sucks in her breath and wipes the blood on the dark blue fabric. Then she tucks in the blouse and wipes her snotty nose. She smooths her hair and opens the door, trying to appear nonchalant.

"This is it!" Rose clutches the white envelope with both hands. Her red lacquered nails like little perfect candies. "The moment we've been waiting for!"

Baker looks at the envelope. Her name, her address, typed in neat, even lines. It all looks so official. It's what they've been waiting for. The admissions letter, expected to arrive during the month of April. Which is now. It was supposed to be so exciting. She could just die.

"Shall we open it? Or wait until your father gets home from work?" Rose swoops in for a hug, and Baker's arms instinctively fly up to protect her chest. "Are you alright, dear?"

"I'm fine." Rose raises a penciled eyebrow. "And yes, let's wait until Dad gets home."

"I'm not sure if I can wait that long, but I'll do my best." Rose puts the envelope in the pocket of her skirt. She looks Baker up and down and glances at the robe on the floor. "This all feels a bit . . . disheveled. Maybe tidy up a bit before he comes home?"

After Baker shuts the door and hears Rose walk away, she drops to her knees, panting. Her stomach churns; her heart thuds; her head spins. She puts her hands on the floor to steady herself. She closes her eyes, but the image of the letter in Rose's hands pulses bright, like the light show at the Fillmore on that dumb night months ago.

She's been imagining this scene for so long: the one where the letter comes, and they open it together, and they toast and cheer and cry. And now it's ruined, along with all the other scenes she's imagined from her amazing future life, including the ones she'd never share with her parents because they involve an existence beyond them. For years she's fallen asleep with fantasies of what an adult life could look like. Baker as a woman in the world: independent, important, intelligent. A writer, the kind of woman who travels so much, she keeps a suitcase of essentials packed and ready to go. She dreams of red wine and deep conversation with influential people in dimly lit restaurants. People who laugh at her witty jokes. People who respect her, who appreciate books and words and ideas. So many times, she has visualized opening a magazine and seeing her name in the byline of a lengthy, hard-hitting article. She has imagined herself up all night working on the final draft of a novel. Interviewing icons, being interviewed as an icon. Giving talks and lectures. Being admired. She's had it all planned for so long.

But in order to even get there, she needs this next step. The college letter, the celebration. The happy send-off from her proud parents. Yes, they think she's going to follow their plans and do an accounting degree. And yes, they'll be disappointed when she changes course and pursues her own dreams once she gets there, but that's a bridge she'll cross much later. First, she needs to get out of the house, to be off on her own. And how is that supposed to happen now? How is any of it supposed to happen? All of the fantasies are just that: figments. Not real. Poof. Gone.

What have I done?

What do I do?

And then another thought: *Does she know?*

The acrid taste fills her, and her mouth waters, her eyes water.

She looks across the room to the wastebasket near her desk. Too messy. She can make it to the bathroom. Quietly. Quickly. *Go.*

Rose is at the end of the hallway, dusting the ceramic figurines on the hutch and the picture frames on top of the piano. She looks up as Baker emerges from her room. Baker sees her mother's smile fade. Her nostrils flare.

"You sure you're okay?"

The vomit hovers at the back of her throat, and Baker knows she cannot open her mouth. She clenches her fists and braces every muscle in her body and takes several shaky strides. The bathroom door is right there. She forces the corners of her mouth to curl upward and wills her head to nod and then she's in, pulling the door closed, lunging for the white porcelain bowl.

Half an hour later, when Baker emerges from her room in a fresh outfit, with her hair brushed and hanging neat around her shoulders, Rose is standing in the kitchen, facing the window that looks out on the side yard. There are blossoms on the lemon tree Gerald planted years ago, and little honeybees buzz around and around. Rose has one hand on her hip, and the other rests on the counter, next to the white envelope and a half-full martini glass. Baker notes the bottle of vodka, the way her mother's nails clack on the counter, how the veins and tendons snake elegantly along the backs of her thin, moisturized hands. How thick the air feels, how heavy her feet seem as she slowly approaches. How her fingertip still throbs from where the safety pin poked it.

The calendar on the wall shows a new car for April. Baker remembers staring at January, feeling so giddy about *nineteen sixty-eight*. Back when it all seemed so exciting, when her plans were all stacked so neatly, delicate cards leaning just so against one another. And now, she can tell, it's all about to fall.

Rose turns around but says nothing. She doesn't have to. It's all right there, in her red-rimmed eyes, her fluttering nostrils, the minuscule lines that radiate out from her tight, pained lips. It's there in her chest, her breaths shallow and rapid. It's there in the way she stares at her daughter, tongue between her teeth, head shaking just a little, like a leaf caught by the slightest breeze.

The invisible cord between them hisses and pulls, magnetic and charged. Rose opens her mouth.

"Are you—"

Baker lunges in front of Rose, grabs the cold metal edge of the kitchen sink, and vomits again. When the heaving has finally settled, she wills herself to look up at her mother, whose face is contorted in horror and sorrow. They cry in such similar ways.

"I'm sorry," Baker gasps, and Rose turns and storms out of the room.

When Gerald arrives home from the dealership, Baker and Rose are sitting in the living room, waiting for him. They're quiet. Unusually quiet. The three-tiered snack tray sits on the coffee table, stocked with nuts and olives and Rose's meat roll-ups. Two martini glasses, filled to the brim, hers with an olive and his with a pepperoncini. And an envelope.

"Why so quiet?" he cries. "Open it up!"

Rose pushes the letter across the table so that it's right in front of Baker. Rose's mouth is tight and Gerald's is a big wide grin. She slides the envelope open and pulls out the folded paper. The letterhead, so formal and important. Her name, right there at the top. And several brief paragraphs outlining a future that two of the three of them know isn't going to happen. Baker hands the letter to her mother and Rose reads aloud. Baker waits for Rose's voice to crack, but of course it does not. Of course she holds it together.

"Hurrah!" Rose and Gerald cheer, clinking their glasses and hugging each other. Gerald whoops and grins at his daughter; he pats her back and ruffles her hair.

"My goodness," he exclaims. "You know what my old man used to say about me not having a son: 'Look at your brothers. Their boys will carry on the family legacy.' And I'd always say, 'I've got Elizabeth.

She's something special.'" He beams at Rose, who's wiping mascara-tinged tears from her lower lids. Gerald's exuberance is a gift to them both. "Pops would be proud if he could see this. Of course, he didn't think girls should go to school past the eighth grade, but hey, maybe he would've come around. To the future!"

After dinner, Baker clears the table and then excuses herself, claiming that the excitement of the day has made her too tired to watch the evening news with them. Gerald is still beaming as he waves her away and settles into his chair. "You've earned it," he crows. "Go take it easy!" Baker half expects Rose to follow her to her bedroom, to pick up where they left off in the kitchen, but she doesn't. Rose says nothing and joins Gerald in the living room.

The pride in his voice makes Baker's heart feel tight and shriveled. It's bad enough to feel her mother's reaction, but the thought of breaking her father's heart, too? She shuts her bedroom door and falls onto her bed. Furious and frustrated, she yanks the bedspread over her body, knocking the algebra textbook and the stupid accounting book to the floor. She glares at the soft white canopy above her, at the awards on the walls and the stacks of books and the pale yellow typewriter. The neglected journal. Everything in her room seems to mock her now, glaring little reminders of all she's just lost. She squeezes her eyes shut and imagines it all just disappearing.

Then Gerald's voice cuts through the house. "God *damn*." Then the sound of his glass slamming down on the side table. Something's wrong.

Baker opens her door and walks carefully down the hall until she can peer around and see the living room, her parents' bodies on the edges of their seats, leaning toward the television. Walter Cronkite speaks with steady authority.

"*. . . They rushed the thirty-nine-year-old Negro leader to the hospital, where he died of a bullet wound to the neck—*"

Gerald is shaking his head, muttering under his breath. Rose is sobbing. A terrible chill runs up Baker's spine; it climbs up her neck and over her shoulders and cascades down over her chest, her clenched heart. The living room seems off-kilter, the house off-balance. The entire planet knocked off its axis. They stare at the television as reliable Walter continues to deliver the news, and the world outside continues to spin, wild, exploding around them.

The next morning, Gerald and Rose don't get out of bed. Baker gets herself ready for school, makes herself toast, puts the empty vodka bottle in the trash, and washes the glasses that her parents left in the living room. Before she leaves, she opens their bedroom door just a crack, wanting a quick proof of life. Rose snores softly, and Gerald shifts under his blanket. Baker is relieved to not have to face them.

Midway through fourth period, Baker gets called into the office. Her heart races as she walks the halls—did Rose tell the school? When she walks in and sees Rose standing there, chatting with Nell, the receptionist, her heart nearly drops from her body. Rose is impeccable in a slimming pencil skirt, crisp white blouse, and long chiffon scarf knotted around her neck. Her makeup is expertly applied, and Baker notices the extra rouge on her cheeks, how the thick concealer falls into the creases below her eyes.

"An important appointment," she's explaining to Nell. "Related to *college*. She's been accepted to Stanford, you know."

Nell smiles and beams at Baker. "We've heard the big news, Elizabeth! How exciting!"

Rose turns to Baker. She's wearing her biggest, brightest smile. "Shall we go, darling?"

They walk to the car in silence. No *How has your day been* or *It's a little breezy out* or *Let me tell you what is happening*. No *How could you do this* or *What's wrong with you*. Not even *Who did this to you*. Not even *Why*.

"Get in the car, please. We can't be late." Baker opens her mouth to ask where they're going, but the words dissolve on her tongue.

The radio comes on when Rose starts the car. *"The disturbances continue, with no signs of ceasing. In over seventy cities across the nation, from Baltimore to Detroit to Washington, DC, the streets are aflame. In Chicago, Mayor Daley has imposed a curfew, and the National Guard has been—"*

Rose turns it off and pulls onto the main road, away from the school. She grips the steering wheel so hard that the pale turquoise veins on the backs of her hands pop out. The thin tendon that runs up her neck to her jaw pulses. When she finally speaks, she doesn't look at Baker.

"We're going to see a doctor."

"Dr. Finley?" Baker imagines her kindly old pediatrician knowing what she's done. She recoils from the thought.

"No. A specialist."

It's warm in the car. Sweat pools on Baker's brow, on the back of her neck, beneath her arms and between her legs and under the itchy elastic of her too-tight bra. She looks out the window at the houses and buildings and people flashing past. She sees an elderly woman walking with a cane, a middle-aged woman exiting a shop, a beautiful lady walking a small brown dog, and it occurs to her that they might all be mothers. Which would mean that they were each pregnant at some point. She watches the women on the street and wonders how this just happens all the time, every day. She wonders if they're looking back at her, if they can tell. Can they sense it? Can they see it in her face? Do women just *know*? Is that how Rose knew?

She'd been feeling so mature, so grown, so ready to burst out into the big world of adulthood, and now she sinks down into the passenger seat of her mother's car, grips her fists, and curls her toes inside her too-tight Keds. She bites her trembling bottom lip like she's four years old, trying not to cry.

The "specialist's" office is in a low beige building. The door has a faux-wood placard: Dr. RICHARD BELL, MD, OB-GYN. Baker's heart races even more. She doesn't know what an OB-GYN is, but she tries to figure it out. She knows that *gyn* is a Greek root, meaning female, so a GYN is a . . . doctor who works with females? She tries to imagine what OB might mean. *Obstinate. Obliterated.*

Rose confers in hushed tones with the frog-faced woman behind the front desk, who glances several times at Baker. The looks she gives are somewhere between professional pity and irritated scorn. She leads them down a hallway into a small white room.

"Remove your clothes and put this on." She hands Baker a stiff blue gown, avoiding eye contact. "Then lie down and wait. He'll be in soon."

"May I wait with her?" Rose asks.

"Sure. But you can't be in here for the exam."

"Of course. Thank you so much."

The exam?

Baker waits for Frog Lady to exit, then turns to Rose. She grips the gown, which makes rustling sounds. "Mother. Please. What exactly is the doctor going to do?"

Rose looks at the brown vinyl bed where Baker will sit. She looks at her balled-up hands holding the stiff blue gown. Then she looks, finally, into her daughter's eyes. She leans in and hugs her, quick and tight, then breathes deep through flared nostrils. "It's better now than it was in my day. It won't hurt, and it will be quick. We can get confirmation." Her breath catches on the word *confirmation,* and Rose's eyes well up. She pulls a handkerchief from her handbag and dabs, catching the mascara before it forms trails down her cheeks. She finds her polite smile again. "I'm okay. We're okay. I'll be in the waiting room."

Dr. Richard Bell is tall and slightly stooped, with graying hair and glasses. Brusque and quick, a doctor of few words.

"Elizabeth Phillips?"

"Yes, sir."

"You know why you're here?"

She doesn't answer.

He chuckles to himself. "I'm pretty sure you have some idea. Lie back, please." She looks up at the ceiling, the light bright in her eyes. Her cheeks burn. Is he laughing at her? "Knees up." Dr. Bell pokes and pushes her stomach, hard, as if trying to find his way in. "And when did you last have intercourse?"

She gasps, then, as she feels his gloved hand enter her, unexpected and cold, nothing like how it felt when Wiley was there.

"Hmm?" He's impatient, waiting for her answer.

"I don't know."

"You must know."

She breathes hard as he seems to twist his hand. "January."

"Just January?"

"And February," she says, wincing, her voice small and strained.

"I see." He looks down his nose at her. "More than once."

Wherever his hand is, whatever it is doing down there, it hurts. She presses her lips together and holds her breath. Hot tears slip from the corners of her eyes and run in little rivers down her temple, into her hair.

"And your last menstrual period?"

One hand is still inside. With the other, he resumes the stomach-pushing, making occasional *hmm* sounds.

"Early January," she whispers.

He says nothing more for about a minute, just pushes and prods in silence until he removes his hands and snaps off his gloves. He doesn't make eye contact, but she can see the disdain on his face.

"You're about thirteen weeks along."

His mouth keeps moving, but Baker can't hear him due to the roaring, whooshing sound that fills the room. It's a cross between a freight train and a massive wave crashing on the shore, and it rattles her brain.

"Thirteen weeks *pregnant*," he's saying.

The whooshing gets louder, and suddenly there is a gaping black hole in the middle of the floor. A swirling sucking whirlpool, and into it goes everything: her diploma, her calendar, her pale yellow Smith Corona, the college roommate, the professors, the crushes, the heady conversations, the books and articles and essays that will never be written, not by her, at least. They'll go to someone else, some other girl who manages to keep her wits about her, who doesn't go and ruin everything.

"Elizabeth? Hello?" He's snapping his thick doctor fingers. "Do you understand what I'm telling you?"

"Yes. Of course. Thank you."

Dr. Bell turns to a calendar on the wall and runs his fingers across the weeks and months. He stops in October. "I'm a betting man, so I'll put my money on . . . October fourteenth. Happens to be my wife's birthday!" He seems satisfied with himself as he gestures for Baker to sit up. "I'm rarely wrong about these things. But for the sake of science, we'll collect a urine sample and see if the rabbit dies."

Baker sits up fast, not even bothering to cover herself with the gown. "The *what*?"

Dr. Bell laughs, a quick sharp bark. "You haven't heard the phrase? We inject your urine into a rabbit, then analyze its ovaries for the presence of human chorionic gonadotropin."

The whooshing sound returns, but she can still hear him speak.

"It's a *hormone*," he explains, as if talking to a child. "People used to think that the urine of a pregnant woman automatically killed the rabbit, but that's incorrect. The rabbit *always* dies. Because we have to dissect them."

She imagines the rabbit, splayed open in a lab, filled with her pee, its little body somehow telling a scientist about her unfortunate situation.

"I'll go speak to your mother. And from now on, young lady, do us—and the rabbits!—a big favor. Keep those lovely long legs shut." He pats her knee, and walks out the door.

And that's that. He doesn't ask how she's feeling, whether she has any questions, if she's perhaps so terrified that she's hallucinating celestial voids. He just walks away, leaving her wishing she'd obeyed the reflex she'd felt and had kicked him when he touched her.

Rose doesn't speak as they leave the doctor's office, but she does hold Baker's hand. Tightly. Baker lets herself be pulled along, and she watches her mother with a kind of fascination as she looks straight ahead, her face serene and tight. Rose is always together, always grace under pressure, calm control, but this is different. This kind of calm seems impossible. Unsustainable. A bomb just *tick-tick-tick*ing.

Baker is consumed by panic, like she was when she was six and broke the arm of Rose's favorite porcelain doll. The one she wasn't supposed to play with. The one she snuck off the shelf because she was just too beautiful. When Rose discovered Baker trying in vain to fix the shattered arm with tape and twine, she'd been so mad that she said nothing. Just frosty silence. It was the worst. Baker wished she'd just yell.

To distract herself, she runs the numbers. *Thirteen weeks.* She tries to count backwards, to figure out when it might have happened, but she gets lost in the math. She can't remember how many days February has, and just the thought of Wiley makes her teeth clench, makes her hands and shoulders tense up tight. Here she is in this miserable car with her devastated mother, her entire future disintegrating before her, and he's probably somewhere with a smile on his face and a nice cold beer in his hand.

She tries to count forward. How many days until October fourteenth? She looks down at her body: her breasts are visibly bigger, but the rest still looks normal. She's *seen* pregnant women before. There's no way her body could transform that fast. Right? She stops trying to do the math. Is anyone going to explain how this all works? Is anyone going to help her?

When they're halfway home, stopped at a red light, Baker can't wait any longer.

"Are you going to say anything?"

"No."

"Why not?"

Rose stares straight ahead. Cars slide through the intersection, filled with people just going about their lives. "Because I'm busy."

"*Busy?*" Baker doesn't mean to snap, but the word comes out sharp.

Rose's head whips around. The light turns green. Her voice is low, controlled. "I am busy figuring out a goddamned plan."

The car behind her blares its horn, and Rose lays her foot on the gas. Baker's body presses against the seat, and they speed home in silence.

Gerald meets them at the door, a drink in his hand, a pained expression on his face.

"Make mine a triple," Rose says.

They sit around the kitchen table. Baker stares at her hands, clasped tight on her lap, knuckles pale, nails digging moons into soft skin. Rose rolls her eyes back and dabs carefully at her lower lids with a fingertip. Baker imagines that she's pushing the tears back in. It seems like a power her mother might have. Gerald stares straight ahead, waiting. Rose exhales.

"Our daughter is—" Her lips seem to freeze. Baker squeezes her eyes shut and pictures herself on the edge of a cliff. Just waiting for the fall.

"Rose?" Gerald's voice has an edge of panic.

Rose spits the word out. "Pregnant." Baker can practically hear it land on the table between them.

Baker opens her eyes. Gerald's mouth is a small open O. Rose's jaw could cut a diamond.

Gerald also seems frozen, so Rose continues. "I thought I was a good mother."

"You are," Baker whispers, surprised by how quickly Rose has made this about herself. "This has nothing to do with you—"

"It has everything to do with me. I'm your *mother*. How could I let this happen?"

Baker examines the backs of her hands. The small brown freckles. She looks across the table at Rose's hands, clasped the exact same way. "It's my fault."

"It started on New Year's Eve, didn't it."

Baker nods her head slightly.

"Some degenerate 'friend' of May's, am I correct?"

She doesn't know how to respond to this, but it doesn't matter.

"Several months now, you've been sneaking around, lying to us."

"But you never lie," Gerald finally speaks, sounding genuinely puzzled. "You're not a liar."

"Well, she is now!" Rose tries to laugh, but it gets caught on a sob in her throat. "And the thing is, I knew it all along."

"Now, Rose," Gerald begins, but she cuts him off.

"Yes, Gerald, I *did*. *Something's not right*, I thought, *Elizabeth seems off, she's distracted, and why does she suddenly want to spend all this time with her cousin?* But I talked myself out of it; I said to myself, *Rose, you're being paranoid. She's a good girl, and it's good for her to go places and make some friends!*" She lights a Winston and takes a long, slow suck. The smoke slips through her painted lips. Her eyes are rimmed red; the thin blood vessels on her cheeks pulse, creating the lacy rash she hates.

"Does anyone know?"

"No."

"Are you *sure*?"

"I haven't told anyone." What does it matter, another lie?

Rose stands and begins pacing the length of the room, carelessly ashing her cigarette on the rug. "It can't be. It just can't. You're too young, you're still a child. You're—you're a Girl Scout!" She spits the last line like an attorney delivering damning evidence, the proof that it cannot be true.

"I'm sorry, Mother."

"You're the daughter everyone envies! *Oh, she's so smart, and so good! And she's even pretty! What a lucky family!*"

"I didn't think this would happen."

"You didn't think at all." The words come out of Rose's mouth like sharp darts, thrown hard. "That's the problem."

It's the worst insult, because Baker knows it's true. She wasn't thinking, or worrying, and for a brief, dumb time, it had felt so good. Her brain has always been her biggest asset, but it's also so exhausting. It was such a relief to take a break from the constant mental gymnastics of being good. It was such a relief to just get to feel.

"We've worked so *hard*. We've worked and we've tried and you're our—you're supposed to be—"

"I get it! I'm the success story! I'm the shiny trophy on your mantel and now—"

Gerald's voice booms uncharacteristically. "Don't you speak to your parents like that!"

Baker is racked with guilt and humiliation, but also rage and disdain. Her chest feels tight, she aches between her legs where the doctor shoved his hand, and she wants to run away. She wants to crawl into bed. She wants to yell at her mother, defend her decisions, her right to live and to make mistakes. Even the ones she regrets so much, even the ones she hates herself for. She wants to be *allowed* to be wrong. She wants to jump in the deep end of the pool and put her head underwater, forever, but she also wants to crawl into her mother's angry arms and be soothed, rocked, told that everything is going to be okay. Why can't they just help her?

"I'm *sorry*, Mother. I don't know what else to say." And she doesn't. The worst has happened. Is happening. She's out of lies, and apologies are futile. It all feels so impossible. So *bad*. She wasn't lying when she said she'd rather have a terrible disease. Then at least her parents would still love her.

A long, miserable silence. Gerald's TV show plays in the other room; an audience laughs. Rose chews her bottom lip, then finally speaks again.

"No one can know. Do you understand?"

"Yes, Mother."

"I'm absolutely serious. *No one.*"

"I get it," Baker mutters. "This is so terribly embarrassing for you."

"Oh, no," Rose seethes. "It's not about embarrassment, Elizabeth. It's not about *me*. They will kick you out of school for this. Do you understand that?"

Baker's body goes cold. Somehow, of all the dark swirling thoughts she's had, this one has not occurred to her.

"Two months before graduation, and they can drop you like that." Rose snaps her fingers. "And then what? You're supposed to be the damn valedictorian, you're not supposed to have—" Her voice drops to a whisper as she barely manages to get the word out. "A *baby.*"

The word seems to change the entire chemical makeup of the room. The temperature, the feel of the air, the light. It all becomes heavier, darker. Real.

"I am protecting you, Baker." She looks at Gerald and amends her statement. "*We* are protecting you. And not every parent would do this, do you understand that?"

Gerald glowers. His voice is unusually deep. "Some people would put their daughters out on the streets for this."

Baker looks at her father with pleading eyes. "Daddy. You wouldn't." Gerald averts his gaze, looks out the window.

"What your father is saying is you're lucky."

Baker almost laughs at that turn of phrase. She couldn't feel further from luck.

"Your mother is right. This information doesn't leave this room." Gerald turns to Rose. "What *are* we going to do?" He speaks as if his daughter isn't sitting right there. He speaks as if she's already out on the streets.

Rose's nostrils flutter; her eyelids lower, then quiver. The slash of turquoise eyeshadow across her lids glints as she lights another cigarette.

"We'll do what's best for our daughter." She looks at them both with the same steely eyes. If there were a plaque to be won for this kind of thing, she would win it. And she knows it. "I will handle this."

Gerald swirls his drink on the table. The ice clinks, loud. "What about marriage? In our day, if this happened, the honorable thing was—"

Rose looks at Baker, who realizes her mother hasn't even asked about the father. "Do you want to marry this . . . person?"

She remembers the view from May's window. How he just walked away, unburdened by not knowing. How she'd tried to envision a kind of life with him. How she'd wanted to scream.

"No."

"What's his name, anyway?"

"Wiley."

"*Wiley.*" Rose nearly spits her drink onto the carpet. "What kind of name is *Wiley*? Sounds like some long-haired loser. Are you going to go be his barefoot hippie wife?"

A wave of defiance crashes against Baker's chest. Her nostrils flare, and she finds herself wanting to defend the man she's so angry with. To salvage some semblance of pride and agency. "He's a good person. But that's not what I want."

"This isn't about what you *want,* anymore. And that's enough about him. We won't speak of him, you won't see him, and he will never know about this."

At least they agree on something. Baker stares at the painting on the wall behind her mother's head: the Virgin Mary, beatific, beaming down at the baby in her arms. Rose isn't religious, but it's a treasured piece—it had belonged to her mother. Baker's always loved how soft Mary looks, how calm and unbothered she and her nice little baby appear. The painting used to make Baker feel calm by extension, but now it makes her even more agitated, embarrassed, inflamed. A bitter taste spreads through her mouth. Mary just up there, gloating. So immaculate and perfect. It's the opposite of how she feels now.

"He's gone, anyway."

"What do you mean, gone? He just used you and left?"

Baker bites her lip and tilts her head back. She pokes her eyelids with her fingertips the way Rose does. The tears come out anyway. "He's in Mexico."

Rose sucks in air audibly. Gerald puts his glass down hard. The table shakes.

Baker imagines running—out of the house and down the street and far away from everything—but she couldn't move if she tried. Shame is heavy. So is guilt. Every angry word from her parents is like a rock in her pockets. If she could get to the pool, she'd sink right to the bottom.

The phone rings, and Rose looks around startled, as if the house were bugged and someone was calling to bust them. She leans in and enunciates every word. "As I was saying: I will handle this. And no one. Else. Will. Know."

Then she rushes off to answer the phone, her chiffon scarf flowing behind her like an angry cloud.

The next day, Saturday, Gerald is at the lot and Rose has two back-to-back events—a fundraiser for the children's hospital, and then the monthly gathering of one of her other lady organizations that Baker can't keep track of. Neither will be home until the end of the day. She has all afternoon to make the call. Or calls. She has no idea how it will work.

She pulls the pamphlet from her purse. She feels a twinge of guilt for dodging May's calls these past few weeks. Rose has taken down a few messages, informing May that Baker has strep throat, and will call when she's feeling better. And she will call her cousin sometime soon. Maybe even later today, after this.

Society for Humane Abortion. It terrifies her, but she knows she needs to try. If she can fix this herself, she'll save her family a world of trouble. She could salvage her dreams, show herself that she can be the competent, smart, worldly woman she wants to be. And what if that works; what if she can make it all go away? Her parents won't have to know how it happened. She can just . . . not be pregnant anymore. Things happen, right?

Before she goes to the phone in the kitchen, she locks the front door and, irrationally, checks each room in the house to make sure that she is, in fact, alone. Her fingers shake as she dials the number. There are several zeroes, and it takes forever for the dial to circle all the way back.

A woman answers. "Hello?"

Baker panics and hangs up.

It's okay. I can do this.

She dials again.

Waits for the zeroes.

"Hello," says the voice again, mildly impatient this time. Baker feels bad for hanging up but reasons that she probably isn't the only one to do that.

"I'm calling about . . . I have the pamphlet?"

"Where do you live?" The voice is warm but detached.

"San Francisco," she lies.

"And you're pregnant?"

Baker stares at the kitchen countertop. Pale yellow with scattered speckles that Rose often mistakes for crumbs. She stares at the specks until they become blurry. Her head swims. Her jaw clenches.

"Hello? Is it safe for you to answer my questions?"

Baker blinks and crouches to the floor. It feels safer, somehow. "Yes, I can answer."

"Okay. You're pregnant?"

"Yes." It comes out as a whisper, but it feels enormous.

"And how far along are you?"

She pictures Dr. Bell's smirking face. "Thirteen weeks?"

"Your last menstrual cycle?"

"Mid-January."

Silence on the other end. Baker hears papers shuffling.

"Almost done with the first trimester. Not much time left."

"Oh." Baker feels relieved and panicked at the same time—there's still time, but also, there's not much time left?

"If you want to proceed, I'll need your phone number. One of our counselors will call you back this evening."

"N-no," she stammers. "My parents will be—that's too late. Is there anyone I can talk to now?"

"I'm sorry, I just pass along the information."

"Can anyone call sooner? Please."

Silence as the woman shuffles more papers. "I might have some-one."

"Before four-thirty?"

"I think so. She'll say her name is Jane. Have paper and pencil ready."

"Thank you so much."

Baker can't help but stand next to the phone as the hours go by. She's hungry and bored, but she refuses to abandon her post, con-vinced that if she steps away for even ten seconds, Rose will sud-denly walk in the door, the phone will ring, and everything will fall apart. She stays put, watching the clock above the pale green oven, picking at her cuticles, chewing on her bottom lip, squeezing her thighs together because she has to pee so bad. If she had her chem-istry book, she could study a little. If she had *Jane Eyre,* she could reread her favorite passages. If she had her journal . . . she wouldn't even know where to begin. Writing it down would make it seem so *real*.

At 4:05, the phone trills, and it's in her hand before the first ring is done. But it's only Aunt Stella, calling for Rose, and Baker explains that she's at one of her meetings.

When it rings again, it's 4:25. Baker's bladder is threatening to spill, and she keeps thinking she hears a car in the driveway. She yanks the phone from its cradle.

"Hello?"

"This is Jane calling." Jane's voice is firm and authoritative, like a teacher. Or a doctor. Could she be a doctor?

"Yes, hi Jane, this is—I'm the one that called the number. For an appointment."

"Tell me your name, please."

She pauses. She hasn't considered what to tell them. "Liz."

"Age?"

"Seventeen."

"How many weeks?"

"Thirteen?"

"Is that a question? We need you to be as certain as possible."

"Thirteen," Baker repeats. "I saw a doctor."

"Okay, Liz. I can tell from your voice that you're nervous. Take a deep breath, okay? We are here to help you."

Baker tries, but her mouth is dry and the air gets stuck.

"Are you interested in having an abortion?"

She looks at the front door; cranes her neck to catch a glimpse of the driveway. She knows no one's home, but she's so afraid to say the words aloud.

"Liz? It's important to be sure."

"Yes," she finally whispers.

"What are the circumstances of your pregnancy?"

"Pardon?"

"How did you get pregnant? With a boyfriend? Was it by force?"

"He's not my boyfriend, but I knew him. Know him. He didn't force me—I mean, I wanted to do it, we weren't exactly dating but—"

"Do you have any health reasons that would make childbirth dangerous or life-threatening?"

"I don't think so."

"Some women can qualify for what are known as *therapeutic abortions*. These are done in some hospitals now, here in California. But it's rare, only allowed in extreme cases. Rape, incest, endangerment of the mother's life."

She is struck first by this phrase, *therapeutic abortion,* then by the mention of these terrible things. How can the mother's life be endangered by pregnancy? Did Dr. Bell neglect to tell her something serious?

"No, ma'am," she mumbles. "None of those things. It's just . . . a pregnancy."

"That's fine, Liz. I'm going to give you an address, and a date and time. We also have a list of names and addresses of doctors outside of the U.S. who we trust to perform safe procedures, but we don't have time to wait for you to arrange all the travel. Better to do it here. You'll need five hundred dollars. And a ride there and back."

"Five hundred dollars," Baker repeats. How on earth will she get five hundred dollars?

"And a ride. You'll be able to get a ride, yes?"

"A ride. Sure." Who on earth will give her a ride?

"Any questions before I give you the address?"

Baker looks at the ceiling. There is a cobweb in the corner by the window, grease stains up above the stovetop. An S-shaped mark from the time Gerald threw a piece of spaghetti up to see if it was done. It stuck to the ceiling for weeks. She wants to ask what *happens,* what an abortion actually *is.* What does the doctor do; what tools does he use? Will she be awake or asleep? Does it hurt? And what exactly is inside of her right now—what does it look like, how big is it? Is it like a tadpole?

"Liz? Any questions?"

"I'm just curious. Is this phone call legal?"

"No. A thousand-dollar fine and up to thirty days in county jail for furnishing this information to a minor, Liz."

"Oh." Baker swallows, overwhelmed by the magnitude of this revelation. It's hard to understand why this total stranger is risking prison just to help a girl who messed up. No questions aside from the logistical ones, no judgment or advice? No asking whether her parents know what she's doing, whether the father knows? Who is this woman on the other end of the telephone? "Thank you, Jane, that's kind of you." *Kind.* It's more than kind, but Baker doesn't have the words.

"Liz, I'm going to give you the address, and some very important instructions. Do *not* let anyone see the address. Except the person who's driving you. Okay?"

"Okay."

*W*hen the day comes, there's no one to drive her. She did finally call May, but she's out of town, visiting her former housemates on their new land down in Santa Cruz. Whoever answered the phone at her place said she won't be back for another week.

So she'll do it on her own. *I got myself into this,* she thinks, as she looks at her puffy face in the bathroom mirror. *I can figure this out.*

She takes a map from the glove box in Gerald's car and lays it out on her bedroom floor. She finds the town—not *too* far—then the street, then the bus line that will take her there. She'll only have to transfer once, and then it looks like a short enough walk from there.

It's Saturday again: Gerald is at the lot, and Rose is hosting a breakfast and then working a catering shift as a "favor for a friend," which Baker knows is code for a way to make some extra cash. Baker waits until they're gone to get dressed. She takes a camel-colored swing coat that Rose hasn't worn for years from the front closet. She puts a scarf over her hair, knotted under her chin, and puts a pair of May's old sunglasses in her purse. She slips on her Keds—they're even tighter now—and looks in the mirror. She sags with disappointment. She wants to project maturity, but the sneakers make her look like a kid playing dress-up in her mother's clothes. She finds an older pair of pale blue satin pumps in the back of Rose's closet. They're at least half a size too small, and so stiff. She'll get blisters, for sure. At the last minute, she grabs a few Band-Aids from the medicine cabinet and puts them in her purse, along with a handful of nickels and dimes for bus fare. Then she tucks 197 dollars in cash into her bra: it's the contents of her childhood piggy bank, plus two twenties that she filched from Gerald's top dresser drawer. It's a meager down payment on the 500 dollars, but she hopes it will work.

When she boards the bus, the driver looks her up and down. Baker keeps her head down but smiles politely, terrified that she'll be recognized. An older gentleman smiles and tips his cap at her. She takes a seat near the back, next to the window, and watches the streets, the towns, the people pass. It gets less and less familiar as they go. She clutches the map from Gerald's car and looks down at it constantly, in case the bus somehow veers off course and she needs to alert the driver. She taps her foot. Her stomach rumbles. She's nauseous; she's tired; she doesn't understand why buses are so slow.

It takes a little over an hour to get to the stop that she's circled in red on the map, but it feels like one hundred years. Finally the driver calls out the name of the street that the lady on the phone had her write down. From there, Baker walks, past a diner, a hairdresser, a vacuum repair shop. Every so often there are a few houses, rundown, front lawns dry and patchy. She sees stray cats slinking around, crows on a wire up above her. She walks quickly, but not too quickly, her nails digging into her damp sticky palms. She hardly sees any people, not even in the shops, but still she keeps her head down. She's far enough from home, but *still*. What if a distant family member lives here? What if a neighbor brings their vacuum to this repair shop? The closer she gets to the number on the paper, the more conspicuous she feels. Like a spotlight is shining on her, like the few cars that drive by are trailing her. She looks for police cars, for nosy older ladies, for men in dark suits who might be FBI agents.

1430 82nd Ave, Suite C. An old brick building with an empty storefront that looks like it used to be a beauty salon. A blank spot where a sign once hung. On the left side of the building is a door. She rereads the instructions she's already read many times.

Ring bell ONCE. Wait. Be QUIET.

"Jane" had raised her voice dramatically on certain words, and Baker wrote them down in capital letters.

Go upstairs to Suite C. Down hall on left.

DO NOT knock on other doors.

DO NOT talk to ANYONE until you are INSIDE Suite C.

She rings the bell and waits. A buzzer sounds, startling her, and she hears the door unlatch. The stairs are dark and narrow and smell like cigarettes and some kind of cleaner. Lysol, she realizes, as she makes her way up the steps. Suddenly she remembers overhearing her aunts talking, at a family party, about a girl, someone's daughter, who'd almost died from drinking a bottle of Lysol. *Spent a week in the hospital,* one of them said. *Would've DIED if her father hadn't found her. Nearly killed her* and *that baby. Who would do such a thing? They should've taken her straight from the hospital to a jail cell.* The memory sends an awful chill up her spine, straight into the base of her skull.

The smell overwhelms her, and her heart begins to race. Her eyes water, and she braces herself in the narrow stairwell, gripping the railing with one hand and the wall with the other. She can't believe she's here all by herself. She's lightheaded, she's queasy, she didn't really eat breakfast, and it's been awhile since she's had anything to drink. Her lungs seem to shrink, and her mouth starts watering, filling with a foul, sour taste. There's one more flight of stairs ahead, and she has no idea what's at the top. Jane's friendly face? Or something else? What if it's all a setup, a trap? What if there is no counselor, no doctor? What if Jane's a spy, or a cop? There's a small window on the landing, and she peers out, scanning the street for suspicious figures. She sees nothing, no one, which also makes her nervous. If she does go through with it, what if something happens to her? She doesn't know exactly what happens during the proce-dure, but she knows, of course, that things can go wrong. Very wrong. *This is why they said not to go alone. This is why you don't show up by yourself. It's not just about a ride. It's the buddy system, idiot.*

Just then, footsteps. A man in a brown suit appears at the top of the next flight of stairs, bald with a thick mustache and shiny shoes. He stares down at her.

"Oh, for Christ's sake," he moans, throwing up his hands. "I'm sick of this. Now turn around and get out of here, or I'm calling the police. *Again.*"

Baker looks up at the man, shocked, her hand gripping the cheap railing attached to the cheap wall of the cheap building. The word *police* rings in her ears. She cranes her neck and tries to see past him. Suite C must be just beyond where he stands. And someone is in there waiting for her. Waiting to help her. She could run past him and find the door—

"Are you deaf?" He takes a step forward, and she stumbles back-wards, nearly tripping on the stairs. Or this could all be a trap.

DO NOT talk to ANYONE.

She turns and she runs, hoping he's not chasing after her. He didn't *seem* like he wanted to hurt her, but she's not taking chances. And he could have called the police—they might be on their way now. She flies down the dark, smelly stairs until she's outside, the door has slammed behind her, and she's panting and gasping in the bright, blinding sunlight. She's got to get out of here. This was *not* mentioned in the instructions. Have the police been there before? Have girls been arrested? She begins to walk, brisk but not too brisk, in the direction she came. Her heart is an earthquake; her whole body shakes.

She doesn't stop walking until she reaches the diner she'd passed earlier. Her stomach rumbles, loudly, and she's desperate for a bath-room. Inside she finds relief, and then a table, where she catches her breath, and orders a turkey sandwich and a lemonade from a busy waitress who doesn't make eye contact. As she waits for the food to come, she sees the large clock on the wall above the counter. It's later than she thought. She has to do that entire bus ride again, in reverse. And she has to get home before five. She wolfs down her lunch, dousing the sour taste in her mouth with too-sweet lemonade, and leaves a big tip.

The bus stop is not where it was before. Or rather: she thought she'd just retrace her steps, but it's all become a blur. She walks and walks in the direction that feels right, keeping her eyes peeled for anything familiar that would suggest that she's on the right path. She wonders if a taxi might be a solution, and how far the remaining wad of cash in her handbag can get her. San Francisco, for sure. Could she go all the way to Los Angeles, to Hollywood? Could she make it to Mexico? She imagines the car pulling up, her leaning in and telling the driver to take her to the border.

Then she comes to a freeway overpass that she definitely didn't cross before. Her heart sinks: in the distance, she can see buildings, and what looks like a downtown area. She's completely lost. And lost in a strange city isn't where she wants to be right now, when cities across the country are still smoldering, still reeling. Just last night, over two thousand people protested at the courthouse in Oakland after the funeral for Bobby Hutton, gunned down by the police. Baker saw it on the news—Gerald cursed at the Panthers, but she imagined raising her right fist in solidarity with them all. He was only seventeen, the same age as her. What if there's a riot up ahead, if buildings are burning there, too? They *should* be burning, she thinks.

Midway across the overpass, she stops and stares down at the rushing traffic, transfixed. Her dress skims the middle of her thighs—it's a dress from *before,* that she can still manage to pull on, but fits a lot shorter now. The cool air rushes up from the busy freeway and gives her goosebumps, makes the fabric—tiny pink paisleys across a pale blue—ripple and move. She feels her feet on the ground, aching from all the walking. She lets her arms float out on either side, imagines them being lifted by the force of the air. Imagines—briefly—her entire body lifted up, off the concrete, over the barrier, and down down down. Maybe the big black hole is down there, maybe it would wrap her in its whooshing arms and make it all go away. It would make sense in the way that nothing makes sense. It would be fast and certain. It would be free.

She's pulled back from the edge by the sound of an approaching car. She whirls around. It's a tan Buick, and Baker sees a woman in the driver's seat. She slows; rolls down her window. Baker knows she should run, but she's also out of options.

"Need a ride, hon?" She has the face of a woman who has seen things, Baker thinks. Rough skin, a deep crease between her penciled-in eyebrows, and a thousand tiny lines radiating from her lips like a soft fringe. But her eyes are kind, and they seem to know that Baker needs help. "It's not safe out here these days. Get on in before someone worse than me comes along, will ya?"

Baker has never hitchhiked before. She's never traveled alone to a strange city to almost get an abortion, either. And she's never considered—not even for a moment—throwing her body into traffic. She's never really done anything controversial or untoward or illegal or even irrational at all. Until this year. Until now. So why not one more thing. She slides into the car.

The woman reaches into the glove compartment and pulls out a wad of lace-edged handkerchiefs and a pack of Winstons.

"Help yourself, honey." Baker takes one of the lipstick-smudged handkerchiefs and blows her snotty nose right into it, then wipes her eyes, and her sweaty forehead and neck. The woman pulls out a cigarette and lights it, handing it to Baker.

"Thanks, but I don't smoke."

The woman shrugs and takes a drag. "You're missing out. Tastes good!"

Baker smiles and finishes the jingle. "Like a cigarette should." She adds, "My mother smokes those."

"Your mother know where you are?"

Baker shakes her head.

"Whatever it is, sweetie, it'll pass. Take it from me, you're gonna be alright." The woman puts her car in gear and pulls back onto the road. "Can't say the same about this damn country. Hell in a hand-basket, and the devil around every corner."

She turns on the radio, blows a cloud of smoke out the window, taps her glossy red nails on the dashboard, and sings along. "Young Girl" by Gary Puckett & the Union Gap. Baker rolls her eyes and groans inwardly. She can't stand this song, and how stupidly perfect for it to be playing right now.

> *You better run, girl*
> *You're much too young, girl*

Outside the Buick, the sun is starting to get lower, and thin clouds lounge across the sky. Baker watches the houses, the trees, the buildings. The white line down the center of the road. She wonders who was waiting for her in Suite C, whether they called "Jane" to tell her that Liz never showed up. Maybe they're worried about her—or maybe they're angry. She thinks about what the woman on the phone risked just to have that conversation. The person in Suite C must be so brave. Braver than her, a girl who fled at the sight of a man. At the word *police*. Suddenly it all seems ridiculous: how scared she got, how she panicked and ran. How she gave up so quickly. That was her chance to solve her own problem. What a coward she is. What a failure.

The woman sings along until the dumb song ends.

"Must be nice, being a young girl. I remember those days." She shifts into high gear and merges onto a busier, bigger road, one that Baker recognizes. She reaches over and grabs Baker's hand, tight. "Gets more complicated as you get older. And us ladies, we gotta stick together."

```
Good afternoon. Welcome to
Good afternoon, and thank you for being here.
I am so happy to be
It is an honor to stand here
```

The night before her high school graduation, Baker is up too late, staring down at her typewriter, trying to write her speech. Trying to figure out how she can keep it short so she can get off the stage as fast as possible. How to sound motivational when she feels miserable. It's nearly midnight, and she can't get past the beginning. She shifts in her chair. Her butt is numb.

```
It is an honor to stand before you, on this
momentous day, during this truly momentous year.
Congratulations to the Class of 1968. We have
done it.
```

No politics, they'd told her. *Keep it inspirational.* The future is exciting! No war, no protest nonsense. She hears Principal Wilson's words in her ear: *Not that we'd expect that from you, Ms. Phillips. You keep it on the straight and narrow. But you never know these days.* Isn't that the truth. Does anyone ever know anything?

```
I stand here today filled with pride for all we've
done, and excitement for our futures. For the lives
we will lead, and for all that we will accomplish.
```

Pride and excitement. She laughs at how wrong it feels to write that. These past months have been anything but exciting, nothing to be proud of. And now she has to stand on a stage and have everyone stare at her while she says a bunch of bullshit about how exciting the future is. To be celebrated as a success when she's anything but. What a hypocrite. She'd wanted to get out of giving the speech, but Rose felt that would draw unnecessary attention. They couldn't give anyone a reason to suspect anything. Proceed as usual. No sudden moves. Get to graduation. Keep the reputation intact. Host the big family party as planned. And *then* what? Baker has asked, several times now, imploring her mother to please just tell her what's going on, please just tell her something about the plan. *Anything.* But Rose is consistent, tight-lipped, a woman who can guard a secret like a sacred temple. *I'm taking care of it,* was all she'd say. *That is the plan.*

```
We have worked hard to get to this moment, but the
truth is, the work has just begun. The tasks that
lie before us are great.
```

On the news the other night, they showed the students in Paris. Chaos in the streets, her beloved fantasy city, now roiling like America. As the television displayed striking students hurling Molotov cocktails at their university buildings, Gerald had muttered, "Shameful, all of it," and even though he was looking at the screen, she knew he was talking about her, too. Shameful, indeed. And to bring a baby into this world, right now? There should be a strike against birthing, Baker thinks. A moratorium on introducing anyone into this mess.

```
This decade is coming to a close, just as our youth
is coming to a close. Our generation has so much
potential. There are so many paths we can take.
```

What the hell else is she supposed to write? She has the radio on low so that she's not in total silence—Gerald's little transistor that he gave to her when he got a nicer one as an end-of-year bonus from the car lot. The antenna is crooked, but it works well enough. "Mrs. Robinson" comes on, but it's staticky, so she adjusts until the reception is clear and she can hear the harmonies, the *doo-doo-doo-do-dos*. She's staring out the window at a patch of night sky when the song ends and the announcement comes.

A man's voice, breaking through to tell the news to everyone who's still awake at this hour. The chaos. The gunshot. Again.

She puts her head down on the typewriter and cries.

She doesn't mention Bobby Kennedy's name in her speech. She doesn't have to. It's on the lips and minds of every person in the audience. They all woke up to the news. They drove to the graduation with their radios on, reporting live from outside his hospital in Los Angeles. They climbed out of their cars and filed into the rows of chairs, and now they're sitting there, staring at her. The collective shock hangs over them all, familiar and unwelcome. Baker and her classmates were in seventh grade when the president died in Dallas, when their teachers screamed in class and they got sent home early to find their mothers slumped on sofas and their fathers crying for the first time. It's unthinkable that his younger brother might die, too.

She doesn't say his name, but she closes her brief speech with his words, which she found in an article in one of Gerald's magazines that she'd remembered reading awhile back. At the time, she'd felt so moved that she'd read the piece out loud to Gerald. She'd looked through the shelves in the living room last night after she heard the news, rifling through the stacks of back issues of *Reader's Digest* and *Life* until she found it.

```
In conclusion, let us remember these wise words
from a great man. "All of us might wish at times
that we lived in a more tranquil world, but we
don't. And if our times are difficult and
```

perplexing, so are they challenging and filled with
opportunity." May we rise to the challenges, and
seize the opportunities.

A vast sea of smiles, a cacophony of applause, the hectic motion of all those hands clapping. Baker takes her seat in between Mary Phail and Michael Price. Baker's eyes dart to the edge of the stage to plan her path to the car.

Now, everyone around her is standing and smiling. They all raise their arms and lift the tassels on their caps, and then all the caps are in the air, like big pieces of confetti. Mary and Michael and everyone around Baker are shouting and hooting, all the proud graduates, they have done it. They shuffle single file off the risers, down the stairs, onto the grass, to flood out into the crowd to find their waving families.

Head down, face flushed, Baker heads straight to the parking lot. She would run if she could, but that would draw attention. She would snap her fingers and disappear if that were possible. Rose and Gerald follow, both wanting to stop her, hug her, congratulate her on a job so well done, but they know they need to get to the car. They can't get sucked into the chitchat undertow, so they smile and wave and act very busy.

They have to get home to set up for the big family party. But really, they have to get out of there before everyone comes to congratulate their daughter. Hug her, shake her sweating hand, pull out the cameras and ask her to smile. They can't risk someone coming too close, getting a glimpse of Baker's swollen body beneath the billowing gown. They can't risk one of the mothers raising her eyebrows, exchanging glances with another, beginning the chain of whispers that could bring it all down.

Once they're in the car, and the doors are shut and the engine's roared to life, they sit in a stunned silence. The relief floods through them all. The unspoken understanding that another hurdle has been cleared.

Gerald turns around and finally lets himself smile. "Well done, young lady. That was a fine speech."

Baker manages a weak smile. "Thanks, Dad. Is there any news?"

He shakes his head grimly. "No."

"Do you think he's going to make it?"

"That's enough," Rose says, her cheeks flushing, and she glances around as the parking lot begins to fill with people. "We won't discuss it right now. And your father is right. Good speech." She pulls a perfume-scented handkerchief from her handbag and dabs at her eyes.

Gerald begins to back out of the parking spot, and Baker turns to watch it all recede: the school, the crowd, the hats and the tassels. The rows of folding chairs, the stage, the risers, the expanse of the green lawn, the scattered old oak trees, the big blue sky, the intense June sun. There's Principal Wilson shaking hands with Kenneth Long, the salutatorian. Kenneth Long with his boring speech about the dumb future, Kenneth Long who's always resented Baker for being a smart girl, for being neck-and-neck in the GPA race. She sees Kathy, Lynn, and Susie, their arms around one another's shoulders, laughing, then shrieking in mock dismay as Peter Kemp runs by and tries to knock off their graduation caps. Sweet girls, fun-loving girls, girls she's known since junior high, girls who have no idea what is really happening.

Baker ducks down in the back seat. "Go!" she blurts out.

Rose turns around and admonishes her. "He's not going to peel out like a race car driver!" Then she leans over to Gerald and whispers, "But yes, dear, let's go."

Baker can hear the cars arriving from the spot on her bedroom floor where she's been lying, flat on her back, still in her graduation gown, since they got home half an hour ago. The carpet is thin, and the concrete subfloor is nice and cool beneath her. She can hear the wheels on the gravel, the slamming of the doors, the chatter of her aunts and uncles and all their kids, the hordes of cousins coming her way. She clenches her fist and braces herself for the family gathering, for the back-slaps and loud jokes and insufferable teasing. She is consumed with the fear of being found out.

She can hear them exclaiming over the decorations, the balloons and streamers that Rose has arranged, the CONGRATS GRADS!!! sign that she hand-lettered and tacked up above the front window. Baker is one of three cousins in the family to graduate today: Timmy, John, and Baker. The soldier, the burnout, and the valedictorian with the shameful secret. Rose had insisted that they go ahead with the party at their house, despite everything.

"It would look too odd if we didn't host," she'd stated when Baker had pleaded with her to cancel it. "And besides, the invitations went out in February."

"But what if I'm showing?"

"You won't be showing."

"How do you know?"

"Because I didn't show with you until I was six months along," Rose had proclaimed with confidence. "And you're built just like me." And that was the end of that discussion.

But Baker knows that's not the only reason for the party. Her parents want to show her off one more time, put the trophy on the shelf and have everyone admire it. They love her, they're proud of her—and they need her. And that's why no one can know what is really going on. Brilliant young Baker is their ticket, the proof to everyone that their little family has made it, *will* make it. The future is bright, because their daughter is bright. No one else in this family has gone to college. Baker is going to lift them to a new level. This has always been the plan.

They're inside the house now, swarming with drinks and cigarettes, the aunts gossiping and bustling, straightening already straight things, offering to help Rose, then wandering away before she can give instructions. The uncles barking, joking, bragging.

Timmy's enlisting next week—he'll ship out real soon, serve like his father.

Best part about John being a pharmacist is the discount on our medications!

And the cousins. The goddamned cousins. She hears their loud footsteps, their grunts and guffaws, knows they'll head straight to the kitchen in search of food like packs of teenage hyenas. They'll swipe unfinished desserts, handfuls of chips, soda pop from the icebox. The boys will belch and kiss their mothers, the girls will eye one another's waistlines, and then they'll all head for the pool.

She knows the drill because it's how it always goes. They'll sneak a joint in the pool house, a flask or two, and John will pass out pills to anyone who wants them. Red ones, blue ones, whatever he can steal.

Eventually they'll get bored and come to find her. They'll barge into her room without knocking. They'll flop onto her bed, peer into her closet, make fun of her books, flip through her records, make barbed little comments.

Last Thanksgiving, cousin Davy, stoned out of his mind, spotted the corner of her precious blue journal peeking out from under her pillow and pulled it out, waving it in the air. She'd tried to stay calm at first, asking him to please put it down, but Timmy egged him on, howling with laughter.

Property of Baker Phillips, Davy cried, clearing his throat as if preparing for a speech. His lips twisted in a sneer. Timmy howling on the floor, Baker screaming as her own words flashed through her mind.

"But someday soon I will be gone, away from this town, this country, finally in Paris, living and writing and hopefully LOVING—"

Baker had lunged at Davy's feet, trying to topple him. *What the hell,* he'd cried, trying to kick her off. That's when May had walked in, screaming *Cut it out, little shit,* running over to her brother and pushing him off the bed, like they were kids again. He hit his head on the nightstand, and he called them both crazy bitches as he and Timmy ran out of the room. May picked up the journal, put it gently into Baker's hands, and whispered, *I can't wait to visit you in Paris someday.*

Now Baker opens her eyes to see Rose standing above her, hands on hips, dish towel flung over one shoulder, kitten-heeled foot tapping.

"It's time, dear."

"For what?"

"That's enough. Get off the floor. No more hiding."

"I'm not hiding. I'm resting."

"Time to get dressed!"

"But I'm *tired,*" Baker exclaims, knowing that she sounds like a petulant child. That's what she wishes she could be. An angry toddler, stomping her feet and balling her fists and just crying *No!*

"So am I, dear. But does that stop me?" Rose gestures to the rest of the house, as if Baker could see through the walls to her kitchen, to the spread of food on the dining table, to the little bowls of mixed nuts and potato chips on the end tables, to the streamers and garlands and balloons. "We have a house full of people. And they're here to see *you.*"

Baker lugs herself up from the cool ground. She narrows her eyes. "I'm not the one who invited them." She regrets the words even before they're out of her mouth. Rose freezes. The only thing that moves is her nostrils. Baker has taken it too far, and she knows it.

"Elizabeth. Baker. Phillips. This is your *graduation*. It is supposed to be a wonderful occasion."

"I'm sorry, Mother. I shouldn't have said that. I'm—thank you. And I'm sorry." A tear slides down Baker's cheek. Then another. Baker's shoulders start to shake. The pit in her stomach is a storm cloud, desperate to release the rain. Rose straightens her shoulders and looks Baker in the eyes.

"We're not doing that right now. We are okay. We are getting dressed, and we are going to the party, and we are happy and having a wonderful time."

Baker wishes she could just wear the big billowing graduation gown forever. But there's a dress hanging on the back of the door, in front of the full-length mirror. It's a mid-calf A-line with a high collar and a busy floral print. Rose worked on it all last week, letting out the bust, bringing down the hemline.

Rose reaches into the closet and hands Baker a shopping bag. Inside is a hideous beige girdle.

"You're going to wear this under your dress."

"But you said I wouldn't be showing! And I'm not!"

Rose cocks her head to one side, her eyes firm and sad.

"Do you want to give your cousins any reason to think anything?"

It's all she has to say. Baker sheds the gown and yanks on the girdle. It's awful. It might as well be a whalebone corset. The elastic cuts into her waist and thighs, cruel and tight. But when she looks again at the mirror, the little bulge is gone.

The dress goes on over her head. Baker sucks in as much air as possible and yanks it over her chest, past her hips. The hem flares out around her legs just fine, but the fabric is still taut across her chest.

"It's fine," Rose says, as they look in the mirror that hangs on the back of the door. "Just don't breathe too deep."

Baker feels puffy and sad and hot, but she tries to smile, because now her mother looks so sad. A current pulses between them—it has always been there—and they can feel how it throbs, overloaded with it all. So much anger that this has happened. So much fear for what's to come. And so much damn love, she can barely stand it.

"One more thing," Rose says, as she adjusts Baker's collar. "I'm expecting a phone call today. About the next steps. The plan. It's obviously not a convenient time to take a call like that, but they're very busy and we are very lucky to even hear from them, so *c'est la vie.*"

"What do you mean?"

"I just told you. Next steps."

"But *who* is calling you? Who's 'they'? Why won't you tell me anything?" Every time she's asked Rose anything about *the plan,* she's received the same answers: *I'm taking care of it. I'll share more when I know more.*

The not-knowing is almost as bad as the situation itself. But there is nothing Baker can do at this point. She tried to fix it, and she failed. She had her chance, and she ran. It's almost relaxing to be this helpless. She can just surrender, just float on the stream of misery and let the current take her through each day. The party is happening. The dress is too tight. The collar is itchy. The phone call is coming. The cousins are here. The world is ending. It was all supposed to be so wonderful, and now it is not. She had a future, and now she does not. She can remember a time when she felt differently, when she was angry and determined and strong. But that feels out of reach, like a dream you can't quite recall, even though you just woke up.

Rose pulls a pale pink mohair cardigan from the closet. "I know it's warm out, but put this on, just to be safe. And button it up all the way."

"Well hello, graduate! Nice of you to show up to the party!" Aunt Carol stands over a mixing bowl at Rose's kitchen counter, licking the end of a wooden spoon. She smiles and offers it to Baker. "I made extra just for you!"

It's her famous orange peel frosting, a special treat that Baker's always loved, cloudlike and flecked with bitter orange zest and sweetened with fresh-squeezed juice and powdered sugar. The white whipped blob glistens, inches from her mouth. She smells the sugar, the orange oil, but she also smells the cold cuts that lie pink and wrinkled on a plate next to slices of Swiss cheese that already sweat in the heat. Someone is opening a can of tuna. An uncle forgot to put the lid back on the rum. She feels her chest contract, her throat tighten. Saliva pools below her tongue. Rose eyes her from the other end of the kitchen; makes the slightest gesture with her head. *Go on,* she's saying. *Eat it. Act normal.* Baker manages a weak smile and opens her mouth. The frosting slides down her throat, sweet and thick.

"What a ceremony!" Aunt Carol exclaims, always the loudest in the room. "And what a speech!"

"It's true, dear," Rose chimes in. "The whole family is so proud of you."

"Wish we could say the same for all our damn kids," Carol mutters, rolling her eyes and plopping the spoon back in the bowl. "Must be nice to have a perfect one!"

The sugary mass bobs in Baker's chest, threatening to come back up.

When May arrives with Auntie Lee, the cousins are in the pool, the neighbors are dancing on the patio, Rose is circulating with a pitcher of punch, and Baker is sitting at the piano in the front room, playing "Chopsticks" on repeat, her fingertips getting numb.

May gives her a hug, and Baker hangs on tight, breathing her in. She smells like the apartment, like incense and cigarettes and soup and suede. But also like something else: she's been down in Santa Cruz, and Baker can swear she smells the ocean, the trees, even the dirt. Her hair is even wilder than usual, tangled and frizzy despite the embroidered headband she's tied around her forehead.

"I'm so glad you're here," Baker says, staring down at May's leather granny boots. "I've missed you."

"I've missed you, too." May glances at her mother, who gives her an impatient look. "Congratulations! Your speech was wonderful."

They lock eyes, and May is asking a million questions without saying a word: *Are you okay? What's been going on? Do your parents know? Why haven't you called me back?* Baker wants to tell her everything, but instead she smiles and accepts the bouquet of carnations that Auntie Lee has produced from behind her back.

"Great speech, Baker!" Auntie Lee is oblivious to the moment the cousins are sharing. "You're such a good egg."

Baker nearly gags at the word *egg*. May notices and stifles a giggle.

Aunt Carol calls from the kitchen. "Is that Lee and May? Come say hello! And help me in this kitchen!"

"Coming!" May hugs Baker again and whispers in her ear, "We'll talk later, okay?"

Just before dinner is served, the phone rings, and through the sliding glass doors, Baker can see Rose gesturing and smiling, speaking the way she does when the person on the other end is especially important. She hangs up and catches Baker's eye. *Come now,* she's saying.

"Follow me, dear," Rose announces loudly, so that all the aunts can hear. "We need to get some extra place mats."

She glides into the back bedroom and shuts the door behind them, glances out the window to make sure there aren't any lurking cousins, then opens the bottom dresser drawer, where she keeps the dining linens. She hands Baker a stack of woven straw mats.

"The phone call came." Rose's cheeks are flushed, and she can't help but smile with relief. She pushes the drawer shut. "Arrangements have been made."

"What arrangements?"

She leans in and whispers, "You'll be going away. It will be safe, and private. All taken care of."

"Where? For how long?" Baker's voice is panicky, threatening to become audible to the house full of guests.

"Until . . ." Rose gestures toward Baker's body and gives her a look. "It's *resolved.*"

"But what will happen to the—"

Rose's hand flies up to Baker's mouth. She doesn't touch it, but her palm hovers close enough that Baker feels the warmth on her lips. "I've made arrangements. You're going to be okay. That's all you need to know right now."

"But I don't understand what you're telling me!"

Rose's face turns a blotchy red. "Never mind," she says, and her voice is almost an annoyed hiss. "I shouldn't have brought it up right now. We'll discuss later."

Linda Moore. The name just pops into Baker's head, out of the blue. Linda Moore. *LindaMoore LindaMoore.*

Rose grabs a stack of cloth napkins from the closet and adds them to the armload of place mats. "Might as well bring more napkins, too," she calls out.

And then she remembers: Linda Moore, a girl two years ahead of Baker, a fast, pretty girl with tight sweaters who smoked and ran with the hoods. They weren't friends, but Baker loved to look at her when they passed in the hall after lunch. Her scent was strong and earthy, not a perfume Baker recognized from the drugstore, but not patchouli, either. Something big and . . . womanly. Linda was generally cool and distant, but one time they locked eyes and she flashed Baker a sweet smile. Her teeth were crooked, her lipstick was thick, but the moment made Baker feel seen in a powerful way.

Then one day, Linda Moore didn't pass by in the hall. Or the next day. Or the next. Baker wondered: Did she drop out? Did she move away? Was she okay? One day she overheard people talking about her. *That fast girl named Linda,* they were saying. *Knocked up and sent away.* Baker didn't know what to make of it at the time—was that just something that happened to girls like that? It made her feel a little sad, but she soon stopped noticing her absence in the hall after lunch. She stopped thinking about Linda Moore altogether. Baker had had better things to worry about, like whether to join the drama club, and what did Mr. Berry think of her essay on *The Grapes of Wrath.* Linda Moore was some other kind of girl, nothing like Baker, and now . . .

Rose wraps her arms around Baker, a sudden and fierce hug. The straw mats crackle between their bodies; their hearts thump against each other's chests. A few cloth napkins fall to the ground.

"Elizabeth," she whispers in her ear. "*I love you.* And I am *helping* you." And Baker wants nothing more than to collapse into her mother, curl up on her lap while Rose strokes her forehead and makes it all go away, like it never happened. "And for the rest of the night, you just play along with me, okay? It's for the best. You *have* to believe me."

Rose uses her apron to wipe the mascara from her cheeks. She pulls a tube of lipstick from her pocket and reapplies without a mirror, then opens the door.

"Here they are! Had to really dig to find these ones."

Baker follows her, again, and if she thought she was in a daze before, swimming in some kind of mist, now she's stumbling through a fog in the dark. Right before they get to the kitchen, Rose leans in and whispers, "It's all going to work out fine." She squeezes Baker's sweating fingers, and her rings pinch her skin. Baker tries to picture Linda Moore's face, but she can't. She's not there.

The uncles crowd around the TV, watching the Giants losing to the Phillies. Baker spreads the place mats around the huge wooden table, the site of so many meals and parties. It's at maximum capacity with the extra leaves inserted, additional chairs pulled up on either end, and still there are two separate card tables set up for the cousins, the overgrown kids' table.

Rose rings the antique dinner bell, then follows with a loud "DINNERTIME!" so the cousins and the ball game watchers will actually pay attention. The aunts bring out the food on Rose's sterling trays: corn on the cob and hot dogs and burgers and shish kebabs and deviled eggs and macaroni salad and green salad and several Jell-O dishes and a platter of fruit and baskets of buttered rolls. On the counter in the kitchen, Baker can see the desserts: two cakes—angel food and chocolate—plus three cherry pies and a platter of Aunt Iris's cherry divinity. On the bar by the table are iced tea and orange soda and tropical punch spiked with rum; in the hands of the guests are beers and martinis and chilled white wine with ice cubes.

"I'd like to raise a glass!" proclaims Aunt Iris once everyone has finally assembled around the table. She hoists her tumbler into the air. "To my son, Timmy. About to serve his country, just like his father and grandfather before him. I love you, son."

Everyone cheers except Baker and May, who lets out a loud grunt at the mention of the word *country*. An uncle shouts *Hurrah!* while Timmy smirks and rolls his shiny eyes, all red from the chlorine and the pot.

Their faces turn now to their hostess, who rises slow with a soft smile. A man on the street once stopped Rose to tell her she looks like a dark-haired Grace Kelly. At the time Baker giggled and thought he was crazy, but it's in moments like this that she gets what he meant.

"What a joy to have you all here, in our home, to celebrate this occasion." The guests at the table fall into an obedient silence. "How blessed we are to have such a wonderful family, with such incredible children who bring us hope for a safe and prosperous future. I know we don't talk politics in this family, but I want to acknowledge that these are . . . trying times." Around the table people bite their lips, clench their fists. "As my daughter said in her speech today, these times are filled with opportunity. Timmy, we thank you for your service. John, we congratulate you. And Elizabeth. My daughter. We are so proud of all you've accomplished. I think this is a good time to make our announcement."

Baker's entire body turns to ice. May looks at her from across the table.

"Elizabeth is going to Paris!"

For a brief, exhilarating moment, Baker believes her. Her heart soars. *Paris? The plan is Paris?! How—*

Rose continues. "She's been accepted into a special program at the Sorbonne, and she leaves next week! She'll spend her fall semester there, studying French history. She'll start at Stanford in the spring!"

No. The soaring heart sinks as Baker realizes it's a ruse. A cruel, cruel ruse. And she's supposed to play along. The sound of applause fills the room, but Baker's vision gets blurry. Everyone is looking at her, but their faces are fuzzy, the outlines of their bodies hazy. Baker feels faint until someone thumps her on the back. The room comes back into focus, and Baker sees her mother's hand, her chunky silver rings and the gold tennis bracelet encircling her wrist as she raises her glass again.

"To Baker! To Paris! To you all!"

Baker forces a dazed smile. Her brain throbs; her mouth feels full of dust; she doesn't understand. *How?* Of all the lies Rose could have concocted to explain the next several months, this is what she's choosing? Does she know how cruel this is? Is this meant to hurt as much as it does? Baker has talked about wanting to travel to Paris someday, she loved to order croissants at the fancy café that Rose would take her to in Union Square, and she had all of the *Madeline* books. But she's never told them that she dreams of moving there. She's never mentioned the plan to switch her major, to buy herself a ticket, to move there and become the woman she knows she's supposed to become. *How did they know?*

Baker looks up at Rose, and it feels like she's looking at a stranger. Rose looks down at her daughter and smiles. *Just play along,* her face says. Timmy whistles, Gerald lifts his glass, and May's mouth hangs open. Cousin John leans over and punches Baker in the arm. "Way to go, smart-shit. Oui, oui."

By midnight, the tikis have burned out, the booze is gone, and the house is finally empty of guests, except for May, who remains behind, washing dishes with Baker in the kitchen, taking sips from her silver flask. Gerald and Rose both had more than enough to drink; once they waved farewell to the last departing carload, they headed right down the hall to their room.

They scrape and scrub the plates, the sink basin slowly filling with half-chewed watermelon rinds, bits of Jell-O and cake, lonely macaroni. They don't talk about Rose's announcement. May tells stories about who's staying at the apartment now, who's moved on or gone back home, who did what at which crazy party. When the sink is empty and the counters wiped down, Baker removes her yellow rubber gloves.

"I'll be right back," she tells May. "Gotta pee. Again."

"Meet me by the pool when you're done?" Neither has to say it because they both know: it's time to *really* talk.

Baker is nervous about what her cousin will have to say, but she's also relieved to finally let it out. "Yes."

Instead of heading to the bathroom, though, she goes into her room, to the bookshelf by the desk. Next to a stack of *National Geographics* are three tall leather-bound books; she grabs the maroon one with '65 stamped on the front in gold and opens it up to the juniors.

Her heart races as she flips through the pages. Linda Moore is right where she should be, in the *M*'s: Linda Moore (*French Club*), smiling tight-lipped, eyes lined dark and thick, brown hair pulled back and teased into a neat beehive. A thin strand of pearls around her neck. Baker stares at her face, remembering how she'd hang out by the parking lot after school, leaning on some guy's car, cool and sleek with her button-up shirt knotted above her navel, nylons shimmering on her legs.

Linda Moore is beautiful, but she doesn't look that different from the girl to her left (Elaine Montana, *Cheer Team, Debate*) or her right (Margaret Nagel, *Dance Committee, Student Government, Art Club, Girl Scouts of America*). Baker grabs the next book in the stack, with the mottled cream-colored cover and a silver '66 on it, and flips to the seniors. There's Elaine, and there's Margaret, but Linda Moore is not between them. Linda Moore's not there.

What happened, Linda Moore? Are you okay?

Baker finds her own face in the small oval mirror above the desk. Her cheeks seem rounder, her lips fuller. She snaps the books shut and shoves them back onto the shelf.

*   *   *

May's sitting on the pool's edge with her bare feet in the water, leaning back on her hands and staring at the moonless sky. They see fewer stars these days, now that there are so many subdivisions with their brightly lit brand-new streets. The sky's just a semi-dark expanse, nothing like the deep blazing blankets they've seen on camping trips. Baker pauses in the doorframe and watches her cousin take a swig from a can of Old Milwaukee.

"Come on. Sit." May waves her over and waits until Baker's there next to her. "Put your feet in, dahling." She dips her hand in the water, then swishes it around.

"Where'd you find the beer?"

"In the pool house. It was only half-full. Or half-empty, depending on how you see the world, right?" May takes another drink. "You're not going to Paris, are you?"

"That was the first I'd heard of that plan."

"So what *is* the plan?"

Baker takes a gulp of May's beer. It's bitter and warm. "'Arrangements' have been made."

"She's going to send you to one of those homes, isn't she?"

Baker shrugs. She parses each word that Rose has uttered, trying to arrange them like blank pieces of a jigsaw puzzle. "I don't know. Someone called her tonight, and she told me that I'll be 'going away.' She won't tell me any details."

"Jesus. That's so like her. Why am I not surprised?" May spits and flicks her cigarette into the pool.

"You better go get that."

May sneers. "She's sending you into hiding. And then making up this stupid story about Paris. God, what a piece of work."

"She says she's doing it to protect me."

May scoffs. "I mean, what, are you a mental patient? A *prisoner?*"

"Something like that."

"It's just not right, this isn't the goddamn *fifties*. Things are *changing*."

"Sure, they're a-changing out there." Baker gestures into the night air. "But around here? Not so much."

"Are you seriously okay with this?"

Baker leans back on her hands. The cool concrete rough against her palms, her body heavy on her thin wrists. She considers the question: *is* she okay with it? Part of her is furious that Rose won't tell her. And part of her is relieved. She tried to take care of herself. She *tried*. And she failed. She wants to tell May everything: How she took the pamphlet and called the numbers and scrounged the cash and studied the map. About the bus ride, the Lysol smell in the stairs, the man in the suit threatening to call the cops, the woman who gave her a ride. But she's too ashamed, embarrassed to say how close she got, how scared she was, and how quickly she ran away. May would be so disappointed.

"I don't know," is her eventual answer.

"Ugh. Snap out of it, Baker!" May whips her hand from the pool and flicks cold water on her cousin's face. "I know this is hard, but come on! You're brilliant. We can figure something out!"

They sit in silence, listening to the occasional dog bark, cars on the highway, crickets in the bushes everywhere.

"I'm thinking of moving," May finally says, carefully. "Down the coast, to that property near Santa Cruz. Where my roommates moved?"

"The commune?"

"It's good people, living communally. Call it what you want."

Baker shrugs, and May presses on, gentle.

"I hear it's really something. It's not chaotic like the city—it's peaceful. Living off the land, in harmony with nature."

"Sounds groovy."

"I'm serious, Baker. I also hear there's a few women there who are expecting, and even one or two who already have babies. I'm just thinking . . . you could be okay there."

Baker closes her eyes. A commune down the coast. Living off the land with other people's babies. Forgetting about college and her parents and just learning to make soup, reading poetry by candlelight. She sees herself in a dimly lit room, a small wooden shack, surrounded by women who sit on the floor and coo at their babies. She's standing off to the side, holding her own baby, who won't stop crying.

"I don't think that's my scene, May."

May shakes her head. "How are you so smart, yet so brainwashed? You're almost an adult. You don't have to be this perfect child who does everything her mother says, okay? You're a *woman* and this is *nineteen sixty-eight* and you're *brilliant,* and you have *rights.*"

"What rights? You think I'm naïve? You don't live in the real world!"

"What are you talking about? I'm making it on my own. You're just doing what your mother tells you, like you've always done."

Baker crosses her arms. "Listening to you hasn't turned out so great."

"I'm trying to help you." May's voice is loud. "You've been ignoring me."

"I've been busy."

"You don't tell me anything!"

"What do you want to know?"

"I don't know, just, like, what do you want to do? How do you *feel?*"

Baker stares at her cousin, who means well, most of the time. The freckles that scatter over the bridge of her nose. Her chipped front tooth. Her big brown selfish eyes.

"How do I feel?" She opens her mouth, and the words just tumble out. "Fat and tired and stupid and embarrassed. Did I mention terrified? My gums bleed every time I brush my teeth, my hair keeps falling out in the shower, and my ankles are *fat.* I'm bloated all over, and my boobs hurt so bad I can't sleep on my stomach, and you know I'm a stomach-sleeper. I just acted like a complete fraud in front of everyone I know, I can't look my parents in the eyes, and I've pretty much ruined everything. Oh, and I'm basically a cowardly child who can't stand up to her own mother, let alone go through with a goddamn abortion."

May's eyes get big. "Wait, did you—"

"Yes, May, I tried. I called the number on the pamphlet, but I chickened out and screwed it up the way I've screwed everything up. And by the way, my whole speech was bullshit today. Everybody with any moral courage in this miserable country gets *murdered*." Baker kicks the smooth surface of the water with her foot, splashing them both. "And you're just going to move to the woods, and Wiley's out there, stoned and surfing, and I'm—" She stops, finally, and takes a ragged breath. "That's how I am, May. Anything else you want to know?"

May shakes her head and holds out her arms. She lets her cousin collapse into her. Baker cries wild, wrecking tears. She doesn't care if she wakes the neighbors or her parents; she doesn't care if Wiley hears all the way down on that Baja beach. She heaves and gasps and drips with spit and snot, and she clings to her cousin for what seems like forever. When she finally catches her breath, she exhales long and slow; it feels as if she's been holding it all night. All day. All year. And she is deeply, utterly exhausted.

"I have to sleep. Like now."

May looks at the aluminum lawn chairs with the faded nylon straps that have been sitting by the pool for as long as they both can remember.

"I'll get some blankets," she says. "Sleep under the stars, just like when we were kids." May lifts her head to the blank sky. "Well, we can pretend about the stars." She tosses her beer can into the pool, hands Baker her flask, and heads inside.

Baker unscrews the lid and takes a sip. Vodka. Straight up. It burns. She grabs the long-handled sweeper and fishes out the can, the butt, May's debris, and then crawls over to the lawn chair and curls up on her side, insides hot from the liquor. She wraps her hands around her belly, feels the stretch of her skin, the mysterious world underneath it. When May returns and drapes the quilt over her, she pretends to be sound asleep.

In the morning, Baker wakes with the hot, bright sun, cramped and sore. May is still completely out, snoring and sprawled, her arms hanging off the sides of the chaise. The yard is silent, save for a few birds, and there's no visible movement inside the house. If this is like every other post-party morning, Baker knows that Rose and Gerald will sleep late. The pool is a perfect turquoise rectangle, the water smooth, glassy, and welcoming. She looks around one more time and confirms: she's alone. She peels off her clothes and slides into the ice-cold water.

It's the most familiar sensation: the initial shock, almost painful as her skin seems to shrink and tighten, quickly covered with goose-bumps. She kicks her legs and moves her arms and relaxes into it, and it begins to feel good. She swims back and forth, freestyle, and then breast, her legs frog-kicking, arms reaching out, around, and up. Then she flips over to her back and floats, arms out, body still and buoyant. For a few minutes, she's just a girl, swimming in a pool. A girl who just graduated high school, who's thinking about summer, sundresses, whether or not to pour peroxide on her hair.

She can believe it's all okay.

That this is not actually happening.

That she's not about to get sent away.

But as she floats her midsection rises just enough. A tiny island on a once-flat surface. She doesn't know what it looks like, but she knows it's there.

She gets out of the pool, breathing heavy, and wraps the quilt around her body. As she stands there, dripping, she feels a tiny pop inside her, somewhere deep below her belly button.

Something that wasn't there before. Moving. A finger flicking, a little hiccup. A bubble filling, then bursting.

Part II

$\mathcal{I}$t's not until they're in the car at 7:00 A.M. on an already hot Friday morning that Rose finally tells Baker the plan.

Rose wears a blue dress, a yellow silk headscarf, and her biggest sunglasses. She sets her jaw and grips the steering wheel, and they drive. Baker slumps against the car door, still sleepy, head resting on the window, cheek pressed against the glass. Her breath makes tiny fog-scapes that expand like magic, then fade away into nothing. Her hands are clasped tightly on her lap. Her feet rest on the plaid suitcase that Rose packed last night.

It contains neat stacks of new elastic waist cotton skirts, billowing dresses in busy florals and dull plaids, with cap sleeves and Peter Pan collars. Button-up blouses with generous cuts. That hateful girdle and several terrible bras that seem comically large. A new towel set, fresh underwear and socks. Once Rose had zipped it up and headed off to bed, Baker had scanned her room, suddenly desperate to pack a few special items, objects to remind her of who she is, and could someday still be. She'd already asked about bringing the typewriter (a definite no). She picked up her journal. It felt heavy, and though she knows very well that it doesn't have feelings, she felt convinced that it might be a little mad at her. She brought it up to her lips and whispered, *I'm sorry. I'll write in you soon. Promise.* It went into the suitcase, along with her fancy fountain pen, black eyeliner, and a half-used tub of rouge May had given her. Then she stared at the stacks of books by her bed. How was she supposed to choose? She closed her eyes and ran her fingers over the familiar spines, the worn covers. She picked three and slipped them into the suitcase without looking. *Little surprises for later,* she thought. Some scrap of something to look forward to.

"I know you're eager to hear where we're heading," Rose finally says.

"That's an understatement," Baker mutters, and again the air from her mouth blooms like a cloud on the glass. She watches it disappear, no trace.

The traffic light up ahead turns from yellow to red. Rose lifts her sunglasses to her forehead, revealing her red, watery eyes.

"I'm sorry that I've had to keep this information from you. I've been . . . afraid."

"Of what?"

"That you'd leave." Rose wipes her eyes with her handkerchief. "I didn't want you to run away. Or to try to . . . deal with it yourself. I didn't want you to get hurt. I've heard of this happening. I had to keep you safe."

Baker is stunned. She'd never even considered running away, and it shocks her to hear that it occurred to Rose. Where would she have gone? And what would she have done with . . . the baby? The words *deal with it yourself* echo in her mind as she remembers the pamphlet, the phone calls, the bus ride, that building. Does Rose know what she almost did?

"You're going to stay in a residential facility."

"You mean a home?"

"Yes, a home."

"What kind? And where?"

"A nice one. A *safe* one. In San Francisco."

The light turns green, and the car behind them blares its rude horn. Rose shifts into gear and accelerates too quickly.

Baker can't help the barking laugh that escapes her mouth. "Is *that* where we're headed?" Of all the places she could go, all the anonymous little far-flung towns in the damn state, and she's getting sent away to the place where it all began. The scene of her crimes. What a cruel, full-circle joke. Like her "trip" to study in Paris.

"What's so funny? You love the city. And besides, the homes in other areas were full."

"Who else lives there?"

"Other girls. In your situation."

"How many?"

"I'm not sure. A woman named Mrs. White also resides there. She is in charge."

"How long will I be there?"

"Until it's done, Elizabeth."

Baker tries to imagine what "done" means. What will actually *happen* to her. What it will feel like, look like, smell and sound like. She wants so badly to ask her mother, but that conversation feels like a box neither of them wants to open.

"You sure you'll want me back?"

"Don't be smart with me. In a few months, you will come back home, and we'll put this all behind us. You'll start your classes in January. I've already arranged it with the admissions office."

"You have?" Of course she has.

"Of course I have. I told them you'll be in Paris, staying with an aunt, studying French history. A once-in-a-lifetime travel opportunity we couldn't pass up."

Of course.

"It was going to be your graduation present, actually," adds Rose. "The trip to Paris. So it doesn't feel like a *complete* untruth."

Baker's heart crumples. A graduation gift. The trip she'd always wanted. She *was* going to get it. Her mother *does* know. Another dream, snatched away. Another beautiful plan, ruined.

They drive for a while before Baker asks her next question. The one she can't not ask. "What will happen to the . . . to *it*?"

Rose answers right away, as if she's been rehearsing for this exact moment. "The baby will go to live with a family, a good family. And they will all be happy, and have a very good life." But her voice cracks on *very good life.* "I promise. Now please, let's get ourselves together. We'll be there soon."

They drive the rest of the way in silence: across the Bay Bridge, past tall buildings, corner stores, stately homes, neat green parks that seem to taunt her. Up hills, down hills, through neighborhoods Baker's never been to. When Rose finally slows the car and pulls up to a curb, she checks her face and hair in the mirror, smooths a few flyaways, and reapplies her red lipstick. She dabs the sheen on her forehead with a yellow cotton handkerchief and hands it to Baker.

"Here, darling. Clean up a bit."

Baker eyes the damp cloth. "I can't imagine they'll reject me for having a shiny face."

"This is not a joke. This is very important." Rose leans over to get her handbag from the passenger side floorboard, and her left arm accidentally leans on the horn. It blares loud. "Dammit!" Rose scans the street to see if anyone's staring. "Now listen: This is it. This is the house."

Baker looks up at the old Victorian home and knows right away that she will never forget this. The fog of her mind parts, lifts, and the world comes into sharp, painful relief. This is really happening. This house, painted varying shades of gray and deep blues, with white trim and faded gold accents, is real. Wide wooden steps lead up to a small porch and an ornate weathered door. All real. Heavy curtains hang in huge windows. Not imaginary. Not theoretical. A tall, thin tree rises from neatly trimmed hedges, and Baker can see a big old oak tree growing in the side yard.

"This is the absolute best option for all of us. It's a lovely house, right?"

The gold curlicues, the delicate pops of color along the rooflines and above and below the big bay windows, the ornately carved old porch posts. This house is beautiful, and real, but it also seems tired. And forgotten. *Just like me,* Baker thinks.

Rose steps out of the vehicle, onto the sidewalk. Two young girls walk by, giggling, and Rose beams at them.

"Come on," she calls to Baker. "Let's not be late!"

"I can't." Baker tries to lift her arm. It won't move. She stares at it, counts the freckles. Tries again.

Rose walks around to the passenger side and opens the car door, ready to drag her daughter out. Before she can, Baker sinks down in the vinyl seat and then collapses onto the black street below. It feels like she's falling through space. Timeless, weightless, conscious but untethered.

"Elizabeth! Are you okay?" Rose's whisper is more like a hiss. "Get up, dear." Baker feels boneless. *Did I faint? Is this fainting?* She opens her eyes and looks at the filthy asphalt beneath her face. Feels the ground, which is colder than she'd expected, like it's held on to the chill from the night before. It feels nice, despite the dirt and sharp gravel. She feels relaxed. Then Rose's firm hand is yanking on her arm.

"I'm fine," Baker mumbles. "I'm just going to rest here for a minute. Or two."

As she lies there on the ground, she closes her eyes and imagines Wiley strolling by. He would notice her in a heap on the sidewalk, her mother in a frenzy above her, and he'd come toward her, his face gentle and concerned, and crouch down. *Hey lady,* he'd whisper; then he'd take her hands and pull her up. Their eyes would lock, and then *poof,* everything would reset, go back to how it was before. *Wanna come with me?* he'd ask, and she'd say *yes!* and Rose would be gone and so would the thing inside her, and the home would become just another anonymous Victorian, in need of new paint.

"*Now!*" Rose pleads, and Baker snaps out of the reverie. She opens her eyes and sees Rose's leather pumps, not Wiley's faded cowboy boots. She lets Rose take her hand, pull her up, brush the dust and debris off her sweaty dress, her itchy tights. Once she's cleaned up, Rose hands her the plaid suitcase. Then she places a firm hand on Baker's lower back and guides her onto the sidewalk, up the faded wooden steps, to the towering front door of her temporary new home.

It has a little window, and several seconds after Rose rings the bell, it slides open. A pair of blue eyes, big and round, appear.

"Can I help you?"

"We have an appointment. With Mrs. White."

"*Ms.* White. One moment, please."

The window slides shut, and they hear the sounds of unlocking: a deadbolt turning, a chain sliding. Baker looks at her feet, the scuff on her left loafer, some dirt still clinging to her tights, the way her ankles turn in slightly, and then it occurs to her that, at some point, she may not be able to see her feet. Will she get that big? Will someone inside this house explain it all to her? She wants to scream: WHAT IS HAPPENING TO ME?

The old brass knob turns, and the door opens just enough to allow entry. The eyes belong to a tiny birdlike woman—a girl, really—in a brown skirt and yellow blouse. Her cornsilk hair is cut in a bob at her chin. With thin arms, she gestures to a small waiting room: several chairs, a bare round table, a closed door and receptionist's window. No magazines, no books, no signs, no indication of what actually happens here.

"For privacy," the girl explains, with the tone of someone who's read the same reaction on many mothers' faces. "The rest of the home is quite grand. It was built in 1884. It survived the earthquake." She clears her throat and continues. "Good morning. My name is Anna. Welcome." She hands Rose a clipboard stacked with forms. "Ms. White will be with you shortly. May I take this?" She picks up the suitcase before Rose or Baker can answer.

Baker strains to imagine what lies on the other side of the closed door. She pictures rows and rows of pregnant girls, sitting in desks, staring at her. Lying on beds weeping or running through hallways laughing. Giggling like classmates, rocking back and forth like inmates.

Anna leads them through the door into the main room. It's enormous, with a soaring ceiling, grand curving stairs, wood-paneled walls, and several stained glass windows. The room is filled with furniture arranged in small clusters: overstuffed velvet armchairs, a lavender chaise longue, a long emerald green sofa. Low wooden coffee tables, end tables with wrought iron bases and slab marble tops, a few rattan pieces. Against one wall is a long buffet cabinet with crystal knobs on its many drawers. Baker can tell there used to be a mirror on its top. Paintings hang on the walls, bordered by thick, ornate frames: she can see faded landscapes, a still life with fruit, and on one far wall, a portrait of an old man. She squints. Or an old woman. Hard to tell. A chandelier hangs above, dusty and missing a number of crystals. It feels fancy but shabby, left behind from a previous era. Around the perimeter are a series of doors leading to other rooms. And, Baker notes, there are no windows. And no other girls.

"The girls are in their rooms," Anna offers, reading Baker's mind. "They'll be coming down for breakfast in just a few minutes. Eight-thirty A.M., sharp." Anna motions to a closed door to their left, at the foot of the stairs. "This is Ms. White's office." She knocks softly.

"Come in." The voice is brisk, official.

It's a stuffy room, small and crowded with bookshelves and file cabinets and tall windows curtained by heavy drapes. Behind a desk sits an older woman with excellent posture, sharp cheekbones, and a thin slice of a mouth. She wears her graying hair pulled back tight, and a navy cardigan buttoned up to her throat. She smiles and motions to the women to have a seat in the two chairs that sit before the desk. Anna stands behind them.

"Welcome, Mrs. Phillips and Elizabeth. It's lovely to meet you."

While she and Rose exchange pleasantries, Baker scans the desk: neat stacks of paperwork, a jar of sharpened pencils, a stapler, a bud vase with a single daisy, an array of brochures featuring drawings of young women with despairing facial expressions. They have big bold titles:

Alone? Scared? Unfit? There's Hope
Give Your Baby the Life She Deserves
A Real Family Is the Best Family

Baker stares at the pamphlets until the words begin to blur.

"Elizabeth? Ms. White is asking you a question."

"I'm sorry. What—can you repeat that?"

"I said, do you enjoy crafts, Elizabeth?"

"Crafts?" Baker stares blankly.

"She's very creative," interjects Rose.

"Wonderful! We offer delightful classes here. Needlepoint, watercolor, even macramé! We're especially excited about a latch-hook rug class that's starting soon. You can take up a few projects while you're here." She pauses, waiting for Baker to respond. "Ms. Phillips?"

"My apologies, Ms. White. Elizabeth is usually very attentive, but she's not feeling so well today. The heat, I'm sure, with her *condition*." Rose drops her voice on the last word, and Baker cringes at the way her mother can still barely acknowledge what's going on.

"I understand, Mrs. Phillips. Believe me." She leans forward and speaks to Baker in clear, crisp tones. "Elizabeth. You're very lucky that we can accommodate you. The room was just opened up recently. We're a small home, with limited beds."

"Why was the room closed?" Baker asks.

"Pardon?"

"You said it just opened up, which means it had been closed. Why?"

Ms. White purses her lips and glances at Rose. "A curious one, isn't she!"

Rose's laugh is sharp. "They didn't make her editor of the school newspaper for nothing!"

"A wonderful trait, indeed. Though within these walls, discretion is key. We value privacy and confidentiality."

"Of course." Baker folds her hands in her lap, while Rose nods emphatically.

"Moving along, Elizabeth, I would like to—"

"Ma'am, I'm sorry to interrupt."

"Then do not."

"I just wanted to say that I prefer to go by my middle name. Baker."

Ms. White raises her drawn-on brows.

"It's a family name," Rose interjects. "And her middle name. It's been her nickname for quite some time."

"Baker. How unusual."

"I still call her Elizabeth," Rose adds.

"Some of the girls here *do* choose to use pseudonyms during their stay, so you won't be the only one with an alternative name. Baker it is." Ms. White makes a note on a piece of paper and continues. "Our job here is to keep you safe and comfortable, and save your family the trouble of having to hide your condition. And to spare you all the shame, of course, if you were to be found out." She looks Baker up and down. "And with that thin frame, you really *are* going to show any day now."

the shame the shame the shame

"You'll remain until it's over. Before you know it, you'll be returning home, ready to put it all behind you and move right along with your life."

"She's going to Stanford," Rose offers.

"Stanford! Delightful. I have a niece who went there. Bright young woman. She married a surgeon!"

Rose beams. Baker grimaces.

"By January, you'll be ready to move forward with your academic career." Ms. White folds her hands and looks, satisfied, at the two women before her. "I'll have Anna lead you up to your room in just a moment. Breakfast will be served momentarily. Are you hungry?"

"No, ma'am," Baker lies. Her stomach is growling, but the

thought of joining the other girls for a meal, right away, overwhelms her.

"That's fine. You can settle into your room. Lunch is at noon, and dinner is at six. Sharp. You'll be pleased to know that we're having an ice cream social this evening, just after dinner. It will be a wonderful opportunity to meet the other girls."

"Isn't that nice, dear?" Rose reaches out to touch Baker's arm.

Baker flinches and finally looks up, away from the pamphlets. "What?"

"The ice cream social. You love ice cream."

"That said," Ms. White continues, "while we encourage you to mingle, we do suggest that you be . . . careful. We are dealing with delicate matters here. Not everyone wishes to chitchat. And while we hope you'll enjoy the other girls, we don't recommend forming attachments. You're all just here for a short time."

A short time. Easy for her to say. "How long *will* I be here?" Baker asks. That doctor had said *I'll put my money on October fourteenth,* but what does that really mean? How can he be sure?

Ms. White looks at the paperwork in front of her. "According to your doctor, you're around twenty-two weeks right now, so your stay will certainly be less than eighteen weeks."

Baker does the math. "That's four and a half months. That doesn't feel like a short time."

"Baker." Ms. White leans in. "I can assure you the time will pass quickly. Just remember: no woman has been pregnant forever."

Rose laughs nervously, while Baker considers this timeline. If she's already over halfway through, and her body doesn't look *that* pregnant yet, when will it happen? All at once? Overnight? She brings her hands to her navel and presses in. It does feel bigger. Bigger than last week, even. She feels movement: a little blip, a flutter.

Ms. White pushes a stack of papers across the desk. "If I can just get your signature, Mrs. Phillips. There will be more for you to sign soon, Elizabeth—*Baker*—but just these for now."

Rose signs a series of papers. Baker watches the way she writes her looping, elegant signature. She can smell the ink; she can smell the paper. She can smell breakfast being prepared. The hands on the clock above Ms. White's desk slide ahead, and Baker hears the quiet thunder of footsteps coming down the stairs. Ms. White and Rose lean in, shake hands.

"We will take fine care of your daughter."

When Ms. White opens the door, the girls are right there, making their way downstairs. Some silent with eyes downcast, others talking and giggling quietly. Some take the stairs with ease while others take it slow, one step at a time, hands pressed against lower backs. One girl waddles so slowly, it looks like she just got off a horse. It's the strangest parade. They all wear similar tentlike maternity dresses, the kind Baker loathes, the kind Rose made her pack. Some of them barely look pregnant, while others are far enough along that their conditions are unmistakable. Baker knows it's rude, but she can't help it, she can't take her eyes off them: their bellies big and round, breasts huge, and one girl with ankles so swollen that Baker shudders involuntarily. She presses her own hard ankle bones together, knocks them once, twice, three times.

They all notice Baker and Rose standing in the threshold of the office, and their reactions vary: some smile politely, some look away, some give Baker the once-over, evaluating her outfit, her face, her midsection. Baker stares back. It's like gazing into a mirror *and* a crystal ball. She feels like she's back in school. Faces laughing, chatting, moving together, all seeming to know one another while she watches, quiet and curious, from a distance.

Rose's goodbye is swift. It has to be. Hug too long, and they might never let go. She shakes Ms. White's hand once more and gives Baker's damp forehead a quick kiss. They lock eyes for a moment, and even that is too much.

"There's a small package for you in the suitcase," Rose says crisply. "A little gift for you to use." Baker tries to imagine what kind of gift could be useful in a setting like this. Then she whispers *good-bye* and Rose whispers *I love you. Be good.* Rose's eyes well up, and Baker's chest feels like it's going to burst open. She wants to throw herself at her mother's feet and beg her not to go.

The door closes, gentle yet firm, behind her. Baker immediately feels alone. Profoundly, incredibly, alone. She wipes Rose's kiss from her cheek, streaking lipstick across the back of her hand. Cherries in the Snow. She remembers her first day of kindergarten, how she was so excited to start school but panicked when she realized that her mother wouldn't stay. Despite the teacher's pleas, she'd stood glued to the windows long after Rose had driven away, silently imploring her mother to come back. She couldn't believe she'd just left her there, and she couldn't imagine what her mother would do all day without her. Now she's wondering the same things. Will Rose miss her? Will she cry as she drives back over the bridge, as she goes about the rest of her day? Will she make too much food for dinner, drink too much white wine? Will she feel relieved?

The smell of breakfast is overwhelming: syrup and sausage and butter and eggs. Baker can hear the clinking of plates and silverware coming from off to the right, where the dining room must be. The muffled sound of girls gathered, the occasional burst of laughter.

"Are you hungry?" Anna appears beside her, ready to get Baker situated.

"No, thank you. I don't have much of an appetite this morning."

"That's what I figured. This is the main room." She gestures to the high ceiling, the worn wood floors covered in enormous Oriental rugs, faded and scuffed from years of footsteps and furniture. "It's where visitors sit. If they come."

At the far end of the room is a fireplace with a massive stone hearth, blackened from years of use. Next to it is a grandfather clock, the biggest Baker has ever seen. Both hands point up to the 12, stopped at noon or midnight.

"At least it's right twice a day!" Baker laughs awkwardly at her own joke, but Anna doesn't. She cocks her head and looks at Baker, and then the clock.

"Is it? I don't really pay attention to time." Anna is flat and plain, like an empty field or a piece of paper.

To the right of the fireplace is another room. A sofa sags against the wall, and a floor lamp with a tasseled shade stands beside it. There's an old rocking chair and an armchair that looks like it used to be comfortable. A narrow bookshelf is lined with faded paperbacks, some old leather-bound classics. Baker sees a stack of *National Geographic*s and a pile of *Reader's Digest*s. A wicker basket on the floor holds balls of yarn, and there are a few board games in a neat stack: Monopoly, Parcheesi, and Baker's least favorite, The Game of Life.

The television is smaller than the one Gerald bought himself for Christmas. A hi-fi is beside it on a low wood table, a few records in a pile below. Behind the television is a window that looks out on a small yard. Heavy yellow drapes hang on either side of the dusty glass pane. Beyond it, Baker can see the oak tree, and a wide patch of dry yellowed grass.

"This is the rec room. TV's on in the evenings, and if you want to sit on the sofa, you better get here early—it fills up fast. The hi-fi's there for anyone who wants to use it. There are only a few records, though. Pretty scratched up, and nothing good, in my opinion."

The record on top is a Mitch Miller sing-along.

"That your thing?" Anna asks.

"Not especially."

"I figured. We do crafts in here sometimes. I like ceramics. I made those birds last summer." Anna points to the windowsill, where several small lumpy creations sit in a line. Baker walks over to examine them. Their bright yellow beaks are comically misshapen, and they don't seem to have feet or wings. "They turned out kind of ugly."

"These are great birds, Anna," Baker offers kindly. "You said you made them last summer?"

Anna looks at the floor. "I've been here awhile."

Baker is about to ask *why*, but then she stops herself—*Discretion is key*—and pulls back the yellow curtain so she can admire the full view of the yard. It's an old casement window, the kind that swing open, like in old movies when a woman flings open a window and calls down to a lover. Baker pushes on it gently, then sees the lock.

"So we don't escape," Anna says, anticipating Baker's question. Her voice is dispassionate. She's given this tour before. "That reminds me. Safety. In the event of an emergency, like an earthquake, we exit through the front door. Single file, calm."

Baker imagines the earth beneath the house shifting, cracking, splitting open. The girls tumbling down all those stairs. "Has there ever been an emergency here?"

Anna grunts, audibly annoyed, and points back out into the main room. "This is just what I'm supposed to tell you. That red thing on the wall is the fire alarm. The glass isn't broken, so I guess that means no one's had to break it. Right?"

Baker returns the shrug.

Anna continues. "Kitchen's over there, through that door, and you can hear where the dining room is. Did you get your chore yet?"

"No."

"We all help with setting and clearing tables for meals, but there are also individual chores." Anna looks around and leans in, offering a secret. "Lunch prep is easy, unless you get sick around food. Dishes is the worst. You get soaked. Also no one wants to clean the floors. They reserve that for punishment."

Before Baker can ask how and why one ends up with a punishment, Anna has turned and walked away. Baker runs her fingers over the smooth glass of the window, then along the backs of the odd little birds. A chill forms between her shoulder blades, spreading along her spine.

Anna is back in the main room. She points out the door that leads to the basement stairs. "They made the basement into classrooms. Classes are down there, two hours a day for the younger girls. You've already graduated, so you don't have to go. You can assist the teachers instead of having a chore. They reserve that opportunity for smart girls. Like you."

Baker gives her a quizzical look.

"I assist Ms. White," Anna says, and shrugs. "I've read your file."

"Is assisting Ms. White your chore?"

"Something like that."

Then Anna leads her back through the main room, to the wide, grand stairs. Anna hurries up both flights, but Baker takes her time, running her hand along the curved handrail, worn smooth by the hands of who knows how many other girls. She admires the balusters, each one identical and intricately carved from a redwood, she imagines, that grew long ago. She pauses on the landing and surveys the room from above, noticing details she didn't see before. The wallpaper with the crowded floral pattern, lots of deep greens and blues and purples. Violets, maybe, and ivy. Across the ceiling, heavy beams form a checkerboard pattern. The table lamps with the Tiffany-style stained glass shades. It's strange here, but it's also beautiful. She looks up at Anna, who stands waiting for her, eyes wide and even paler than before.

"Are you okay?"

"I'm just taking it all in."

At the top of the stairway is the tallest stained glass that Baker's ever seen, taller even than the bleeding Jesus she stared at when she went to Catholic Mass with the O'Farrell kids one Christmas. The glass panels are deep rich hues that depict a flower—an iris, Baker guesses—in full giant bloom.

"Your room is here, on the second floor. I think we have about eleven girls here right now, including you."

Baker's not sure how many girls she expected there to be, but something about the number *eleven* feels comforting. "And all of them are . . ."

"In the same predicament? Yeah."

It amazes Baker that there are ten other girls like her. For the first time since Rose left, she feels the slightest bit less alone.

Anna leads her down a long narrow hallway on the second floor. It smells like dust and wood and Breck shampoo. In some ways, it reminds Baker of May's place—faraway ceilings, too many doors, intricate light fixtures and architectural details from another era. The bulbs dim, the ceilings dark. Baker runs her hands over the wallpaper; it peels and flakes at the seams, and she pulls off a tiny strip as she goes. It crumbles in her damp palm.

Anna points to the two doors on the left. "That one's the toilet, that one's the washroom. There are two more downstairs."

"That doesn't seem like enough."

"It's not. The lines get real long. Try to go early if you can. Or late, after everyone's in bed." Anna opens the washroom door, and Baker sees two pedestal sinks and a clawfoot tub with a dingy shower curtain around it. "At least there's two sinks, so you don't have to wait as long to brush your teeth."

They continue to walk, and Anna names the girls who live in each room. "Janey's in here with Lydia; Marcy's with Carol."

The doors—one after the other, worn wood with dull brass knobs and gaping keyholes—are all shut.

"More locks," Baker notes.

"Mm-hmm."

"Do we get keys?"

Anna shakes her head and laughs for the first time. It's like a small sneeze pushed through a smile. She doesn't actually answer Baker's question. Then she motions to an open door toward the end of the hallway. Beyond it, at the end of the corridor, is another small stained glass window. The sun is coming in just right, and the glass glows red and green and purple. More flowers—a rose and a poppy.

"This one's yours. Your roommate is a girl named Michelle. She's . . . well, you'll see. My mother would say she has *a big personality*."

The room is narrow, like Baker imagines a college dorm room

might be. On the far wall is a small window, no curtain, with a view of the same oak tree she saw out the window when she arrived. There is a twin bed pushed up against each wall. One mattress is bare, except for a plastic fitted sheet. A yellow chenille bedspread sits folded at the foot. Baker turns to talk to Anna and sees that she's still standing in the hall, just outside the door.

"Would you like to come in?"

Anna's face flushes, red and blotchy, and she shakes her head. "No, thank you. I'm fine right here." Her voice sounds strained.

"I assume this one is mine," Baker says, pointing to the bare bed. "Do I have to use the plastic cover?"

"We all have them. In case your water breaks in bed."

"My *water*?"

Anna doesn't offer an explanation, just stands at the threshold, watching Baker. The other bed is unmade, sheets twisted, a brown-and-white crocheted blanket draping over the edge of the bed, onto the floor. Below it, a pair of crumpled socks and what looks like a nightgown. A macramé plant holder hangs above the bed, with no plant in it. *Michelle's a mess*, Baker thinks. A stack of books on the small bedside table—Baker can't make out the titles, but she can see the cover of the record that leans against the bed. The slightly blurry photo, the wild hair, the chiseled jaw, the scarf around his neck. Baker smiles and picks it up, a warm feeling spreading across her chest. Maybe Michelle won't be so bad. Maybe she'll actually be a friend.

"That your thing, then?"

"Yeah," Baker says, a little wistful. "I love Bob Dylan."

Baker notices that Anna is squinting, trying to see the album cover without entering the room, so she holds it up. Anna examines the photo. "He looks like a hippie."

Baker walks over to the small window and scans her new view. She can see the oak, its branches tall and far-reaching, its leaves various shades of pale green and golden, quivering in the breeze. She pulls up on the window sash, but nothing happens. She pulls again, harder, and manages to open it about two inches. The breeze is warm, and Baker realizes it's the first fresh air she's felt since she and Rose walked through the front door.

"It won't open any further," Anna offers, her thin arms crossed.

"Why not? It's so stuffy in here!"

"You're smart. Take a guess." Anna shifts her feet and clasps her hands behind her back. "Any more questions?"

"Just one, thank you. Who was in this room before me?"

Anna's eyes get narrow, her jaw tense. "Michelle got here a few weeks ago."

"Right. But before that. I was told the room was opened up recently?"

Anna points to the window, clearly trying to change the subject. "You got a nice view!" Her voice sounds weird. Falsely chipper and still strained.

"I just thought that since you've been here for a while, you might know who was—"

"You should unpack now." The fake-nice voice is gone. Baker freezes. It's clear she went too far, said something wrong, but she's not quite sure what. Is she not supposed to ask about the other girls? Was that rude? *Discretion.*

"Thank you, Anna. I'll do that."

Baker lifts the plaid suitcase onto the mattress and unzips it. The plastic sheet crinkles. The present from Rose sits on top, wrapped in plain brown paper. Inside is an envelope with *Elizabeth* written on it in Rose's beautiful script. There's also a packet of cream-colored stationery, and a thin stack of postcards. The one on top has the Eiffel Tower on it. The one beneath it shows the Seine. The next has several shots of Paris at night, all lit up, stars twinkling— *Paris à nuit,* it reads. Baker opens the envelope, removes the note inside gently, tapping and shaking as she draws it out. Small puffs of sweet white talc waft into the air, settling on the bed. The smell of her mother fills her nose, the room. Lilacs and baby powder, the soft scent of her skin.

Dearest Elizabeth,

I hope this package finds you well and settling in.

I have included a new set of stationery for letter writing, as well as several postcards from Paris for us to display at home.

I hope that you are feeling well, and getting rest. If you feel ill, remember that a hot water bottle can do wonders. If they don't have one there, I can send one.

I will think of you every day until you return. Please write often.

With love,
Mother

"Your mother's signature scent?" Anna still stands there, just outside the doorway. Baker thought that she'd left.

"How'd you know?"

"My mother used to do the same thing." Baker hears the stress on *used to* and wants to ask more, but doesn't. She doesn't want to upset Anna any further.

"Does she keep a little bottle of it on her desk?"

"Of course. I mean, she did. I haven't been home in so long, maybe she's moved things around."

"I'm sure it will still be there when you get home."

Anna tucks a few strands of pale hair behind her ear. "Just so you know, it's common. For girls to do this. Send postcards from places we're supposed to be."

"Really?"

"It's part of how we cover our tracks."

*   *   *

Once Anna has left, Baker doesn't know what to do with herself. She wiggles her swollen fingers, then bends down to touch her toes. She's aware of the extra heft, how it swells a little more each day, how it brushes against her thighs as she folds herself in half, lets her head hang down, heavy. When she stands up, she's dizzy, and the room goes blurry, so she spreads the yellow chenille blanket onto the bed and lies down. She looks at the ceiling. She looks out the window. She bites her cuticles; then she looks at the ceiling again. She turns on her side and looks at Michelle's bed, the clothes on the floor, the record, Bob Dylan's face staring back at her. She wants to rifle through Michelle's things, peek in her closet, sniff her clothes, get a sense of who she is. But that would be rude.

She sits up, legs over the edge of her new bed, hands curled around the edge of the metal frame. Feet on the wood floor. She flutters her lips and lets her breath make a buzzing sound. She closes her eyes, sits perfectly still, and listens to her pounding heart. She stands up again, desperate to distract herself.

"Time to get cracking, Baker. You can do this." Her voice echoes in the small narrow room, and she looks around, sheepish, as if someone may have secretly been in there the whole time. But there's no one. It's just her.

The clothes look so sweet and unassuming, everything folded neatly, eager to go on a trip. As if she really were going to Paris. She opens the closet, but there are no hangers, just a few old metal hooks nailed to one of the inside closet panels. *That's odd,* she thinks. *What's the point of a closet if there aren't any hangers?* Then she feels worried. *Was I supposed to bring my own?* She hangs a few dresses on the hooks, then balls up the rest of her clothes and shoves it all into the drawers of a small dresser that's been pushed against the wall. The few pairs of shoes get lined up at the foot of the bed. She pulls out the books she grabbed blindly before she left and is relieved to see the bold cover of *The Colossus,* Sylvia Plath's name across the bottom. She's less excited to see the old Shake-speare anthology. She hates to admit it, but she finds him so boring. The third book is, of all things, her dictionary. *Great. What's the definition of* misery?

At the bottom of the suitcase is her journal. She knows it was right to bring it, but she still doesn't want to look at it. She knows that the last entry is from February, when she sprawled across her bed and gushed like a fool about Wylie. How embarrassing. She reaches under the bed and wedges the journal between the mattress and the metal bedframe slats.

And then it hits her. The exhaustion. She yawns, and yawns again. She'll lie down for a moment, just a minute. It's warm in the room, but she pulls the bedspread up anyway, just beneath her nose. The smell of Ivory Flakes mixed with the sharp scent of mothballs . . .

She wakes to a loud knock on the door.

"Hey, Baker," a voice calls from the hallway. "It's Michelle. Din-ner's in like ten minutes, and I gotta get my sweater."

Baker's mouth is bone-dry. Her empty stomach rumbles, and the sheets are twisted tight around her. She's sweaty and sticky, and it takes her a few seconds to process what's happening. She's been asleep all day. In a new bed, a new room. The home. She's in the home. And that voice is Michelle—her roommate. She sits up too quickly, then runs her fingers through her hair and instinctively pinches her cheeks for color. This place may feel strange, but she still wants to make a good first impression.

"Of course! Come in!"

The door swings open, and there's Michelle. Black frizzy hair, skin tan like an acorn, and a big crooked smile. "Finally! I thought I was gonna have to sleep in the hallway."

"I'm so sorry, I've been asleep. You could've just come in."

"Well, I did. I peeked in a few times, and you've been sound asleep all day. Didn't wanna disturb you. It's all so exhausting, isn't it?" She sticks out her right hand; the stack of brass bangles clank against one another. "Let's make it official. Hi. I'm Michelle." Her voice is loud in the little room, like a hardcover book dropped on a library floor.

"I'm Baker. Your new roommate."

They shake hands. Michelle has what seems like a hundred different brass rings stacked on her fingers.

"I like your rings."

"Thanks. I'm stuck with them for a while!" Michelle holds out her hands, tugs on a few stubborn rings. They don't budge—her fingers are too swollen. "See? My fingers are like sausages! Are yours?"

Baker wiggles her fingers. They're okay, but she doesn't want Michelle to feel bad. "A little bit. And I'm plenty swollen in other areas."

"What a racket, huh?" Michelle shrugs, then puts her hands on her hips. Baker tries to hold eye contact, but she's too distracted by the hem of Michelle's crocheted crop top, how it grazes her bare middle. Michelle looks further along than Baker, and she's not hiding it. It's right there, swelling gently, a hill in a field. An undeniable reminder of why they're all here.

Michelle rests her hands on either side of the belly, as if presenting it. "I like to let it get air, you know? Ms. White hates it, but I don't give a shit."

Baker clasps her hands behind her back to keep from reaching out to trace it, touch it, rub the taut skin. She's overwhelmed, too, with the urge to taste it, and that thought makes her feel ridiculous. But her desire to closely examine a pregnant body, so that she can understand what actually happens, what might happen to her body, is so strong. She clenches her jaw and knits her fingers behind her.

"It's okay," Michelle tells her, and Baker feels herself blush. Was she that obvious? "You can touch it."

"Oh, no, I couldn't." But oh, she wants to.

"Really. You can." She puts her hand on Baker's arm and gives a gentle tug. "You've never felt a pregnant body before, have you? I mean, aside from your own. Which isn't very big yet. How far along are you?"

"Twenty-two weeks."

"Huh! You're gonna pop any day now!"

Baker shudders at the word, goosebumps coating her arms.

Michelle laughs. "I just mean, you're gonna get big. Soon. Bet you'll be one of those girls who looks like she's smuggling a cute little volleyball." Michelle takes Baker's hand and holds it so it hovers over her skin. Her smile is easy and warm. She presses Baker's clammy palm to her body. It's like touching a beach ball that's been warmed all day by the sun.

So soft, Baker thinks, *and strong.* That feels like a strange way to describe skin, but it's true. There's a power to Michelle's body, a strength in her skin.

"I'm apparently due at the end of September," Michelle continues, "but we'll see. I already feel huge. Let's go eat. Aren't you starving?".

"How did you know?" Michelle feels safe and familiar. A little like May, but better, because she actually gets what Baker is going through. "I'm positively voracious. I could chew through these floorboards." She hasn't eaten since this morning, when Rose wrapped lightly buttered toast in a cloth napkin and handed it to her in the car. *Eat it,* she'd insisted, and Baker did, letting it scrape the roof of her mouth on its way down.

The girls are already sitting around tables in clustered little groups when Baker and Michelle enter the dining room. Some girls have just a dinner roll and some lettuce, while others have piled on the food: Baker sees vegetables and buttery potatoes and some kind of roast meat. There's an audible murmur when Michelle walks in with the new girl, and at least one disapproving teeth-suck. Baker thinks it's directed toward her at first, but then remembers Michelle's barely-there top.

Ms. White meets them at the door, a smile for Baker and a sharp look for Michelle.

"Ms. Larson. We've discussed the dress code."

Michelle produces a tan cardigan from behind her back. "I was just about to put this on. Ma'am."

Ms. White turns to Baker, smiling again. "I trust you've settled in?"

"Yes, thank you. I've been resting."

"Rest is so important. And you've clearly met your roommate."

"I have."

Ms. White's voice drops to a stage whisper. Her breath is warm and thin, like broth. "It's not the most ideal pairing, for your sake, but it's all we have available. Please let me know if there is any trouble."

Baker's eyes dart over to Michelle, who stands fiddling with the pearl buttons on the too-small cardigan. Baker doesn't want to make trouble with Ms. White, but she already feels protective of her roommate. "Michelle is already a wonderful roommate, Ma'am."

Ms. White turns to face the room. She clears her throat, but the chatter doesn't stop. Once more, louder. The room goes silent, and all the girls seem to turn at once. Baker's heart races. It feels like the first day of high school.

"I'd like you to meet our newest guest, who has just joined us today. Please welcome her as warmly as you recall yourselves being welcomed, and please take a moment to say hello during our after-dinner ice cream social."

Baker manages a polite smile. So many eyes, all on her. And her body. "Hi everyone. I'm Baker."

A blonde with two perfect spit curls stuck to her temples speaks up. "Like, bread?"

"Excuse me?"

"Bread. *Baker.* Like, a baker of bread?"

"It's a family name."

The girl with the curls snickers and turns back to her friends, a round brunette with full rosy cheeks and a slim girl wearing a long dress. "A baker with a bun in the oven," one of them whispers, loud enough for all to hear. Baker's face burns, and Michelle groans.

"So clever of you, Vivian," Michelle says, then she leans over and whispers in Baker's ear. "Just ignore them. They're not so bad—all bark, zero bite."

Michelle leads Baker to the back of the room, where their dinner options are displayed on a long table. The carrots look mushy, and the mashed potatoes seem dry. Baker passes on the mystery meat but takes several buttery-looking Parker House rolls.

"Good call on the rolls," Michelle says. "I usually get a few extras and smuggle them out in my pockets. I get hungry late at night."

"Like Heidi." Baker smiles, remembering the story about the little Swiss girl that Rose used to read to her. "Thanks for the tip, Michelle."

"No problem. I'll fill you in on all you need to know."

After dinner, the girls get their scoops of ice cream—chocolate, vanilla, strawberry, or orange sherbet—and move into the main room to eat it. The room fills with the hum of girl voices.

Michelle leans against the doorway, spooning chocolate ice cream into her mouth. "Main thing here is you gotta stay busy. Chores, art classes, whatever—you gotta keep moving. Otherwise you'll go mad." She bugs her eyes out and gives Baker an exaggerated grin. "It's weird in here, but you'll get used to it."

Baker looks at the girls, then at her new roommate's still-visible skin. Then down at her own body. Her ankles already look like someone else's. "That's hard to imagine. But it's nice to hear."

Michelle squints and leans in close, looking Baker up and down. Then she draws back. "So. You're a good girl."

"Excuse me?"

"That's my guess. And I'm pretty good at guessing. Everyone in here's got their own trip, sure, but when it comes down to it: you're either a good girl or a bad girl." She takes another bite, smearing a little chocolate on her lips and chin. "Your parents were either totally shocked . . . or everyone knew this was coming."

"Which one are you?"

"Guess."

Baker grins and feels herself start to relax a bit. Michelle *is* a big personality, and Baker likes it. After all these months of tense secrets and anxious whispers, it feels good to have someone to talk with. Without crying or apologizing. "You probably assume I'm going to guess *bad* because of what you're wearing, but I'm not. If the criteria is whether or not your parents were shocked—"

"That's not the *only* criteria, Ms. Facts and Information." Michelle raises one eyebrow in a comical way. Baker responds by lifting her chin and putting a pointed finger in the air, a saucy expert ready to prove a point.

"Well, then, the additional criteria would most likely be your prior behavior, and I have no way of knowing that. I just met you. I don't even know where you're from. You could've been class president. You could be a preacher's daughter."

"Then you'd *know* I was a bad girl!"

"Fair point."

"You overcomplicate things, sister. But that's cool. I like it, Good Girl."

Baker considers the options. What if she's both? Or neither? "I think I'm more of just a Normal Girl. I've done a lot of good things, sure, but I'm not exactly perfect . . ." She gestures to her midsection and shrugs, then feels an unexpected lightness. It's a relief to be able to joke about it.

"Another fair point, but we're operating on basic Judeo-Christian principles here. Light or dark. Heaven or hell. Saint or sinner!"

"I choose C. None of the above." Baker crosses her arms in mock defiance.

"Heretic!" Michelle throws her hands in the air like a preacher, and they both burst into giggles. Some of the other girls glare, but Baker sees smiles on a few of their faces. "Blasphemer!"

Baker can tell that Michelle likes her, and she's surprised by how good that feels. How relieved she is to make an actual connection with another human who understands what she's experiencing. But she can also feel Ms. White's eyes from across the room, and she remembers the warnings from her meeting with Rose. *Discretion.* She shifts gears, hoping for a less-animated topic. "How long have you been here?"

"Two interminable weeks. I was the new girl until you showed up. But I work fast. You want the scoop on everyone?"

"Sure."

"Got pen and paper? You seem like the kind who takes notes."

Baker grins. "My memory's superb."

"Alright." Michelle leans back, her head close to Baker so she can whisper. She motions to Anna, who sits by herself a few tables over, a *Life* magazine open on the table next to her bowl of orange sherbet.

"We'll start with her."

"Anna," Baker says.

"Yup. Sad Anna. You met her. She's not actually pregnant any-more, that's why she's so thin. What do you think: good or bad?"

"I don't really . . ."

"Oh, come on!"

"Bad?"

"Bingo." Michelle drops her voice even lower, and Baker has to strain to hear her. "She got knocked up by the next-door neighbor. A *married* neighbor."

"Why is she still here?"

"She's got nowhere to go. Her dad won't let her come back. The neighbor denies the whole thing. So she's here for a while, working to earn her keep, until she figures out something else."

"What about her mother?" Baker thinks about the bottle of scented powder on her desk.

"A drunk. According to Anna." Michelle shifts, arches her back, and huffs. "Damn sciatica."

"Do you want to sit down?"

"Naw. That's no better." Michelle points to a group of girls sitting around a coffee table near the fireplace.

"Blond one: Marcy. She's good. But you knew that. Yell team, total deb. I call her the Golden Girl. She's about seven months along, though you can barely tell, huh? Perfect little bump. And a surprisingly good sense of humor. Next to her is Lydia. I call her The Pledge—college girl, real sweet, goes to Cal. Jewish. She'd get kicked out of her sorority if they found out. She's not here for much longer—she's going over any day."

"Going over?"

Michelle raises an eyebrow. "That's what we call it here. It's the *polite* way to say it without saying *it*."

"I see. And do you have nicknames for everyone?"

"Most of them. Across from The Pledge is Carol, aka Christmas Carol. The one with the brown curls and the puffy cheeks. Her birthday's on Christmas, so that's an easy nickname. Plus, she's super into Jesus. She's the oldest one here right now—I think she's twenty. But she might as well be thirteen, she's so naïve. She's about five or six months, and according to her roommate, she is *very* gassy. Next to her is Farmer Janey. She's from Iowa. Or Ohio. Idaho? One of those. She's also six months along, total doll, totally heartbroken. She wanted to marry the guy, but his parents freaked and shipped her as far west as they could without putting her out to sea."

Baker imagines Farmer Janey adrift on a raft in a sea of corn, her parents waving from a ship in the distance. A teenage boy trying to swim after her, thrashing in the kernels, while Janey sails to California. She watches Lydia, who leans back slightly, closes her eyes, and rests a hand on her enormous belly. A grimace on her face as she grunts. Her friends don't seem to notice.

Michelle goes on. The girl with the spit curls is Vivian—goes by Viv—and she's "hard." Keeps to herself. A very young-looking girl with a mousy face and pigtails, who apparently cries in the bathroom every night, is Ida, but Michelle calls her Sobs. Baker is impressed by the litany of details.

"How do you know all of this?"

Michelle shrugs. "I watch. I listen. And I ask questions. Most of them take awhile to open up. The short one over there with the long bangs and big boobs? That's Debra—I call her Bangs. She's shy at first, but she's a total chatterbox. A good girl chatterbox, to be exact."

"So what's your story?" Baker has been observing Michelle as she talks and gestures. There's a rough edge to her, but she's also sharp. Smart-assed and just plain smart.

"I'm from Florida." She notes Baker's surprised reaction and shrugs. "I know, right? I went as far away as I could. I mean, once my mom kicked me out, I did."

"What's she like?"

"Mama? Highlight of her week is playing the organ in the church choir. Other than that, she's mostly into the three B's—Bible, bridge, and booze."

"So she kicked you out of Florida and you came here?"

"You're not so bad at the Question Game yourself, Baker. And no, first she kicked me out of the house, and then I came to the Golden State. On my own. The promised land! Fresh start, free love, all that good stuff. Then I met Barry." Michelle stops talking for a moment. Her mouth slides into a wide smile, and she bites her lower lip. "My boyfriend. We were shacking up with his Auntie Brenda."

"Here in the city?"

"Yeah. The Fillmore. But then he got called up, right when we found out I was knocked up. And Brenda said I had to go. She's a good woman, but she's got enough on her plate. Always taking care of everyone else: her own kids, their kids, her friends' kids. Her pad is small, and she's busy. She couldn't take me on, too."

Baker is surprised by how forthcoming Michelle is, especially after Ms. White's warnings. Michelle is anything but discreet, and Baker is fascinated. "That makes sense."

"It's not Brenda's fault. She says if Barry wasn't gonna serve, and if we got married and everything, then she could maybe help us out. She says she wishes I could keep her. But it's just that if something happens to Barry . . ."

Baker can't help but ask. "You just said 'her.' Do you . . . know?"

"It's just a feeling." Michelle rests against the wall, grand and lanky, and scratches her navel with one long-fingered hand, her rings clinking. "But I don't know if anyone will even want her."

"What do you mean?"

"Mixed babies aren't exactly flying off the shelves." Baker stares, perplexed. Michelle drops her voice to a whisper again. "They probably wouldn't have let me in here if I'd told them the truth about the father, so *shhhhh*. This baby's gonna be some kinda brown, and those upstanding couples out there? I hear they're a lot more eager for the all-white ones."

Baker tries to keep her expression neutral, but she can't hide her surprise. It's not something Baker has considered, the skin color. That it has skin, will have skin, will have skin of a certain shade that could then determine its desirability, its place in the world. Will it be tan like Wiley? Pale like Baker? Will it have freckles and a birthmark like the one on her hip? Why should its color matter, anyway? Can a couple really be *upstanding* if they're choosing babies based on skin color?

In the far corner, a girl with a dark ponytail sits alone, ankles neatly crossed, crocheting. Baker recalls seeing her earlier in the day, yarn in hand as she descended the stairs.

"Who's that?"

"Oh. Helen."

"What's she making?"

Michelle pauses, as if not sure how to answer. "Sweaters."

"Only sweaters?"

"*Baby* sweaters."

"Oh."

"She's been here awhile, I guess. She keeps them in a box under her bed. She's probably made like fifty of them by now."

The bowl of ice cream in Baker's hands has melted; she now holds a soupy chocolate mess. The carrots on her dinner plate were pale and soft; when Rose makes them, they still have some crunch. She feels them now, uneasy, somewhere between her throat and stomach, as she watches the girl, her fingers hooking and looping, the string of lavender yarn hanging between the wound-up ball and the tiny half-formed sleeve. Someone turns on the TV; the theme song for *Let's Make a Deal* begins. Gerald loves that silly show, and Baker pictures him watching it now, back home in his chair, in a home that continues to exist without her. Her mouth tastes sour. Is real life really this unfair?

"Thanks for the intel, Michelle. I don't know how it's possible, but I'm tired again. I think I'll head up to bed."

"The sweaters really get ya, don't they?"

"I'm fine. Just tired."

Tired is an understatement, a euphemism. *Fine* is a flat-out lie. The most far-off feeling she can imagine. Her mind whirs with faces, names, and stories. Sweaters and boyfriends and sororities and ice cream. Florida, the Fillmore. Free love, heartbreak. Dinner rolls, a bun in an oven. So many intimate details contained in one strange place. Baker looks toward the stairs, feels the pull of sleep. It may not be the most comfortable bed, but she's so exhausted, she could sleep back on the asphalt out front if needed. She could sleep for days, for weeks. *Wake me up when it's over.*

When she gets ready for bed, Baker decides to pretend that she *is* on vacation. That the home is a hotel in Paris. That the other girls are guests there, that a maid will come and clean the bathroom tomorrow morning, that there's a possibility of room service—croissants, chocolates, maybe even champagne. That she'll sleep well and wake up and read poetry in bed and drink coffee from a small thin-rimmed cup and then maybe take a walk, have an adventure in this new city.

She brings the toiletry kit that Rose packed for her into the bathroom, and when she unzips it and pulls out a washcloth, it smells so much like home. She tries to imagine what a Parisian bathroom would smell like. Roses and perfume. Faint hint of cigarettes. When she slathers her face with Noxzema, a scent she normally loves, she feels nauseous. She heaves over the sink, the thick white cream still all over her face, but nothing comes up. She brushes her teeth, and when she spits, there's blood in the sink.

"That happens to me, too." The voice comes from behind, startling Baker. "Sorry, didn't mean to scare you. But my grandmother says it's normal for your gums to bleed like that. You have, like, *extra* blood in you right now."

It's Marcy, the Golden Girl. She wears a yellow Swiss-dot nightgown with a bow at the neck, and she carries a toothbrush wrapped in a pink terry washcloth. She turns on the faucet and begins rinsing her face in the other sink.

"It can get pretty crowded in here. Some girls don't like it, and they skip their beauty regimens entirely!" She leans close to the mirror and begins smoothing Pond's cold cream across her forehead, under her eyes, onto her slim throat. "Not me. This time here? Temporary. But I'll have this face forever."

"My mother uses Pond's," Baker notes.

"Mine, too. And she still has a lovely complexion, even at her age." Marcy dries her face gently, dabbing the towel on her cheeks and forehead. She looks at Baker's reflection in the mirror and smiles. "It's not so bad in here, you know. I'm sure Michelle has all kinds of things to say, but she can be so negative. For the record, I am happy to be here."

Baker isn't sure whether to believe her, but she smiles politely. No point in arguing, and maybe Marcy really is happy here. "That's nice to hear."

"Honestly, it's a godsend. You think I want anyone to see me like this?" Marcy steps back so she can see more of her body in the mirror. She frowns and wrinkles her freckled nose. "Ugh! Disgusting!"

Sometime in the middle of the night, Baker wakes to a terrible howl. It sounds like an injured animal, something clearly suffering—and it's coming from outside the room, down the hall. Soon there are doors opening and shutting; there are feet in the hallway, the dark muffle of urgent voices.

"What's happening?" She doesn't mean to say it out loud.

"It's someone's time," Michelle mumbles from her bed, pulling her quilt up over her head. "Probably Lydia. She's like a week late."

Baker sits up in the dark, straining to hear what's happening. Lydia from dinner, the college girl, eyes closed, grimacing while all her friends giggled. She was just right there, like everyone else.

More voices, more howling, and then moaning. Someone runs past their room, down the hallway, in the direction of the stairs. A voice cries "Quick! Help!" Another door opens, then slams shut. It sounds like an emergency.

Ms. White's voice rises above the rest. Baker's heart races, and she hears loud chanting: "Breathe! Breathe! Do not stop! Breathe!" Why does Lydia need to be reminded to breathe?

"Michelle! Wake up!"

"Sleeping," is Michelle's muffled reply. Baker doesn't understand why she's not more worried.

"Do you think she's okay? What if something goes wrong?"

"Too many questions, sister." Michelle goes quiet, and within seconds, she's snoring. Now there are more footsteps in the hall, fast and urgent, then doors slamming as Lydia and her howls grow farther and farther away.

*I*n the morning, no one mentions Lydia. Not in the bathroom, where the girls splash cold water on their faces and pick at blemishes in the mirror, groggy and slow in their sunrise haze. They say *hello, good morning, did you sleep well,* but that's it. Not a word about the cries in the night, the fact that one of them has gone. *Gone over,* Baker mumbles to herself. No one mentions Lydia in the hallway, where the girls walk in silence toward the stairs, both lured and repulsed by the breakfast smells. And not in the dining room, where Baker follows Michelle's lead, grabbing a plastic tray, standing in the line. She feels dizzy and unsettled as she grabs some kind of muffin and a mug of hot coffee and follows Michelle to a seat.

Lydia is just not here. Not in her sorority house, not attending class at Cal, not here in this dining room. Her friends are here, a group of three instead of four, munching on grapefruit, dry toast, cereal. Janey laughs as Carol burns her tongue on too-hot tea. Marcy picks at sliced peaches in a bowl of cottage cheese. And Lydia is just a girl in the night, gone.

"She's probably still in labor," Michelle whispers, reading Baker's mind. "In the hospital."

Baker opens her mouth, about to ask Michelle more about the hospital: What happens there? Will Lydia come back afterwards? Will they see her again? But the dining room door swings open, and Ms. White appears with a clipboard, ready to start the day.

"Good morning, girls. I have this weekend's schedule, if you'll please listen carefully." Baker turns to give Ms. White her attention, then notices that she's the only one to do so. The other girls whisper and giggle like they're in homeroom. Ms. White clears her throat and glances down at her clipboard. "Visiting hours will be between ten A.M. and noon. Please remember that if your visitor is not already pre-approved, she will not be allowed in. I don't want a repeat of last week." Her stern glare sweeps the room, a searchlight shining on each girl's face. "And please note that I said *she*. We do not allow male visitors, including relatives. Fathers may send letters and make phone calls. Boyfriends and other male acquaintances may not."

She scans the room again, her eyes resting on a few faces. Janey ducks her head and looks sheepish. Viv lifts her chin, the tiniest bit defiant.

"Lunch is at noon, of course, and today is Saturday, so chores must be done. There's a two P.M. outing for those who are on the approved list. Keep in mind that we are having some unusually warm weather for San Francisco in the summer, but you must still dress according to our guidelines. Modest and concealing, please. Mail goes out Monday morning at nine A.M., so have all letters in the box by then. Thank you, and have a lovely day."

Again, no mention of Lydia. Baker's not sure what she expected— a brief update, a word or two about her condition? An acknowledgment that something very important happened? She knows there won't be a celebration, no cigars or bouquets, no joyous cries of *It's a Boy!* But not even a brief *Lydia is resting and doing well*? She can't tell whether there's some kind of rule against mentioning it, or whether they just don't care. Either way, the strange erasure makes Baker feel very far from home, far from herself, far from anything she's known.

The girls gather for the walk, waiting in the front room wearing lipstick, too-nice shoes, and coats, despite the summer heat. The morning grogginess that Baker observed during breakfast is gone, replaced by shiny rouged cheeks, bright eyes, pearl earrings. Marcy totters in crocodile pumps, ankles swelling over the sides; Janey clutches a pink satin handbag in front of her, as if it might hide the obvious bump. Michelle wears a navy wool peacoat barely buttoned across her middle.

Just after breakfast, Michelle and a few others encouraged Baker to join them, and she decided to make the effort. Going outside is appealing, and she doesn't mind the thought of spending more social time with the others. Baker tried on three different dresses that Rose packed before settling on the least-hideous one, and she grabbed a green cardigan to cover the puffed sleeves. She worried she'd feel overdressed, but now that she's down here and sees how done up the others are, she feels the opposite: frumpy, plain, a shapeless bore.

But despite her self-conscious feelings, the excitement is electric, palpable. The girls joke and tease and giggle like schoolchildren about to go on a field trip.

"I hope we go by that bakery again," gushes Marcy. "The one with the raisin sweet buns."

Janey swoons. "Those were to *die* for."

"I could eat a dozen!"

"If I recall correctly, you did!"

"Think we'll go to the park?"

"You just want to see your *boyfriend*."

"Stop that! He's not my boyfriend!"

"We've seen the way you smile at each other!"

"We've never even met! He's just some man who works at the gas station!"

Marcy turns to Baker. "You're a local gal. What are your favorite spots?" The others lean in to hear her answers, but the door to Ms. White's office opens, and they grow quiet. Ms. White carries a clipboard and a long slim box. She places the box on a mahogany side table and stands next to it. The girls crowd around. Michelle joins them, but Baker hovers on the outskirts, on the bottom step, where she can watch the scene unfold.

"Are we ready?" Ms. White calls.

Michelle glances back at Baker. She winks, then whispers, "Are *you* ready?"

Ms. White opens the lid and holds up the box. Baker can see several rows of glinting gold and silver rings, some with stones that sparkle in the light, some just simple bands.

Marcy leans over and whispers to Janey, "I want the ruby this time."

"That's fine," replies Janey. "Pearl's my birthstone."

One by one, each girl steps up and chooses, then slips the ring onto her left hand. Baker is baffled until she's not—a stroke of realization, and it all makes sense. They're wedding rings. Fake ones.

Michelle steps up for her turn and selects a gold band with a single stone. "Pretty far-out, huh?" She turns and waves to Baker, flashing her hand with a wink. It looks out of place next to her chunky silver rings, her turquoise and moonstone.

"Isn't it just divine, darling? Can you believe the size of this rock?"

Marcy joins in the joke. "Oh, yes, I just couldn't *believe* that he would get me a diamond this big!"

Baker doesn't know whether to laugh or scowl or cry. She likes the camaraderie between the girls, but at the same time, it feels cruel, making them pretend like this. Like pouring salt on the wound and asking them to smile.

"Girls," Ms. White chastises. "That's enough. These rings protect your dignity, and that is *no* laughing matter."

Baker stands up and approaches Ms. White, who stiffens when she sees her.

"I'm quite sorry, Baker, but you won't be joining us." The girls exchange concerned glances. "Per your mother's instructions." Ms. White gestures to her clipboard, as if that explains it all.

Baker's heart sinks, and her cheeks burn. "May I ask why?"

"Discretion. The risk of being seen. You know, most of our girls aren't from this area. Janey is all the way from Ohio—"

"Iowa, ma'am," Janey interjects quietly.

"They're all rather anonymous. But given your mother's involvement in so many local organizations . . . well, she just doesn't feel that it's prudent."

The murmurs intensify, laced with a sense of injustice. *How unfair,* Baker hears someone say. Michelle whispers, "Bullshit," and Ms. White's head snaps around to see who swore.

"So I can't leave?"

"We have so many ways to keep busy in here."

"I can't even go outside?" Baker knows she needs to stay composed, but she can't help the panic that creeps into her voice. The room feels warmer all of the sudden. Stuffy and thick. The walls look too dark. Too close. Ms. White raises an eyebrow and speaks slowly, with some force.

"Not unless you're accompanied by your mother. You can use this time to settle in a bit more. You did *just* arrive. Write your letters. Do some puzzles!"

Her voice leaps unnaturally at the end of the world *puzzles,* like a diver who's bounced too hard on a board. Baker feels everyone's eyes on her. The icy feeling returns, wrapping around her like a freezing ribbon until it can't wrap any tighter. Her ears ring; her breathing feels compromised. *Trapped,* she thinks. *I'm trapped.* She looks at the heavy front door, at Ms. White's clipboard, at the faces of the girls who now pity her. *We all are.*

"Will you be okay, Ms. Phillips?"

Baker squares her shoulders. "Of course. I'm looking forward to the quiet time."

The girls shuffle toward the door, giving Baker little half waves and shrugs.

"We'll bring you back something," offers Janey.

Carol's face brightens. "How about a pastry?"

Baker shakes her head. "That's so kind, but I'm just fine. You all enjoy."

Michelle waves her hand in the air and mouths *Fuck this.*

Then she calls out, "Ta-ta, darling, I'm off to shop for the wedding!"

When the door is shut and the girls have gone, Baker wonders about their route: Will they stroll through the Financial District, scandalizing the businessmen? Toddle around Fisherman's Wharf, slurping chowder and dodging seagulls like tourists? They could crack open fortunes in Chinatown—*A stranger will soon come to visit*—or climb Telegraph Hill, huffing and puffing to the top of Coit Tower. Cable car rides seem too bumpy, and no way would Ms. White let them go near the degenerates of Haight Street. Definitely no stroll across the Golden Gate Bridge. Too tempting to jump.

She pushes that dark thought from her head and turns around, alone in the big empty room. In the big empty home. And maybe that's not so bad. She smiles at the sound of all this silence and heads up to her room. As she climbs the wide wooden stairs, another dark thought appears, unbidden: *Has anyone ever fallen? An accidental slip, or maybe even—*

She shudders. All that hard wood. It would probably knock you out. It just might work.

> *Dear Mother,*
>
> *Thank you so much for the stationery.*
>
> *There's not much to report so far, aside from everyone being very nice and the food being just fine. My roommate, Michelle, is helpful. I look forward to trying some activities.*
>
> *I miss you and I could really go for a swim right about now. Do a few laps for me, please.*
>
> *Your daughter,*
> *Baker*

Dear May,

Greetings from my new "house." It's OK, but it doesn't feel like I'm in SF at all. I feel very far away. My roommate is named Michelle and I think you'll dig her. Come visit and I'll introduce you.

> *I feel nauseous and a little trapped.*
> *Please come visit me ASAP.*
> *Did I mention to please come visit?*
> *Say hi to everyone at your place.*

Destroy after reading,
B

She writes her postcards, then decides to try the Shakespeare. It's an old edition, cloth-bound and faded, the kind of book that used to feel special and grown-up. Now, as she tries to make her way through a few pages of *King Lear*, it just feels old and dense. It's hard to focus. She can't get comfortable.

Her eyelids droop, and the small type blurs together. She has to reread lines again and again, and has no patience for the language. The mattress is lumpy, her neck is stiff, her lower back itches, her hip is asleep. She needs to pee, *again*.

For the first few months, it was easy enough to *not notice* being pregnant. Or at least, she could ignore it more easily. Yes, there were the tender breasts, the bloating, the nausea, but for a while it seemed possible that she might not ever *really* change. It was one thing to feel sick, but maybe her body wouldn't blow up like a balloon? Maybe her body wouldn't expand; maybe she'd stay small and slim and could just wear long voluminous dresses and get away with it. Maybe she could just carry on, as if everything were normal.

But that was the first phase of the moon, when she was just a sliver. That's not, she realizes, what's happening now. The truth is she's changing every day. When she sees her face in the bathroom mirror, she can't deny her round, full cheeks. Even her hair feels thicker than usual. Her fingers are puffy, and by evening, her ankles are the same size as her calves, and while she's never considered herself to be terribly vain, she doesn't like to see it. Will she get as big as Lydia was at the end?

Her stomach rumbles—she's hungry, but it's not just that. The thing inside her is moving. Again. It's been happening more and more. Not all the time, but it's definitely more frequent. Sometimes it feels like a gentle rolling. Or like something is knocking on the inside of her body. What is it doing? And what *is* it? Her brain conjures images of the only newborn creatures she's actually seen— just-hatched baby birds, or pink writhing kittens—and then she feels freaked out. She's never even *seen* a newborn baby. Toddlers, yes, but an actual human baby, freshly into the world? Never. How big are they?

The girls joked about her name that first day. *A baker with a bun in the oven.* She pictures a tiny little bun inside of her. Round and soft, golden dough. It's much less grotesque than a damp squirming animal, and somehow, much easier to accept than something human. Another little shift from deep within. She puts her hands on her sides and imagines a doughy bun tumbling, floating gently inside her. It puts a smile on her face. It almost makes her laugh. *Hello, Bun.*

She puts the Shakespeare down and stands up, then pauses for a moment as a dizzy spell washes over her. She chooses a spot on the wall just behind her bed and tries to focus, tries to make the spinning seasick feeling go away. The Bun is still, but she swears she can feel the blood pulsing through her body.

Her nightgown is still draped across the foot of the bed, and her blouse from yesterday is on the floor. It's not like her to keep a messy room, but she's so tired, and bending down to pick things up is sometimes just too much. But she makes herself do it, crouching down slow. She opens the door to the small closet at the foot of the bed and hangs up her blouse and nightgown on one of the hooks. Then, on some strange impulse, she pushes the other hanging clothes out of the way and steps inside, inhaling the scent of cedar and spray starch. And then she sees something on the back wall.

It's a list. Handwritten words, starting at the top of the wall and running down in a column.

At the top: MARGARET WAS HERE is written in neat script, in faded pencil.

And then below it:

DONNA WAS HERE, in pencil. Also faded.

Then:

PATTY WAS HERE

CATHERINE WAS HERE

MARY WAS HERE

Baker runs her finger over each name, each repeated phrase. *Was here was here was here was here.* They all look like they were written some time ago, messages from a secret past. The last one, though, looks fresher. Bold and dark, the graphite still sharp. Neatly in pencil, in all capital letters:

KITTY WAS HERE

And then in smaller letters, underneath:

but she didn't want to be

Baker reads it to herself several times. *Kitty,* she whispers, feeling her tongue touch the roof of her mouth each time she says it. *Kitty kitty kitty,* like she's calling for a pet. She touches the words again, careful, not wanting to smudge. She realizes she's been holding her breath, and when she breathes in, the closet smell is no longer nostalgic. It's nauseating. She backs out of the closet and looks around the room, as if Kitty might be standing there behind her, watching. But everything is quiet, and Baker is still alone.

*   *   *

That evening after dinner, Michelle tells Baker that she's going straight to bed. "That walk *exhausted* me," she groans. "Why does this city have to have so many hills?"

Baker doesn't want to go back to the room, especially if Michelle is going to crash right out and leave her lying there with her thoughts and the wardrobe of names, so she joins some of the girls in the rec room. She's missed the evening television routines of home: most nights, they'd eat at the dinner table, then after she'd cleared the plates and helped with dishes, she'd join Gerald for the evening news. On weekends, though, they'd have their meals on TV trays, sitting together to watch their programs. She wonders what she's missed since being in here.

The girls in the room—Janey, Carol, Marcy, and the girl Michelle calls "Sobs"—have claimed most of the available seating, so Baker perches on the edge of the couch, trying to stay balanced and appear friendly.

"Mind if I join you? I always watch the evening news with my dad. And I think there might be a Giants game on after that. Does anyone like baseball?"

Janey examines her. "It's Saturday. We watch *Jackie Gleason* first, and then the Saturday Night Movie. We don't watch sports."

"And the news is so boring," Marcy adds, her big eyes rolling. "So *depressing*."

Carol smiles kindly. "But you're welcome to join us, Baker." She scoots closer to Marcy and pats the small patch of cushion next to her.

Baker swallows, and squeezes in next to her. She can't stand Jackie Gleason, but it's better than nothing. Maybe someone can bring her a newspaper the next time there's an outing. At least she could get a little bit of information from the outside world. She makes a mental note to give Michelle two dimes from her coin purse.

Dear May,

Just a reminder that I'm allowed to have visitors between 10am and noon every Tuesday and Saturday. My mom hasn't even come yet. You can be the first!

Did I mention that they won't let me go outside? How's everything?

Love,
Me

On Monday morning, Baker receives her chore assignment. Anna was right: rather than laundry duty or dishes, she will have one of the coveted classroom assistant positions.

"I think you're an excellent fit," Ms. White says, beaming. "A smart girl like you. You'll assist Mrs. Williams. She was an English teacher for many years, and now she volunteers here, with our younger girls who are still in high school. They're currently reading *Jane Eyre*. Are you familiar with it?"

Baker tries to stop the smile from spreading across her face, worried that Ms. White might change her mind if she sees how happy this makes her. But she can't help it. Is she familiar with *Jane Eyre*? She's only read it a hundred times. She remembers when she first pulled it from the bookshelf behind Rose's recliner. It was hardbound with a faded red cloth cover, gold gilt lettering, and decoration on the spine. Baker curled up in the chair and began reading, stopping only because Rose called her name a third time for dinner. If she had been allowed to read at the table, she would've, and once she was excused from dinner, she'd rushed right back to it, enamored of poor Jane. Since then, she's reread it many times and has gone through a significant phase of being infatuated with the Brontë sisters. All that genius and wild imagination, all that sickness and suffering. Their pseudonyms and secret worlds! Their novels and unfinished manuscripts! Their brilliant lives, cut short so young.

"Yes, ma'am," Baker says. "I know the book well."

"Wonderful. You'll start tomorrow after breakfast."

*   *   *

Baker is surprised by her reaction when she enters the classroom: it's just four girls sitting around a single table, listening to an older woman with thin frizzy hair and wire-rimmed glasses. The space is plain: a chalkboard on one wall, a small bookshelf, a wastebasket in the corner. It's nothing like her high school classrooms, which were crowded with desks and books and teenagers, but it still feels familiar, and her heart races at the scent of chalk dust, the sound of a teacher leading a discussion. Baker stands at the back of the room, taking it in and awaiting instruction.

"There are five primary settings in the book," Mrs. Williams intones. "Let's begin by discussing the names of each place. Do you think there is any *symbolism*?"

"I think it's called *Lo*wood because the orphan girls who get sent there are the lowest," offers Janey. "The girls that no one wants."

The girl that Michelle calls "Bangs" speaks up. Beneath the curtain of hair that covers her forehead, she has enormous eyes, and so many freckles. "Maybe it's called *Thorn*field because it's . . . complicated. You know, like it's thorny?"

Mrs. Williams beams. "Nice, Debra. Very astute."

"Or it can hurt you if you're not careful," adds Janey. "It's beautiful, but there's danger, too."

Helen, who's wearing her dark brown hair in long braids down her back, nods in agreement, along with Ida ("Sobs," as Michelle calls her). Baker gets a good look at her—short dirty blond curls, chapped lips, shy eyes, a big round middle—and nearly gasps. She can't believe how young she looks. Ida looks down at her hands on the table, then winces as she shifts in her seat.

"These are excellent observations, girls. Sharp thinking." Mrs. Williams looks at Ida. "Are you alright?"

"Yes, ma'am." Even her voice sounds young. "Just a little cramping."

Mrs. Williams seems unfazed, as if she's quite used to girls in pain. Then she looks up and notices Baker. "Ms. Phillips, correct? Please, join me up here. Do you have a copy of the book with you?"

Baker shakes her head. "I didn't bring it, Mrs. Williams." She knows exactly where it is on the bookshelf in her bedroom back home. She can picture it: top shelf, on the left. Red with gold. Next to the hardcover copy of *East of Eden,* which is blue, and her Nancy Drews, some the original grayish blue, others with the yellow spine. She knows her books by color. She wishes she'd brought them all.

Mrs. Williams points to the small bookshelf below the chalkboard. Old paperbacks are lined up neatly; some hardcovers, too. "There are a few extra copies on the shelf. Please select one, and join us."

Baker scans the books, noting the faded spines and worn edges. There are three additional copies of *Jane Eyre,* and she takes the one that looks most well-worn, most loved. She opens to the title page and sees that someone has drawn on it. Doodles cover the page: hearts, stars, spirals. A bird, a moon, a row of flowers growing up from the bottom edge. She imagines a girl here before her, bored and restless, a pencil in her hand, the thrill of making marks you're not supposed to make. Then she sees the name written in the upper right-hand corner, and her breath catches in her throat. Surrounded by stars, in the same handwriting she saw in the closet: KITTY.

Baker snaps the cover shut and takes a seat with the girls, gripping the book in her hands and trying not to think about this mystery girl. *Who was she?*

The discussion picks back up, and Baker is able to put Kitty out of her mind. The conversation energizes her, and soon she's able to forget why she's there, why they're all there. Though she's probably only a year or two older than the other girls, Baker feels wise and important. They look to her, and she has something to offer. At one point, she mentions that the Brontës originally published under a different name, and the girls are surprised.

"Why did she do that?" Janey asks.

"Maybe she was afraid people wouldn't like it," suggests Ida.

Debra mutters, "I think it was because no one would believe that a girl wrote it."

Janey looks up and squints. "Were girls not allowed to write books, or was it just not acceptable?"

Mrs. Williams looks at Baker encouragingly. "Go on, Ms. Phillips."

"It wasn't illegal, Janey, but it was unusual. In fact, all three Brontë sisters used pseudonyms." Baker notices Janey's furrowed brow. "That's a fancy word that means a fake name. Charlotte was 'Currer Bell,' Emily was 'Ellis Bell,' and Anne was 'Acton Bell.' They kept their initials, you see." The girls are paying close attention, and Baker buzzes with the power of being listened to.

"Thank you, Ms. Phillips," Mrs. Williams says, with a tone that indicates she's ready to have her class back. "Is there anything else you'd like to add today?"

Caught up in the moment, Baker feels open and bold. "I was in eighth grade when I learned this. I was fascinated. I didn't know you could do that, just go by a different name. I figured if Charlotte could do it in nineteenth-century England, I could do it in modern-day California. I loved how Currer sounded, and I realized that my middle name sounds a little like it. And that's actually how I started going by Baker." As it comes out of her mouth, she realizes that she's never told anyone this, not even her English teacher, not even Rose or May. She blushes. Suddenly it feels so silly, copying a long-dead novelist, assuming a new name as if she, too, would someday be known.

But the girls love the story. Ida gazes at Baker.

"I've always wanted a different name."

"Ida is a lovely name!"

Ida shakes her head. "It's an old-lady name. Maybe I can change it when I'm done here?"

"If I was going to publish a book, I would definitely use a different name," says Janey. "I wouldn't want everyone reading what I wrote. I would use the name Jacob."

"Jacob," Baker repeats. "A strong name."

"It would've been my name if I'd been born a boy. That's what my dad wanted."

Mrs. Williams turns to Baker. "This has been a lively discussion. Thank you for your help today, Ms. Phillips. I usually end my classes by reading several pages aloud. Would you like to read today? We're on chapter twenty-three. The dialogue between Jane and Rochester. A pivotal moment."

As Baker flips to the page, she realizes that her hands are shaking. She's proud of herself for leading the discussion, and for telling them the story of her name. She'd always figured that people would laugh if they knew why she changed it. Rose wouldn't get it, nor would her aunts and uncles, and the cousins would be relentless with their teasing. Her classmates couldn't care less about old books, and while her teachers always praised her intelligence, it felt one-dimensional to Baker. Like it was never actually about *her,* her loves and her interests and all that made her tick deep inside. But somehow, in this small makeshift basement classroom, with these girls, she feels understood and accepted. Appreciated, even. The quiver in her hand calms, and she scans the page. There they are, Jane and Rochester, so tortured, so beguiled.

"'*Jane, do you hear that nightingale singing in the wood? Listen!*'"

Baker pauses and looks up; the girls lean in, transfixed.

"*The vehemence of emotion, stirred by grief and love within me, was claiming mastery, and struggling for full sway, and asserting a right to predominate, to overcome, to live, rise, and reign at last: yes,—and to speak.*"

Baker has the rest of this part memorized. She looks up from the book. Debra and Ida are leaning forward, their eyes open wide; Ida is twirling one of her curls around a finger. Janey sits with her eyes closed, hands gripping the seat of her chair. Without looking, Baker recites:

"*Jane, be still; don't struggle so, like a wild frantic bird that is rending its own plumage in its desperation—*"

Then a bell chimes, loud and sharp. Baker stops, her mouth still forming the next word on the page. Class is over. Mrs. Williams stands and rings the small brass bell once more. "That's our time for today!"

"But ma'am, I wasn't finished," Baker begins, and Debra and Ida chime in.

"Yeah, Mrs. Williams, it was just getting good!"

Mrs. Williams's head swivels quick, and her voice slaps like a ruler. "Do not 'yeah' me, young ladies. It is time for lunch. We'll continue next week."

The girls groan, but they all stand obediently and gather their things. No one is going to risk upsetting Mrs. Williams further or being late to lunch. Baker remains in her seat, the book in her lap, still startled by the interruption. The next sentence sits full in her mouth.

Mrs. Williams finishes erasing her chalkboard. "Thank you for your assistance, Ms. Phillips. You're a *very* smart girl." It's a compliment, but Baker sees how the woman purses her lips and shakes her head slightly after she says it. No words are needed. *What a waste,* Baker can tell Mrs. Williams is thinking, and she can't help but agree in spite of herself. Her cheeks burn, suddenly filled with a new kind of embarrassment. The familiar sheepish feeling of being publicly praised combined with the hot shame of her new situation.

"Thank you, ma'am."

"Please join us again next week. Go ahead and borrow that copy until then. It clearly gives you pleasure to reread such a classic."

She hugs the book to her chest. It feels charmed or cursed—she can't tell which. When Mrs. Williams leaves the room, she opens it back up and finds the place where she left off. That's when she sees the mark on the page. The sentence that sits full in her mouth, firmly underlined with the same blue ink. Her heart races as she finally speaks it out loud:

"I am no bird; and no net ensnares me; I am a free human being with an independent will, which I now exert to leave you."

Dear Elizabeth,

I hope this letter finds you resting and feeling well.

Your father and I are adjusting to you not being in the house. When I walk past your room I still expect to see you on your bed, reading a book or working on homework. At least once or twice a day I call your name for some reason or another—to help with the laundry, to unload the groceries. What I mean to say is that you are always on my mind. You are missed. But I know that this, like all difficult times, is temporary.

Ms. White says that it is best to give girls a few weeks to settle in before coming to visit. I will wait a bit before coming to see you.

Your father is pleased that the Giants are having such a good season. He wonders if any of the other girls enjoy watching baseball, and whether you'll be able to catch the Game of the Week on Saturday.

Regards,
Mother

Hey kid,

How's it going? You doing OK? Are your boobs big yet? I'll come visit soon, I swear. I've been real busy lately, picking up extra shifts, saving all the tips I can.

I keep trying to picture this house you're in, but every time I do I imagine that awful hospital from Cuckoo's Nest*! Isn't that terrible? I'm sure it's really nice, Rose* *would never send you somewhere like that! You're a writer—describe it to me!*

I wish you could've just come here. *I'd take great care of you! All the Saltines you can eat, kid. Although to be honest it's not feeling great around here lately. A lot of dark energy. I'm trying to just steer clear of it but it's not easy.*

Ok gotta run to work but love ya and thinking of ya!

XOXO
May

*B*aker's first group counseling session happens on a Friday after-noon, in a downstairs room next to the English classroom. The chairs are arranged in a circle. Ms. White is already sitting in the stifling room, wearing a pair of dark wool slacks. Baker is in her lightest cotton dress, the sleeveless one with the daisies, but sweat still builds on her temple, and she feels a single drop roll down her back. Ms. White looks up as each girl enters—Michelle, Janey, Marcy, Carol, Helen, Ida—and checks names off her list.

Next to Ms. White is a younger woman with a jet-black updo and enormous smile that spreads across her face like a lava flow. Black cat-eye glasses; flawless coral lipstick that perfectly matches her pumps. A tiny pearl glistens in each earlobe. On her lap is a clip-board with a pen attached, and a spiral bound notebook. On the floor next to her is one of those expanding file folders. It has a little black handle, and a bright paisley print that seems too bright and fun for the setting.

The woman smiles, and then gestures with a sweeping arm. "Please. Sit in the chair most comfortable to you."

Baker looks at the identical chairs and wonders what that could possibly mean. She chooses the one as close to the door as possible. The Bun has been quiet all day, but Baker feels it shift a little as she sits in the hard wooden chair. Michelle sits beside her, one arm casually slung across the empty chair next to her.

Ms. White checks her watch. "Let's begin then. You all know me, and let's welcome back Mary Ann, our social worker."

Her smile grows even bigger, somehow. "It is my pleasure to be here today. How is everyone feeling?"

Silence.

"Remember: I cannot counsel you if you don't participate. Once again: *How is everyone feeling?*"

"Better," offers Marcy. "Last week I was quite ill."

"Excellent. I recall that you felt ill and am so glad you've improved. Thank you for that, Marcy."

Christmas Carol looks up. "I finished the owl I've been working on."

"Wonderful. Tell us about your owl."

"It's macramé. It took a long time to get the knots and pattern just right. I'm really proud of the wings. And it has wooden beads for eyes." She pauses. "I imagine it going in the nursery, above the bassinet."

Mary Ann looks away from Carol and carries on. "Anyone else?"

"I think the baby will like to look at it," Carol adds.

"I'm sure it's a fine owl," Mary Ann purrs, as she jots something down on her clipboard. "But we've discussed this before, remember? Does your mother like owls?"

Carol stares straight ahead, a dazed look on her face.

"I'm sure your mother will love the owl. Anyone else?"

"I feel like shit," Michelle says, shrugging. Ms. White winces and begins to scold her, but Mary Ann holds up a manicured hand and smiles at Michelle. She flips to a new page on her clipboard and writes without looking down.

"Such strong language, Michelle. Tell us more about these negative feelings."

"Nothin' new. It's a million degrees out, and my feet are sandbags. I'd give anything to be outside right now. I wanna go swimming, I don't care where. A dirty old pool, a scummy pond. Even your freezing cold Pacific Ocean!" The girls murmur and smile as Michelle adds, "And my hips feel like they're gonna break apart."

"I remember that from my own pregnancies," says Mary Ann.

"It's not uncommon. But it *is* uncomfortable. What else can you tell us, Michelle?"

Michelle cracks the knuckles on her right hand. *Pop pop pop.* "I got a new roommate! And Helen made another sweater."

Helen's eyes get wide at the mention of her name. She's wearing a long-sleeved navy blue dress, and Baker can tell she's trying to sit properly, but her belly is making it difficult to keep her ankles crossed and her hands folded on her lap.

Helen's cheeks flush. Mary Ann's eyes narrow, but her smile remains. "The sweaters will keep nicely in your hope chest, Helen. You have a hope chest, yes?"

"I do," says Helen, always polite.

"And Michelle, I was asking about *you*. Perhaps you tried to redirect our attention to your new roommate and Helen in order to avoid having to be honest?"

Michelle's nostrils flare. Baker is surprised to see her so rattled, so quickly.

"Let's talk about what awaits us back home." Mary Ann pivots, leaving Michelle to seethe in her seat.

"I miss my mother," whispers Janey. "Even though I'm still mad at her. I've just never been away from home before."

"What do you miss, Janey?"

"Her Sunday roasts. Her pancakes."

"Delicious," murmurs Mary Ann. "Think: just a bit more time, and you'll be back there, enjoying that roast with your family. I can picture it clearly, Janey. Can you? There's your mother, bringing you dinner on the good china. She's wearing . . . an apron?"

Janey's eyes are closed, a small smile on her lips. "Yes, ma'am. The blue one with the red trim."

"Who else is there?"

"My father; my younger brother. My sister. Maybe my aunt and uncle, since it's a Friday. Right? Is today Friday?"

"Yes, yes it is. Just imagine that you're with them. You will be so soon. Isn't that nice?"

Janey's eyes pop open. "Yes ma'am. So nice. But I'm only six months. It feels like it'll be forever."

"But you'll be home by Thanksgiving. With so much to be thankful for."

"Right."

"Who else is longing for a home-cooked meal? Anyone?"

Baker sits as still as possible, but her eyes scan the group, trying to get a read on the faces of the others. Do they find these questions sincere and helpful—or a little bit off? Baker's gut leans toward the latter, but the girls around her are lost in the memories of their mothers' food.

"Okay. I know we have someone new here today." She reaches into her bag and pulls out a folder. She smiles as she says "Baker."

"Hello, ma'am." She sits up straight and keeps the polite smile on her face, but inside, she's glaring, suspicious.

"How are you today, Baker?"

"I'm fine, thank you." Rose's words ring in her head: *Be gracious. Be polite.* She glances at Michelle, who now scowls. "Grateful to be here."

"Tell us about yourself. What are your interests? What do you want to do with your life?"

The questions surprise her, and she worries that this is a trap. The answers fly around inside of her—*I love to write and tell stories, I've always loved poetry, and novels, and I love journalism, and I want to travel the world and meet new people, and hear their stories and just explore and see new things*—but she can't seem to arrange them into sentences. There's so much she could say. But she's not sure she trusts these other girls with her information yet. Or Mary Ann, for that matter. *Be discreet,* she recalls.

"I'm seventeen. I just graduated from high school. My best subject is English. Um, I like to swim."

"And what do you want from your future, Baker?"

"I plan to attend college. And then work with my father. We have a family business."

"What else would you like to do, Baker?"

"What else?"

Mary Ann leans in, like a friend. "Come now! An intelligent girl like you must have other big dreams, aside from working for your father."

Baker stares at Mary Ann. How can she tell? Baker has a hazy sense that she's being tricked somehow, but the feeling of being understood by this stranger overrides it. She wants to be truthful. Maybe she does want this woman—and the other girls—to know who she really is.

"You're right." Baker says cautiously, and the other girls seem impressed by Mary Ann's perceptiveness. "I've always dreamed of being a writer. That's my goal." Mary Ann's eyes light up. Baker regrets the words the moment they leave her lips.

"A writer!" Mary Ann claps her hands and looks around at all the girls, her face imploring them to be as impressed as she is. Baker ducks her head, wishing she'd just lied. "How wonderful. You have so much ahead of you."

A few of the girls exchange glances; Marcy leans over and whispers to Helen.

"Thank you."

"But you haven't quite figured it all out yet, have you?"

Baker shifts in her seat. All eyes are on her. She can't *not* answer the questions. "No," she says quietly, hoping that Mary Ann will move on if she agrees.

"That's fine. To be expected." She looks around the circle and nods at each girl, as if they're all in basic agreement about this. Then she glances into the folder she holds, examines a piece of paper. "You plan to attend college, yes? And to live in the dormitories?"

"Yes, ma'am."

"And you'll make good grades, of course."

"I plan to."

"I understand that you're interested in travel, as well."

"Yes, ma'am." The short answers have sufficed, but now Mary Ann looks at her, expectant. "I'd like to study in Paris."

"Paris!" Mary Ann lights up. "Gorgeous city. Have any of you girls been?" They all shake their heads no. "You really must go. Add that to your lists!"

As Mary Ann consults her folder again, Baker feels a chill run through her body. It's not right, this line of questioning. It doesn't feel like it's going anywhere *good*. Baker looks to the door; she could say it's a restroom emergency. But Mary Ann is quick, and Baker is hesitant.

"Now. Can you do any of that with a baby? Can you bring a baby to—where is it you plan to attend college?"

"Stanford."

Mary Ann laughs. "Can you imagine a baby in a classroom at Stanford?"

Baker looks to the girls for some kind of support, but they all look away. At the floor, at their feet, at their hands. Janey waves a home-made fan on the back of her neck. Michelle just shakes her head.

"How much money do you have right now, Baker?" Mary Ann's tone has changed. She's no longer a friend. "Can you imagine pursuing these dreams with a child? They have so many needs, you know."

Baker tries to agree in order to get her to stop. "I know that."

But the woman is in motion. It occurs to Baker: Mary Ann has done this before. "You can't take your baby all by yourself, on a plane, to a foreign country. You can't sit at your typewriter all night, working on a story. Listen!" Mary Ann flings her arms wide, looks around the room, an actor in a dramatic scene on stage. "The baby is crying! The baby is sick. The baby needs medicine! Who can give that to her?"

Baker can't help but picture the scenes that Mary Ann describes. She imagines her room back home, a baby in a bassinet on the floor near her bed. She's sitting at her desk, trying to type. She resents how right this woman is. "I don't—"

Mary Ann stands and begins to walk around the circle. She

touches each girl on the shoulder. "We know the answer. We do. We know. I know. Ms. White knows. And though you may have mixed-up feelings, even some very sad moments, you know, too." Mary Ann stops when she gets to Baker's chair. She leans in, close to her ear. She smells like fresh-cut flowers. "The baby is crying. Who can help her?"

A wild rage bubbles in Baker. Mary Ann is supposed to be on her side, but she feels like an opponent in a game Baker didn't know she was part of. She's using Baker's private fears to score public points. And it's so unfair.

"I don't understand why you're doing this, ma'am—"

"Who can help her," Mary Ann cries again, ignoring Baker as she arrives, breathless, at her conclusion. "Her family! There is a family waiting to give that to her, a fine family who is ready, prepared. *Fit.*"

Baker feels the heat and pressure in her face like a rumbling volcano. She swallows hard, tensing each muscle in her jaw, her throat, her neck to keep herself from erupting. She can't deny Mary Ann is right. Isn't she?

"A wonderful family, Baker. That's why you're here. That is how we help you. The baby gets a family. And you *both* get a future." Mary Ann looks at Ms. White, who beams with approval. "Remember, girls: you *will* move on. You *will* be great wives with beautiful families! This"—Mary Ann flicks her slender hand around the room—"will be a distant memory. A blip in your great life."

Marcy looks up and whispers. "But what if I don't want to forget? What if I can't?"

"You will. You absolutely will." Marcy looks satisfied, until Michelle stands up, her face red and furious.

"Bullshit," she yells, and runs out of the room.

Baker's breath is still ragged as she heads to art class; her face and shoulders are still taut. She takes long, deep breaths. *What happened in there? What* was *that?* She'd thought it was supposed to help them, not make them feel trapped and terrible, not send them out of the room crying. *Am I crazy?* she wonders. *Do the other girls see how cruel that was?*

Marcy's in the class already, seated and running a brush over a stiff piece of paper. Baker takes the open seat across from her. Marcy's face is also tense, her eyes also red. *She feels it, too. She must.*

The tables hold white rectangles and several tins of watercolor paint. Wooden brushes poke out of glass jars, coupled with bowls of murky water. In the front of the room, a painting rests on an easel: a barren landscape with three sloping hills in the background, a handful of scrubby trees and bushes in the foreground. A blue sky with white cloud wisps. Black Vs to indicate birds. A yellow-brown to indicate earth. The art instructor, Ms. Charlotte, is an older woman in an embroidered smock who smells like cigarettes and Jean Naté. She brings Baker a piece of paper and a jar of brushes, and watches as she picks up a brush, dips it in the bowl, and swirls it around the blue paint square in an automatic, obedient motion.

Ms. Charlotte begins her lesson. *Clouds should be gentle. Hills are not pointy. Don't try to add other animals, only the V birds for now.*

Marcy exhales, and the small watery globes of paint quiver, then scoot across the paper. She smiles, and does it again, watching the faint streaks.

"It's like tears," she says to Baker. "So many damn tears."

Baker nods in understanding.

"Days like this," Marcy whispers, looking right into Baker's eyes, "and I really wish I'd had that damn abortion."

Keep your brush light on the paper, now. No need to be forceful.

"Excuse me?"

"You heard me," Marcy says softly. "I was gonna go to Mexico. I had a ride and everything." She keeps her eyes fixed on Baker's face. "Know what I mean?"

Baker looks around the room at the other girls, dutifully moving their brushes along imagined horizons. She'll tell Marcy more, at some point, but this room feels too small. She holds the wet brush above her paper and lets it drip, drip, drip. Each dark drop splatters, creating a spreading, bruise-like stain. She does it over and over, in spite of Ms. Charlotte's scolding expression, until the whole white sheet is a big black mess.

Baker's feet feel extra heavy as she heads up the stairs to her room. Like her shoes are concrete, not canvas. Each foot drags up each stair in slow motion, one at a time, and she's self-conscious of how loudly her steps echo in the vast space. The wooden banister is smooth and cool against her sweaty palm. When she gets to the stained glass window at the top of the stairs, she pauses to catch her breath—how embarrassing to be winded from walking up one dumb flight of stairs—and as she stares at the colored pane, she's surprised by how badly she wants to break it. Her left fist clenches, her hand raises, and the wild impulse frightens her—is she really capable of that? She shoves the fist into the wide pocket of her dress and hurries down the hall.

The door to the room next to hers is open, which is odd—everyone seems to keep their doors closed. It's Debra and Helen's room, and Baker pauses. Helen sits on the edge of a small bed that looks identical to Baker's. She's looking out her window that looks like Baker's window, but the view is different—no oak tree, no broad branches. Helen's view is all sky. She turns and notices Baker standing in her doorway. She doesn't smile, but her face is kind. Her eyes are deep ponds.

"You can join me if you'd like," she whispers. "I'm cloud-watching."

Baker enters and sits next to Helen. She notices a ball of yarn, and what appears to be a single sweater sleeve on the bedside table. She follows Helen's gaze and looks out the window.

"That one looks like a dragon." Helen keeps her voice soft, as if she doesn't want to disturb the sky.

The clouds are big and dramatic, riding a strong breeze, shape-shifting and languid. Baker imagines her heavy breasts as light clouds.

"A pirate ship." Baker pictures them floating out the window and sailing away on it.

"Do you see the one that looks like a heart?"

Baker doesn't really see it, but she plays along. "That one is like a cigar."

"Look," Helen points to a fluffy formation. "It looks just like my cat. His name is Socks."

Baker's heart breaks a little at the thought of Socks the cat, curled up in Helen's home somewhere. She always wanted a little cat who would sit at the foot of her bed and purr while she read. But Gerald is allergic. And Rose doesn't care for pets. She wonders if Socks misses Helen. If he notices her absence.

In the next cloud, Baker sees a teacup, like the one she broke when Rose tried to take her to the Wendy Ward Charm School, and she clinked the delicate china too hard on the little saucer, even though the instructor said not to.

Then she sees a car, cruising the strip, teenage girls packed into the back seat.

Then it's a big white wave, tall and towering. Wiley on his surfboard, cutting across the sky. Does he think about her still? Does he lie awake at night on the beach in Mexico, looking at the stars and wondering where she is? Does he even remember her? Does he give a shit?

"Michelle will be okay," Helen says, still staring out the window. "She cries a lot, actually. Before you got here, I heard her almost every night. She acts tough, but she's just as scared as the rest of us."

Baker looks at Helen, impressed.

"I just don't want you to worry about her. I can tell you're already close."

"Thank you, Helen. That's sweet of you."

She shrugs. "People think I don't notice things because I'm so quiet. But I notice everything. I always have." Her smile is crooked, and a little sad. Then she gasps and points out the window. "Do you see that one? It's a rabbit!"

"I do! Good call." They watch as the big fluffy cloud with two long earlike wisps floats by.

"You're probably also wondering whether all the counseling sessions are like that."

Baker's heart skips, and she turns toward Helen. Maybe keeping her distance from these girls is not the best strategy. Maybe she's going to need them. "That was really messed up. Right?"

Helen smooths her long braids with both hands. She's so slight, you can hardly tell she's pregnant, but in profile, her bump is clear. She sits up straight and lowers her voice. "I agree with you. But remember: we're not here for long, Baker. Don't stir the pot, that's my advice. Well, it's my mother's advice. But it helps."

"That's definitely something my mother would say."

"They're usually right, you know." Helen folds her hands in her lap. She has excellent posture.

"What other advice do you have, Helen?"

"Have you had your meeting with Ms. White and Mary Ann? Or your appointment with Dr. Sullivan?"

Baker shakes her head.

"Those will come soon. When it comes to questions, just answer them. Don't ask them. Just play the game, Baker. It's easier that way."

"The game?"

"And don't think too much." She gestures to her yarn. "When I really get going on a sweater, I can almost forget that I'm here entirely."

"I wish I could do that. I have a very busy brain."

Helen laughs and taps her forehead. "You should see what goes on in here!"

"Seems like we have a lot in common, Helen." It feels so good to see and be seen that Baker wants to reach over and hug Helen. She settles for a genuine smile. "Except I don't know how to knit."

"It's crocheting. I'm happy to show you sometime. And don't worry, Baker. We all get through it somehow."

Michelle is quiet all evening. She barely eats dinner, then skips television time to go to bed early. When Baker comes in to put on her pajamas, Michelle is staring at a book but not, Baker notices, turning any pages. She walks softly to the washroom with her toiletries, and when she returns, Michelle has pulled the covers up over her head. Baker turns off the light. The moon is out, and the room is lit with its soft bluish glow.

"I'm not actually asleep," Michelle announces from beneath the blankets. "Just so you know."

Baker is glad to hear Michelle sounding at least a little like herself. "Feel like talking?"

"Depends."

"Do you want to talk about what happened earlier? With Mary Ann?"

"Nope."

"Okay. How about I ask you some questions?"

"What do you wanna know?"

"How about your favorite color?"

"That's easy. Blue."

"What kind of blue?"

Michelle pauses and makes a humming sound. "I don't know what the proper word for it is, but it's a specific blue you see in the ocean. In Florida. In the waves, just before they break on the shore. Kinda green but also blue, and when the sun hits it, there's a little bit of gold."

"That sounds beautiful."

"It is."

"How about your favorite holiday?"

"Halloween. Hands down. I love candy and costumes."

"Me too! And the smell of pumpkins."

"Okay, that's weird." Michelle's voice sounds lighter, and Baker feels a warm satisfaction knowing that her efforts to cheer her roommate up are working. "But I do love carving them. Next question."

"Best dessert you ever ate?"

"That's a good one. I'm gonna say my grandmother's special fudge. With walnuts. What about you?"

"I also love blue, specifically the sky above my swimming pool in the summer when there's no clouds at all. And I love angel food cake, with orange peel frosting."

"Yum." Michelle cracks her knuckles. "That wasn't so bad. Anything else?"

"I do have another question."

"Shoot."

"Do you know who used to be in this room before us?" As if on cue, Baker hears muffled sounds from the room next to theirs.

"Nope. No clue."

"And you've been alone in here since you arrived, right? You didn't have another roommate before me?"

"Again, nope." Michelle emits a dramatic sigh. "It was my own private suite until you showed up!"

"I'm so sorry that they let me in to crash your party, darling!" They laugh, and then both fall silent. The sounds from next door continue. The bedframe squeaks. Feet walk across a room. A door opens; the hinge creaks; it closes. The feet walk down the hall.

Michelle props herself up on her elbow. "Why are you asking? What is it you wanna know?"

"I'm just curious."

Michelle chuckles. "So I've noticed!"

"I'm just wondering if you've heard anyone mention a girl named Kitty?"

"Doesn't ring a bell. Is she someone you know?"

"Not exactly. Just someone who I think maybe used to . . . be here."

"I've never heard anyone talk about girls who were here before. Like once you're gone, you're gone."

"I guess it's better that way." Baker stares at the closet at the foot of the bed.

"Better than what?"

Baker rolls onto her side. She can feel her small bulge as it touches the cool sheet. The Bun pushes and shifts. Baker lowers her arms and cups her hand gently below her navel. "I don't know."

Michelle is quiet for a while more, and then she sits up suddenly, her arms crossed so tight, she's almost embracing herself.

"You don't forget, okay?"

"What?"

"I said, you don't forget. They tell you that you will, and it's a lie. No one forgets this."

Baker knows it's true. She can't imagine forgetting any of it. "I thought you didn't want to talk about what happened with Mary Ann."

"I don't, but I can't help it." The moon makes Michelle's tan skin look darker, a little luminous. "Here's the thing, Baker. It's not my first time."

"What do you mean?"

Michelle gestures to her breasts, her round middle. "*This*. Not my first time with *this*. I was in a different home, and it was back in Florida."

Baker sits up and looks at Michelle. She wants to be fully awake for this. Michelle drops her voice to a whisper and seems to spit out the words. "*I've been pregnant before.*"

Baker's response is a sharp gasp. "Oh!"

"Yeah, hard to know what to say to that, isn't it? That's why I don't make a habit of mentioning it." Michelle rubs her face, hard. "I think about him every day. And I'm gonna think about this one, too. Forever, probably."

Baker sits with this new information, trying to wrap her mind around it. Initially, the revelation is surprising: Michelle has already *had* a baby? Then it becomes a little exciting, like finding an answer key to an impossible quiz: Michelle knows what's going to happen. She might have answers to all the questions Baker has; she might be able to shine some light on all the dark hidden parts that no one wants to talk about. But then it sinks in more, and Baker feels so selfish. Michelle has had *a baby*. This isn't good news. Michelle has had a baby, and she misses him. And now it's going to happen again. This isn't confusing, and this isn't great news: this is heartbreaking.

"Oh, Michelle. I'm so sorry."

"Yeah. Me too. Six-six-sixty-six."

"What's that?"

"His birthday." Michelle pauses, then surprises Baker with a chuckle. "That *really* put my mom over the edge. The Devil at work!"

Baker laughs along with Michelle, but this is all far from funny. She purses her lips to hold back all the things she wants to ask. Finally, carefully, she whispers, "What was it like?"

"Which part?"

"The birth, I guess."

"I don't really remember the details. They knocked me out cold once I got to the hospital. Those doctors got the good drugs."

Baker feels relieved that Michelle doesn't have a horror story. But it also frightens her to imagine being unconscious during something as momentous as a baby being born. She feels an ache in her groin as she thinks this, and a tingling tightness in her chest.

"Next thing I knew, I woke up alone in a room with my tits all bound down and no clue what happened. Less than two years later, and *boom*, again, here I am."

The tingling sensation increases. Baker feels like overinflated balloons. She crosses her arms to try to ease the pressure, but it doesn't help. The tingling runs all through her chest. Her nipples feel almost electric. "Did you say your breasts were bound down?"

"I said *tits*, but that's cool." Michelle manages a snotty laugh.

"I'm not trying to freak you out. It's just something they do when you're not gonna keep it. They wrap your chest. With cloth strips, like a mummy. Keeps your milk from coming in. Since you're not gonna need it. Otherwise you'd go back home with leaking udders. That'd be a dead giveaway."

"I didn't know that."

"Why would you? No one tells us this shit." Michelle grabs the corner of her sheet and wipes her eyes. She looks over at Baker, who's curled into a ball. "Hey—you okay?"

Baker thinks of Ms. White commanding Lydia to breathe, and she releases another exhale. The throbbing lessens, becoming more of a light pulsing. The tightness eases. She slowly moves out of her curled-up position.

Michelle continues. "Anyway, I think I'd keep this one, if I could. But Barry's about to get shipped out, and I don't want to do it without him. I don't think I'd know what to do. I'm not 'fit.'"

Baker feels her heart beating slow inside her chest. The Bun tosses and turns. Her breasts relax, falling to either side of her rib cage. "They love that word, don't they?"

"What does it even mean to be 'fit' to be a parent? My folks sure as hell weren't fit."

"And look how you turned out!" A smile creeps over her face, and she can feel a giggle about to emerge. "You're perfect!"

They try to keep their laughter quiet. Baker hears the feet again in the hallway, the door opening and shutting, the feet on the floor, the bed creaking. Muffled sobs again. Baker knows they should be asleep, and she feels a little bad for laughing, but this moment feels too important.

Then she whispers to Michelle, "Can I ask another question?"

Michelle blows her nose on the bedspread. "Fine."

"Do you want a hug?"

"Yeah," Michelle says. "I think I do."

Baker moves from her bed to Michelle's. She pulls the blankets back up, then wraps her arms around her new friend, smelling her salty skin, her sweet scalp. Her soft, wild curls. Her heat. Michelle's heavy body begins to relax, collapsing quietly against hers. Their breath gets slow and steady as Baker murmurs, "It's okay, Michelle, it's okay," into the moonlit room.

Dear favorite cousin,

Thanks for writing. How do I feel? Puffy. My fingers are puffy, my calves are puffy, and my ankles are still just plain fat. *My hair is puffy too, which I guess is kind of nice. You'd like it. In short: everything about me is bigger.*

And hey, if you want to know what it looks like here, how about you come and visit! If and when you come please bring me a newspaper or two and some magazines and something delicious to eat. Tuesdays and Saturdays between 10am and noon. You can wake up that early for me, right?

I better go—I can hear Nurse Ratched coming down the hall right now!

Haha,
B

Dear Mother,

Thank you for your letter. I am feeling rested. And restless, if that makes sense. The other girls here are very nice and I do wish I could join them on their weekly walks. I miss fresh air! It gets really stuffy and hot in this

old house. I get that you don't want anyone to see me,
but who would I run into, anyway? And even if I did see
someone we know, would they even recognize me? I
don't look like myself at all.

If you don't mind making the trip over here, I would
really like to see you.

Please tell Dad that, so far, it seems I'm the lone
baseball fan here. I'd love to hear the bats cracking and
the fans cheering.

See you soon?
Baker

May,

Just in case my last postcard got lost in the mail . . . I
can have visitors on Tuesdays and Saturdays between
10am and noon.

See you soon? Please?

Hey kid,

Ok ok I get the message! I'll try to come next Saturday,
promise. Gonna ask my boss if I can switch shifts. I'll
bring you the news and some cookies, how's that sound?

Xo May

*   *   *

When the day of May's visit finally comes, Baker wakes up extra early, a kid on Christmas morning, giddy at the thought of having something to look forward to. She lies in bed, letting the early morning light stream in, imagining how May will smell, what she'll wear, what goodies she'll bring, what bits of gossip she'll share. Who's sleeping with whom? Who's sick, who's gone, who got too high and did something wild? Who's in May's bed, and who's got her heart now? What did they eat for dinner last night, who's plotting the revolution in the living room, who's hanging out on the front porch? She wants to hear it all.

She smiles to herself all through breakfast. Marcy finally points it out.

"Okay, Baker, what gives? You're like the Cheshire Cat over there."

"I'm expecting a visitor," she answers, blushing slightly. "My cousin May. She's really more like a sister. You guys will dig her."

Ida smiles wistfully. "I don't have any cousins; can you believe that?"

"That's wonderful, Baker," says Carol, beaming. "You're so lucky to have family close by."

"At least, family that you actually want to *see*." Marcy snaps. "Yes, everyone, Grandmother is coming again. With that cake you all love. And her Bible."

Carol shoots Marcy a disapproving look. "I would love to have a visit from my grandmother, Marcy. *And* her Bible."

"So who else is *not* getting awkward conversation and cookies today?" Michelle asks, clearly eager to change the subject. "As usual, please feel free to join my Lonely Hearts Club Band. New art class starts today! Who's making rugs with me?" Michelle holds up her hand, ready to high-five.

"I'll join you," says Debra. "I'd like to make a wall hanging."

"Sounds like a blast," grumbles Viv.

"My mother's cousin is driving up from somewhere kind of far away, I guess," Debra offers. "Mother says she's coming to pray for me. I guess we'll have more than one Bible."

At 9:45, Baker is in the front room, ready. She settles into her favorite chair, the one in the far corner beneath the grandfather clock. She figures May will be late, so she grabs a worn paperback from the shelves in the rec room. There's a cowboy on the cover, and a woman in distress. She leans back and tries to get comfortable.

Marcy sits with her grandmother in silence, eating slices of frosted cake; a black leather-bound Bible sits on the table between them. Soon Debra is joined by an older woman with a neat brown bob and too much lipstick. She can't stop glancing around the room, as if someone is about to sneak up on her. Then she bows her head and clasps Debra's hands in hers. Carol comes in around 10:30, a polite smile on her face and her own Bible tucked under her arm. She looks quizzically at Baker, who stares at her book and pretends she doesn't notice.

By 11:00 A.M., May still isn't there, and Baker has to pee. Bad. It feels like the Bun is sitting right on top of it, like she might lose control and soak the chair. But Baker doesn't want to get up. If she can just sit there and wait, May will show up. She feels stubborn and resentful of Marcy and Debra and their prompt, respectful visitors. She feels annoyed at herself for getting her hopes up. And she feels full of rage toward May, the person who got her into this mess in the first place. The person who invited her to that concert, who let her go off with Wiley, who could have done more to prevent this all from happening.

Baker holds out for another thirty minutes, staring angrily at the same page in her book. Then she throws it to the floor and rushes to the bathroom in as dignified a manner as she can manage, despite the thin trickle of urine that makes its way down her inner thigh. May's not coming, and it's not because Baker couldn't wait any longer. She didn't get lost; she didn't have some emergency. May isn't coming because she's May. Because she's got better things to do than visit her silly little cousin in her depressing asylum. Because she's carefree and unburdened and selfish, and she has no idea what this is actually like.

When Baker finally emerges from the bathroom, her eyes red from crying and her mouth bitter with disappointment, she finds a slice of cake on her chair. Thick layers of white frosting, coated in perfect coconut flakes. She looks around the room. Everyone is gone except Carol, who's buried in the New Testament, crumbs stuck to her full rosy cheeks.

It's two days before Baker finally hears from May, in the form of an old cardboard hatbox, chaotically wrapped with tape, postmarked Santa Cruz, California. Ms. White raises an eyebrow when she delivers it to Baker at mail time.

"Quite a package. From whom?"

"My cousin."

Ms. White leans in close and sniffs the package, then looks hard at Baker. "I smell *incense*. This cousin of yours wouldn't be sending any contraband, would she?"

"No, ma'am." She shakes the box weakly. "It's probably magazines and newspapers. She knows I'm a reader. And besides, my cousin's the type to keep the contraband for herself."

Baker takes the box to her room and tosses it on the bed, too mad to open it right away. She's been stewing in her disappointment, and she's not yet ready to let it go. She goes to help Mrs. Williams with English class again, and when she returns, it's still there waiting for her, the familiar smell of sandalwood and frangipani seeping through and perfuming the room. She tries to resist the urge to open it, but her curiosity and desire to see *anything* from the outside world is too strong.

The smell comes whooshing out, transporting Baker instantly to May's flat. To her bedroom, to her porch, to memories of Wiley and those sweet, free times. It's the smell of the incense, yes, but it's also beeswax candles and the musty scent of antique store fabrics-turned-curtains and couches found on the street. It's the smell of the Indian spices always in use in the kitchen, of cheap Chianti and bundles of dried herbs, cigarettes and pot smoke.

The contents of the package are wrapped in a hot pink silk scarf, and when Baker unties the knot, it slides back to reveal a note, which she puts aside, and then a cookie tin. Baker's heart leaps. She pries off the lid and gasps. There they are: Auntie Lee's snickerdoodles, perfectly round, stacked neatly, each one dusted with cinnamon and sugar. The best cookies on earth. She puts one in her mouth, letting it sit on her tongue for a moment before biting into it. As her teeth sink through the soft dough, she tastes the warmth of the cinnamon, the sweet of the sugar, and that perfect slight tang from the cream of tartar. She chews slowly, savoring every moment, letting the crumbs dissolve in her mouth, and then she eats another one. And another. Nothing has ever tasted this good.

After her sixth cookie, she begins to explore the rest of the box. There's a letter addressed to Baker. Baker recognizes Auntie Lee's handwriting on one, and it hurts her heart to see how carefully she wrote out the fake Parisian address that Rose must be giving out. Baker feels excited as she picks up an issue of the *San Francisco Chronicle*, but she deflates when she sees the date. It's from a month ago. Before she was even here. The tattered issues of *Life* magazine aren't even from this year. Baker pictures May rushing around her flat at the last minute, looking for any old magazine to throw in the box.

Underneath the magazines are an assortment of objects that Baker recognizes from May's room. A hunk of some kind of purple crystal; a tattered matchbook from The Golden Cask, the bar down the street that May likes to go to; two tortoiseshell hair combs; a bracelet made of antique coins from other countries; and a butterfly cast in resin, its wings an iridescent blue. There's also an assortment of the small round pin-back buttons that May always has adorning her purses and hats and sweaters: one says FREE HUEY! above a prowling black panther, and one just says LOVE in a swirly red script. Baker feels a pang of grief when she sees the blue and white SOCK IT TO 'EM BOBBY! pin. It seems like so long ago that he was gunned down in that hotel in Los Angeles. When she stood on that stage and gave that speech. How many days, weeks, months, has it been? Then she sees the one that says GOD IS A TEENYBOPPER, and she laughs. Mixed in with the buttons are a bunch of cat-eye marbles that roll around the bottom of the box, like the ones she and May played with when they were kids. She puts them in her palm and lets them clink against one another, then slips one into her skirt pocket. Then she eats another perfect cookie. Under normal circumstances, a box of May's special knickknacks would be a welcome delight. But now, each tiny treasure just reminds her that there's an entire world out there, just going on, without her.

Hey kid,

I'm really really sorry I couldn't make it, I truly am. I hate to let you down but things got kinda hectic here. Some bad stuff went down with a couple of the roommates and I had to skip town sooner than I thought. So I made the big move! I'm down at the property I told you about. It's amazing here. The trees are enormous, the land feels alive, the people are something else. I WISH you were here with me.

I put the stuff I was gonna bring you in this box, plus a few extra goodies I found in my room when I packed up. I took the magazines and the letter from my mom from my parents' house last time I was there.

Look, I know you're probably mad at me for not coming. If and when you forgive me, here's what I want

*you to know: this property's called the Grove, and it's on
Redwood Rd. There's not an exact address but they tell
me that if you get to Santa Cruz and ask around,
someone will know where it is. The invite is open. You
can come any time. I really mean that.*

XOXOXOOXO May

*p.s. I made the snickerdoodles myself, fingers crossed
that I did right by my mom's recipe! Are they any good?!*

One week later, a new girl comes to take Lydia's place. During lunch, the news of her arrival spreads, and the girls buzz with excitement over ham sandwiches and potato chips. They know her name—Lizzie—but nothing else, besides the glimpse Janey caught while Anna whisked Lizzie and her mother into Ms. White's office: ("She's pretty, and she has long hair, and I think her shoes were blue?")

When lunch is over, Baker and a few others settle on the couches in the main room, pretending to read magazines, waiting for the new arrival to emerge. Baker is struck by how eager she feels to see a new person, and it occurs to her that this might be how the girls felt when she arrived, just a few weeks ago. Or was it several months? Sometimes it feels like an entire year has gone by since she laughed with her friends in the hallways at school, a lifetime since she gave that speech at graduation. Time seems to have flattened, warped. Whatever the duration, her initial arrival feels like a million years ago, and it also feels like yesterday. She'd felt invisible then, but now she realizes that they were excited. They felt about her the way they feel about Lizzie. She wonders what they noticed, what details stood out, and what they thought they knew about her.

When Lizzie finally appears, the girls peek over the tops of their magazines and check her out. She's tall and striking, with dark wavy hair, tan skin, and eyelashes so thick they seem to weigh down her lids, giving her a look somewhere between sleepy and sultry. Her lips are curved down in a mild frown, and she holds a small vinyl suitcase with both hands. Baker can tell that beneath her unseasonable peacoat, she's far enough along that a stranger on the street might look twice, but she could still pass for normal in a billowy dress. Baker pegs her as cool and confident, the kind of girl who's admired by many and friends with few.

Marcy leans over to Baker. "I don't know about her," she whispers, her voice tinged with a bit of envy. "She looks stuck-up."

Michelle glares at Marcy. "Girl, you're just jealous of that hair. How do you think she gets it so shiny?" She winks at Baker, while Marcy wrinkles her nose.

"I bet she rinses with apple cider vinegar," Carol offers sincerely.

Baker grins and surveys the group. "What on earth did you all say about me when I walked in here?"

Marcy is about to answer when Lizzie's mother emerges from the office, sobbing audibly. The girls bury their heads back in their reading material, pretending not to watch. But there's no way to not hear the woman, overdressed in a church hat and floral dress, as she wails and moans. Ms. White is speaking quietly to Lizzie's mother, who keeps shaking her head, reaching for her daughter, crying. Ms. White puts her hand on the mother's back and guides her to the door while Lizzie watches, still clutching the suitcase, her chin lifted in what looks like slight defiance. Baker wonders how Rose reacted after she left. *Did she sob in the car as she drove over the bridge?*

Once the door is closed behind the mother, Lizzie turns around and faces her audience. She raises her hand and offers a wave, then a shrug and a crooked smile.

"My mother, everyone," she calls out dryly, like a comedian. "Thanks for watching." Then she leans down and picks up a black guitar case. The girls collectively gasp when they see it, and Baker's heart jumps a little at the sight. Anna begins to lead Lizzie up the stairs, and the guitar case bumps against each step. Halfway to the landing, Lizzie stops and looks down at the girls.

"See you in bit," Lizzie calls down. "Something about crafts? We're making rugs?"

Ms. Charlotte starts the latch-hook rug class promptly, sitting at one of the larger coffee tables in the main room and taking the day's supplies out of the large tote bags she embroidered herself. She arranges small bundles of pre-cut lengths of colorful yarn, then hands out the latch hooks, funny little tools consisting of a short metal crochet hook protruding from a rounded wooden knob. Then she pulls out the rectangular canvas mats, each with a different pattern printed over a grid of tiny holes.

The girls begin to sort through the canvases, exploring their options. There's one with two kittens sitting underneath the moon, and one with two swans in front of a rainbow. A bouquet of tulips, a smattering of daisies, and one that's just a big sunflower. Janey selects the daisies. Marcy goes for the kittens. Baker considers a beach scene, but then thinks of Wiley, and she opts instead for pine trees with a mountain background. It reminds her of camping trips. Of childhood. Of being outside, and free, and very far away. She grips the latch hook and begins to pull the yarn through the tiny holes.

Lizzie is the last to select her pattern. She frowns as she studies them carefully, appearing dissatisfied with the options. "Do you have anything more . . . contemporary?"

"Pardon?"

"Like, from *now*? A guitar? A peace sign? I'm not really into . . ." She scans the remaining designs. "Geese."

"Maybe it's a goose who plays guitar," whispers Baker. Lizzie grins, and the others giggle. Ms. Charlotte shoots them a look, and they fall silent again, back to their crafts.

Michelle mumbles under her breath, "Hang tight. Just wait five minutes."

Ms. Charlotte leans back in the high-backed green velvet chair and begins to methodically wrap the yarn around her hook, then poke it through the hole, then pull it through. Again and again. After a few minutes of this, Ms. Charlotte reaches for her purse and stands up.

"I need to step out for some air," she announces. "I'll be back in a bit."

Once she's out the front door, Marcy guffaws. "She acts like we don't know she's going to smoke!" She looks at Baker. "She does this every class. Like clockwork. Now we can dish!" Then she turns to Lizzie, looks her up and down. "Your mother seemed *very* upset. And what's with the *guitar*?"

Later that evening, Lizzie brings her guitar to the rec room and begins playing an impromptu concert, not asking if it's okay, or whether anyone minds. She just plops down on a chair, while the television drones at a low volume, and begins to strum. It turns out she can really play—and she can sing.

Her voice switches easy from sweet and light to deep and heavy, and Baker watches in awe as she sings and plays, eyes closed the whole time. Her fingers know where to go, moving along the frets; just a few simple chords, but it's all she needs. She rests the instrument on her body awkwardly—"It's really changing the way I play," she says. "It's a bummer"—and rocks back and forth.

The girls who haven't gone back to their rooms or stayed in the kitchen for cleanup and dish duty are enthralled. They gather around and listen as Lizzie sings Janis Ian; Peter, Paul and Mary; Bob Dylan. She sings Odetta, soaring protest songs that Baker knows from records played at May's place. Lizzie takes requests, even the square ones from Carol, who joins in a few times, revealing a beautiful, deep voice.

"You're so good," Baker whispers to Carol, whose face turns bright pink. "Choir," she beams, and then opens her mouth again to join Lizzie in perfect harmony.

Ms. White hovers just outside the rec room, arms folded, watching and listening. After a few songs, she seems convinced that the girls are safe, and she retreats into her office. Once she closes her door, the home feels like a different place. Baker can almost imagine that they're just a group of college friends in their dorm, pals hanging out at a coffee shop in the West Village, in Golden Gate Park, at one of May's parties. Just a group of teenage girls, singing some songs, but they all happen to be pregnant. Some of them, Baker realizes as she looks around, are crying. Carol sings along to an old folk song, one hand resting on her heart. Marcy stands, rocking her body back and forth, hands resting on her lower back, tears slipping past her jaw. Even Michelle's eyes are welled up. Baker feels it, too, how the need to release just builds and builds. And then she senses the movements within, as the Bun makes what feels like a series of distinct little pops. She hasn't felt the movements all day, and now here it goes. She nearly gasps—can it hear the music? No way. She shakes her head and comes back to the image of the small blob of dough.

Lizzie finishes the song and then begins to tap on the body of her guitar. A drumbeat, familiar. Michelle bobs her head and begins to sing along. Then Baker joins in, singing through the warm tears that she just can't hold back.

One pill makes you larger
And one pill makes you small

At the start of Ms. Charlotte's next class, she pulls new canvas patterns from her tote bag. "They're flags!" she exclaims. "Stars and stripes, just in time for the holiday."

Janey and Carol make sounds of approval. Helen smiles and rubs her middle, which is looking even bigger. Anna has joined the class today, but she sits quietly by herself, off to the side of the group. Michelle rolls her eyes, and Baker is sure she's about to make a snarky comment about patriotism, but she holds her tongue. Ms. White is planning a party for the Fourth, with actual visitors, and rumor has it that there will be tons of food—good, *homemade* food.

"Thank you, Ms. Charlotte," says Janey. "Fourth of July is my favorite."

Baker agrees. Despite her feelings about war and the turbulent times, she's always loved the day itself. The fireworks, the block parties, the sparklers. She has no interest in owning an American flag rug made of yarn, but she takes one of the special canvases anyway and gets to work. It's a good feeling being here, with these girls. The hooking and pulling is meditative and relaxing, even in this strange stuffy room on another hot summer day. Ms. Charlotte fans herself with a magazine, then stands. Baker can see beads of sweat forming on her forehead.

"I think you're all doing just fine," she says, satisfied. "I'm going to step outside for some fresh air. I'll be back in a bit. Carry on!"

Marcy was right—Ms. Charlotte's smoke breaks are a regular occurrence. Once she's shut the front door behind her, the girls giggle and exhale dramatically.

Baker can see why they love this little pocket of free time. They can sit together and talk, unmonitored, without supervision or the pressure to be "discreet." Ms. White is in her office, door closed, likely on the phone. This is how Michelle learned so much about the other girls, Baker realizes. And she wants to know them, too.

She turns to Lizzie and smiles. "I really enjoyed your singing. How'd you learn to play guitar?"

"At sleepaway camp. In the Catskills." Lizzie is still struggling with her goose rug. She's hooked half the yarn through, but it looks scraggly, and she's messed up the color pattern of its wings. She holds it up and wrinkles her nose. "Best summers of my life. When I was a counselor, we'd all sneak out after the campers were asleep and meet the boys from the other side of the lake. They'd bring guitars, and I would borrow them. I watched them play, and I figured it out. We'd sit out under the stars all night, just roasting marshmallows and singing songs."

Marcy grins. "Sounds like heaven."

"Oh, it was." Lizzie's face lights up, then she shakes her head. "Until it wasn't."

"Lemme guess," pipes up Michelle. "One of those boys landed you here. Right, counselor?"

"Good guess. It only happened a few times, but that's all it takes, apparently."

Michelle leans in, her canvas mat and latch hook set aside and forgotten for now. "And where is he now?"

"*Harvard*. Studying *literature*." She says it with a mocking accent and a wry grin. "It was just a fling, you know. Nothing real."

Baker surprises herself by speaking up. "Does he know what happened?"

Lizzie is quiet, and for the first time since her arrival, she seems just like every other girl here: confused, vulnerable, trying to hold it together but in danger of splitting open like a too-ripe plum. "No. It's better that way."

Baker feels a jolt of connection, like finding out they're on the same team. She wants to shout in agreement, but she doesn't want to spook Lizzie. Or upset the others. "Same with me. I mean, with him." It's the first time she's said that out loud, in front of the other girls. She scans the room, trying to read their reactions.

Lizzie gestures to the front of the room, where the black phone sits, a quiet reminder of the outside world. "I *could* tell him if I wanted to. I could call him right now. I could write him a postcard. But I won't."

"What's the point?" Michelle shrugs. "Would it change anything?"

Baker is relieved to hear Michelle chime in.

"Exactly! He just gets to live his life. And I get a trip to San Francisco." Lizzie looks around at the windowless room, to the stairs, to the sagging furniture and old framed paintings. "Not what I had in mind."

"I think that's just wrong," declares Janey from her spot in the corner of the couch. She's been hooking stars, but her face has turned bright red. Her thin lips are pinched so tight that little lines radiate out like cracks in concrete.

"What's wrong?"

"I think it should be against the law not to tell them."

Anna and Carol nod in quiet agreement.

"So you think I should be arrested for not chasing him down at Harvard Yard and telling him he got some camp girl knocked up?" Lizzie cocks her head and stares at Janey.

"You don't have to be rude about it. I just think it's unfair."

Carol interjects politely. "I believe a man has a right to know that he's a father."

"*Unfair.*" Marcy, who has been sitting quiet on the couch, twirling a long curl around her fingers, speaks with such force she practically spits. "I can think of all kinds of things that are *unfair*. Right here in this room." Baker takes in all these faces and bodies, newly aware of the endless stories and secrets behind them. Wiley on the beach. His stupid grin as he rides a perfect wave. She makes eye contact with Marcy. *Thank you.*

Janey stands, steadying her swollen body by placing one hand on the wall. "I know *plenty* about *unfair,* Marcy. At least you have a nice grandmother to eat your cake with. And Lizzie, you just got here. You too, Baker."

Michelle raises her hands in the air. "Ladies! Enough!" She drops her voice to a whisper and gestures to Ms. White's office door. "Do we need another sing-along? Lizzie, you know 'Kumbaya,' right?"

"It's okay," Lizzie says. "We're allowed to talk in here, right? What are they gonna do?"

"Put muzzles on us," cracks Michelle, smirking. Baker laughs, but the image freaks her out.

"I'm serious," Lizzie continues. "Are we supposed to just act like we're not all . . ." She gestures again, this time to the round breasts and bellies of this grouping of girls.

Baker holds her breath as they all look at one another. She takes a risk and cracks a joke. "That we're not all expert rug-makers?"

It works—the girls all laugh, and the tension breaks. They loop their yarn and continue chatting, until Anna raises her pointy chin from its resting place on top of her knees and speaks, barely above a whisper. "You know, some of us are grateful to be here." The room falls silent again. "Some of us have no other place to go."

$\mathcal{M}$s. White is calling the Fourth of July party an "indoor picnic," and it's co-hosted by members of one of the local women's auxiliary leagues. They arrive in the morning, all decked out in red, white, and blue dresses; patent leather heels; festive hats. They're chipper and polite, and very good at pretending like everything is normal and this isn't a house full of wayward pregnant girls. Baker can imagine Rose volunteering for something like this, leading the procession of proper ladies, gently barking instructions on where and how to set down the platters.

The house is filled with the smells of summertime. Macaroni salad, potato salad, ambrosia, pigs-in-blankets. Butter-soaked corn on the cob, baked beans, hamburger patties, steamed buns. A Texas sheet cake, strawberry shortcake with real whipped cream. Pitchers of iced tea, punch, and lemonade, everything laid out on portable tables that are dragged into the main room. Ms. White puts a Sousa record on, and the home is filled with the tinny sound of marching bands.

Once all the girls have gathered downstairs, Ms. White explains the day: eat a delightful lunch, then play some fun games. There will be dessert, and when evening comes, she will let them watch fireworks—from the roof. The girls are amazed. They'll get to be *outside*? It's a major piece of news. Baker feels a thrill—she loves fireworks—and then the sinking sensation as the joy sags, and she realizes that she's missing the annual Fourth of July block party back home. The homesickness is sharp and bright.

Rose is likely setting up now. She's done all the baking, and she's tidying. She's making iced tea. She's doing her meat rolls. She's smoking a cigarette and dancing in the kitchen. Is she missing her daughter? Is she wondering how she's doing? Is she practicing her answers to the questions they'll ask? *Baker is loving Paris! She's having the time of her life! She doesn't want to come home!* A thought strikes her, ice-cold: *Will the cousins hang out in my room without me?*

When it's finally time to eat, they pile their plates high. The potato salad isn't as good as Aunt Stella's, and the corn has gotten cold, but Baker still goes back for seconds. Marcy's fingers and cheeks are stained with barbeque sauce, and Michelle eats three pieces of pie. Debra is huge and slow and keeps saying she doesn't feel well, but Baker sees her eat several helpings of baked beans and at least two hamburger patties. When Debra notices Baker watching her, she shrugs.

"I never cared much for beans, but now I can't stop eating them. I think it's the molasses."

After lunch, there's a beanbag toss, and a silly round of pin the tail on the donkey. When a blindfolded Ida pins the tail on the donkey's big round belly, they crack up, and even the polite volunteer ladies chuckle. Michelle is in fine form, cheering everyone on and leading a few hilarious rounds of charades. It's nowhere near a normal celebration, but it's better than expected. It feels good to just be girls playing games, eating food, acting silly.

After the games, Lizzie gets her guitar out, and indulges the volunteers with "America the Beautiful," "Yankee Doodle," and "Home on the Range." Then she goes into "This Land Is Your Land." The entire room sings along, an unlikely but beautiful chorus of women's voices. Baker closes her eyes and imagines herself in that redwood forest. She pictures that golden valley, that endless skyway, the wheat fields waving, and the way the thick fog eventually lifts, even when it seems like it's permanent.

After the sing-along, the girls help clean up; then they gather in the rec room to wait until it's time to go up to the rooftop.

Michelle pipes up. "Pretty wild that a year from now, we'll all be back to normal. Watching the same sky, but from different places."

"I hope I'm on a lake," says Helen. "In my cousin's boat."

"I'll probably be working," Janey offers. "The fireworks go all night where I live, so I'll get to see some after we close."

"I'd like to be sitting on the pier at Fisherman's Wharf, eating crab and sourdough with Barry," says Michelle, with a far-off stare. "The view of the Bay is perfect from there."

"I miss our neighborhood block party," offers Baker. "But maybe I'll finally be in France. I can see the fireworks on Bastille Day."

"What's Bastille Day?"

"It's like the Fourth of July. Except French. And *better.*"

Then Ida speaks up, her soft voice a little shaky. "What do you think it will be like? You know, *after*?"

Lizzie tilts her head. "After what?"

Ida points to her midsection. She's looking huge, like she's going to tip over any moment. "This. Like when it's over."

"You'll jump right back in where you left off," declares Marcy.

"Back to normal, baby," Michelle mutters in retort.

"*Normal.*" Lizzie scoffs. "Come on, Marcy! Who wants to be *normal*?"

Ida shakes her head. "I do! But I don't think I will be. I can't imagine I'll ever be normal after this."

Then she starts her trademark sobbing, and Baker realizes that she'll miss it when Ida's gone. It's part of the soundtrack of this place: Ida's sniffling nose, the little gasps, the way she usually ends up with delicate hiccups.

"I agree," Baker offers. "I mean, I *want* to move on with my life. But I'm never going to forget being here. With all of you." She wonders if someday she'll be able to choose what she does and doesn't remember. Can she keep the faces and voices of the girls she's met, but forget the reason that they're all here?

Ida looks up, hiccupping, then embraces Baker in a damp, warm hug. She puts her lips to Baker's ear and whispers, "I won't forget you, Baker."

Lizzie concurs. "I just got here, and I already know I won't forget, either."

Michelle rubs her eyes and walks away. Helen follows, slipping her thin arm around Michelle's slumped shoulders.

Marcy stands up, hands on her round hips. "My mother says that we'll treat this time like a dream that no one knows I'm having. When it's over, I'll wake up, and *poof!*" She snaps her fingers. "Back to real life. That's my plan."

"Like Dorothy?"

"Sure. But this is definitely *not* Oz!" She laughs. "Now let's watch some fireworks!"

When Ms. White unlocks the door to the small roof deck that none of them knew existed, they cram onto it. At first, it feels amazing to be outside for the first time in a month. Baker breathes deep: the air smells of smoke and trees and heat and BBQ. The fog has rolled in, and she relishes the cool, damp air on her arms, her cheeks, the back of her neck. *Fresh* air—not stale, trapped in the same old building all day. She would gulp it like a frosty cold soda if she could. Ms. White has warned the girls to *please keep it down,* but the excitement is impossible to silence.

Fireworks explode, streaking the night with reds and greens and glittering golds. The air is pierced with flashes and bangs, the echo of explosions happening out on the Bay, as well as the street displays happening all over the city. As Baker laughs and claps along with everyone else, though, she feels a growing sense of unease, almost terror. The outside world feels so big, so loud. Another explosion, and she imagines what it sounds like for some of the boys she went to school with, so far away, hearing blasts in the jungle. Her heart races, and her body fills with a panicky feeling, like she's a vessel slowly filling with a liquid she doesn't want. Suddenly the entire day feels absurd—the games, the food, the ladies pretending that nothing is wrong, the girls goofing off and acting like they're not trapped in this strange limbo. The whole world in pain, and this house filled with it, too. *How can we be celebrating anything right now?*

She feels a pop from deep within. The Bun is like a finger flicking her from the inside, and then a whole hand, pushing. A tiny firework.

Pop. She worries she has frightened the Bun with her anxiety. *Does it know what I'm thinking?*

POP—the sky explodes, the bombs bursting in air.

Pop, the Bun echoes inside of her.

No one notices as she slides her hands beneath her blouse, as she holds herself tight, pats gently, tries to calm the Bun, keep it safe. No one notices as she backs away, finds the door, and makes her way through the now-dark house to her soft small bed. Everyone else's face stays glued to the glittering sky.

That night, while the girls toss and turn in their beds, dreaming of fireworks and apple pies, or racked by relentless heartburn, Baker wakes to loud sounds coming from the room next to hers: an urgent wailing. Desperate. It's Debra, Baker's sure of it. She lies still in her bed, wondering if she should get up and help. And if she does, what she would even do. How do you help someone who sounds like *that?* The wailing gets louder, and it sounds like she's right there, at the foot of Baker's bed. What does it look like? What does it smell like? Is there blood? Vomit?

Then Helen's voice, loud and clear, calling for Ms. White, for help. Then footsteps coming up the stairs, down the hall, back down the stairs. Running and whispering and doors opening and closing. Footsteps on the stairs again, the wailing grows faint. Outside the window, Baker sees headlights, a flash of yellow under the lone streetlight. The front door slams, muffled voices out front. A car pulls away. The night is quiet again.

Dear May,

I have no idea if this letter will reach you there, but I'm going to write it anyway. It sounds pretty far out, literally. If you do get this, I hope all is well there. I hope you're settling in and enjoying the scene.

It must be really nice to just pack up and go when things are feeling too hectic. I'm not going to lie, I'm still pretty mad that you never showed up here. The box of stuff was nice but I would've preferred your company. You want to know about my body and how it's changing? You could've come to see for yourself. I don't want to write it down. I'm too tired. And annoyed. It'll be over soon anyway, that's what they keep telling us.

I'm mad, but I still love and miss you. A lot.

—B

p.s. Yes, the snickerdoodles were delicious.

Baker's so good in the classroom that Mrs. Williams asks if she'd mind helping some of the girls after class, as well. Janey, in particular, is struggling with the essay she's supposed to write. Baker watches as Janey's small freckled forehead scrunches up in frustration as she tries to think of a thesis sentence. Her pale eyebrows knit together, and she chews her thin lips.

"I'm just not smart like you," she whispers. Her midwestern accent shows up sometimes, like when she draws out the word *smart*. "I wait tables; why do I need to be good at writing essays about old books?"

Baker smiles patiently. "You're plenty smart, Janey! I've heard you discuss the book in class. You have great ideas."

"I'm surprised by how much I like it, actually. I'm not usually much of a reader."

"Think of the essay like a class discussion. You're just going to tell Mrs. Williams which character you identify with, and why."

Janey shifts in her seat. "It's funny, when I first started reading it, I thought that I was a little like Jane. Plain and lonely, but also real romantic. But now I think I'm more like Bertha." She looks at Baker. "You know, a crazy lady trapped in a room that no one knows about. And I actually have a pretty loud laugh."

"This is all great, Janey," Baker says. "You can use this in your essay."

"To be honest, I don't blame Bertha for any of it." Janey lowers her voice, as if she might get Bertha herself in trouble. "I know she's mad, but how could she *not* be?"

"See, Janey? That's your main argument right there."

Janey is riled up. "The way they treated her! Locked up like an animal! No wonder she did what she did. She was just so heartbroken. And *ignored*. They pretended she wasn't even there! I think that's what really drove her mad." Janey ruffles her hands through her pale hair and makes a snarling sound. "Being ignored can really push a woman over the edge!"

Baker laughs and musses up her own hair. She growls back at Janey. "You can't ignore us now, can you!"

"One of these days, we just might bite!"

"Or set the whole place on fire!"

They collapse into giggles. Mrs. Williams pokes her head into the room. "Everything okay in here, girls? I didn't realize you found Brontë so humorous."

"Just fine, ma'am. Making great progress with the essay." Baker lowers her voice, tries to stifle her laughter. "Okay, Mad Woman. Let's finish this paragraph before we burn it all down."

An hour later, Janey has finished her opening paragraph and made it halfway through the rest of the essay. Janey beams at Baker, her eyes the color of what Baker imagines an Iowa sky to look like.

"Thanks for the help. I get so frustrated. My boyfriend Carl's usually the one helping me with my assignments."

"Carl," says Baker, careful. "Sounds like a nice guy."

The little blue eyes get faraway. "We've been together two years. It's real, you know."

"I believe you," says Baker, and she does.

They head upstairs together, and Janey invites Baker into her room. It looks just like the others: same narrow beds, nightstand, single window looking out on trees and the building next door. Next to Janey's bed is a framed photo of her and a boy Baker assumes is Carl. His chubby, ruddy cheeks bracket a big smile; his tan arm wraps around a happy Janey's waist.

"Can I show you something?" Janey pulls a small box from beneath the bed and lifts the lid. The necklace is dainty, the chain a bright gold.

"It's a pearl. My birthstone. He got it for me when we found out. I don't know where he got the money, but I just love it. I don't wear it, because I don't want anyone to take it away."

She puts the pearl back in the box and shoves it under the bed.

"His mother hates me." She pulls her thin shoulders back, shakes her hair. Her nostrils flare in defiance. "'No son of hers,' she said." Janey's impression of her boyfriend's mother is a pinched, nasty drawl. "She threatened my mother. Said she'd spread rumors. And then she paid us off. Made all the arrangements to send me here. We told everyone I'm helping a sick aunt in Kansas. I'm supposed to be in Wamego."

"What will happen when you go back?" Baker asks. "Will you see him?"

"He'll be gone. University of Iowa. I was supposed to go with him. The plan was to get an apartment." Janey puts her hands on her middle, rubs it gentle and soft. "I think we could've been good parents."

"I'm sorry, Janey." And she really is. Sorry for Janey, for Carl, for empty Midwest skies and apartments. For a diner in Iowa missing a hardworking waitress. For poor, ignored Bertha, and all the mad women.

That night in her room, Baker reaches under the mattress. Janey hides a necklace; she hides a journal. It's still there, waiting patiently for her to remember that she needs it. Once it's back in her hands, she leans against the wall, cross-legged on the narrow bed. She closes her eyes and, for a moment, feels that she's back in her own bedroom. Safe and protected, alone with her thoughts and dreams, recording all her potential selves on page after page. She feels her body on this bed, and it's different—this mattress is lumpier, this body is a stranger—but her mind is the same. Her self is the same. The pen has the right weight in her hand; the blank page of the journal is smooth and familiar. Her eyes open, and she remembers.

For the first time in months, she writes. She begins with Debra: how she ate all those beans, how she raised her hand so sweet in class, how the night before she went over, she'd asked them all what it would be like. *And what is it like, Debra? Can you come back and tell us?* In her journal, Baker imagines the answers. Writes down just some of the possibilities for Debra's future.

Then she writes down Janey's story. She tries to get it word for word, like she's transcribing an interview logged in her memory. *Sometimes it feels like all I got, ya know?* The story of Carl, his mother, the apartment she thought she'd live in. The fake sick aunt in Wamego. It all feels urgent, like she has to get it down before Janey is gone. Lost in the wheat and corn.

She writes and writes, her hand aching from gripping the pen so hard. When she finishes Janey's story, she keeps going, and suddenly she's scrawling sentences about herself. How heavy she feels, how tight the bras that Rose bought for her already are, how she has to pee all the time, how she's cranky and bloated, and how sometimes she feels like she's swallowed an ocean. She details her bleeding gums, her thick hair, her aching hips, the flush in her newly full cheeks. She writes about her body, but what she doesn't write about, what she *can't* write about, is the baby. The Bun. What it might look like. What it will look like. And what, if she *could* choose, she would do about it.

When she gets there, the pen stops. Her hand cramps. That's when Michelle comes into the room and sits down on the edge of her bed, bouncing slightly and snapping Baker out of her reverie.

"Hey, girl," Michelle says. "You writing poetry over there or what?"

Baker's cheeks burn, like she's been caught in a very private act. She shakes her head but doesn't look up. Her heart is pounding. She can tell that she's unlocked something powerful.

"Will you read me something when you're done? Carol picked the channel tonight, and if I have to watch another episode of *Lawrence Welk*, I'm gonna jump." Michelle lunges over to the window, and pantomimes throwing it open and diving out.

Baker closes the journal. Her entire body is buzzing, as if all those words carried tiny electrical charges.

"I'll read you a poem. But it's not by me. I don't write poetry. This is . . . nonfiction."

"Ooh, nonfiction! Baker is sooo serious!"

Baker groans. "Nice, Michelle. You sound just like my idiot cousins."

"I'm just kidding, pal. I love your big serious intellect. Now read me someone else's poems! Distract me!"

Baker picks up her copy of *The Colossus*. Her hand is still vibrating with creative energy, and she waits for Michelle to ask why on earth she's shaking. But Michelle just smiles, expectant and ready to be read to.

"How about something from this?"

"Speaking of taking one's own life . . ." Michelle lies down on her bed. "Of *course* you like Sylvia Plath!"

"Do you know the poem 'Metaphors'? I haven't read it for a while, but it's pretty apropos."

"Oooh, fancy French word. Let 'er rip, sister."

Baker clears her throat. It's a short poem, just nine lines, each one filled with images that are deceptively whimsical—but definitely about pregnancy.

"I'm a riddle in nine syllables," Baker begins. She reads on, her voice easily finding Plath's rhythm as she lists each metaphor: the red fruit, the loaf, the purse, the cow. The apples. When she gets to the last line, her voice catches in her throat. "Boarded the train there's no getting off."

"Holy shit," Michelle murmurs after a few moments of silence. "Can you read that again?"

Baker does, and when she finishes, they stay quiet, this time for longer. Footsteps echo down the hall; a toilet flushes. A siren wails somewhere outside, and a crow sits cawing on a nearby roof.

"A loaf."

"A ponderous house."

"A *cow!*"

"No getting off. Indeed."

"Indeed."

Dear Elizabeth,

I have talked with Ms. White and she thinks that next week would be a good time for me to come visit. She says you're doing well, and are a great help in the English class in particular. While this doesn't surprise me, it does ease my mind.

I will see you soon. Until then, please continue to be good, and to keep in mind the fleeting nature of this

whole ordeal. Let us get through, so that we may
move on.

With love,
Your Mother

Michelle was right on that first night when she told Baker to stay busy. It's the only way to make the long days bearable. She counts down the hours and minutes to anything that gets her out of her room and into a space with the other girls: English class, mealtimes, evening television, and most of all, the latch-hook rug class. It's there that the girls get to sit together, sharing stories while their hands stay busy, and during that precious time, Baker is able to put aside the stories that constantly swirl in her own head. How abandoned she feels by May, how guilty and shameful and stupid she feels, like she pulled a trick lever and opened a trapdoor beneath her. When she's listening to the others, she doesn't have to think about college or Paris or how 1968 was *supposed* to go.

Because what she realizes as she talks to the other girls is that she's not as isolated as she'd believed. She's not the only one to feel this, to have this happen. Other girls are angry and ashamed. Other girls are embarrassed. Other girls are full of rage. Other girls know how she feels, even if they don't talk much.

Michelle tends to hold court, almost like a hostess, and Baker watches her fondly. Anna stays quiet, but she doesn't get up and leave when they talk about the real stuff. Sometimes she puts down her rug and rereads an old Sears catalog, holding it close to her face, staring at draperies and china patterns, but Baker can tell she's listening. Lizzie will talk about anything, Helen is always good for a supportive smile, and even Viv has started to join the group, often bringing her roommate, sweet young Ida, with her. Carol is reserved, but when someone mentions that she got pregnant on her first time, Marcy offers up her own story.

"I didn't even think we'd done it right," Marcy explains in a hush. "It was dark, and it just felt like all this . . . fumbling. It only hurt a little." A small giggle escapes her mouth, and she clamps her hand right over it. "I'm sorry. I laugh when I'm nervous. Such a stupid habit."

"It's better than crying," Viv says dryly, without looking up from her craft.

"My mother figured it out; she just *knew*. I begged her not to tell my dad, but she did. It was like I became invisible to him. My parents told my high school that I have mono. I'm supposed to be 're-cuperating' with my grandparents, up the coast in Oregon. 'The cool sea air is good for tonsils,' they're telling people. I've been writing these postcards to my friends, pretending I'm in Oregon. I'm just making it all up! I haven't been there since I was six; I don't know anything about Oregon. I'm so worried because in one postcard I wrote that I saw a bear! What if I'm wrong, and my friends get suspicious? If anyone finds out, I'm completely ruined. Do you guys know if they have bears there?"

Viv laughs, and Michelle reaches over and pats Marcy's back. "There are definitely bears in Oregon, Marcy."

Then Viv speaks. "Believe it or not, it was my first time as well."

"I believe you." The words come out of Baker's mouth automatically. She sees Marcy raise her eyebrows, how Michelle and Lizzie look at each other. Even Helen looks surprised.

Viv laughs. "Sure you do."

"Why wouldn't I?" Baker isn't sure what Viv thinks of her, but it doesn't matter. She does believe her.

Viv gives Baker a watchful side-eye and pulls a compact out of her dress pocket. She reapplies her black liner, drawing the wings out even farther. Then she smirks and leans in.

"It was my teacher. *Advanced* English Lit. My favorite class. I was an outstanding student, he said. Best essays he'd ever seen."

She puts the compact away and looks right at Baker. "I could teach that class you're helping with. But they don't see me as the teaching type. I'm too *bad*."

Baker still can't tell what Viv's deal is, but she doesn't take the bait. "Maybe we can ask Mrs. Williams if you can join me sometime?"

Viv lifts her long arms above her head. She rolls her wrists and then her shoulders, taking her time before she answers. "It's okay, Baker. I'll be out of here soon enough. He promised he'd wait for me, and since I won't be a student when I get out, we can be together." She looks Baker right in the eyes and continues. "You should see the bookshelves in his apartment. Every book you could ever imagine. You'd love it."

Helen tells them she was with her boyfriend for a year, but they weren't planning on marriage. "We were just being kids, you know. Having a steady is what you do. It wasn't forever. I'd never even *thought* of forever. I wasn't even thinking of next month. Then next month came. And another month. And no sign of . . . you know." She looks around, blushing. "It didn't come. I kept checking and checking, and it didn't come."

The other girls know exactly what she means. They've all hidden themselves in bathrooms, checking their panties for signs of blood.

"When I realized what was happening, I told him, and he just . . . stopped talking to me. Radio silence. He ignored me at school; he wouldn't even look at me." She begins to cry, and Carol reaches out and takes her hand. "I must've used every safety pin in my mother's sewing basket. I let out every skirt I had, cut slits up the backs of all my blouses and wore my heaviest coat, even though it was warm out. But we can't hide it forever, can we?"

Michelle lets out a low whistle and shakes her head.

"My parents made me go see our priest. He's the one who had me sent here. He knew all about it. I don't think I was the first girl in town to come to him in trouble."

Carol makes a loud *hmph* sound when Helen mentions the priest, and the girls turn their heads to hear more. Carol's eyes get wide, as if she hadn't realized the sound was audible. She smooths the front of her plaid dress and tugs at the Peter Pan collar. "Sorry, I didn't mean to say . . . it's just that . . . we're really not supposed to be saying all this. We're supposed to be discreet." She looks at Helen. "But I'm glad your priest was able to help you. That's not always the case."

That's when Michelle turns to Ida. The group is on a roll, swapping stories, feeling open and safe. She gives Baker a confident look, like *Watch how I get everyone to talk.*

"So, Ida, what's your story? You look so young. How old *are* you?"

Viv puts her arm around Ida's shoulder, protective.

Ida looks at Viv before she speaks, as if seeking assurance. Then she answers in the quietest voice: "Fourteen."

Fourteen? Baker works to make sure her face doesn't show the shock, but it hardly matters. Everyone looks stunned. Michelle's eyes bulge, and her mouth hangs open, frozen in the shape of whatever she was planning to say next. No one asks any follow-up questions.

Viv pulls Ida close. "But she's a good girl. It wasn't her fault." Viv scans the room, making sure everyone is paying attention. "You get what I'm saying? And she's going to be just fine. Right, Ida?"

Baker can see Ida's face beginning to mottle, the water forming instantly in her eyes, a few droplets of snot leaking from her round, freckled nose.

"You'll be more than fine, Ida," Baker says with forced enthusiasm, and the others chime in.

"Better than ever," says Marcy.

"This will be over in no time," offers Helen.

Michelle heaves her body off her chair and walks over to crouch, awkwardly, in front of Ida. "You will absolutely be okay."

Ida sniffs and wipes the sleeve of her sweater across her blotchy face, now streaked with snot. "Really?"

Viv puts her hands on Ida's shoulders and kisses her gently on the forehead. "I promise, Ida."

"But how do you know?"

Viv looks at Michelle, and then at Baker, some kind of twinkle in her eye. "Because we're really smart. Like Baker."

This seems to comfort Ida, who sits up straight. She looks at Baker with pleading eyes, and Baker realizes that she's an authority figure to Ida.

"We are all certain, Ida. You're doing great."

"Now go upstairs and get some rest." Viv pats her on the back. "You can finish your rug during the next class. We'll see you at dinner." Ida heads up the stairs, and the other girls pick their rugs back up. They loop the yarns around their swollen fingers and try to remember their patterns. They switch back to small talk; try to remember how to be discreet. The word *fourteen* echoes in Baker's head.

Baker takes it all back to her room again, holding the details in her mind like precious liquid in a pitcher, and then pouring it all into the journal. Marcy pleading with her mother, how awful her father's silence must have felt. Helen and her boyfriend, the heartbreak when he ignored her. Her angry parents, an old priest in a big dark church. Viv and her teacher, his bookshelf, his praise for her essays, the idea that he's waiting for her somewhere. And the way Ida said *fourteen*. The way she cried. The way Viv protected her, and made sure they all understood. *It wasn't her fault.* The way their hearts all broke for her. *What happened, Ida?* Baker feels like a reporter covering a story that no one else cares about, like she's back in her journalism class, trying to get the school paper edited before the deadline. But this feels bigger than a 200-word blurb on the varsity basketball game or the homecoming parade. This is bigger than her unfinished editorial. With this work, Baker feels like a comrade, like a correspondent, recording dispatches from the trenches of a forgotten war that she knows will matter someday.

It's the opposite of the fake postcards that the girls are sending home, the ones Baker hardly bothers to write anymore. This writing is an act of solidarity. She takes great care to be respectful, to transcribe the conversations without judgment, without editorializing. She works to capture each girl's voice, her gestures, the way they react to one another. The shock and the defensiveness. The hurt and the care. She feels a rush when she writes, a kind of release, and also a sense of satisfaction as the words bloom and fill each page, detailing how they're suffering, how they're persevering, how they're *real*. How they got here, and where they want to go. She's memorializing them, proving their existence before they go and disappear.

When she's done writing, she bends down to hide the journal under her bed. It's not that she thinks that Michelle or another girl is going to sneak it and read her words. She just can't be sure that Ms. White doesn't check their rooms from time to time. Or Mary Ann—she can imagine that woman snooping around, trying to dig up details to use against them.

When Baker bends down, her breasts nearly spill out of her bra. Her firm belly against her thighs, the twinge in her hips as she leans down. The Bun moves around, like it's trying to get out of the way but can't. She feels even more like Plath's ponderous house as she lowers herself onto the floor, onto her knees, and then leans down until she can just see the dark zone under the bed. She reaches under and wedges the journal between the mattress and one of the metal slats. Then, curious, she pokes her head deeper into the shadowy space.

She cranes her neck and scans the darkness, ignoring the cramp in her right hip. She can make out the dirty worn baseboards, the slats and the bottom of the worn mattress. A few spots where the sagging springs poke through the faded fabric. *How many other girls have slept in this bed?*

Then she spots something else: a white envelope, also tucked up between a slat and the mattress, all the way back toward the wall.

She sticks her arm under and waves it around, trying to get it, but it's just out of reach. She curses and pants, out of breath from the exertion, but determined. She has to get that envelope. Kitty put it there—she knows it.

She sits up too fast, and the blood rushes from her head. She's dizzy and frustrated when it occurs to her that she can just pull the bed out from the wall and reach down from the other side. She laughs at herself, then grabs the corner of the bedframe, gives it a yank, and reaches under to grab the envelope.

It's addressed to a P.O. Box in Berkeley, California, each letter and number printed in a steady, familiar hand. There's no return address and no postage stamp, but the envelope is sealed. Someone clearly intended to send this letter, but then hid it away. *Why?* A chill falls across her back, and the pit in her stomach lurches upward. A gurgling heartburn feeling, right beneath her sternum. She goes to the door and opens it, peers up and down the hallway to make sure there's no one coming. Then she slides a finger under the seal and slowly pries it open, her breath held, her eyes wide. The date at the top reads *July 15, 1967.* One year ago.

Dear Mrs. Pat Maginnis,

My name is Kitty, I am 16 years old, and I'm in trouble. I'm writing you from a home in San Francisco, my parents had me sent away. I just don't know what to do. Another girl told me your name and said you're someone people write to for help. She said you work for a special Society that helps girls like me. So, at your earliest convenience, can you please help me? Can you tell me about the Society? Am I too late? I'm afraid I will try to

do it myself if I don't get help. I am desperate, Mrs.
Maginnis, I cannot go back home. Please help.

Thank you,
Kitty

She holds her breath until she gets to the last word. Then she reads it again, the thin paper quivering in her shaking hands. This letter has been here, hidden and unsent, for one year. It was supposed to leave the house, to go out in the mail, into the world. But for some reason, it didn't. It's been trapped, right there under the bed. Baker is racked with questions: *Who is Pat Maginnis? How did she "help" girls like Kitty?* She thinks of the pamphlet, the Society for Humane Abortion, that woman Jane on the other end of the phone. *Is that the same Society? Was Pat Maginnis part of that group? What was Kitty going to do to herself?*

Why didn't she ever send the letter?

And: *Was she too late?* She reads it several more times. The words feel mysterious but familiar. As if she could have written them herself.

in trouble
my parents
sent away
afraid
desperate
please
help

She has no idea who Kitty is, but she can sense her. It feels like she knows her. No, it's not that. She can't shake the feeling that she *is* her. Or rather: that she could be her. Baker closes her eyes and tries to picture Kitty, in this room, writing that letter. The vision comes quickly, and it's sharper than her usual daydreams.

She is in the room, this room, and she is watching a girl hunched over on this very bed. Her hair hangs down, blocking her face. Her posture blocks the full view of her body, but Baker can tell the girl is pregnant. The girl is writing, furiously, on a piece of paper that sits on a book on her lap. Baker can hear the pencil scratching on the paper. She can hear the girl breathing hard. It feels . . . real.

The pencil stops moving. The girl folds the letter, puts it in an envelope. She begins to get up from the bed, her hair still a curtain across her face. Then: the sound of footsteps in the hall. Someone is coming. A knock at the door. Baker's heart pounds. The girl drops to the floor, hides the letter under the bed, and then—

Baker opens her eyes. The knocking continues.

"Baker? Can I come in?"

It's Michelle at the door. Baker shoves the letter under her pillow.

"Come on in! I'm just getting in bed." She climbs under the covers and pulls the sheet over her head. She pretends to fall asleep while Michelle gets ready for bed, but her eyes are wide, and her mind is spinning. She stares at the wall until the lights go out and the dreams take over.

When she wakes in the morning, her throat feels raw, and her hands are clenched in stiff, tight fists. Michelle's sitting up in her bed, humming.

"What song is that?" Baker whispers.

"Good morning, sleepyhead! Name that tune." Michelle starts over, hums louder.

Baker recognizes it this time and joins in, singing the words quietly over Michelle's hushed hum.

Don't question why she needs to be so free
She'll tell you it's the only way to be
She just can't be chained

Michelle's humming stops. "It must be a Tuesday if this is the song that's stuck in my head. You never sleep in like this. You okay?"

"I didn't sleep well. Weird dreams. Again."

"Last week I dreamed that this baby clawed her way out of me!" Michelle shudders, remembering the gruesome dream. "It was like an episode of *The Twilight Zone*. You ready for breakfast?"

"After that visual, I'm not so sure."

Michelle laughs. "Sorry about that. You have your meeting with Ms. White today, right?"

"I do, after breakfast. She told me last night. What is it about?"

"It's mostly just paperwork, signatures, all the logistics. But it's still pretty heavy. You don't want to go in on an empty stomach."

"The logistics of what?"

"Of who gets these babies, Baker. You know, after they emerge into this wonderful world."

Baker shakes her head, as if that might clear the foggy feeling in her mind. She wonders if Kitty had the same meeting with Ms. White. If she did paperwork. What her logistics were.

trouble
afraid
desperate

"Right. Of course."

Michelle looks closely at Baker, squinting. "You're not really thinking about it, are you?" When Baker doesn't respond right away, Michelle keeps talking. Her voice softens. "That's how I was the first time around. I felt like if I pretended it wasn't happening then, I don't know, maybe . . ."

"Maybe it wouldn't happen?"

"Maybe it wouldn't be as sad."

"Yeah."

"Yeah. It's really real, ain't it?"

"I know my body is changing. I can see that. But it's hard to think about much beyond today, you know? If I think about what's actually inside me . . . and what I'll look like in a month, or two months . . ." Baker's hand moves to her chest, then she flinches and pulls away. Her breasts feel like sandbags. She wiggles her swollen toes and winces at the *crick-crack* sounds they make.

"Told you it's heavy stuff."

"Can I ask you a question?"

"Go for it."

"I know you said you don't really remember having your baby before . . ."

"Ah. *This* kind of question."

"But do you remember anything? What's it like when you actually have the baby? How do you know when it's happening?"

Michelle wraps her arms around her chest and walks to the window. She opens it as far as it will go and stares out. "I remember feeling like an animal. A caged one. Angry. How's that?"

"Okay. Is there more?"

"You'll know when it's happening. You just will. It's obvious. And all I remember is that once I was at the hospital, I really wanted to be in the bathroom. It was so nice and cool in there, but the bathroom was in the hallway, and they wanted me to be in a room, in a bed. They let me use the bathroom, and I went in and just laid down on the tile floor, but I guess I was taking too long, because they came in and pulled me out, back to the room. That's when I felt like an animal. I fought back—the poor nurses. I'm pretty sure I growled. I may have kicked one. They wanted me in that bed so bad."

The image of Michelle fighting and growling is awful, near impossible to imagine. Baker knows that childbirth isn't easy, that it isn't necessarily pretty, but she's never imagined that a woman becomes some kind of wild creature. "Why?"

A pause. "That's the way they do it, I guess."

"So what happened?"

"One of those bitches went and got the doctor, who brought a security guard, and they pulled me back to the bed and held me down, and that was it."

"That was *it*?" She was held down?

"Everything went dark. I woke up who knows how much later."

"Were you still . . . ?"

"I remember looking down, and my body was like a deflated balloon. I told you about the tits. Wrapped up like a mummy. And I hurt everywhere. Like I got hit by a fuckin' truck."

Baker shudders. She pictures herself standing on a dark highway at night, a huge truck bearing down on her. She tries to stop the unwanted thought before the moment of impact, but she can't. *Bam.* She explodes into a million aching pieces.

"And the baby?"

"What about him?"

"Do they let you hold it?"

"I never saw him. They took him away before I woke up."

Baker gasps. "Michelle. That's terrible. Right? Is it worse to not see him?"

Michelle chews on her fingernails. "It's just how they do it. I didn't even know it was a boy. I found out a few months later, when I snooped through some paperwork my mother got in the mail." Michelle smiles, but it's a sad one. "I do wonder what he looks like. I always picture a generic baby face, like the Gerber Baby, you know? Happy and healthy, fat and round. He's almost two now, so I guess he walks and talks and all that stuff. But when I think of him, he's tiny, wrapped in a blanket, being rocked to sleep. I'll probably imagine him like that forever, you know?"

"Maybe it is a good thing you never saw him." Baker mulls it all over, tries to weigh the pros and cons of an impending yet abstract situation. If a tree falls in a forest, does it make a sound? If you give birth but never see the baby, did it really happen? "Maybe that is the best way."

"Who knows. They say it's for the best. But I would've liked to say hello. I know I act all tough, Baker, but the truth is, I'm sad. And scared."

"I know, Michelle."

"You do? How?"

Baker smiles. "Because you care too much to not be scared. Or sad. You've got a big heart, Michelle."

Michelle's face softens, and she looks relieved. She lays a hand across her chest, over her big heart. "Pretty wild to think that there's gonna be another one. Just out there in the world somewhere."

"Whoa. What if they—"

"Look exactly alike? Run into each other someday? Now *that* feels like a *Twilight Zone* episode."

The door to Ms. White's office is closed, and Baker stands outside for a full minute before she knocks. She breathes deep, in slow and out slow, remembering the time May tried to teach her about meditation. But her stomach is roiling: she tastes the fat of the bacon, the bitter edge of the coffee, the thick milky cream. The scrambled eggs were too watery. The banana was mushy. It feels like it's all rising up. She puts her hand against the door to steady herself.

"Yes, Baker," Ms. White calls through the door. "You may come in."

You will not throw up, Baker tells herself. *You. Will. Not.*

She hasn't been inside the office since the day she arrived with Rose. The windows still seem like they've never been opened; the filing cabinets are still there; the wide wood desk still holds stacks of paperwork, folders, and pamphlets. Ms. White sits behind her desk, and next to her sits Mary Ann, her hair pulled up tight, just like it was during the miserable counseling session. She wears the same glasses, the same bright lipstick. Same clipboard. A thin strand of pearls sits just above her collarbone. Baker brings as much air as possible in through her nostrils and then lowers herself into the empty chair.

"Good morning, Baker. You remember Mary Ann, our social worker. How did you find the session with her?"

"I learned so much," Baker says, and it's not a lie. The two women raise their eyebrows.

"Wonderful to hear. Mary Ann actually works for the county. Our facility no longer handles the placement process for the babies, so Mary Ann is here to assist with paperwork, legal matters, any questions that you might have."

"Hello again, Baker," purrs Mary Ann. "I look forward to working with you."

Baker exhales slowly.

"Are you winded from the stairs? Your lung capacity *is* diminished by this point." Ms. White looks down at her desk as she says this and begins to shuffle through the stacks of papers.

"No, ma'am," Baker scrambles to cover up her anxiety. "I've just been . . . meditating."

"I've heard good things about meditation," chirps Mary Ann.

Ms. White pulls a folder from the pile, and Baker can see her name written in black ink. Ms. White flips through it, running her index finger down the pages, as if reminding herself of Baker's existence. Mary Ann does the same. As they review the pages, Baker's eyes survey the desk. She spots the top half of a piece of paper and can clearly see the name *MICHELLE*. She squints and tries to read the typed words beneath it, but it's too small for her to see. She looks back at the pile in front of Ms. White and sees the corner of another envelope that juts out. The first few letters of a word, stamped in red capital letters: C O N F I—*Confidential,* she thinks. Above the stamp is a name, written in small black script.

Without looking away from Baker's paperwork, Ms. White tucks the envelope back into the stack, but not before Baker's quick eyes can scan it. *Kitty.* She's certain that it says Kitty. Ms. White keeps her hand firmly on top of the pile of papers and sits up straight.

"How are you finding your time here so far, Elizabeth?"

She hears Rose's voice, reminding her to mind her manners. "It's fine, thank you."

"You're enjoying the activities?"

"I am."

"Mrs. Williams says you're wonderful in the English classroom. That seems a good fit for you."

"I really like helping the other girls. And I do love talking about books."

"Excellent. This home is intended to be a place of compassion and support. We hope you feel both. Do you have any questions?"

Of course she does, but she hears Helen's voice. *Answer the questions. Don't ask them.* "Not at the moment."

"Good. Now, there's something we want to discuss with you. Mary Ann tells me you had some challenges during the counseling session."

"I did?"

"You seemed a bit defiant during our session, Baker," says Mary Ann. "It's so important for you to have a positive attitude. It's critical for the placement process. But it's also important for the *baby.*"

Baby. Ba-by. Bay. *Bee.* Sometimes the word just hurts, a sharp punch to a bruise. It's why she prefers Bun. Harmless, inanimate. Baker pinches her lips together and looks up. An abandoned cobweb floats from a corner.

"We just need to finalize a few more details to make this official. On paper, you're great. Just what we like to see."

Baker jolts at the phrase. What does that even mean?

"Of course, we don't *like* to see young women like yourself in this situation, but when it happens . . ." Mary Ann trails off, then clears her throat. "You have married parents, correct?"

"Yes."

"No major illnesses or diseases running in the family?"

"I don't think so. One of my grandmothers died before I was born."

"Maternal or paternal grandmother?"

"My mother's mother. Ma'am."

"And your mother, she's well?"

"I suppose. She gets headaches sometimes."

"Don't we all. And your father?"

Baker pictures Gerald in the backyard. He's smoking a cigarette, cleaning the pool. He's waving and laughing as she does another silly dive off the concrete edge. *Splash.* "He's fine."

"And it looks like you've been a very healthy young woman so far. Aside from this, of course."

Another strange phrase that makes her cringe. Her reply is sharper than she intends. "I'm not *sick*."

"Of course not. But just to be safe, we've scheduled an exam with Dr. Sullivan, to do one more check on the baby's health before we move forward with the placement. It's part of our process here. All the girls see him. You'll do that in just a few days."

Ms. White clears her throat. "Any more questions, Baker?"

She understands why Rose wants her to be polite. And why Helen told her to play the game. But she loves questions. "Yes."

"Go ahead."

"How does this all work?"

Mary Ann blinks. "Pardon?"

"What's actually going to happen to me? And *when*? How will I know when it's time?"

Ms. White glances down at the papers in front of her, runs her fingers down one of the pages. "October is likely your time."

"With all due respect, Ms. White, I don't see any calendars around here. I barely know what today's date is."

"July twenty-fourth. Wednesday," Mary Ann answers automatically.

"Thank you. But most of the girls in here, we don't *know* that. And I'm just trying to understand."

"Her mother did describe her as curious." Ms. White speaks as if Baker has already left the room.

Baker persists. "Will it hurt?"

"Have you experienced menstrual cramping before?"

"Yes."

"When it is time, you'll likely experience what feel like menstrual cramps. You will feel a tightening within. Possibly a rush of fluid. When this happens, it is time to go to the hospital."

She pauses, as if the story is done.

"Which hospital?"

Ms. White sighs, clearly irritated.

"Will anyone be with me? Will someone call my mother? I've heard some of the other girls when their time has come and it sounds—"

Mary Ann stands up. "Your mother will be notified. Some do choose to accompany their daughters. Others do not. At the hospital, you'll be attended to by a doctor. You'll be given medicine to help you relax. You'll likely go to sleep. Before you know it, it will be done. The baby will be safe in the nursery, and you'll rest. I'll visit the following day, with the final paperwork. Then the baby can be released to the family, and you can return to yours. Any further questions?"

Baker's mind whirls with images: hospital corridors, doctors in masks, Rose running from room to room, an eager new family with arms outstretched. A baby crying somewhere in the distance . . .

"The family?"

Mary Ann's smile spreads wide across her face. "We have wonderful news. We've found a match. A good family who can offer proper care. This doesn't always happen, you know, a match like this. Many babies go to foster care before we can place them. But your baby will go *straight* into a perfect home."

Your baby. She feels the Bun begin to stir. *Not right now.* As if Ms. White and Mary Ann can see it. As if she needs to keep it hidden.

Ms. White opens a new folder. "Now we just need your signature for the adoption paperwork."

"A formality, really," adds Mary Ann. "It's mostly settled by now."

Baker looks at the books on Ms. White's shelves, the tall metal file cabinets filled with papers and folders and faded shaky signatures by girls still studying penmanship. What is in there? Who else was here? She wants to throw open those long-closed windows, push the cabinets out, watch them smash on the ground below. Stacks and stacks of secrets and mistakes, alphabetized and orderly, locked up and sealed, all these names and lives released, flying through the air, whipping on winds like scattering seeds.

She looks back at Ms. White and Mary Ann, and a thought begins to knock at the door to her brain. *What if you don't do what you're supposed to do? What will happen? Aren't you curious?*

Her life has been a series of tasks and responsibilities, coupled with potential for consequence, success or failure. Do it right or get it wrong. But what if there's no right answer? What if everything feels like failure? What if anything can be a success?

"Ms. White, I've been thinking—"

"You're six months along, Elizabeth. At this point, it's best not to."

"With all due respect, ma'am, I'm not exactly capable of not-thinking. I have an active brain. I believe that to be a *good* quality. And yes, Mary Ann is correct: I am having challenges. I'm not sure what I want to do. I'm not sure about anything, really."

Ms. White folds her hands tight. Small brown spots spread over her swollen knuckles. "Well, we are sure. And so are your parents. It's not actually up to you."

"Then why did you even call me in here? Why do you need my signature?" It's too much, and she knows it. Rose would be appalled. Baker thinks about her roommate. *Michelle would cheer me on.*

"Your mother described you as a courteous young woman, Ms. Phillips."

Baker looks right at Ms. White, blinking back tears. Did Kitty cry when she had her meeting?

"Elizabeth," Ms. White intones. "There is a family waiting to relieve you. He's a *doctor*, Ivy League–educated. The wife is lovely, and they have a beautiful home. This baby won't want for a thing. All will be provided."

Mary Ann is enthusiastic. "Ms. White is so right, Baker. Our studies all clearly show babies thrive when they have a mother and a father who are *ready*."

"Married," chirps Ms. White. "Employed. Upstanding."

Mary Ann continues. "Baker." Her voice is careful, like a mother trying to prevent a toddler's tantrum. "I know how you're feeling. Trust me, I see it all the time. This can end well, but you must understand that we know best."

Baker crosses her arms. *But what if they don't?*

Ms. White leans back in. "We can tell you're confused. But let me remind you: you got yourself into this situation. We are helping you out of it. Do you realize how lucky you are to be here?"

Baker considers this. Is she lucky? She thinks of Marcy, who's grateful to have a safe place to hide out. Anna, who has nowhere else to go. And Carol and Helen—they don't seem to resent being here. What other options do they all have? Now Baker begins to worry: *What's wrong with me? Am I being ungrateful?*

"Maybe she doesn't realize it," adds Mary Ann. "Baker, you know we have a waiting list. You got a very coveted spot. This city is teeming with young women in your situation. It's a regular epidemic."

"All this 'free love' has consequences," Ms. White says sharply. "You've got a lot going for you, Baker. You're smart. Your parents still speak to you. You're going places. Some of the other girls in here? They don't have that."

"So let's not waste time, okay?" Mary Ann's voice rises up on the *kay*, a helium balloon released, rushing up into a gray sky. She pushes the paper across the desk again; extends a pen. As it slides, it uncovers the now-hidden envelope, and once again Baker sees those letters: *C O N F I D E N—*

"Baker? Take the pen, please. It's just one signature, right there."

The phrase forms clearly in her mind. She knows she's going to say it. She doesn't bite her tongue. She doesn't stop herself. "I don't want to." Once the words are out, a smile threatens to slide across her face. She straightens her mouth and sits up. Serious.

"Excuse me?"

"Not right now."

Ms. White closes her eyes and bows her head slightly, like she's done for the day. When she opens them, she smiles, then takes the paper from Mary Ann and puts it back in the file.

"We'll revisit this soon, Elizabeth. You can go now."

Baker leaves the office and beelines for the downstairs bathroom. The Bun kicks, and she vomits it all up: the bacon, the banana, the awful shame of it all.

That afternoon, the girls gather for another latch-hook rug session, but Ms. Charlotte is nowhere to be found. After a few minutes, Ms. White appears, well-dressed in one of her nicer tweed suits.

"I'm sorry to tell you that Ms. Charlotte is ill today. I need to leave for some important business, so you'll be on your own here. Ms. Charlotte says you're all quite skilled and that you'll know how to proceed with your . . ." She glances at the half-finished yarn projects in front of each girl, but her eyes skip right over Baker. It's such an uncomfortable feeling, knowing she's defied an adult. Especially *this* adult. Baker keeps her eyes fixed on the yarn tangle on her lap.

"Lovely creations. I will see you all for dinner."

The girls pick up their mats, quietly looping yarn until Ms. White is gone. They wait about twenty more seconds, then burst into giggles.

"Woohoo," cries Marcy. "Party time!"

"I'm going to get my guitar." Lizzie heads up to her room.

"Oh, good, another sing-along." Viv rolls her eyes. "Let's dish before she gets back. I have a question."

This delights the girls, who let out a collective *Ooooooo!* Janey claps her hands. "For who?"

Viv holds a ball of orange yarn. "For the Smart One." She looks at Baker and tosses the yarn her way. "It's your turn, Baker."

They all turn to look at her. She holds the yarn ball and feels her cheeks get hot.

"What's *your* story?"

Everyone is eager to hear the answer.

Baker smiles. "That's an excellent question."

"Yeah," crows Janey. "You're always asking about us, but we hardly know anything about you."

"Was it your first time?"

"Who's the daddy-o?"

"And what did your cousin put in that package? Anything good from the outside?" Viv winks at Baker and mimes smoking a joint. Michelle, who relaxes against the wall in an attempt to keep her sciatica at bay, watches with delight, her eyes twinkling as she waits to see how her roommate handles the interrogation. Baker is blushing, but she opens her mouth to answer.

Marcy interrupts her. "Wait, wait. We already have you all figured out."

"I can't wait to hear this," Michelle cackles.

"Straight-A student," Marcy continues.

"Val-e-dic-tor-ian!" Janey enunciates each syllable carefully. Anna, who sits quiet in her preferred chair by herself, her canvas mat a mess of knotted tangled yarns, agrees.

So far, Baker doesn't mind the attention. "Excellent guesses."

Helen joins the challenge, sweetly asking, "Girl Scout?"

Baker raises her right hand and extends her index, middle, and ring fingers. "On my honor, I will try . . ."

Helen grins and finishes the sentence. "To serve God, and my country."

Carol, Marcy, and Janey all raise their right hands, too, and the five of them recite the rest of the pledge. "To help people at all times, and to live by the"—they all shout the last three words—"*Girl Scout Law!*" Then they dissolve into giggles.

Once they've recovered and quieted down, Viv continues. "We know you're a bookworm. Who wants to be a *wriiiiiiter.*" She delivers this line with drama, rolling her eyes and assuming the imagined voice of a haughty literary type.

"Only child," calls out Lizzie as she descends the stairs with the guitar case in hand. "Am I right?"

Baker is impressed. "How can you tell?"

Lizzie grins. "We recognize our own."

"We're on a roll," Marcy exclaims. "Next I'm gonna go with . . . knocked up by your sweetheart! A star quarterback who's already in college?"

"No way!" It's a game now, and even Carol joins in. "He's a hood!" The girls yelp with delight that square Carol would suggest such a thing.

Viv bites her lower lip and leans in. "Or maybe he's a radical, you know, an underground Leftist type . . ."

"It's Abbie Hoffman!" Lizzie cracks herself up, and then laughs even harder when Helen asks who Abbie Hoffman is.

"I think you're in love," offers Janey, always the romantic. "You seem like the type who has a steady. A brainy college guy."

That first night with Wiley unspools in her mind. The music, the smoke, the cool midnight air. How free she felt, how unleashed and unmoored and dizzy and *real*. The next day in Golden Gate Park, walking and talking for hours, the encounters that followed. It seems like forever ago, a strange blur from an ancient era. They weren't in love; that's not what it was. She'd felt something, that was for sure, but not *that*. It was something bigger than love, she thinks. It was freedom. He'd offered an escape, a glimpse into a different way of being. Like a portal into a wild world, a magic potion that makes you grow and shrink and fall and fall. Everything with Wiley was fun, but nothing was real. With one very incontrovertible exception.

"Okay, okay! Pipe down, everyone!" Baker surveys the girls like a schoolteacher waiting for her kindergartners to settle down. "He wasn't my sweetheart, and he wasn't a hood. He's definitely not Abbie Hoffman. His name was—is—Wiley. He's a . . . hippie, I guess that's the box you'd put him in. Though he'd definitely get mad and tell you he can't be contained." A few of them snicker, familiar with the type. "We were just having fun, you know. It wasn't super serious, but it was a big deal. At least for me. I'd never done anything like that before. Being with him was like . . . like the record got flipped, and I was living the B-side of my life. Does that make sense?"

Lizzie strums a chord dramatically and turns Baker's words into a little song. *"The record got flipped / And there I was / Livin' the B-side of my liiiiiife!"* Helen applauds.

"Sounds like a hit, Lizzie. And you guys are pretty much right, I'm a 'good girl,' like Michelle says. I always told my parents the truth, I always followed the rules. And then . . ."

"And then you didn't."

"And then I didn't."

"And here you are," states Carol. "Here we *all* are."

Baker continues. "Let's see, what else? He likes bad poetry, he smells like mint and cigarettes, and he wears cowboy boots. He has really nice white teeth."

"So what happened?"

"Is he waiting for you back home?"

"Does he know you're here?"

She thinks of that day at May's when he came to find her. Hearing him say her name to those guys on the front stoop. The image of him walking away, up the street, his boots on the sidewalk, no consequences. Probably right back into Fur Hat's arms, until she gets in trouble, too.

The thought startles Baker. What would Fur Hat do if she got pregnant? Would a girl like her end up in a place like this? No, she thinks. Fur Hat would call that number. Fur Hat would go to the appointment. Fur Hat wouldn't think twice. Would she? "Turns out I wasn't the only girl he was having fun with."

"Ouch," says Lizzie.

"And no, he doesn't know I'm here. And I think that's just fine. Last I heard, he was in Mexico."

They hear footsteps coming down the stairs, and they freeze. It's just Ida, coming down to find them. She waves to the tight-knit group. "I heard your voices from my room. Can I join you?"

"Sure," calls Michelle. "We're just grilling Baker. Now where were we?"

"Mexico," says Helen. "He went to Mexico."

The girls look at one another, exchanging whispers.

Marcy looks directly at Baker. "I have a question. Do you wish you'd gone to Mexico, too?"

Baker's heart pounds. The other girls don't seem to catch on, but Baker knows what Marcy's after. She wants to know she's not the only one.

"Yes, Marcy."

"You know what I mean, right?"

"I do. I had an appointment and everything."

The other girls look confused, but Michelle's eyes get wide. Baker knows her roommate understands exactly what she's saying.

"Not in Mexico; it was up here, actually. But when I got there, I just . . . I panicked. I was all alone, and I panicked, and I left." It's terrifying to say it out loud, but she is comforted by the understanding in Marcy's expression. "I was too scared."

Marcy grabs Baker's hand. "That's what happened to me, too. I mean, probably not in the same office. But I got scared, too."

The other girls stare, some of them catching on. Michelle leans over and hugs Baker, and then Marcy. Viv bites her lip and shifts in her seat. Lizzie watches closely, and Ida's eyes dart from face to face, trying to get a read on the reactions.

Janey is lost. "Wait, *what* are we talking about?"

"Shhhhh!" hisses Anna. "Don't say it!"

Lizzie doesn't listen, or she doesn't care. "*Abortion*, Janey!"

They all go silent again. A toilet flushes upstairs, and they hear the sound of someone's feet going back to their room.

Janey's puzzled expression turns to horror. "No! You can't say that word, Lizzie."

"Says who?"

Ida looks confused. "Why not? What does it mean?"

"It's just not right." She looks to Baker and Marcy. "Y'all know it's wrong, don't you? It's not a Christian thing to do."

"I'm not a Christian," Baker says. It's just a statement of fact, but Janey looks like she's been slapped. She narrows her eyes. "It's also *against the law.*"

Carol and Helen cross their arms. Anna gets up and moves to another chair.

"For now," says Lizzie.

"What are you talking about?"

Lizzie crosses her arms, assuming an air of superior knowledge. She drops her voice low. "It's going to be legal. Soon."

"That's not true. It's *a crime.*"

"Not for long. My aunt told me so. She lives in Boston; she's a women's libber *and* a lawyer."

"A libber lawyer," laughs Viv.

Lizzie glares, then continues. "My aunt is friends with a lot of *very* smart people. Including doctors. She says it's a matter of time before it becomes legal. The world is changing, gals. Get with it."

The information ripples through the group, hitting everyone differently. Baker feels breathless with this knowledge, like a whole new world is cracking open. She also feels resentful. Why couldn't this liberated future have come sooner? Like, a few months ago?

Janey remains steadfast, indignant, her fists in tight balls. "The laws can change, but that doesn't make it right."

Baker is irritated by Janey, but she also feels protective over her. "You can believe that, Janey. But that's why we have separation of church and—"

"This isn't Mrs. Williams's class, Baker. I don't need a lecture."

Carol looks concerned. "I don't even know how it works, but I know it's very dangerous. You can *die.*"

Ida's small voice pipes up again. "I still don't know what you all are talking about."

"My aunt also says it doesn't *have* to be dangerous. And you can think it's wrong, but women have been doing it for centuries, all over the world."

"She's right," says Viv. "Women have been figuring this shit out since we've been women. My grandma told me about it once. She's no libber lawyer, but she still knows a lot."

"Did your *grandma* have an abo—"

"Don't *say* that word, Marcy!"

"I don't know. I just remember one time when I was twelve, my grandma and me helped care for her sick neighbor, this woman named Mrs. Wallace. She had a fever and couldn't get out of bed, so I watched her kids while grandma took care of her. She had so many kids, seven or eight of them, including two sets of twins! And she was married to a monster—he was awful. Grandma just told me she'd had 'a procedure.' She said, 'People might talk, but don't you listen, cuz that woman did what she had to do.' Mrs. Wallace wasn't a criminal. She was just . . . doing her best."

"What else did your grandma tell you?" Baker is fascinated by these revelations, these aunts and grandmas and the secrets they've shared. She tries to imagine Gerald's mother, sweet proper Nana Anne, saying anything like this. She tries to imagine Rose talking about this, but it seems near impossible.

"She told me if I ever got into trouble, I could come to her."

Michelle doesn't miss a beat. "So why didn't you?"

"Because she's dead now. And my mother is nothing like her. Her house, her rules. And here I am."

Lizzie smiles at Viv. "My aunt was gonna help me, too. She'd already gotten me the pill, but my mother found out and freaked. She threw them away. Wrong move, ma. Look at me now." She looks down at her body. Her voice grows angry. "I told my aunt when I realized what was going on. She was going to take me to a real doctor, to one of her friends."

"What happened?"

"My father overheard us talking on the phone. He felt so betrayed that they haven't spoken since. She was just trying to help me. I know she'd come visit me here if she could. But they won't tell her where I am."

"I wish your aunt could come visit us all. I bet we'd have such great conversations."

Baker's heart hurts for Lizzie. It hurts for Janey, and for Michelle, and for Viv. And for herself. Her belly tightens, her heart pounds, and the anger and sadness and shame swirl inside her like a twister. It gets in her throat, it gets in her fingers, it gets trapped in her rib cage by the too-tight elastic band of her bra. Her fingers start to itch for her pen and her journal, for a moment alone to write all these new stories down. The Bun jumps and tumbles, as if reminding her why she's there. She wonders if the Bun can hear. If it heard them talk about abortion. It makes her feel guilty. *It's complicated,* she wants to tell the Bun. *Someday maybe you'll understand.*

Lizzie lets herself be messy, hiccupping as she talks. "You'd love her, Baker. She reminds me of you, actually."

Janey's face is drawn and sad. Her body seems to droop. "I just don't understand. I thought you were good people."

"We *are* good people," Baker says. Her words come out hot, with force. "This is all very complex."

"And unfair," mutters Marcy.

"And scary," adds Viv.

"And confusing," says Ida, with a shrug.

"And *hard,*" offers Lizzie.

Michelle yawns. "My feet hurt."

Baker reaches out and begins to rub Michelle's swollen arches. She looks at the group of girls and feels flooded with admiration and care. Each one so different, so full of flaws and fears and love, each one holding her frightened, pounding heart in her hands, presenting it to the others, because why not? What have any of them got to lose now?

As she takes Michelle's rough heel in her palm, she muses. "Can you imagine if we all just got to decide?"

Michelle scoffs. "Decide what?"

"What to do! How to live! What's best for ourselves. Instead of letting all these people make decisions for us."

"Sounds like a dream," agrees Lizzie.

"Sounds scary, if you ask me," interjects Ida.

"And what if we don't know what we want?"

"We help each other," Baker says with confidence. Then she winks. "Maybe we should all just move to a commune in the woods and live together."

"Don't threaten me with a good time," cracks Lizzie.

Janey puts her hands together in front of her face and bows her head. "I'm still going to pray for each of you. And your babies."

After dinner, Lizzie plays another concert in the rec room. The girls gather around her, humming and swaying and stealing small glances at one another. No one mentions the conversation that afternoon, but Baker can tell they're all thinking about it. Marcy leans back on the couch, her feet propped up and her arm slung, surprisingly, around Viv, who seems relaxed and content. Janey keeps to the edges, but she hums along. And Carol seems to know the words to every song. She sings, letting her voice be a little bit louder this time. There's new energy among them, a new level of connection. Baker can sense it.

On top of that, it seems like each song Lizzie plays has a new kind of poignancy. All the lyrics land different, and so does Lizzie's voice. Once you've heard a girl cry like that, you can hear it in her voice forever. She does "If I Had a Hammer," and they all chime in, their voices rising in unison on "a hammer of justice!" "Puff, the Magic Dragon" makes them wistful, and "Scarborough Fair" is extra haunting and sad. Carol's voice breaks the last time they sing "She once was a true love of mine." Lizzie doesn't start another song right away. She sits quietly, like the rest of them, absorbing the moment.

"Any requests?"

Baker grins. "Know anything off *Blonde on Blonde*?"

Lizzie grins back, sensing Baker's request for a change of pace. "If only I had a harmonica!" Then she moves her hands to the body of her guitar and pats out the opening beat of "Rainy Day Women #12 and 35." Michelle hoots with approving delight, and she and Baker begin to slap their thighs and tap their feet, keeping the bouncing beat while Michelle strums, hard and rollicking. They sing the first verse together, while the other girls look on with amusement.

> *Well they'll stone you when you're trying to be so good*
> *They'll stone you just like they said they would*

They don't get all the way through, because no one can remember how the last verse goes, so they repeat the first verse several times. Marcy is standing and doing a pantomime of a marching drum majorette. Viv is dancing from her comfy seat on the couch, and Janey and Carol are clapping along, clueless about anything Bob Dylan–related but delighted by the shenanigans. By the time Ms. White comes into the room to tell them that's enough, time to head upstairs, they can barely hear her over all their laughter.

*B*ack in their room, once they've washed their faces and dressed for bed, Baker and Michelle whisper in the dark. They're not quite ready for the day to be done.

"I have another question for you, Michelle."

"Hit me."

"How did you end up here? It seems like most of the girls got sent here by their parents. But you'd already left home . . ."

"This inmate checked herself in to the asylum."

"You did?"

Michelle throws her hands up in the air and shrugs. Her hair is wild in the moonlight. "What else was I gonna do? I got sent to one of these homes the first time, so I knew if I came here, I'd at least have this cozy bed and three meals a day and, you know, a television. And of course, I'm passionate about latch-hook rugs, so that was a big draw."

"But how'd you get the spot? Ms. White makes it seem like it's near-impossible to get one of these coveted beds."

"Let's just say I have my ways. And I'm very good at impersonating my mother's voice. And forging her signature." She shakes her head. "I'm so messed up."

"You're not messed up, Michelle."

"Then what am I?"

Baker pauses. She can make out Michelle's body in the darkness: her knees, her arms, her hips, her hands. She looks down at her own body, so different yet so similar. "A woman?"

"Same difference. Now I have a question for you: what you said tonight, to Marcy . . . was that for real?"

"I wouldn't have said it if it wasn't for real."

"I was just surprised, that's all."

"Because I'm a 'good girl'?"

Michelle pauses. "Pretty much."

Baker feels satisfied, a little proud that she's not such an easy read after all. "I guess you can't guess everything about me."

"Touché."

"And good girls do all kinds of things. Including chickening out of abortions."

"It's okay that you got scared. I don't blame you."

"Did you consider that?"

Michelle pauses. "I guess deep down, I believe some of the religious stuff I grew up hearing. I figure I've already sinned this much, so if I went and did something like that, I'd be like extra punished. You probably think I sound ridiculous."

Now it's Baker's turn to be surprised. Michelle, worried about sinning? She's seemed so dismissive of her religious upbringing, so blasé about the past she left behind. "You're neither messed up nor ridiculous."

"I think it's cool that you got as far as you did, though. Made the appointment and showed up for it and all that, right?"

"Sometimes I wish I'd been brave enough to see it through."

"I get it. We're all just trying to do our best."

"Thanks. But I don't think this is my best."

"Unwed teenage mothers generally don't feel that way."

"What if Barry wasn't getting called up? Would you keep the baby?"

Michelle doesn't answer. It's quiet long enough that Baker sits up to look over and make sure her friend is still awake. She is. The whites of her eyes glint in the dark. "Why even ask that? It's just gonna make me feel worse."

Baker stops herself. One question too far. "I'm sorry, Michelle. Scratch that from the record, please."

The moonlight casts shadows from the oak outside the window. Gnarled branches, fluttering leaves. Outside the room, in the hallway, footsteps shuffle. Doors open and close. The toilet flushes, the faucet runs; someone turns on the shower. Ms. White doesn't like bathing to happen this late at night, but she won't come up to stop it. Some of the girls need the blast of hot water to relax before bed.

Baker thinks they're done with the conversation, but then Michelle rolls over and props herself up on her elbow. "What about you, Baker? Do you want your baby?"

It's the question that no one has asked. The words sound so unexpected, so foreign, that she has to repeat them to herself, as if translating from another language. *Your baby.* That is not how she's allowed herself to think about it, as something she could possess. Something that belongs to her. *Does* she *want* the baby? *Want want want.* The word loops in her mind.

"That's not an option."

"That's not what I asked."

Baker's face flushes. She understands why Michelle reacted the way she did to this awful question.

"I don't know, Michelle. I don't really think about it."

"Bullshit. We're *all* thinking about it. All the time."

Baker trembles. Michelle is right, of course. "Okay, let me rephrase it. I'm *trying not* to think about it."

"That's better. But it's still kind of bullshit."

Baker tries to stay calm, but the words leap out, loud. "Okay, fine! I'm full of shit!"

"That's not what I'm saying."

"I don't want any of this. I don't know who to trust, and I don't know what the right answer is. How am I supposed to? I've never done this before!" Baker realizes how big her voice has become, and she lowers the volume but not the intensity. "And I *hate* not knowing the answers!"

"Those are all fair points. No one gives a study guide for this part of the test."

"I think I deserve the chance to figure it out, though. To figure myself out. You do, too."

"Now you're talking!"

"And they don't want that to happen here. Not in this house."

"And ain't that the truth."

They go quiet again, hearts racing, fists clenched, insides churning. Michelle leans over and pops open her container of contraband Tums. Baker hears her chomping a handful in the dark.

"Want some?"

"Sure." The plastic bottle arcs across the room, and Baker manages to catch it. She puts several tablets in her mouth and bites down. The minty, chalky dust fills her mouth, coats her throat.

"Good night, Baker. And thank you. Feels good to talk about it."

"Same here. Sweet dreams, Michelle."

Baker doesn't fall asleep right away. She can't. Her body is too amped up, her mind too active, her tongue too dredged in Tums. She stares at the now-familiar ceiling and feels her body: she wiggles her faraway toes, rotates her swollen ankles, listens to her joints snap and pop. She twists her head back and forth to relieve the tension in her neck, then yawns and feels her jaw relax. She looks down at the dome of her body, the hill that rises beneath the blankets. It's big. Bigger than last week; bigger than yesterday, even. She rubs the taut skin, runs a finger around the rim of her stretched-out navel, strokes the sloping sides. It feels soft and warm, and it's all so weird and unbelievable that she almost giggles.

Inside, the Bun is still. Resting. She thinks of the yeasted rolls her grandma used to make for holidays. How she'd mix the ingredients, then knead the small blob of dough, then put it into a big wooden bowl beneath a flour sack towel. Baker loved to sneak peeks, watching in awe as the blob transformed, growing, rising, expanding like magic. She falls asleep to images of the dough overflowing, rising so much that it spills from the bowl, onto the counter, into the outstretched hands of the young girl who's watching.

*T*he next morning, Ms. White calls Baker into her office again. She doesn't mention their previous meeting. She holds Baker's file in her hands and taps it a few times on the desk.

"Today you have an exam with Dr. Sullivan. He is very discreet. It's a routine third-trimester appointment to make sure everyone is healthy. Follow me." Ms. White stands and leads Baker out of the room, down a narrow hallway just past the front door that Baker hasn't been down. Ms. White pauses at a door and smiles when she notices the perplexed look on Baker's face.

"Many girls are surprised when they learn that we have a doctor's office on the premises." She opens the door, revealing a clean, sparsely furnished exam room. "Dr. Sullivan will be right in, Elizabeth. Undress from the waist down and wait on the table. Put this on."

She hands Baker a worn cotton apron with tattered strings on either side and then leaves the room, closing the door noiselessly behind her. Baker takes it all in. The long table covered in crisp white paper, the silver stirrups that jut out on either side like suspended insect legs. The white metal tray and its neat array of shiny instruments. The sink, the cupboards, the lack of windows, the jars of cotton balls and Q-tips, the fluorescent light overhead. The life-sized anatomical diagram of a pregnant woman that hangs on the wall: a side view, as usual, her body cut clean in half, the upside-down fetus snuggled in a tight, patient ball. It's not unlike the office she went to back in Berkeley all those months ago.

Then she sees it: the full-length mirror. As tall as her, if not taller, mounted flush against the back of the door, reflecting back to her a person she's never fully seen. The mirrors in the washroom are small and round, resting high enough above the sinks that a girl can only see her face, neck, shoulders. She's gone as high up on her tiptoes as she can, and she's glimpsed her hazy reflection in windowpanes, but this is the first time she's seen herself, full-length, full-on, for months. And it takes her breath away.

She looks like . . . a pregnant woman. Like an actual *woman*. It's unlike any version of herself that she recalls, more like a familiar stranger you pass on the street whose face you just can't quite place. She's in there, somewhere, but it's an entirely different body. She remembers one of the girls at school telling her she looked like Grace Slick. How cool that made her feel, how womanly and mysterious. *Now I look like Grace Slick's knocked-up little sister,* she thinks.

Her hair is longer and thicker. Her cheeks are puffy. The eyes are hers, but they're tired and sad. The mouth is hers, but the lips are fuller. There's more neck, more flesh on her arms, more flesh in general. She wants to look away, go back to not knowing what she looks like, what's really going on, but she knows that time is over. That ship has sailed. It's time to be strong, to face all this truth. She reaches up to undo the top button of her blouse and notices that even her hands look different: a little pink, kind of swollen. Her chest is blotchy, and the maternity bra Rose bought her months ago is too tight. The blouse falls to the floor. She struggles to reach her arms back to unhook the bulky bra, and when she finally does, she peels it off, along with her elastic waist skirt, which puddles down around her swollen ankles.

There she is. All of her. She stares first at her breasts: how big they are, how grown-up looking, how *ponderous* is the word that pops into her head. *Sylvia Plath was so right.* She *is* a melon, a loaf, a ponderous house. A cow. Her nipples are the red fruit—they used to be small and pale, and now they're dark, spread out, the deep color of a berry jam—and her skin is ivory, nearly translucent. Then she focuses on the thighs, thick and sturdy, and the hips, which didn't really used to be there at all. *She's got a figure like a little boy's!* Rose would often say.

Finally she lets her eyes settle on *it*. The big, round beach ball that now lives in her midsection. It's all she can see when she looks at the place where her ribs and stomach and waist used to be. It's streaked by tiny red marks, crisscrossed by bluish-green veins. The skin is pale, tight, almost shiny. Similar to Michelle's, but also unique. Her once-puckered little belly button is now a taut lower-case *o*. And there's a line, a dark vertical line that runs from the top of her panties up to the crest of the mound. She traces it lightly with her finger, up and down, up and down. Then she spreads her palms and presses them on either side, firm and tender. She feels the stirring within, as if the Bun is moving in response to her touch. She leans as far down as she can and whispers.

"Hello."

More movement.

"Can you hear me?"

She rubs her hands around in circles.

The rapping on the door startles her. "Knock knock!"

It's the first man's voice she's heard in months. It's so loud, so intrusive. She grabs the cotton apron and wraps it around her body as she climbs onto the exam table, her clothes still in a pile on the floor. For one brief and bizarre moment, she's terrified that her naked reflection will still be in the mirror when he comes in, and she turns to the glass to make sure she's not still in there. But she's right here, on this table, fully aware of what she looks like.

Dr. Sullivan is tall and slightly stooped over, wearing glasses that sit at the tip of a long nose. His mustache is a miniature version of the ring of hair that circles his head, just above his ears.

"This won't take long," he assures her. "Just want to make sure everything's where it's supposed to be."

She closes her eyes while he puts on rubber gloves, and then begins to press: the sides, the bottom, down from the top. He pushes hard in some places, and Baker gasps.

"Apologies," he says. "I know it's not the most comfortable." He touches the belly button, which tickles, and he examines the dark vertical line that she just stroked. "Everything feels fine. Baby's right on track, a good size. Must be making you tired. You've been working hard to build a human."

She hasn't thought about it this way, that she *built* this baby. That she has been working hard, building a body, cell by cell, day by day. She's felt more like a container for some strange phenomenon, not a key player or active participant. It makes her feel proud. And sad.

While he does the pelvic exam, Baker closes her eyes tight and imagines herself as a scientist in a lab, constructing a human, building and creating. Like Dr. Frankenstein, but less monstrous. She's read the classic novel several times, and she remembers learning in English class that Mary Shelley was just a teenager when she gave birth to a premature baby who didn't survive. Her mother was long dead, and she'd already infuriated her father by running off with her poet boyfriend (and his mistress). She was haunted by visions of her deceased daughter, and one year later, when she was eighteen, she began writing the story that would become *Frankenstein*.

For a brief second, she feels tethered to Mary Shelley, connected in some tortured-soul way. A line from the novel pops into her head, and while Dr. Sullivan pushes his gloved hand against her cervix, radiating a deep pain throughout her lower body and inner thighs, she repeats it to herself: "Thus strangely are our souls constructed, and by such slight ligaments are we bound to prosperity or ruin."

"What's that now?" Dr. Sullivan peers up from between her stirruped feet. "Thought I heard you say something?"

"Just trying to distract myself, doctor."

He snaps off his gloves and tosses them in the trash can. Her groin throbs.

"Like I said, everything's in the right place. I'll give Ms. White the good news." He picks her clothes up off the floor and hands them to her. "I *am* going to add a note that this baby appears to be pretty good-sized. You have a small frame, so if it keeps growing at a steady pace, I'm going to recommend that we give you something to help you relax when the time comes. A little twilight sleep. You won't feel a thing."

"I won't?"

"You'll go to sleep like *this*." He flings his head and arms back, lets his tongue loll from his mouth. It's an unsettling sight. "And then you wake up like this." He stands up, wipes his hands together a few times, and puts them on his hips. "Any further questions?"

She has lots of them, still. But not for him. Not for another man who thinks that he knows how she feels just because his gloved hands have touched her. He doesn't know her, or her story; his examination can't decipher her heart or her mind or the thousands of feelings that bubble just beneath the skin. "Just one. Were you Kitty's doctor, too?"

Dr. Sullivan's nostrils flare, and the glint in his eye disappears.

"How do you know about her?"

"It doesn't matter how. I just want to know more about her."

Dr. Sullivan walks to the door in silence and opens it. "It's time to head up to your room and get some rest. I'll let Ms. White know that I've prescribed a quiet evening for you."

"That's it? You're not going to tell me anything?"

"Let's make that a quiet week. We don't want you getting overexerted."

Baker narrows her eyes. She's not afraid of this man. "You can't make me be quiet."

Dr. Sullivan ducks his head and exits without saying another word.

Baker balls her fists, clenches her jaw. She bites her lip and puts her clothes back on. Then she takes another long look at herself in the mirror. She wonders what Mary Shelley wore when she was pregnant; whether Sylvia Plath wore maternity clothes. She imagines Mary suffering in corsets, crushed under the weight of petticoats and woolen skirts. She imagines Sylvia balancing her journal on a small, round belly. In the mirror, Baker's cheeks are flushed and, briefly, she sees herself as beautiful. She smooths down her dark hair and purses her lips, sharpens her gaze. She juts out a hip and pushes her bust up and out.

The sound of footsteps snaps her out of this trance. It's time for the girls to go on their walk. She presses her ear to the door and listens, certain that she can tell who's who by the sounds of their footwear on the stairs. Lizzie clomps in those wood-soled sandals she's still wearing. Marcy's heels make dainty clacks. Anna's pumps give a gentle thump. Baker hears them whisper and laugh as they line up to get their rings, then the swishing of their coats as they head to the front door, exiting the home one by one, a neat line of young women in unseasonable outfits and gleaming wedding bands.

When she pushes open the door to the no-longer-secret doctor's office, she feels like she's stepping out of one world and into another. One with no mirrors, no men, no stainless-steel stirrups. Just a big empty room with once-grand furniture and a clock that doesn't work, old magazines and faded paintings and walls that have heard and seen it all. Closed doors, layers of wallpaper, worn wood. An in-between place for temporary secrets.

Dear Mother,

Your visit can't come soon enough. To be very honest I am just dying to get out of this house. I know it is temporary, and I know that I should be very grateful to be here, and I am, but I cannot tell you how cooped up I feel. I just want to walk on the sidewalk and look at the sky and ride in the car with the windows rolled down. I would also love to drink a cold Coca-Cola.

They keep telling me that after this is over I can put it all behind me and pick up right where I left off but that's very hard for me to believe. Sometimes I think I will always be sad, and you will always be disappointed. I don't know if that's true. It's hard to tell what's what when you're in here.

Your daughter,
Elizabeth

$\mathcal{B}$aker has been sitting on the long green couch near the stone hearth since 9:00 A.M. Rose is scheduled to pick her up at ten, but she knows her mother will be early. She skipped breakfast to get ready for Rose's arrival. Her hair is clean and brushed and pulled back from her face (the way Rose prefers it) with the tortoiseshell combs that May sent her. She's terrified of how Rose will react when she sees that her daughter does, in fact, look pregnant. She tried out ten different outfit combinations before settling on the skirt, blouse, and sweater that make her look the least enormous. Her lips are shiny and pink, thanks to a lip gloss borrowed from Marcy.

When the door finally opens and Rose walks in, Baker's heart pounds. Her hands rush to cover her middle as the Bun kicks, pops, seems to be doing flips. Rose looks beautiful. She wears a crisp white blouse knotted at the waist, and pastel floral culottes, the silk ones that flow when she walks. Her makeup is subtle but classy, her eyebrows arched and lips outlined and cheeks a little rouged. Her scent is strong, and Baker imagines her perfume wafting up the stairs, under the doors, filling every room with the scent of a mother.

When she sees Baker, her eyes go wide, and then she smiles and holds out her arms. Baker wants to jump into them and cling to her like a baby animal. She wants to let her mother lead her out the door and back to her bedroom, back to her childhood, back to the beginning of it all. She wants to leave her own body, dissolve into her mother's chest and curl up next to the beat of her heart.

But instead she walks carefully toward Rose, head bowed slightly, and they exchange a brief, tentative hug. Unspoken words begin to pile around them as Rose fills out a sheet of paper on the clipboard that Anna hands her. Then Anna reaches into her pocket and pulls out a gold ring. When she holds it up, it glints in the light.

"Here," she says to Baker. "You finally get to wear one."

No! is what Baker thinks, but she doesn't say it. She takes the thin band and begins forcing it onto her finger. It's too small, or her hand is too swollen, or both. She finally gets it over her knuckle, and a flash of discomfort moves over Rose's face. Anna opens the door.

When they step outside together, Baker gasps. It's her first time in the world as a visibly pregnant young woman. Aside from her time on the roof on the Fourth, it's her first time out in the world since she *arrived*. The air feels so fresh and crisp and alive. The grass is an electric shade of green, the clouds look cartoonishly fluffy, and the buildings up and down the street seem to sparkle in the sunlight. Each car that passes is so loud and fast. Each person she sees looks so free. She breathes so deep that her throat tickles, and she barks out a cough.

"Are you okay, dear?" Rose asks.

Baker feels sheepish. "I haven't been outside for so long."

A flash of recognition comes over Rose's face like a midday shadow. "I read your letter. I understand."

Baker doesn't ask Rose where they're going, because it doesn't matter. She would happily go anywhere. Maybe they'll end up in Sausalito, eating fresh fish at that Italian place Rose loves. They could get enchiladas from the Hot House, the ones that come on the paper plates that get soggy from all the sauce and cheese so you have to eat them as fast as possible. Then for dessert they could get fat slices of lemon meringue pie from the pie shop up the street. Or maybe, she imagines, they'll just keep going, up Highway 101 until night falls and Rose is too tired to drive and they're where? Oregon? Washington? Canada? How far could they get?

Rose talks nonstop for the first half of the drive, navigating busy city streets and heading out along the Presidio, toward the Golden

Gate Bridge. The details of the upcoming tea party to benefit the Children's Hospital are endless; the latest drama at the dance studio is Joan's fault, yet again. And believe it or not, but plans for the annual Christmas auction are already under way.

As they approach the bridge, Rose finally grows quiet. Baker isn't sure if she's run out of things to complain about, or if her mother feels the majesty of crossing the deep water on the suspended span of orange metal just as much as she does.

Baker leans her head out of the window and looks up as they pass beneath the first of the two towers. It's always been a dizzying delight to do this. She feels so small and always marvels at the fact that the whole thing was built by men with nothing but nets between them and the water below. The Bay glistens, its deep blue pierced by the white caps of waves, the sails of boats that glide along. It's a long way down. A long, dizzying dive.

Once they're over the bridge, Rose takes the first exit—*I was right,* Baker thinks, *Sausalito lunch it is*—but then loops around and heads west, toward the headlands. Desolate beaches, whipping winds, rolling hills, and hiking trails that cling to the very edge of California.

"I thought we'd admire the view," she explains. "I packed us a picnic. Fried chicken and potato salad. Your favorites."

Of course, Baker realizes. *She can't go parading me around Sausalito. Or San Francisco, or Pacifica, or any damn city.* It stings, but it also makes sense. Would she really want to risk running into an acquaintance, feeling their eyes on her body, having to stand there and experience their reactions and judgments, her mother's embarrassment? It's an awful thought, but at the same time, there's a very small part of her that desires an awkward encounter. The chance to just get it all out there. To stop hiding. She remembers a term her history teacher had once used, one that stuck with her for its poetic sound, how it rolled off the tongue. *Persona non grata.*

The car climbs the narrow, winding roads. Rose grips the steering wheel tightly, her eyes locked on the road ahead. Baker stares at the world below, slightly nauseous, slightly thrilled. At the top of the hill, Rose pulls the car over. Below them spreads the Bay, the water, the entire city of San Francisco. The glinting dome of the Palace of Fine Arts. Alcatraz sits stoic to the left, and to the right, past the Golden Gate, the land ends, California bows into the sea, and there is nothing but blue until the far-off horizon. Seagulls and hawks swoop overhead; aside from their distant calls, it is quiet.

"I'll get the food." Rose opens the trunk and returns with a small picnic basket. "We'll eat in the car." Baker can tell how paranoid Rose is, as if someone she knows might come around the bend at any time. It feels absurd—they're so far from home!—but not worth an argument. "We can just put the plates on our laps. Carefully."

Rose places two plates, two sets of cutlery, and two tiny salt and pepper shakers on the car's expansive dashboard. Then she arranges the food: deep golden hunks of cold fried chicken; creamy potato salad with flecks of celery; rolls with butter already spread thick; two bottles of Coca-Cola. Baker spots dessert in the picnic basket: two slices of angel food cake. The smells are unreal. Baker's mouth waters, and pangs of hunger radiate.

Rose lights a cigarette and inhales deep. "Don't just stare at it! Eat!"

One bite of the fried chicken, and Baker is flooded with pleasure, with memories of childhood picnics, summer dinners at her grandmother's house. It tastes perfect and overwhelming. It tastes like home. She dips a fork into the potato salad and swoons over that, too: the potatoes soft but not too soft, the slight tang of Dijon mustard, the sweet homemade relish, the crunch of celery. When she bites into one of the rolls, she realizes how hungry she's been this entire morning.

Rose lets her daughter devour the food, nibbling here and there at her own plate. She waits a few minutes before resuming the chit-chat.

"So," she finally asks, "how is everything going?"

An impossible question. How is Baker supposed to answer?

Should she tell her about the latch-hook rugs and all the stories she's heard? How she's nowhere near the only girl who's messed it all up? Should she tell her mother about Michelle, how it's her second pregnancy? Or about Viv, pining for her teacher? Does Rose want to hear about the one who's just fourteen years old? Should she explain that she feels connected to Marcy because she, too, almost got an abortion? And what about Kitty? Does Rose want to know about the mysterious girl who left clues for Baker? No, none of that was in the plan. When Rose asks about *everything,* what she really wants to hear is *very little.*

"Fine." Baker's lips and fingers are slick with grease from the chicken. Crumbs cover the cotton napkin on her lap. "Everything is fine."

"Wonderful."

"Except the food." Baker grins between bites. "It's nothing like this."

Rose beams. "Are you getting along with the other girls?"

"Of course. My roommate Michelle and I are getting pretty close."

"Not too close, I hope." When Rose breathes out the smoke curls upward in intricate swirls.

"Of course." Baker stuffs another roll in her mouth. She feels the butter coat her tongue, her teeth, her throat. "You're the one who asked."

"You know, not every girl in your situation gets to do what you're doing. Live in this nice home, get taken care of, get to preserve your dignity. It could be much worse, Elizabeth. Much worse."

"I know." And she does.

They sit for a while more, Baker eating and Rose smoking.

"The boy that did this to you, is he still in Mexico?"

The question is a bit of a trap. "I guess so. I don't know."

"You haven't heard from him?"

"No. But if I told you I *had* heard from him, you'd be mad about that, too."

"True." Rose takes a long drag from her cigarette. Baker listens as it crackles. "I went away once, too, Elizabeth."

"Pardon?"

"To Chicago. I was sixteen years old, and I was in trouble."

Baker puts the half-eaten chicken thigh back down on her plate. She glances at her mother, perplexed, unsure where she's going with this.

Rose continues. "There was a doctor there; he'd done the same for the teenage daughter of the woman I was working for. Mrs. Carlson was her name. I cleaned her house twice a week—I've told you that before, haven't I? After my father passed, and I needed to help mother with the bills, I took on a job. She was a good woman, Mrs. Carlson. Wealthy, and very discreet. When she noticed that I wasn't well, she helped me arrange it." Rose sips her Coca-Cola. The amber bottle trembles in her hand. "You know what I'm speaking about, right?"

Holy shit. Baker does know. It's hard to believe what her mother is telling her, but she knows. The way she knew when Marcy mentioned Mexico. The way, Baker realizes, women seem to understand. Because this is something secret that so many share. Baker nods, her heart racing, her eyes wide, her chest tight.

Rose continues, calm and composed. "We were living in Nebraska then, you'll recall. The small town outside of Lincoln. The boy, he came with me. I'll always be grateful for that. He stole the money from his father. I remember thinking that was a very gentlemanly thing to do. Mrs. Carlson gave me an envelope with paperwork, a map, an address. I carried the money in my bra. We took the train all the way there." Rose smiles wistfully. "It felt so grown-up. It would have been so fun if it weren't for the circumstances."

Baker has never heard her mother share this much personal information. She's hardly considered the fact that her mother *has* personal information, that she's had an entire life of experiences and feelings. And secrets. She's terrified to move, worried that she might startle Rose and snap her out of this honesty trance. When Rose continues, her voice sounds lower, and faraway.

"I don't know what I expected, really. At least a clean office, I think I expected that, but that wasn't the case. It was a rowhouse, very rundown, not the kind of neighborhood I was used to. There was an older woman there who didn't speak, just took the money and led me to a dark room with a table and a lantern. The boy had to wait outside, so I was alone. Then a man came in; he spoke very broken English. I've always imagined he was Eastern European, but I have no way of knowing for sure. I don't remember much after that, except the pain. And the dog."

She turns and looks at Baker, who notices the lines around her eyes and her lips, the two parallel creases in her forehead, like the number 11, the way she looks young and old at the same time. "The worst pain I've ever experienced. I don't think the man numbed me at all. And midway through, the door opened, and a dog came into the room, sniffing around and panting, and I was so shocked. *A dog.* Can you believe that?"

Baker doesn't know how to answer. She can't believe *any* of it, dog or no dog. She can barely believe that this woman in the car, spilling her deepest darkest secret, talking about having an abortion, is her mother. The same woman who's been acting like Baker's pregnancy is the end of the world. The same woman who boxed her up and sent her away. Baker has no words. She still doesn't move a muscle.

"Can you?"

Baker jerks her head back and forth. Rose continues.

"I thought the dog might eat me! I was delirious. And I was so tired afterward. Everything ached. I thought I was dying, I really did. I don't even remember the train ride home; I must have slept the entire time. And then I developed a terrible fever."

Rose pauses and lets out an audible shudder. Then: "Dessert! We can't forget dessert."

She pulls the cake slices from the basket, unwraps the thin plastic film, and places one on Baker's plate, next to the abandoned chicken thigh. Baker sees how her hands are shaking. She pulls a fresh fork from the basket, its sharp tines glinting in the sun. Rose brought the good silver.

"Here. You don't want your cake tasting like your lunch."

"Thank you. I don't . . ." She searches for something to say. The fork is heavy in her hand. She has no appetite for cake, for any of it. And she needs to know the rest of the story.

"Were you okay?"

"Oh, no, not at all." Rose takes a bite of her cake. "Delicious! Try it."

Baker puts a small bite of cake onto her silver fork and forces herself to raise it to her mouth. She wills herself to chew, and to swallow. She tastes nothing. The frosting is thick. She smiles politely. "It's perfect."

"Isn't it? Anyway, where was I?"

"You had a fever."

"That's right. I had told your grandmother that I was spending the weekend with girlfriends, and next thing she knew, she was with me in the septic ward. She must have known right away what I'd done, why I was so sick. The doctors did. I could tell by how they looked at me. Like I was a whore, Elizabeth. That's what they thought of me. That's what people think of women like us."

The phrase nearly knocks Baker from her seat. Her heart lurches. *Women like us.* Does Rose think they're the same?

"But my mother, she never said a word about it. She stayed by my side and prayed until I was well, then took me home. She knew, though. We never recovered from it. Ever."

Ever?

"I remember a few months later, I broke one of her favorite teacups. She slapped me so hard, I thought she broke my jaw."

They hear a rustle and look up: a hawk takes off from a nearby tree, swooping over them as it soars up and over the hills. Its wingspan is immense, its feathers dark and shiny.

"I should stop," says Rose. "I've said far too much."

Baker can't stop herself: she falls into her mother's lap with no hesitation, burying her head in the soft silk of Rose's pants, fitting herself into Rose's curves, trying to get as close as possible. Rose allows it, and soon Baker feels her mother's hand stroking the top of her head. Baker lies there in Rose's lap, letting this new information settle inside her, the way she's done with the other girls' stories. This is entirely different, though; this is so far beyond anything she has experienced. She'd never really imagined her mother as a young person, as a girl who existed before her, as a teenager who was loved and harmed and slapped and scared. She feels connected to teen-aged Rose, heartbroken for her, and also for grown-up Rose. At the same time, she's angry at her. Furious. Why didn't she tell her daughter this story sooner? Did she not realize how much it would mean to know this? Was she trying to forget? Whom was she trying to protect?

"You weren't supposed to be born, Elizabeth. The doctor in that ward told me I'd never be a mother. That I'd ruined myself forever. When we got married, I didn't tell your father. I was afraid he'd re-ject me, and I just crossed my fingers and prayed that doctor was wrong. And he was. Somehow, you happened. But that was it, just you. Your father wanted a son. I would have been happy with three, even four children. But it wasn't to be."

Baker tries to imagine having three siblings. The hawk swoops back by, something in its beak this time. They can hear the swoosh of its wings, the air breaking over its body. Wind in the eucalyptus trees; the thick, salty smell as a breeze blows up from the water below.

"And everything's been fine. Everything turned out just fine. This is a fleeting time, really. You *do* move on. You have to."

Rose shifts in her seat, and Baker sits up.

"Why didn't you tell me this sooner?"

Rose looks indignant. "I just didn't think it was necessary. It wouldn't have changed the situation."

"But it might have made me feel better."

"*Feelings* have not been my primary concern, Elizabeth."

The warm connection between them feels frayed. A static in the air. Then:

"If you did it a long time ago, why wasn't it an option for me?"

"Are you asking me why I didn't arrange for my daughter to undergo an illegal procedure that could kill her? That could get her—and her parents—arrested?"

"It's not like that anymore. It's not . . . as bad."

"And you know this how?"

Baker considers telling Rose everything. Opening her mouth and letting more truths come out. The phone calls she made, the money she took from Gerald's dresser, the clothes she borrowed from Rose's closet. The strange town she went to, the man in the suit, the woman who gave her the ride. Rose would *hate* that part. *You hitchhiked?* It's too much. They've gone far enough today.

"It's just different now. Everyone knows that."

Rose picks up her napkin and wipes frosting from the corners of her mouth. The lipstick traces on the napkin look like little bloodstains. "There are no easy answers here," Rose says quietly. "No perfect options. I don't care how much the world has 'changed.' What I experienced is not something I would wish on my worst enemy, let alone my own daughter. I couldn't risk putting you through that."

Baker begins to cry. The sobs are big and ugly, raw and untamed. "It's just not *fair*," she wails. "It's not *fair* that I'm the one stuck with all of this, it's not *fair* that you had to go through that, to be there in that room with that *dog*. It's just awful, and I wish the doctor had been right, I wish you hadn't been able to have me." Baker looks at her face in the rearview mirror. A hideous crying monster. "Then you never would've had to deal with *this*."

Without hesitation, Rose grabs Baker's shoulders and spins her around, their faces inches apart.

"Don't you *ever* say that again!" Rose's eyes burn, her nostrils flare. Baker flinches as saliva flecks fly from Rose's lips. "Now listen to me. This has been happening to women since the dawn of time. We don't discuss it because it's private, and it's painful. And we have to stay safe. So we can carry on. Head high, mouth shut, eyes on the future. Not the past."

"Easy for you to say." Baker tries to pull away, but Rose's grip is strong.

"You think you're the only one? Of course you do! You're an only child; you think it all revolves around you." Rose releases her, and slaps her hands on the steering wheel, exasperated. "Oh, you have no idea. Your great-aunt Eleanor—my aunt—she had a daughter when she was fifteen. She got pregnant by a schoolteacher. A married man. Eleanor's mother Hazel kept the whole thing a secret, then raised that child as her own, as Eleanor's baby sister. Told everyone she was a little surprise baby, a Christmas miracle. Little Aunt Jeannie, who was really my cousin. Did you know that?"

Baker feels small. Her shoulders ache. She shakes her head obediently. "No."

"Of course you didn't. And that's how it's supposed to work. Last year, Joyce from my bridge group, her middle daughter was only fifteen—" Rose catches herself, a tipped glass spilling, and stops. "That's enough."

"Tell me." Baker's voice is a whisper. "I can keep a secret. Obviously." She can't help but smirk at her own dark humor. Rose's mascara runs in black lines down her cheeks, but she smiles, too.

"Fine. Sarah, you remember her. Lovely girl. She had *twins*. And now her father won't speak to her. Not a word. That poor girl came back from the home, and he won't even *look* at her. Joyce is just beside herself, and the only reason I know is that she had too much brandy at last year's Christmas Auction and had a near breakdown in the bathroom. In fact, that's how I learned about Ms. White, and the home. From Joyce, bless her heart." She looks at Baker. "You're lucky your father is a good man. This is *very* hard for a lot of men to understand."

Baker thinks about Wiley, lounging in a hammock on a beach.

She thinks about Gerald sweeping each leaf from the long blue pool. She thinks about Janey's boyfriend Carl back home; Lizzie's camp counselor at Harvard. Barry, getting ready to go to Vietnam.

"If men could get pregnant, I bet it would be different."

"That, my dear, is certainly true."

Baker shoves the rest of the slice of cake into her mouth, chews it, manages to swallow. "Why didn't you tell me any of this before?"

"I already told you. Discretion isn't just about manners. It's about safety, too." Rose picks up a napkin and reaches over, wipes frosting and crumbs from Baker's face. "There's much about the world I can't explain, my love. We do what we have to do, and we make it through the damn day. Then we wake up tomorrow and do it again."

Baker shakes her head. That's it? *That's* the advice? She looks at her mother and feels crushed by a new wave of tangled feelings. Pity and grief, regret and love. And the distinct feeling that something *has* to change. Somehow, someday, her tomorrows need to be different.

"Someday you'll know what I mean, Elizabeth. It might not seem like much, but believe me: it can take everything you've got."

*T*hat night Baker lies restless in bed, too hot, hips sore and tingly, her mind still dizzy as the details of the day finally begin to settle into something she can begin to understand. Like the moments after a whiteout blizzard has ended, and the world is just a vast blanket of snow. She replays it all: the winding roads, the picnic lunch, the hawk overhead, the waves down below. The lines on the backs of her mother's hands and the tiny Coca-Cola bubbles fizzing and burning as they rushed down her throat. Rose's perfume. Rose's gaze. Rose's story.

Rose, a teenager in the 1930s. Rose, a pregnant teenager with a boyfriend who stole money from his parents. How long did it take to ride a train from Lincoln to Chicago? She pictures the boy in a button-up shirt, thin suspenders holding up his pants. Rose in a fitted wool suit. Beautiful. Baker had been so paralyzed during the conversation, letting Rose's words just gush over her like a reservoir undammed. Now the questions come: Why did Rose do it? Why did she go to such lengths? What other options could she have had? Did she consider having the baby? Did the boy ask her to? And how would Rose's mother have reacted if she'd known?

Rose never liked to talk about her childhood. Baker knows that her mother's family struggled, that there wasn't much money and they had to move often, especially after her father died. *Those were hard times*, Rose would say whenever it came up, and that was usually the extent of it. Baker never got to meet her grandmother, who died two years before Baker was born. If she'd lived, would Rose have let her meet her daughter? *We never recovered from it. Ever.*

She has only seen a few photos: black and white, creased, edges tattered, one of them torn in half and held together with crumbling yellowed tape. She has stared at the image of her mother's mother, at her stern, hard face, her dark hair pulled back tight, her thick sturdy body. Did she ever smile?

The question that won't stop rattling around remains: Why couldn't Rose have shared this sooner? She could have said, *I know how you're feeling. It happened to me. I understand.* She could have made the appointment; she could have given Baker the ride. She could have been with her in that stairwell. She would have known what to say to that man. Rose would have told him to be quiet and mind his own business. She would have marched Baker into that suite the way she marched her into Dr. Bell's office.

In the dark of her room, Baker shakes her head. *No way.* No matter what Rose held in her past, she never would've taken her daughter to do something like that. Not now. She's come too far to take risks like that. She's upstanding, she's holding it all together—but it's tenuous. Delicate. Baker knows that Rose doesn't want to rock the boat. But did she truly believe that this option, this situation right here—Baker in this narrow bed, alone but surrounded, in a home but not at home, hidden in plain sight, secret and learning secrets—was the best option?

Baker hated the drive back to the home: the return to polite chit-chat, as if the world as she knew it hadn't just cracked open and flooded her entire heart. The brisk goodbye; the awkward hug on the faded porch; Rose's back, walking away. Baker was overwhelmed by the loss she felt as her mother drove away and she reentered the home, swallowed up by its dark walls. She moped through dinner and tried to soothe herself with cinnamon toast and Ovaltine for dessert, the comfort foods that Rose used to bring her after hard days, or as a peace offering when they had their disagreements. But she didn't get the cinnamon-to-sugar ratio right, and the Ovaltine was too weak.

Is Rose able to sleep tonight, or is she sitting outside on the patio, under her broad-leafed tropical plants? Is she replaying the visit, too, with a cocktail and a cigarette and the saccharine scent of the purple wisteria? Does she worry that she said too much? Or does she wish her poor daughter was still lying across her lap?

Baker forces herself to switch gears by picturing May's new place: ramshackle wooden houses? Tents in a clearing in the forest? She imagines redwood trees, the sound of the ocean, birds over-head. Hawks, crows, bluejays. It must be foggy there, and chilly, but there is probably a fireplace. She sees herself sitting in a room like May's old bedroom, but with a crackling fire, a bowl of soup, and nothing out the window but branches and sky. It's a relaxing thought. It might not be that bad.

When she wakes in the middle of the night, she has to pee, as usual. She gets up, feels her way through the dark to the door. Michelle's snores are soft; moonlight slips through the window and illuminates her sleeping face.

She hears it as soon as she opens the door. It's different from the normal nighttime crying, which usually comes from behind a door, muffled by a pillow or blanket. These cries are harsh, unfiltered, and very close by.

The door to the washroom is ajar, and there she finds Anna, curled on the tile floor, her small body heaving. Her eyes are closed tight.

"Anna?" Baker whispers and touches her arm. It's cold, damp with sweat, prickled with goosebumps. "Anna, it's Baker. Are you all right?"

Anna doesn't respond. Her eyes remain shut; her cries continue.

"Anna, wake up!" She gives her a soft shake. Then a harder

shake. Anna's eyes fly open, pupils dilated big and black like eclipsed moons.

"I saw her," she gasps. "It was so real. I saw her."

"Saw who?"

"I saw her here, right here." Anna points to a spot on the floor, next to where Baker is crouched. "Right where it happened."

"I think you've had a nightmare, Anna." Baker tries to soothe her, but Anna's entire body is rigid. "It's okay. It wasn't real."

"But it was; it all really happened."

"Shhh." Baker is sure that someone else will hear them. She doesn't want the whole floor of girls crowding in here. But she does want to know what Anna saw. "Do you want to tell me about it?"

"It was the night my water broke."

"Who did you see?"

"It was dark, like this. I woke up soaking wet, in so much pain, and she wasn't in her bed. I came in here, dripping all down the hall, and I saw her, on the floor."

"Anna, *who?*"

Anna blinks and looks right at Baker. "My roommate. She was right here, right on this floor. Blood everywhere." Anna points to various spots on the floor. She seems more alert, her voice calmer and clear. "There was other stuff. Towels, a long rubber tube. A coat hanger. All bent up and bloody."

Baker tries to swallow, but her throat feels swollen. She knows she should get Anna out of here, back to bed, but she can't stop. She has to know the rest of the story. "What happened next? You can tell me."

"I screamed. *Kitty! Kitty!*"

Baker's body turns to ice. Her vision seems to tunnel; her head begins to throb. Her hands tingle. *Kitty.* Anna's roommate was Kitty.

"I touched her arm, her face. She was . . . burning."

"A fever," Baker whispers, and Anna reaches out and grips Baker's forearm with her small cold hands.

"I went on the floor next to her. All the blood and everything, and I heard the voices and footsteps in the hall, and then she grabbed my arm."

"What did she say, Anna?"

Anna blinks. Her lips part, and she whispers. "She said *help*. She said *I don't want to die*."

Baker gasps. "Then what?"

Anna just stares, her eyes glassy. Baker knows she should just take her hand and lead her to her room.

"What happened next, Anna? What did Kitty do?"

"I helped her stand up. And she ran."

"Where?"

"To the stairs."

Baker's heart knocks against her ribs, bangs on her lungs. She feels the rumbling sensation of movement inside of her. The Bun is awake. She wants to throw up.

"I said *Kitty wait,* and she said *I've got to get out of here.* I heard her on the stairs. The whole way down."

"Oh my god."

"She didn't mean to fall, Baker. I know it. She didn't mean to."

"What happened next?"

"I don't know. I fainted. There's nothing else."

"What do you mean nothing else?"

"I woke up in the hospital. Empty. No more baby. When I came back, Kitty was . . . gone. Her bed was empty, her closet was empty."

"Where was she?"

Anna looks at Baker. Wide eyes even wider. She doesn't blink. "She was gone."

"Anna." Baker's voice shakes. "Was she . . . ?"

Anna's body stiffens, and she looks away. She sits up straight, crosses her arms. "She was gone. And so was my baby."

"Anna. I'm so sorry."

Anna clears her throat. "We don't need to talk about it. We moved on."

"Anna," Baker whispers, and she reaches out her hand to stroke the girl's head.

Anna jerks away from Baker and stares at her with sudden suspicion. "Why are you asking me so many questions?"

"I'm sorry, I just—"

"I already answered. They told me no more questions." She stands up and crosses her arms. "We shouldn't be in here. Back to bed now. It's fine."

Anna heads back to her room, leaving Baker alone in the cold, bloodless room that pulses against the now-silent night.

Part III

August, 1968 (at least I think it's August . . . we don't have a calendar here!)

Hey kid,

I wish you could see my view right now: the pointy green tips of 1000 trees and the biggest bluest sky. I can almost see the ocean from the second floor of this house. I'm getting good at kitchen work. We make bread from scratch just like Nana Anne. I learned how to make a pie even! Your mom would be proud. Speaking of moms, there's a few mamas here, and a mama-to-be. It's really accepted. No one's hung-up about anything.

You'd love it here. Ok, maybe love is a strong word. I know it's not "your scene" but I imagine you here and it makes me feel . . . better. I worry about you. And also, OK I'll admit it . . .

I miss you.

Peace,
May

p.s. If you ever decide to come, there's a guy with a beard at the donut shop in town who can give you directions. Tell him you know me.

"nstable."

Michelle spits out the word as she enters the room after breakfast. Her face is flushed, and her eyes are blazing. She says it again: "*Unstable!*" She waves a piece of paper in the air and then flops onto her bed, wincing as her body hits the mattress. It's still possible, sometimes, to forget how these bodies have changed. She looks up at Baker. "Damn. My lower back. Can you rub it for just a second?"

Baker puts her book down and lifts the hem of Michelle's tank top. She spreads her hands over the warm bare skin, pushing with her palms, and her fingertips, slow and steady. She imagines her own lower back, her tense thighs and aching pelvis, and she rubs the way she'd want someone to touch her. Michelle's flesh is soft and grateful as her fingers press deeper.

Michelle groans. "That feels so damn good."

Baker slides her hands up Michelle's spine. She feels the tension in her friend's neck and shoulder blades. "Wanna tell me what this is about?"

"It's the latest addition to my file. I took it from Mary Ann."

"What?"

"Ms. White doesn't lock her office door. Or her file cabinets. All the other doors and windows in this place are shut tight, but not these precious files. Did you know that?"

Baker shakes her head.

"We had another meeting a few days ago, when you were out with your mom. Mary Ann asked me all these questions. I don't trust her, and I wanted to see what she wrote down. So this morning, I snuck in and swiped it from the office. And now I know: I'm *fucked*. This baby is fucked."

Michelle hands Baker the piece of paper.

Baker's body tightens, and she feels a spasm that begins somewhere behind her navel and radiates down through her inner thighs. The questions Mary Ann was asking, the answers she pretended to know. How Mary Ann told her it was just a formality.

LARSON, MICHELLE

The Mother was a high school drop-out who left
home mid-way through her junior year. She has some

secretarial training but has not held a job. The
Mother was of Swedish, Italian, Scotch, and "other
unknown" background. She was 5'5" in height and
120 lbs, with dark brown hair and hazel-green
eyes. She was interested in art and music. The
Mother's father was a high school graduate and
business owner. His health was described by the
Mother as "okay." The Mother's mother was a
homemaker who played organ in the church
choir. The Mother does not speak to either
parent.

Baker glances up. "It seems okay so far, I guess? It's weird that
it's in the past tense."
"Keep reading."

The Mother was dishonest about the baby's Father,
claiming to be "unaware" of his identity. She has
stated that the pregnancy was the result of a "one-
night stand" with a "stranger from a bar."
However, an internal investigation confirms that the
Mother does know the biological Father. Interviews
with parties with personal knowledge of the situation
confirm that the Father was a Negro with dark brown
skin and black hair worn in an "afro" style. He had
no known criminal record. No information known about
his father. His mother worked as a domestic and ran
a boarding home. The Father had one year of Junior
College. He had athletic interests. He was "against
the war."

The Mother complained of lower back pain but aside
from that had no immediate serious physical health
problems. The pregnancy was normal, though The Mother

```
stated that she used marijuana and LSD during the
early stage of the pregnancy.


The Mother was known to have fits of depression and
mood swings. When asked to describe her mental and
emotional state she said "Pretty unstable." The
Mother had one previous pregnancy and live birth, in
Spring of 1966. That baby was adopted through a
private agency in Florida. Exact DOB was unclear: The
Mother was unable to remember. The Mother "blacked
it all out." The Mother was described as talkative;
stubborn with a temper; defiant; beautiful; unfit.
```

"It's such bullshit," Michelle spits. "An *internal investigation?* They're spying on me?"

"Why did you lie about Barry?" Baker regrets the words immediately.

Michelle narrows her eyes. "Why are you asking me that? Are you on their side?"

"I'm so sorry. I shouldn't have said that."

Michelle sulks for a moment. "I know. I'm just upset."

Baker turns the paper over in her hands, examining it from all angles, until Michelle snatches it away and begins pointing to the bold, black words.

"The mother *was*," Michelle hisses. "The mother *was*. Like I'm not even *here*."

"It makes it sound like you're . . ."

"Dead?"

"Gone."

"And I never said that I'm unstable. They're putting words in my mouth to make me look bad. On my *permanent record*."

"But that's not right," Baker insists. "They can't just lie like that. Can they?"

A sharp laugh bursts from Michelle's full lips. "They can, and they do. I lie, they lie, we all lie. This is how they get us, Baker. This is how they keep us. Up against the wall. Trapped."

"What do you mean?"

"I'm marked for life now! Unfit, liar, druggie, all that. They might as well add *stupid idiot*."

"You're none of those things!"

"How else do you describe someone who checks into this place on purpose?"

"Hopeful?"

"Desperate."

"All of the above?" Baker looks at the paper again. "Did you really use LSD?"

"I didn't know I was pregnant, okay? I don't know why I ever told Mary Ann that. That's what I get for trusting her." Michelle is up now, pacing around the small room. "And the thing is, it's not even all about me, Baker, it's about *her*." She points to her belly. "A head-case druggie hippie having a Black baby? That's a one-way ticket to foster care. Do you understand? She's not even born yet, and I'm screwing it all up! Again."

Baker reaches out once more, this time bringing Michelle in for a hug. She feels her friend's body shake against her own quivering frame. It's rage, and it's fear. It's everything. Baker rubs Michelle's back, her mind spinning as she desperately searches for the right thing to say.

"She's not gonna end up in foster care, she's gonna have a great home with great parents and a great life."

Michelle pulls away. "You sound just like them. You don't know that, and neither do they. It's just what they tell us so we agree to give them our babies."

As if on cue, the Bun is suddenly awake and moving, pushing its foot or hand up under Baker's right rib. Baker puts her hand over her big round bump and tries to calm it all down. She thinks about the meeting she had with Mary Ann and Ms. White, and the first group counseling session. She tries to remember all their questions, all her answers. If they lied about Michelle, they'll probably lie about her. Did they really find a nice family for the Bun—for her *baby*? She breathes in and out, then looks her friend solemnly in the eyes.

"Michelle. We've got to get out of here."

Michelle opens her mouth to reply, but a wailing howl pierces the air. It comes from down the hall.

"It's Marcy," says Michelle, and they rush to the door. "I know it. She kept stopping on the walk yesterday because of cramping. She's past due. It's gotta be her."

They see Marcy at the top of the stairs, leaning against the banister, fingernails digging into the polished wood, barely able to stand. Anna is with her, and Baker hears footsteps coming up the stairs. Ms. White appears with a damp cloth and ice pack. Now Marcy's on her hands and knees, grunting, her pretty hair hanging in sweaty clumps.

Michelle rushes forward and takes the cloth from Ms. White, applies it to Marcy's forehead. Baker stands frozen, unable to move. It's the first time she's actually seen this. The other girls have all gone over in the night, which has led Baker to the false sense that it only happens in the dark.

Marcy heaves, then pounds her fist into the floor. Fluid spreads like dark ink spilled. Other girls gather, murmuring, *What should we do? Is she okay?* Baker feels someone gripping her hand, and she looks over to find Helen standing beside her.

"Poor Marcy," she says. "It looks so *painful*."

Ms. White begins to bark orders, and most of the girls spring into action. Lizzie goes downstairs to call Dr. Sullivan. Carol runs to get a glass of water. Anna appears with a stack of towels and a plastic container of pills that she hands to Ms. White.

Marcy vomits on the stairs. She pushes Ms. White and the pills away. Anna swoops in with a towel to mop the carpet.

"Breathe! Through your mouth! That's right! Don't hold your breath! Breathe, Marcy, breathe!" Ms. White is firm and in charge. She knows what she's doing, and that gives Baker a sense of comfort. This version of her feels so different from the dour lady who glares at her from across the desk in the office.

Helen grips Baker's hand even tighter, crushing her knuckles. Michelle catches Baker's eye across the chaos, and Baker gets it. *Not like this,* she imagines Michelle is thinking. *I'm not doing it like this again.* Michelle backs away and heads toward their room.

Soon they hear the sound of the front door opening and closing, then boots on the ground, a distinctly masculine stride. Two paramedics with a stretcher rush up the stairs, followed by Dr. Sullivan, who hasn't even had time to put on his white doctor coat. The men are an alien presence, like a father walking in on a sleepover party.

Once they've carried Marcy down the stairs, Baker eyes the stains left behind. Anna runs rags over them, but that seems futile. She can't tell what it is—blood? Urine? Sweat? Tears?—but it seems like gallons. Like an ocean. Like Marcy has liquefied, absorbed into the floor of the home forever.

"The dog days are here," Gerald always said once August rolled around. And then for the rest of the month, on the really hot days, he would squint at the outdoor thermometer on the fence by the pool, and go "Woof, woof!" It always made Baker laugh, but now the swollen heat of August is anything but funny. It's miserable. And the coming of September is no relief, either. It used to make Baker feel so happy—the return to school, the crisp leaves and structured days—but now it looms as something else entirely. Because after September comes October. She hears the voice of Dr. Bell back in Berkeley. *October. I'm rarely wrong.*

These August weeks feel extra long. Something shifted once Marcy went over: everything feels ready to blow. The walls of the home, the world beyond, and every girl in there. Bursting at the seams, all of it. Their bodies get bigger by the day, their due dates inch closer, and their tempers fray like old rope in the sun. The home is a vast field of land mines, and every interaction holds the potential for explosion. Viv is back to her surly self. Baker accidentally spills coffee during breakfast, and Lizzie snaps at her when a few drops speckle her shoe. Helen cries during a commercial for dog food, and then yells at Carol when she tries to pat her back. Janey's middle protrudes like a giant torpedo, ready to launch, and she looks like she'll tip over at any moment. Every time she gets up from a seat, she groans and grunts and has to pause to let the dizzy spells pass.

Baker finishes another latch-hook rug and helps Mrs. Williams grade the girls' *Jane Eyre* essays. Janey did a good job comparing herself to poor tortured Bertha, and it gives Baker a brief moment of joy to write a big red A on the top of her paper. Ida struggles with organization and sentence structure, but her ideas are solid, and Baker tries to highlight that in her notes in the margins. She discovers that Lizzie is a baseball fan, so they manage to watch a few Giants games together. Mays and McCovey, Marichal on the mound. It's a decent distraction, but Lizzie remains moody, and Baker can't shake the gnawing anxiety that something is not right.

And then there's Michelle: ever since she found the file, she's been off. She sleeps in past breakfast, and for a few days in a row, she barely gets out of bed at all. She blames it on the lower back pain, but Baker can tell it's more than that. It's an emotional exhaustion. A surrender. Baker starts sneaking pastries and coffee up to the room for her, trying to get her to eat something. But Michelle just lies there, barely picking at the food. She doesn't crack her usual jokes, she stops staying up to gossip in the dark, and she doesn't seem to care if Baker reads Plath poems out loud or not. When Baker brings an apricot Danish, her favorite, she doesn't touch it.

By the last weekend in August, Baker's hot and tired and crabby, too. To cool down, she wets her washcloth and lays it across her forehead, drapes it around the back of her neck. She lies on her floor with the lights off, and Michelle doesn't even seem to notice that she's sprawled on the dusty floor. Kitty's unsent letter is still tucked up between the mattress and the bed slats, her name still written in graphite in the wardrobe.

KITTY WAS HERE
but she didn't want to be

Kitty was here. She *was*. And Baker can't escape the feeling that, somehow, she still is. What did she want? She wanted help. She wanted to get out. She wanted to be okay.

Anna tried to help. But Kitty ran. And then she fell. And then she was . . . *gone,* Anna said. She was gone. Gone like Marcy, and Lydia?

Or gone like . . . *gone*? Baker knows she needs to tell Michelle about it, but now it seems too late. Michelle has given up. She gets out her journal and writes in the dark, tries to capture the details of how it all feels.

She covers them all—snarling Viv, emotional Helen, giant Janey, precious Ida—and she envisions where they'll go, what they'll become. She writes about Michelle, catatonic and sad; how she wishes she could make a phone call to someone, anyone, and fix it all for her. She writes about Rose at home, deep into a lifetime of compromise and cover-up, composure and constraint. Waiting for Baker to be done so they can all move on. So they can all forget. Her former classmates, probably off partying and preparing for college. And Marcy—will she get to go back to school soon? Reenter the world with her big smile, tell everyone about her time recuperating with the bears up in Oregon, and then forge ahead with college like nothing ever happened?

She writes about May, living off the land, and her invitation. Would it be better than this? Of course, Baker reasons. Most things would be better, including whatever damp, dusty hut May might offer. But then what? Communal forest living doesn't exactly appeal to Baker—she never felt like she fit in with May's friends. Does she want to share her daily life with them? So cut off from the rest of the world? It's hard enough being trapped in here, no consistent evening news, no daily paper to read. Baker hates not knowing what's happening in the world, and May's friends have always been the opposite. *Turn on, tune in, drop out.* Baker has already been forced to drop out, and she can't stand being tuned out, too. And, of course, the bigger question: What about the Bun? *The baby?* The reality. It doesn't even seem possible to imagine another option than the one she's being . . . offered? Provided? Forced into? She tries several words and phrases, but nothing quite captures the depth and breadth of what it all is, what it all feels like. *Maybe that's part of keeping it all a secret,* she writes. *If we don't have the language for it, we can't tell anyone what happened.*

$\mathcal{R}$ose calls on Monday afternoon, and they discuss the weather, a little bit of news: the bomb scare that cleared the dugouts at Shea Stadium; the Democratic National Convention in Chicago and Rose's worries about people making trouble there. She doesn't mention May, and Baker wonders if Rose even knows that her niece now lives on a commune. It seems plausible that May could get away with failing to mention to her parents that she's left San Francisco. As long as she calls home once in a while, they likely won't suspect a thing.

It's hard for Baker to make light chitchat over the phone with Rose after their visit. She has so many follow-up questions, but the distance feels too great. It was different when they were together, in the car. Just as Baker is about to start saying her goodbyes, Rose's tone shifts.

"We are almost to the end of this," Rose says. Baker wants to scream, *What do you mean* we? And then Rose brings up Mary Ann, who has called Rose to discuss some "challenges."

"This is unacceptable, Elizabeth," Rose continues. "We are all working very hard for you. You will meet with Ms. White this week and sign the documents. There is nothing to discuss or negotiate. Please just do what is asked of you."

Baker leans against the wall, curling the long black phone cord around her finger, tighter and tighter until the circulation slows and the tip of her finger turns white and numb. She scans the room as her mother lectures her: all the paintings on the wall, the stained glass, the old hearth, the sagging furniture. Janey, sitting in her favorite chair, fat feet propped up on an ottoman. The red fire alarm that sits on the wall.

IN CASE

OF EMERGENCY

BREAK GLASS

"Is this clear, Elizabeth?"

"Yes, Mother."

"You will take care of the paperwork?"

"I will," Baker says, but behind her back, she has her fingers crossed. Like she's seven years old and doesn't want to get in trouble for lying. It's not *untrue,* she reasons to herself. She *will* take care of the paperwork. She's just not sure what, exactly, she will do with it.

That night, dinner is pork chops and applesauce and mushy carrots bathing in butter. The girls take their seats and eat like they do every night, like nothing has happened and nothing will happen. Marcy's seat remains empty. No one's going to sit in it, just like no one's going to touch her half-empty jar of cold cream that still sits on the ledge above the bathroom sink.

It's the inevitable ending to everyone's stay there. No point in rehashing, or in asking questions out loud. But they hang suspended, unanswered, like the cherries in the too-sweet lime Jell-O they're served for dessert: Will Marcy be okay? Does she get to see the baby? Will they ever see her again?

After dinner, Lizzie goes to get her guitar, while the rest of the girls turn on the television. Baker remains at the table, picking at the crumbs from her cornbread muffin, when she hears her name being called.

"Baker! Come see this." It's Viv, calling from the rec room, and her cool, collected voice has a hot streak of urgency. Baker heaves herself up and walks over, pausing at the doorway to observe the scene. The girls are transfixed, eyes glued to the television, hands over their mouths. Ms. White is there, which is odd, and she looks like she's working hard to appear not-worried. When a few girls glance at her for reassurance, Ms. White gives a thin smile. But when they turn back to the screen, her hand flits to her mouth, and Baker watches as she chews on a cuticle.

It's the Democratic National Convention in Chicago, and the scenes playing out on the evening news are chaotic. Huge crowds of people, mostly young, chanting *PEACE NOW! PEACE NOW!* And so many police.

They march in a thick line: helmets on, visors down, wielding black batons. Like a storm front over a war zone. The sound of their boots stepping in unison. Then the tanks, and the bus: CHICAGO POLICE DEPARTMENT big and black on the side. The vehicles push against the defiant crowd; arms and fists pump in the air. Bottles are flying, voices are crying, the police lines are pushing with plastic shields against the crowd of protesters until it seems to break open, and the police are pouring into the crowds.

Janey looks up at Baker, her big eyes even bigger. "They punched Dan Rather," she whispers.

Baker has seen America's upheavals on TV before. In April, she watched the streets of Chicago, Baltimore, and DC burn and bleed in the wake of Dr. King's death, neighborhoods aflame, caskets on the tarmac. She watched those students marching and chanting at Columbia University, and last summer, too, the long hot one when Detroit exploded and Gerald shook his head in dismay.

But this feels different.

When tear gas is released, the girls gasp. White clouds billow; the crowd panics and runs; the police give chase. It's all there, right in front of their eyes, and they cannot look away. The shaky camera captures young men in horn-rimmed glasses climbing trees, screaming insults from above like furious birds. From a distance, the movement of the bodies is almost beautiful, this mass of figures moving so fast, all at once, together. But there are up-close shots, too, and this is when Janey begins to cry, and Lizzie shouts, and Viv grips the arm of the sofa and gasps.

The batons rise and fall, smashing down on the bodies. One of the young men looks like Wiley, with the cowboy shirt and everything. Baker gets closer and squints at the screen. *Is it him?*

Ida shrieks. "I didn't know police were allowed to do that to people!"

Lizzie rolls her eyes and scoffs. "What else do you think pigs do?"

"That's enough," snaps Ms. White.

The camera cuts to a woman in a pink dress and overcoat with a matching handbag who steps out of the crowd, waving a hand at an officer as he shoots blasts of stinging pepper spray. She looks like one of Baker's aunts, a nice older white lady. *No,* it looks like she's saying, *No no no!* She steps up onto the back bumper of a packed paddy wagon and appears to be singing. Her eyes are closed, and she holds on to the doors, refusing the orders of the officers. An officer pulls her from behind while another pries her hand from the wagon door. She's still singing as they push her in and slam the doors.

"The crowd behind me is chanting," yells the broadcaster, trying to be heard over the persistent shouting. "They're saying *'The whole world is watching. The whole world is watching.'* We are live in Chicago on August twenty-eighth, 1968, and *the whole world is—*"

"Well, we aren't. Not anymore." Ms. White turns the silver knob, and the TV is off. "We don't need to see this madness."

The girls cry out, their own small protest.

"This is important," cries Lizzie. "This is *real life.*"

"Please," says Janey. "I've never seen anything like this."

"The television is off. Your lives are real enough."

"Turning it off doesn't mean it's not happening, ma'am," says Viv.

"How else are we supposed to know what to expect when we leave this place?" Lizzie crosses her arms and pouts. "If you really cared, you'd let us watch."

"Ha!" The sharp crack of Ms. White's laugh stuns them all into silence. Her eyes narrow as she scans the room. Her voice stays even, but the veins on her neck reveal her anger. "I'm not sure that any of you realize what we've done for you, what I'm doing for you, each and every day. Maybe you never will. But I do. I know." She takes a deep breath, smooths the front of her skirt and jacket, and walks out of the room.

In the morning, Baker goes to breakfast while Michelle stays in bed, her pillow pulled over her head, her sheets and quilt twisted around her legs. Baker sips her tea and nibbles on coffee cake with brown sugar crumble on top and isn't surprised at all when no one mentions what they saw on TV last night. They don't say a word about Ms. White's outburst, but when she walks into the dining room to say good morning, they exchange knowing glances, wordlessly noting the dark circles, her slightly puffy eyes, the fact that she seems to have forgotten to pencil in her right eyebrow.

Ms. White keeps her announcements brief: "Good morning, girls—that coffee cake certainly smells delicious. Eat up, enjoy. I'll see you at two P.M. for our outing."

Baker's heart begins to race at the mention of the outing. Since her phone call with Rose, she's been forming a plan, and she's been running it over in her head all morning. Plotting each move and analyzing all possible outcomes. She's got it figured out. Today's the day, and if she's going to break the rules, she's going to do it perfectly. She glances around, convinced that the other girls can sense her nervous energy. But they're wrapped up in their conversations, downing their glasses of juice and chatting about the day. She feels like an undercover operative, a potentially heroic spy.

At 1:45, Baker is sitting in the front room, pretending to read a magazine while she waits for the girls to gather. She watches as they get their rings, then follows them to the front door to send them off.

Ms. White looks at Baker. "No Ms. Larson today?"

"No, ma'am. She's still in bed with back pain."

"I do wish you could come with us, Baker," says Helen. "It's not fair that you still have to stay behind."

"Life's not fair, kiddo," cracks Lizzie. "Have you learned nothing?" Then she turns to Baker and puts a firm hand on her shoulder. "But I agree that it's bullshit you can't come."

"Language, Lizzie," squawks Ms. White as she puts on her hat and opens the front door. Baker leans toward it, gulping in the fresh air. It smells like sidewalks and grass, eucalyptus and cars, dirt and electricity. It smells like a city. She breathes in again as the girls file past.

Mary Ann is joining the walk today, and she glances at Baker. "I look forward to our meeting this week, Elizabeth."

Viv leans over and whispers to Baker as she heads out. "Hey, I know Michelle always brings you treats. I'll try to bring you back something nice."

Ms. White closes the door, and Baker hears the lock click as the key is turned outside. She opens the peephole and watches them head up the block. Lizzie swings her arms like a little kid, Janey and Anna stay close to Ms. White. Viv struts, and young Ida loops her arm through Viv's. Helen holds out her hand as they pass a row of overgrown shrubbery, lets her fingers trail over the little green leaves.

Once they're out of sight, Baker is ready. She knows exactly what needs to happen. First she walks a lap of the first floor of the home, scanning each room to make sure there's truly no one else there. The kitchen, the dining room, the rec room: all empty. Michelle's upstairs, probably asleep. For at least an hour, the coast is as clear as it's going to be.

Michelle was right: Ms. White doesn't lock her office. Baker slips inside and closes the door behind her. The curtains are drawn tight, and only slits of sun sneak through. Her eyes scan the dim room, in search of the pieces of paper that, according to Michelle, will determine the future. Her future, and her baby's. What are they saying about her? What's on this permanent record? Have they made up any lies, twisted her words? She also wants to know about this perfect family who wants her baby. Are they real? What if she could just *see* a photo of them? Glimpse their faces, judge whether they seem kind, capable, *upstanding*.

She heads across the room to the file cabinet, passing Ms. White's desk. The drawer labeled PA-PR slides out smoothly; she flips through folder after folder until she finds the one labeled PHIL-LIPS, ELIZABETH B. It's right there, in her trembling hand.

She backs away from the cabinet slowly, like it might come after her, lunge like a monster in a horror film. She doesn't see the small cardboard box on the floor until she's stumbling over it.

The box is light, and it makes little sound when she picks it up and shakes it. It's addressed to Mr. and Mrs. H. G. Miller of Sioux Falls, Idaho, but written in large letters next to the names, it says:

PARCEL REFUSED

RETURN TO SENDER

Baker opens it. On top is a sweater, then a skirt, then a floral cotton dress. She lifts the pale pink sweater and holds it up. It has tiny pearl buttons, and a name embroidered on the chest in delicate white script. Her breath catches in her throat for one, two, three full seconds.

Of course it's you, Kitty.

Then she remembers the envelope she'd seen on Ms. White's desk. The one labeled *CONFIDEN*—. She tries to look through the piles of paper and stacks of folders and envelopes as quickly—and neatly—as possible. At the bottom of a pile near the edge of the desk, she sees it. The red capital letters telling her not to look. She pulls the envelope toward her:

C O N F I D E N T I A L.

Secret. Dangerous.

She tears it open.

Sheaves of paper come tumbling out, some falling onto the floor. Baker grabs them, trying to reorganize them as fast as she can.

A police report. Pages and pages of what she realizes are witness statements. A letter from a doctor. A single page with a header that includes the word *CORONER*. Baker sinks to the floor and tries to take it all in. The type is small and hard to read; her hands shake; her eyes leap across the pages, landing on words and phrases she can barely believe:

```
subject found unconscious
base of stairs
non-responsive
broken neck
Time of death: 4:45am, July 18, 1967
Cause of death: Suicide
```

Baker clutches her chest. Her fingers dig into her skin. She is a petrified statue for a few seconds, until her body remembers how to release. She reads the page again.

"This isn't true. She didn't want to die." She can't help but say it aloud, even though she's trying to be quiet. Anna told her. Kitty didn't mean to fall. Kitty was trying to get help. She looks at the witness statements.

```
Anna Brown, age 16:

I saw her in the bathroom. Then she ran away and I
heard her fall down the stairs. That's all I
remember.

Mrs. Mary Ann Carver:

She was a troubled girl with a history of behavioral
problems that preceded her time here. In our sessions
she expressed gratitude for the care she received
here. Sadly, she also expressed a desire to take her
own life.
```

Ms. Carolyn White:

I am heartbroken over this tragic and isolated
incident. We all did our best to care for the young
woman but sadly her will to end her life was too
strong.

Baker has seen enough. She's aware, suddenly, of the temperature, and feels overwhelmed with a feverish flush. Sweat pools on her brow, the nape of her neck, beneath her bra so her blouse becomes damp. The room begins to tilt, and she feels like she just stepped off an out-of-control merry-go-round. A wave of nausea rises up, and she shuts her eyes tight.

Kitty is dead. Not just gone, but dead.

Kitty was desperate.

Kitty was just trying to save herself.

She was doing her best.

Kitty didn't mean to die.

But now that's her permanent record.

And Kitty is trying to warn me.

Baker puts her file, and the confidential paperwork, in the box, snuggled underneath the sweater, and gets herself out of the office, up the stairs, into her room. She tries to be quiet, not wanting to wake Michelle, who snores softly underneath her quilt. She puts the box in the wardrobe but keeps the file with her name on it. She sits on her bed, panting heavily, shoulders heaving, and begins to read:

The Mother was the valedictorian. She was in perfect
health. The Mother was from a very good home. The
Mother was deeply remorseful about her situation. The
Mother was eager to place her child with a good
family. She never considered anything else but the
adoption process.

The Father was a soldier. His parents are deceased.
The Father was known to be healthy and widely seen
as handsome.

The Mother was bright and ambitious, yet naïve and
frightened.

Baker gets the journal from under the bed. It all pours out of her,
line after line and page after page, and soon it becomes clear. She
thinks of her mother, spilling her secrets, passing on her advice:

> *We do what we have to do*
> *We make it through the damn day*
> *Then we wake up tomorrow and do it again*

Baker knows what to do, and she needs to tell Michelle. She
stares at her sleeping friend. "Michelle! Are you awake?"

From under the blankets, Michelle issues a muffled "No."

Baker has no time to waste. If she wasn't so big, she'd be bouncing on the bed, dragging Michelle out by her arm. "Wake up. *Now.*
We have to talk."

"Can it wait?" Michelle's body stirs, but the covers stay over her
head.

"NO." Baker yanks the blankets off, exposing a curled-up, now-
angry Michelle.

"Hey!"

Baker wants to scream, but she knows she has to keep it down.
She has to be careful. She leans in close to Michelle.

"We're leaving." The words may be whispered, but they're loud as
hell.

Michelle rubs her eyes and sits up. "What?"

The smile on Baker's face is wild, undeniable. She looks like a
captive who's learned that the cavalry is coming. Like a captive

who's figured out how to free herself. "Or at least, I am. And I want you to come with me."

"What are you talking about?"

Baker walks over and sits on the edge of Michelle's bed. She strokes Michelle's sweaty, matted hair.

"I know this sounds crazy, but I've made up my mind. We gotta get out of here."

Michelle squints up at Baker's determined face.

"When?"

"As soon as possible. I have a plan."

"A *plan*?"

"It's solid. We can do this, Michelle."

"Baker, I'm so confused." Michelle holds out her arm and pulls up the bell sleeve of her blouse. "Go ahead, pinch it. I'm obviously dreaming."

She gives Michelle's soft skin the slightest tweak, then kisses the spot. "See? You're wide awake. And so am I."

"This isn't like you."

Baker laughs and gestures to her body. "Neither is this! Look, I've thought it over." She drops her voice to an even quieter whisper. "We'll go down to the Grove, where my cousin May is living."

"The commune?"

"Shhh! May says anyone is welcome there. And there's women there with babies. Pregnant ones, too. It's not really my scene, but it's better than this. You could stay there, Michelle, you really could."

"And what if it's not my scene, either? Did you think of that? I'm having a baby any day now, my friend."

"We'll figure it out."

"And what about you? If it's not for you?"

"I still don't know."

Michelle laughs. "Some plan!"

"All I know is I'm going to figure it out. But I can't do that in here. We gotta go." She points out the window and takes a deep breath. She feels her words forming in her chest, as if they're hatching from her heart. "I'm done letting other people decide for me." It feels triumphant. And terrifying.

"Whoa!" Michelle runs her fingers through her tangles and rubs her massive middle. "And how are we going to get out of here, boss?"

"I'll tell you after dinner."

"And how will we get there?"

Baker takes a deep breath. "You're going to call Barry. For a ride."

"Oh, really? And if I decide not to come? What's your plan then?"

Baker sits up straight, pulls her shoulders back. "I'll hitch. I've done it before."

"Damn, sister." Michelle whistles. "I did not see this coming."

"That's precisely why it's going to work."

"You good girls are really something."

"So what do you say? Will you come?"

"I have to think about it." Michelle winces and puts her head in her hands. "This is unexpected. And heavy. And, like, really fucking nuts."

"I'm sorry to spring it on you like this. It's been on my mind, but I didn't know if I could really do it. I had to consider all the angles. And then today was just the last straw."

"What happened?"

Baker walks over to her bed and holds up her file.

Michelle groans. "Fuck."

"Exactly. But it's not just this, Michelle." Baker's face gets tight, and her eyes narrow. She gets the box from the wardrobe. "I need to tell you about Kitty."

The latch-hook rug group is small today, and Baker is relieved. Marcy's gone, of course, and Helen isn't feeling up for much these days, so she stays in her room, along with several others who are just too far along to want to come downstairs to hook endless pieces of yarn.

As they pick up their projects and get to work, Baker's heart is about to burst out of her body. She taps her foot and bounces her knee until Michelle leans over and puts a hand on her thigh.

"Relax," she whispers.

"I can't!"

Viv glances over and raises a thin eyebrow. Lizzie catches on and gives Baker a quizzical look. Baker can't stop glancing at Ms. Charlotte, who seems to be panting in the heat. Sweat glistens on her pink forehead, and a single drop trickles down her cheek. She doesn't move to brush it away. Finally, she stands up, clasping her handbag.

"Goodness, it's warm! I'm going to step outside for some air, girls. Carry on with your work."

The door has barely closed behind her when the girls all look to Baker.

"Spill it," says Viv.

Lizzie puts her hands on her knees and leans forward. "Something's up. We can tell."

Baker looks around at each girl's face. Lizzie's dark eyes are narrowed. Anna looks confused, like she's in the wrong meeting but doesn't know how to walk away. Viv sits back with her arms crossed, and Janey looks nervous. Michelle stares back, head cocked, ready to hear the plan.

Baker takes a deep breath and begins. "I need to tell you something. But I need to know I can trust you."

Lizzie raises her right hand. "Scout's honor."

"I'm serious," Baker says, her voice heavy and hard.

"You can trust me," Janey says.

Viv leans in. "We're in this shit together, aren't we? Semper fi, soldier."

Baker glances toward Ms. White's office, then begins. "It's about a girl who used to live here. Her name was Kitty."

Baker looks at Anna, whose already pale face goes even whiter. Baker tries to speak with her eyes. *Is it okay if I talk about her?* Anna bites her lips. Baker continues.

"She died here. In this house."

The girls begin talking over one another, but Baker just keeps speaking. "And Ms. White and Mary Ann have been covering up the truth about it." She pauses as the girls' chatter turns to looks of horror. "Kitty lived in my room, in my bed, and I don't know how to explain it, but it's like she's still here."

Lizzie is fascinated. "Like a ghost?"

Anna grips the carved wooden arms of the chair she sits in, and whispers, "Have you . . . seen her?"

"Not quite. It's hard to describe. It's more like . . . a presence. She left things for me. Clues, notes, her name written in the wardrobe, and in my copy of *Jane Eyre*."

Anna closes her eyes, and Baker wonders if she'd had any idea that her roommate was in such a bad state. Did Anna know that Kitty had written in the wardrobe? Did she see her hide the letter under the bed? Did she know she was trying to get help? Or was Kitty always good at keeping secrets?

Viv crosses her arms and looks skeptical. "You think this *presence* is trying to tell you something?"

"Yes, Viv. I'm certain of it. She wants us to know she was here. She wants us to understand what really happened."

The girls go quiet.

"So what did happen to her?"

"Anna knows. She was there."

Anna looks up. "She hurt herself."

"How?"

Baker remembers how distraught Anna was that night in the bathroom. She feels protective, and a little guilty for the way she pressed Anna to keep talking that night. "Anna, you don't have to—"

"It's okay," Anna whispers, looking at the floor. "I can talk about it. She was the sweetest girl, but she was always so sad. She was my roommate, and my first friend here. My only friend, really. She didn't talk about it much, but I know she was really scared. Something bad happened to her back home. With her father." Anna pauses and looks up. The girls are stone-faced. "She really didn't want to go back there. And she really didn't want to be pregnant. I mean, none of us really do, right, but she was . . . she was trying to make it go away. She did things to herself, you know, things that are supposed to end it." So Anna did know something. In an impossibly quiet voice, Anna tells them what happened that night in the bathroom. The girls sit in stunned shock.

"Poor Kitty," says Lizzie.

"Poor Anna," adds Viv.

Baker continues, her voice solemn and clear. "I found documents in Ms. White's office. Police records." The girls raise their eyebrows, shoot one another looks, but Baker just keeps talking. "They ruled Kitty's death a suicide."

Anna cries out. "But that's not true! She didn't want to die; she told me so. She was trying to get out!"

Baker continues. "And the report leaves out what else Anna saw—the rubber tubing, the coat hanger. The stuff she used to try to . . . end it."

"But why would they—" Janey stops herself before the other girls can scoff at her naïveté. "Never mind. I get it. They wanted to cover it up, didn't they?"

Viv claps Janey on the back. "That sure is what it seems like. If a girl died on accident here, they'd be in big trouble."

"Probably get sued," Lizzie adds with authority. "Lose their license."

Viv whistles and shakes her head. "And if they found out she was trying to give herself an abortion? Not a good look."

Anna's eyes are closed. Her nostrils flare, and she clenches her fists.

Janey scoots over and takes Anna's hand. "Why didn't you tell us any of this, Anna?"

"I couldn't. They told me if I say anything, I can't stay here anymore. And now I just told you all. What if they find out?"

"Your secret is safe with us," Baker reassures her. "And besides: they're about to have other things to worry about."

"Like what?"

"This is the other secret. Promise again that I can trust you all?"

Viv sticks her little finger out. "Pinkie swear." The other girls hook their pinkies. Then Janey looks at Baker and puts her hand over her heart.

"I swear to Jesus. That's a way bigger deal than a pinkie swear."

"Thank you." Baker breathes deep again. "I don't have much time to explain, but first I want to tell you that I really love you all."

The girls are both flattered and confused.

"We've gone from being total strangers to being . . . friends." Baker chokes up on the word. She's always been content with her solitude, her lack of a big social circle. She's had May, her other cousins, friendly acquaintances at school. But this is different. What if she'd had more friends, *true* friends, back when she'd made that appointment? If there'd been someone other than May to drive her, to talk to, to help? "Good friends. *True* friends. I've never really had that. And I need to know if you'll help me."

"Of course," Lizzie says right away.

"It depends," says Viv.

Janey's voice shakes. "What do you need, Baker?"

"Get to the point," hisses Michelle. "Ms. Charlotte's smoke break won't last much longer."

"I'm leaving. And I'm going to need—"

Michelle interrupts. "Correction: we're leaving."

Baker whips her head around. "We are?"

Michelle takes her hand. "We are."

The girls explode in hushed tones, spilling over with questions and concerns. Baker's not the kind to break the rules—they all know that.

"And we'll need you to cover for us so we can get as far away as we can before they realize we're gone."

Janey's face is solemn. "But you *can't* leave. You'll get in trouble. And I'll miss you."

"I'll miss you too, Janey. But we all leave at some point. We're just going . . . on different terms."

"Where are you going? And what are you going to do?"

"I can't tell you, because I know they're going to ask you. And I don't want you to hold any more lies."

Viv crosses her arms. "That's smart. But they're going to find you. You're willing to get in this much trouble?"

"This already *is* trouble, Viv. I need to make my own decisions."

"Can they arrest you for this?"

"I don't know. But I'm willing to risk it. I'm done being told what to do. By anyone. Except Kitty, that is." Baker smiles, and she and Anna both look up, as if Kitty might be hovering above them, watching and approving.

"I'm in," says Janey. "And I wish I could come with you."

"I wish you could, too. I wish we could all leave. I mean, if you want to, we could probably—"

"Let's just stick with you and Michelle for now. Okay?" Lizzie smiles and sticks out her hand. "Shall we discuss details?" Baker shakes it, and Michelle puts her hand on top of theirs. Anna adds hers.

*I*t takes another week to get everything set. To make the phone calls to Barry while the girls are out on their walk with Ms. White, to send a postcard to May, to gather up the courage and the will to go through with it. Michelle is getting bigger and slower by the day. Dr. Sullivan told her that second babies can sometimes come sooner, that she should be ready for anything, so Baker begins sneaking extra towels and washcloths from the bathroom and hiding them in the plaid suitcase that sits under her bed. Just in case. She's seen enough girls go over now—she knows it gets messy. She wants to be prepared.

When they finally decide that the plan is a "go," that the girls can be trusted, that Barry is on board, Baker prepares to leave. That evening before dinner, she cleans their entire room. She wipes down the windowsill with a damp cloth, then runs it over the nightstands. Then she does it several more times, her heart racing and her body jumping any time she hears footsteps outside her door. She sweeps the floor and empties the wastebasket and wipes down the bedframe and the dresser and the little lamp beside her bed, and when there is absolutely nothing else left to clean, it's time to pack. She still can't believe they're going to do this, and she worries that if she stops moving, she'll lose her nerve entirely.

She decides to leave most of the ugly maternity clothes, so she packs just enough clothing to get her by for a few days. The necessities: giant underpants, a few pairs of socks, the big ugly bras she unfortunately needs. A few cotton blouses, one pair of pants, and the simplest dress that she has. She is *not* bringing those awful girdles. Maybe the other girls can use them.

She opens the closet and breathes in. The smell of cedar, wool, a weak lavender sachet, the industrial strength detergent they use in the home. She gets the box and places it on the bed. Then she stares at the stupid dresses with their high collars and floppy neck bows. The fussy blouses. The itchy wool skirts with the busy patterns to "distract the eye." She feels a pang of guilt, knowing that Rose spent good money on the clothes, and then she remembers what she's about to do. She laughs at herself. *Someday you'll know what I mean,* Rose had said, and Baker hopes her mother remembers her own words. *We do what we have to do.* Left-behind clothes will be the least of her worries. She stares at the list of names that she found carved into the wood.

MARGARET
DONNA
PATTY
CATHERINE
MARY
KITTY

She grabs a pencil from the pile of belongings on the bed and writes herself in:

Baker "a free human being with an independent will"

Next, she sorts through her pile of May's treasures and locates the matchbook from the Golden Cask. It goes into her pocket. Then she reaches—slowly, awkwardly—under the bed to retrieve Kitty's unsent letter. She opens the cardboard box and takes out Kitty's pink sweater, and all of her files: the police reports, the witness statements, the letter from the coroner. All of it goes in the small suitcase. It's getting crowded.

You're coming with me, Kitty.

I'm getting you out of here.

I'm setting you free.

She places her journal on top and smiles. She's going to do something with all these stories. Something that matters.

You're ALL coming with me.

She's going to do right by all these good girls.

One last thing: she gets her file, the one labeled PHILLIPS, ELIZABETH B, and puts it in the cardboard box. From beneath Michelle's pillow, she gets the one labeled LARSON, MICHELLE. That goes in the cardboard box, too.

She hears the doors opening and footsteps in the hallway. Dinnertime. She puts the box back in the wardrobe and begins to zip the plaid suitcase. It seems unbearably loud, and she freezes, terrified that Ms. White might hear it from all the way downstairs. But no one else hears the tiny metal teeth of a single zipper as they slide together, leaving the smooth closed line behind.

They all work hard to appear as normal as possible during dinner. Michelle sits next to Baker, like they've done every evening since they've been there, and they eat and chat with the other girls as if it's not their last night, as if everything is not about to change.

After dinner they go into the rec room for an episode of *The Dating Game,* a show Baker really can't stand. Usually she insists that they change the channel, and if the girls are set on watching the wide-eyed ladies asking pompous men inane questions, she leaves the room. But tonight she stays right there, wedged between Viv and Janey on the couch. Lizzie sits on the floor, her legs straight out ahead of her, her ankles thick, her bare feet swollen. Anna sits in the rocking chair, crocheting something pink.

Baker looks around at each girl, their faces relaxed and happy, temporarily transported. She's going to miss them. The thought makes her sit up straight, a new pang in her chest. She's learned bits and pieces from each of them, and she's imagined and written them various possible futures, but suddenly she worries that she doesn't know enough. That she should have asked them more questions: what they fear and believe and think and dream of. She knows a little about what they'd *like* to do next. But nothing is certain. Their stories will unfold, and she won't get to know them.

On the TV, a pretty blonde with giant eyes is asking questions of three men in suits who sit grinning behind a partition. They smirk and try to one-up one another with their clever answers. *What's your best feature? Are you wild or tame?* Then she asks:

"If there were no rules, what would you do first?" It gets the girls' attention.

Viv barks out a laugh. "What the hell kind of question is that?"

"Does she mean no rules *at all?*"

"Is gravity a rule? Because I'd like to fly!"

"If there were no rules, none of us would be here in the first place," Viv points out.

"I'd be wearing a bikini, floating in a pool at some rich person's mansion, sipping on a daiquiri," says Lizzie. "I'd look like Humpty Dumpty, but I don't care."

Then Baker opens her mouth. "If there were no rules, I'd leave here tonight."

She can't believe she said it out loud. She sits frozen on the couch, bracing for the reactions. What if she blows their cover? But the girls are game, ready to play along. They crack up at the sheer absurdity of Baker breaking the rules.

"But you'd *never* do that," Viv says loudly.

"I don't think you'd even know how!" Lizzie glances to the main room, checking to see if Ms. White is in earshot.

"Can you *imagine*," Michelle howls.

Viv keeps it going. "She'd probably ask permission before busting out!"

Baker ducks her head. "Okay, guys, you got me. What can I say? I'm a good girl!"

They turn back to the TV to see what these men would do in a world with no rules. Viv reaches over and squeezes Baker's shoulder. Lizzie nudges her lightly in the ribs, which actually hurts a little. Every part is feeling so tender these days. Baker takes in their faces as she's done so many times. But this time, she realizes, is probably the last. The truth is jarring: she'll never see them again. Will Viv's teacher really be waiting for her? Did Carl wait for Janey? Will Anna stay here forever? When does Ida turn fifteen? Will she see Lizzie's face on an album cover someday; will she buy her record and recognize that voice? And is Lizzie's libber lawyer aunt right—is everything actually going to change? It's gutting to realize that she won't get to follow all these stories. But Baker is glad she at least knows this chapter. And these magnificent, complicated characters.

Baker is heading back to her room when she hears someone call her name. It's Helen. Her door is open. She wasn't downstairs with the others watching TV.

"I have something for you, Baker."

"You do?"

Helen is huge now. She stands up slowly and squats down next to her bed, huffing and puffing with each movement. She pulls out a box of yarn and picks up the item on top. It's folded, so Baker can't tell what it is, but she can see the warm colors. And how soft it looks.

"It's a scarf. I was making it for myself, for winter, but I think you should have it." She offers a small smile, her wise eyes soft as moss. "In case it's cold where you're going."

"Where I'm going?"

Helen leans in and whispers. "It's okay. I'm not going to say anything."

Baker peers into Helen's kind face. "How do you . . . ?"

Helen shrugs. "I told you, I pay attention. And for what it's worth, I admire you. I think you're really brave, Baker."

"You can come with us."

She shakes her head. "I can't. But I'm happy for you."

Baker lifts the scarf to her face and breathes it in. It smells cozy, and the yarn is soft against her cheek. "Thank you. Good luck, Helen."

"You, too."

Baker wraps the scarf around her neck and heads to her room, her heart rattling in her chest.

Baker and Michelle brush their teeth and wash their faces. They rub on the cold creams, they make small talk in the bathroom line. They get one last little sip of water, say *good night* as if it's just another night. And then it's lights out. Their last one. Michelle's bag is packed, stashed under her bed. The phone call to Barry has been made, and the plan is set. They're ready to go. Somehow Michelle manages to fall asleep, right away, while Baker lies there, blinking in the dark. She listens to the sounds outside her room as the girls settle down, toss and turn, the old bedframes creaking and whining under the restless bodies. She watches the moon rise in a slow arc across the night sky outside. The Bun seems to be moving more than usual, and Baker thinks it must feel her nerves. She rubs her belly and whispers softly.

It's okay, baby Bun, it's okay. I told you, I've got this.

When she feels the response, how it seems to tap from within, she can't help but tap back, say hello through layers of skin and muscle.

Around midnight, when the house is finally silent, she stands up slowly and begins to move in the dark. She's rehearsed each step, each move, each word.

She checks to make sure her suitcase is under the bed, ready to go.

She makes her bed and fluffs her single pillow.

She wraps Helen's scarf around her neck.

She gets the cardboard box from the wardrobe and wedges it under one arm.

She whispers to Michelle. "Here I go. See you soon."

She opens her door and steps into the dark hall.

She pauses at each door to say a silent goodbye and to leave a little gift.

She slips the comb under Janey's door. *Goodbye Farmer Janey, This comb can hold your hair back while you're waiting those tables.*

She puts the "God is a teenybopper" pin under Lizzie's door, even though Baker wants to keep it. *Take care, Lizzie—maybe you can wear this pin when you play your first concert.*

She leaves the Shakespeare for Viv, one of the old *Life* magazines for Anna, a marble that looks like the sky for Helen. Then she heads to the stairs and pauses at the top. The stained glass iris is a muddy blur in the dark.

She absolutely should not be doing this. But she absolutely is going to anyway.

Her heart is a bell, ringing loud in her chest. She grips the box with one arm and squeezes the railing with the other hand, feels the smooth worn wood on her damp palm.

The main room is dark and still. She marvels at all it contains: all these girls, the wood walls absorbing how many years of whispered conversations, stifled cries, unanswered prayers and pleas. The screams of at least one girl as she fell down these stairs.

Baker feels winded and tired; a cramp grips her inner thighs.

It's time to stop thinking and to start doing. She swears she feels a soft push at her back, an invisible force that moves her down the stairs, along with another *Jane Eyre* line that she whispers to herself: "*Night was come, and her planets were risen: a safe, still night: too serene for the companionship of fear.*"

Too serene for the companionship of fear. *Yes.*

She repeats it as she tiptoes to the rec room to make a few donations. She pulls several records from the box under her arm and sneaks them into the tired old stack of albums by the record player. Then she puts her copy of *The Colossus* on the bookshelf, along with Michelle's copies of all three *Lord of the Rings* books. She's sad to say goodbye, but she likes to think of future girls sitting in here, listening to Dylan, lost in Plath's imagery and the depths of Middle Earth.

She creeps back into the main room, letting her fingertips brush the soft velvet of the couches, the lacquered tops of the end tables. She runs her hand across the cool stone hearth, the thin glass that protects the intricate workings of the broken grandfather clock. The walls are smooth and beautiful in the dark; the ceilings are high and grand. She realizes how loud a scream would sound, how deep it would pierce the night.

The office door swings open with a creak that echoes, it seems, throughout the entire house. Baker halts and holds her breath, but the house stays silent. She enters with purpose, the box held tight, and goes straight to the wastebasket next to the desk, which is filled halfway with wadded-up papers. The box fits perfectly in the wastebasket, just as she's been picturing it. She pulls her own file from the box and holds it up in front of her. Then she gets the matchbook from her pocket.

This is not what a good girl does.

She strikes the first match on the side of the desk. It hisses in the dark, then illuminates the room. Baker gasps, stunned that she lit it on the first try and awed by what she's about to do. She holds it to the bottom corner of her file and watches as the flame takes hold.

This is not what is expected of her.

She drops the burning paper into the cardboard box and grabs one of the pamphlets from the desk.

Scared? Unfit?

She lights that one on fire, as well.

This is not discreet.

At her feet, the contents of the cardboard box are burning. Michelle's files. All those lies.

Unstable. Unfit.

This is not upstanding.

She drops the pamphlet into the basket and watches the fire spread, devouring the box itself, catching on the wadded-up papers now, too.

Naïve.

Scared.

Soldier.

All those lies going up in smoke. Smoke filled with secrets, smoke filled with shame.

She grabs another pamphlet, strikes another match. Then another, and another, and then she leans over the desk, extends her arm, and sweeps the stacks and piles onto the floor.

This is not just about her and Michelle. This is about all of them. The records are no longer permanent.

Nothing is.

The flames leap. The smoke thickens. The fire is growing bigger than she expected, spreading fast, fueled by so much paper. Her eyes sting. She tries and fails to suppress a cough.

She backs out of the room, marveling at this massive mess she's just made. She feels exhilarated. And terrified. And proud. She closes the door behind her and gets ready to sneak back up the stairs so she can evacuate with the entire group, as if she'd never been down here at all. But first she goes to the red box on the wall by the front door.

IN CASE

OF EMERGENCY

BREAK GLASS

A small silver hammer hangs from a chain next to it. When she smashes the glass, it cracks like an ice sheet, and as the shards fall at her feet, the alarm begins to ring.

The smoke is seeping out from under the office door as Baker sneaks back up the stairs to meet the stampede of girls who will come rushing down the hallway. She knows that as soon as she heard the alarm, Michelle grabbed their bags and squeezed them through the small window opening. Now, she sees Michelle join the sleepy-eyed procession moving toward her. They murmur in confusion and excitement as the smell of smoke fills the hallway.

"I thought it was going to be a false alarm?"

Janey looks worried. "It's a *real fire*?"

Viv mouths *What is happening?*

Lizzie looks impressed and a little shocked.

Michelle grabs Baker's hand and pulls her into their ranks, hissing, "An *actual* fire? Are you mad?"

Baker shrugs, says nothing, and falls in with the girls as they head down the stairs to evacuate the building.

Ms. White, her hair in curlers, her face coated in cold cream, is at the front door in her robe and slippers. She is screaming for the girls to hurry, hurry.

"Anna," she cries, "Anna, I need your help! Headcounts, please!"

Anna rushes to the door, and Ms. White dashes around the main room, trying to gather valuables. The smoke is getting thicker, and the flames from the office reach beneath the door. Anna announces each girl's name as they slip out the door, into the night, and when Baker and Michelle go by, she makes a point to say their names extra loud. She gives them each the slyest smile, then calls out, "Everyone is accounted for, Ms. White!"

The fire trucks come screaming down the street, lights flashing.

In the chaos that ensues on the street outside the home, as the girls form little huddled clusters, as the neighbors spill from their homes to watch the spectacle, as the firefighters shatter the front windows of Ms. White's office and climb in to face the flames, thick hoses snaking across the lawn behind them, as the girls gasp and Ms. White sways and holds Anna's thin frame for balance, no one notices the two figures that make their way to the crowd's outer edge. No one hears their soft footsteps as they melt into the shadows of the trees that line the block. No one sees when they slip around the side of the burning home and then reappear with two bags. And as the hoses pump water and begin to drown out the flames, no one pays attention to the two silhouettes, pregnant, terrified, ecstatic, as they get to the corner and begin to run.

They can't go very fast: their chests hurt, their heavy bellies weigh a ton, and within a few seconds Baker realizes that she is going to pee herself. But neither of them is willing to stop. At one point it's too dark to spot the rosebushes planted near the sidewalk, and Baker's arm gets caught in the briars. She feels the scratches but doesn't stop to look. This is their chance, and they need to get as far as they can, as fast as they can, before anyone notices that they're gone.

The night air feels cool on their faces, their throats, their bare legs. Their lungs feel like exploding, their chests burn, the bags that were lightweight in their rooms seem like they're full of rocks now. Baker's suitcase clomps against her thigh, its handle blisters her fingers, but she doesn't let go. They trot up the block, eyes peeled for the destination, and then they see it: the orange 76 sign that glows like a neon oasis.

As they get closer, they can see the beat-up yellow Beetle idling at the curb, the passenger door open and waiting.

It worked.

Barry came.

Their getaway car awaits.

Michelle gets a new burst of adrenaline and sprints ahead of Baker, charging toward the Beetle and the grinning guy in the driver's seat. Baker catches a glimpse of a few faces in passing cars who spot the incredibly pregnant young woman running at full speed toward a gas station at 2:00 A.M. A few slow down, and one car pulls into the gas station, but it's quickly clear that this is not an emergency—

it's a reunion. Barry gets out of the car as she approaches, and Baker looks on as he admires Michelle, her body huge and round and full. Barry is gorgeous. His eyes shine, his teeth gleam, he radiates joy as he watches her head his way. It's the definition of love, Baker thinks, the most beautiful thing she's ever seen. Michelle nearly crashes into him, immediately wrapped in his arms. Their hug lasts forever, and Baker wishes she were part of it. When Barry finally looks up to introduce himself, she waves and smiles and squeezes into the tiny back seat, content to absorb the welcome by osmosis.

"Holy shit," Baker says, panting. "Holy *shit*."

Michelle lets out a *whoop,* and Barry reaches back and squeezes Baker's sweaty hand.

"Nice to meet you, Baker," he says with a grin. "You smell like roses."

And then she finally laughs, louder than she has all year. Barry puts the Beetle in gear, and they fly up the street. Each red light seems to last forever, but soon they are out of the city, no cars behind them, no one on their tail. Free. Barry's Beetle heads to the edge of California, the vast Pacific appears on their right, the twists and turns of Highway 1 lie ahead. In the cramped back seat, Baker cries, laughs, shudders, squeals. Michelle does the same in the front seat, her left hand rubbing Barry's neck, stroking his cheek, playing with his ear. Baker rolls down the window and lets the air rush at her face, which gets lit by the glow of the fat round moon that hangs above the sea.

It's exhilarating, just the feeling of being in a car, in the world again. The taste of the salty night air, the sound of the crashing waves far below. The moonlight is like spilled opal on the vast expanse of the water, and every headlight that comes toward them is a bright diamond in the velvet night. They're all so wound up and wild that it takes a long time to come back to earth, to begin to actually communicate.

Barry's the first one to share.

"Baby, I've got big news," he begins, as he downshifts and takes a sharp turn.

Michelle's shoulders droop. "Oh no, don't—"

"No, it's good! It's good news! I'm 4-F!"

Baker watches Michelle's tan face in profile, her perfect cheekbones flushed and rosy, her lips full and parted, dark eyebrows furrowed. She doesn't seem to get it, either.

"*Medical exemption,*" Barry continues, but Michelle still doesn't react. "I don't have to go to goddamn Vietnam."

Michelle lets out a yelp, followed by a howl, followed by unbridled sobs. Barry keeps one hand on the wheel and uses the other to pull her close.

"I went a few days ago to get the physical, and they found something in my x-ray, a spot on my lungs. It's probably leftover from when I had TB as a kid; I'm not actually sick."

4-F. Phillip Castle, who graduated the year before Baker, got 4-F status because he'd had childhood polio and couldn't bend his right index finger all the way. *Broken trigger finger,* he'd said with a shrug, and just like that, he got to live.

Barry continues: "They saw the spot, and the next thing you know, *BAM!* A 4-F stamp right on my permanent record! Just like that! 'Unfit for combat.'"

Baker and Michelle cannot believe it. They throw their heads back and roar with laughter, baffling Barry.

"What's so funny?"

Baker reaches over the seat and grabs Michelle's hand, squeezing it as hard as she can. They are giddy, bursting from the sheer absurd perfection of it all.

"Unfit!"

"Aren't we all!"

When they've finally calmed down, and Michelle has caught her breath, she registers the reality of this new information.

"So does this mean we can . . . I mean, do you want to . . ."

"I already talked to Brenda. She says we can come back. It's not permanent, but it's something. We don't have to decide right now, baby." He puts his hand on her soft center and grins. "I mean, we clearly gotta figure it out *soon*."

"Holy shit." Michelle turns around and looks at Baker. "Holy shit. Thanks, sister. I really owe you one."

Barry adjusts his rearview mirror so he can see Baker's face clearly.

"I owe you some gratitude, too. Thank you for getting my girl out of there."

Seeing the two of them together makes Baker's heart swell. It also makes it ache. "I owe her a lot, too. She's taken good care of me."

"And thank you for the invitation to this . . . whatever this place is that I'm driving us to. There will be a bed for us, right? Not just some hay on the forest floor?"

Baker laughs. "It's not like *that*. At least, I don't think so. My cousin definitely mentioned an actual house."

Barry's eyes flicker to his right real quick, and he catches Michelle's gaze. "So I gotta ask, Baker. You worried? You smell like smoke, and Michelle said something about a fire. Are people gonna come looking for you? Like . . . the fuzz?"

"They might. But I covered my tracks pretty well," Baker explains. "I burned lots of files in the office, so that it wouldn't just be ours that were missing. I threw the matches I used into the fire, and no one saw me in there at all. They might suspect me, but there's no evidence. And I trust the girls to cover for us." She pats the dented and dirt-covered suitcase that sits at her feet. *And I brought Kitty with us.*

Barry whistles. "Okay, Agatha Christie!" He pushes on the gas pedal and takes the next downhill stretch of road with speed and grace. Baker reclines as best she can, extending her aching legs and swollen feet. Barry fiddles with the radio, turning the knob from fuzzy station to fuzzy station. Finally he finds the familiar rasping voice of Wolfman Jack.

"Man, with so much bad stuff goin' on in da world, we just want to have fun on da Wolfman show," growls the beloved late-night DJ. "We gonna have one big love-in on the big X."

> *When the truth is found to be lieeeeessss*
> *And all the joy within you dies*

Baker sings along, loud and free. Her shirt slides up and over her expansive body to the base of her bra. Her instinct is to tug it down, but she stops herself and allows the exposure. She drapes an arm over her head and lets the full expanse of her body match the moon. The fire is probably out by now. Maybe the girls are back in their rooms. It makes her feel good and calm—less guilty, perhaps, for nearly burning down the house—to picture them, snug in their beds after the exciting night. It distracts her from thinking about Ms. White realizing that two girls have gone missing.

Wolfman plays a James Brown tune next. Barry turns it up, Michelle laughs, and they speed toward the little beach town of Santa Cruz. And then, of course, Michelle and Baker's bodies both finally remind them that they have to pee. Like *now*. Barry asks if they can hold it for just a little bit more, but when Michelle asks if *he's* ever held a bowling ball on his bladder for an hour, he pulls over, on the edge of the winding road.

Baker follows as Michelle walks up to the edge, hitches up her dress, and squats, bare ass to the sea, waves churning and crashing way down below. There's no other option, no tree or bush or building to hide behind, so Baker joins her, and together they giggle at the sound of their urgent streams, nearly crying at the immense relief of emptying their bodies, sending all that pressure over the cliff.

After they're done, they stare out at the vastness. The stars are going wild, sprayed all over the sky.

"I can't believe we did that," Baker exclaims.

"Me neither, Baker. That was the craziest shit I've ever done."

"Really?"

"I've done a lot of things, but this really takes the cake. You're a brave woman. Thank you."

"You're welcome. Thank *you*."

"So tell me honestly: what was the final straw?"

Baker watches the glint of the moon on the edge of a set of waves that roll in.

"I didn't feel safe there."

"I hear you."

"Not that it's that much safer elsewhere."

"No shit."

"Except maybe here. I feel okay right here." She takes Michelle's hand and squeezes it gently.

"Nothing safer than two girls standing in the dark on the edge of a crumbling cliff in the middle of the night."

For the rest of the drive, they let Wolfman do the talking. There's so much more to say, but it can all wait until tomorrow. No more questions about what will happen, what to do, how it will all work out. Just the knowledge that there's a place to stay at the end of this drive is enough.

It's still dark when they roll into town. Barry pulls into a grocery store parking lot so they can get some sleep. Michelle leans her body down and rests on Barry's lap in the front seat, and Baker balls up a sweater to use as a makeshift pillow. When the sun is up and the streets show signs of life, Barry quietly opens the car door and heads out in search of the twenty-four-hour donut shop that May mentioned in her letter.

When he returns an hour later, he's got a pink pastry box with two coffees balanced on top of it, and a big grin. "Rise and shine, ladies. I got donuts *and* directions. Turns out we're not far from the spot at all."

Baker's entire left side has fallen asleep, and the Bun is stirring, and her face is streaked with drool, but none of it matters now that Barry is handing her an old-fashioned, no glaze, her absolute favorite. How did he know? She sinks her teeth in and nearly passes out from the cakey thrill.

"God. I've missed this."

He hands her the hot coffee, and she gulps it, no cream or sugar, just black and bitter. It burns her tongue and the roof of her mouth, but she takes another sip, then another. She feels warm and satiated, ready to get moving. Barry heads back toward the main road and turns toward the mountains, away from the sea. Michelle wakes up and yawns, twisting her body to pop and crack her aching joints, then begins to eat one donut hole after another. After half a dozen, she finally asks where they are.

"Almost there, baby," Barry says, as he downshifts around a hairpin turn. "Almost there."

The narrow road winds and twists around redwood groves and tall eucalyptus trees. A thick mist hovers above the asphalt, and Barry flips on the high beams, slowing to a crawl in some spots. They roll down the windows, and the morning air smells like damp earth, ferns, the little eucalyptus buds that Baker used to collect as a child, pretending they were teacups for fairies.

Barry tells them the bearded hippie in the donut shop had said to look for the "big green arrow," and finally, there it is. A large arrow cut from plywood, painted green, nailed to a tree, pointing to the left. Barry turns right, onto a rocky, narrow road.

"What are you doing?" Baker asks.

"This is what the guy at the donut shop told me to do. *Turn right at the arrow that points left.* Guess they're trying to keep people out." The narrow road curves, and they can just barely see a valley down below, and the warm glow of a few lights.

The VW crunches the gravel so loudly that Baker is sure they're waking everyone as they reach the end of the road. They can make out a few figures approaching, holding lanterns that bob and bounce as they walk.

When May's face comes into view, Baker gasps. Her cousin lets out a holler.

"It *is* you!" May turns to the figures holding the lanterns. "It's Baker, the one I've been telling you about. She came!"

May's eyes go right to Baker's big round belly—so much different than when she last saw her—and she lets out her own gasp before pulling her in for the biggest hug.

"Good morning, everyone, I'm Baker," she says, once she's extricated herself from the embrace. "And these are my friends, Michelle and Barry. We don't want to intrude, but May said . . ."

A thin, bearded man steps forward and waves his hand dismissively. "All are welcome here! Any cousin of May's is a cousin of ours." He turns to Michelle and Barry, who stand next to the VW, lost in a deep embrace. He bows to Michelle, then extends his hand to Barry.

"What's happening, my brother. My name is Dov." Dov attempts a high-five, but Barry ignores him and stays locked in on Michelle. Dov puts his hand in his back pocket.

A pretty woman with rosy cheeks and long thick braids steps forward, arms extended. "We're glad to welcome you all. You must be ready to crash. We can show you to the sleeping barn."

May hugs her cousin again. "You can sleep in my bed, okay?"

Baker nearly collapses into her arms. A wave of exhaustion sweeps over her as the adrenaline of the long wild night dissipates entirely. Her body wants nothing more than to lie down, preferably somewhere soft, warm, and quiet.

The rosy-cheeked woman leads Michelle and Barry to a big barn, while May brings Baker to her cozy little room, located right off the barn. It smells and feels like all the other rooms she's ever had, and Baker feels safe immediately. She crawls into her cousin's bed, and May piles wool blankets on top of her. Baker's hips ache from the drive, her toes are cold, and the Bun won't settle down—a foot in her rib cage, an elbow in her side—but she's so tired that she falls sound asleep.

Many hours later, Baker wakes to the sound of May coming into the room. She's wearing ankle bells and holding an old chipped mug filled with steaming peppermint tea.

"Hey, sleepy bear."

Baker extends her aching arms above her head. "You know, you'll never catch a mouse with those bells on."

"Meow!" May laughs, then throws her arms open and gives Baker another long hug. "Oh, kid, I'm so glad you came. When I saw those headlights coming this morning, I just knew it was you. Your friends are already up in the main house. Let's get you dressed." She opens Baker's suitcase and begins to rummage through.

"Slim pickings, I know," Baker says. "Fashion hasn't exactly been a priority."

May holds up a blue polyester dress, knee-length with cap sleeves and oversized pockets, and frowns. "I'll be right back, okay?"

She returns with a new dress: purple, with flowers embroidered across the chest. "It's from Mexico," she explains. "I just brought it back from Baja."

"You were in Mexico?"

"Just a little road trip. If you'd come last week, you would've missed me!"

"Cool." May, just out there in the world, cruising down to Mexico because she can. Did she pass Wiley on some dusty highway? Did they camp on the same beach, marvel at the same sunsets? Baker sits up and slips the dress over her head. It smells like the inside of a van, but it actually fits comfortably, which seems like a small miracle. As she raises her arms above her head she catches a whiff of her body's intense scent—musty sweat mixed with smoke. "Is there a bathroom?" Baker asks. "I think I need to wash up."

May leads her to a tiny crude bathroom behind the barn. A jagged shard of mirror hangs above the sink, and Baker hardly recognizes the face that stares back. Exhausted, red eyes; cheeks ruddy and puffy; her usually smooth hair tangled and frizzy. She looks at her hands and sees the dirt under her nails, the black ash smudged all over her fingers, the scratch across her left palm and along her arm, dotted with dried blood, from the rosebush. *That was just last night,* she thinks. It feels like forever.

A small washcloth is draped over the edge of the sink, and when she picks it up, she finds a sliver of soap stuck to it, a little gift. She scrubs her hands, arms, and armpits, then, without thinking about who the cloth belongs to or who might want to use it next, she soaks the cloth with hot water and runs it between her legs. It's a deep, soothing relief. Then she splashes icy water on her face until her cheeks feel numb. She digs through a small woven basket until she finds something resembling a comb—it's handmade, clearly, and the rough wood snags on her tangles. It's better than nothing, she reasons. An unlabeled vial of scented oil sits on the window ledge, and she applies it to her throat, wrists, and pits. Rose, sandalwood. Maybe jasmine, too. It makes her feel just this side of decent, and as she steps out of the bathroom and heads toward the main house, she realizes she feels self-conscious. Aside from Rose, no one in the outside world has seen her like this.

The main house is a huge rambling wood-shingled structure just across the road from the barn, flanked on one side by steep tree-covered hills and on another by a vast stretch of what look like apple orchards. The house has several floors and curved turrets topped with broken weather vanes. There are balconies with intricately carved railings around them and a mishmash of windows—some circular, some enormous and rectangular, some tiny with colored panes of glass. The wood shingles that clad the entire exterior are sometimes square, sometimes rounded, like scales on a mermaid's tail, and sometimes missing altogether. The house looks old, but its style has no clear decade or time period.

Beyond the main house, Baker can see a series of small structures scattered among the gnarled spreading oaks and tall bay laurels, the towering redwoods and stately madrones. Some structures look like regular wood cabins, some like two-story treehouses, and some are round with canvas walls instead of wood. There's a building that looks like an octagon, as well as a tall tepee.

"We got all kinds of dwellings," says Dov, the bearded guy from the night before. He's in the doorway of the main house, waiting for Baker to enter. "Everyone's encouraged to design their own. I'm real proud of my tepee."

"It's . . . tall," Baker offers.

Dov beams. "I'll give you a tour after breakfast. Come on in. We've a got a plate waiting for you."

The kitchen is massive, and it opens onto a large living area, where Baker finds people in various stages of breakfast. Some are still digging into heaps of food, while others lean back, content, with clean plates on the table or floor in front of them. Baker giggles to herself—it couldn't be more different from where she's just been. The space is big and open, with high ceilings crossed by thick beams. The walls are redwood-paneled, so there's a dark coziness to it, like being inside a tree. On one wall of the open kitchen Baker sees a large framed map that details the property they're on, and the wooded trails that snake across the land, up into the surrounding hills. An assortment of paintings hangs on the walls, most of them just a bit crooked. Some are abstract, with dark swirling designs, and some are landscapes—classic California coasts, with crashing waves, jagged cliffs, and little black checkmarks to indicate seabirds. A few enormous macramé pieces are tacked to the walls. She's surprised not to see any bookshelves—a big living space like this, devoid of books, makes her suspicious.

Michelle and Barry sit on a beat-up Naugahyde love seat, talking to May and a guy in a cream-colored tunic. A girl who can't be older than sixteen sits cross-legged on a thin embroidered hassock, eyes closed, lost in meditation. Baker feels shocked that someone so young is here, then remembers her own age. She remembers Ida. Most of the people here, she guesses, are at least a few years older than she is.

A woman with long red hair hands Baker a plate of food and a glass of juice.

"My name is Freya. Welcome." She grins and places a hand on her middle. Beneath a faded floral apron, Baker sees a small but distinct bump. "What else can I get you?"

Baker takes a long sip. It's apple juice, thick and perfectly sweet. She looks at the generous plate of food. It reminds her of home—her *actual* home—and long weekend mornings when she and Gerald would eat together in the kitchen while Rose cooked and bustled. They'd read the entire paper, section by section. She misses that. "This is lovely," Baker replies politely. "Do you have a newspaper, by chance?"

Freya looks confused, so Baker explains. "My dad and I always read the newspaper with our breakfast. I just thought you might have one?"

Freya shakes her head and laughs. "I haven't seen a newspaper in months!"

Freya stands and watches while Baker devours the bright yellow scrambled eggs ("Fresh from the chickens," says Freya), the fried potatoes ("They grew on their own in the compost pile!"), the scoop of brown rice ("We're looking into how to grow our own here"), the thick slab of brown bread ("The girls are making more loaves this afternoon, if you want to help out"). She drinks another glass of apple juice ("Just pressed!") and a mug of Constant Comment tea ("It's like the only commercial thing we have in this kitchen," Freya confesses. "That, and French's mustard. I can't help it. They're too good").

Baker has a mouthful of toast when Freya leans in and asks:

"How far along?" As if it's a normal question to ask over breakfast, in a room full of people.

Baker feels disoriented, disconnected from time and place. She has to think for a second. "About eight months."

"Cool." Freya's smile is a gentle glow. "I'm just behind you," she says, beaming. "So, what's your story?"

"Oh, it's pretty complicated."

"Aren't we all. Your cousin says you escaped from a burning building?"

Baker swallows, and the brown bread hovers in her throat, slow to go down. It occurs to her that she needs to be careful with what she does and doesn't reveal. She's still gaming out her plan. "May's such a storyteller." She laughs and looks over at Michelle and Barry, wanting to protect them, too. "Fire?! I'm just a normal girl who thought I'd come visit my cousin at her new place."

"Come on," Freya chides her. "You're not *normal*. Look around you! No one here is normal. We come here to get *away* from normal."

Dear Mom + Dad,

This is just to let you know that I am alive, and OK. You know by now that I am no longer at the home. I'm sure you're very angry, and very worried. I am truly sorry for that, but I did what I believe I had to do. I could not stay there any longer.

I promise I'll write again soon, but for now: I am safe. And I will be in touch again soon. And I love you.

B

For the next few days, Baker tries to give the Grove a chance, to ease into it all. The routines, the freedom and the space, the outdoorsness of it all. She appreciates how alive the trees are, how bright the sun is. The air feels fresh and clean, she walks around barefoot, and even though her feet are tender and always a little cold, she loves the feeling of actual earth, the soft dirt beneath her toes. She explores the vegetable gardens, picks wildflowers and lets May braid them into her hair. When her thighs get too crampy and painful, she goes for slow walks up the driveway, which for some reason relieves the tension. She stops when it gets too steep and catches her breath while she looks out at the entire property.

She tries to *be present in this moment,* like May always says; she tries not to think about the mess she's left behind, but that doesn't seem possible. She's still piecing it together, not quite believing what she did. A *fire?* Was that really her? Ms. White must be beside herself. Rose must be through the roof. Maybe they *will* call the police. She wonders what the girls are doing, what they're watching on TV, what they've had for breakfast, if anyone has gone over in the few days since they left, and what they think when they walk past the empty room she and Michelle shared. Did anyone claim the clothes she left behind? Did people like her little gifts? Are they envious? Proud? Does it even matter? *Once you're gone, you're gone.*

Barry and Michelle spend most of their time huddled up in the little structure (it's called a "yurt," they're told) that May and a few others cleaned out for them. They emerge for meals and for careful, slow walks, and Barry does join some of the men for wood-chopping duty. But mostly they're cocooned, "reunited and reconnecting," says Michelle, who looks radiant, her crop top framing her very pregnant body. She's just a few weeks from her due date, and she moves at a gentle pace, often short of breath, but she has a kind of peace that Baker hasn't seen before. Barry stays by her side, holding her hand and steadying her as they walk on the path through the apple orchard, getting up to make her tea and get her slices of fresh bread slathered with bright yellow butter. On the third day, Michelle lets one of the girls paint her body with some kind of natural dye. A fine-lined spiral swirls out from her belly button, and the women *oooh* and *ahhhh*. The girl is eager to paint on Baker next, but she politely declines. *No, thank you. Not today.*

After breakfast on the fourth day there's a gathering of women, including the handful who've birthed their babies already, as well as Freya and a few others who may or may not be pregnant (Baker can't quite tell from looking at their bodies, which are draped in loose fabrics). They sit in a circle beneath an enormous fig tree, its leaves broad and green. They've spread several worn quilts on the ground, and two babies crawl and roll in between them, playing with a green apple and a large wooden spoon. One woman is folding cloth diapers, placing them in neat stacks beside her, and another woman leans in and coos at the babies. Another has her baby draped across her lap, her blouse unbuttoned and its little face attached to a dark nipple. It clutches a clump of her long hair in its chubby hand, but she doesn't seem to mind.

Baker and Michelle eye the circle from the porch of the main house. Freya spots them and waves. The morning sun hits her face, lighting her like a friendly paper lantern.

"Hey! Come on down!"

Michelle waves back, then turns to Baker. "You sure you don't want to join?"

KATE SCHATZ

Baker looks down at the circle of women, at the two tiny creatures rolling around on the ground, at the small body squirming in its mother's arms. The babies are adorable, and the women are welcoming. But while there's something familiar about the way they cluster together, leaning in to talk and share, it could not be more different from where they were just one week ago. She thinks about the latch-hook rug group, what they looked like when they sat together and talked, shut in and shamed, kept in the dark. Her eyes burn, and she feels an undercurrent of dark anger begin to stir. These mamas, beautiful and open, communal and blissed. How did they know to come here? How did they make this choice? It's not *them* she's mad at, but it's just not fair. Lizzie would love this. Janey could use this. And Kitty. What would Kitty have thought of this scene?

One of the babies makes a loud shrieking sound, and the women erupt into laughter. Freya swoops the baby into her arms and spins around. The shrieking turns to a gurgling laughter that seems to carry on a current directly into Baker's ear, right into her brain and down into her heart. The Bun kicks and pushes. Her breasts tingle and become painfully tight. Her entire chest suddenly constricts.

Michelle reaches over and takes Baker's hands. "Baker . . ." Her voice has a serious tone. "Barry and I are leaving. Tomorrow."

Baker's chest tightens even more. She had a feeling this was coming, but it's still hard to hear. She bites her top lip, and her nostrils flutter. "Are you sure?"

"Never been more sure. We gotta get back to the city. I don't think I have much more time. This has been so good, these few days. And I don't even know how to say it, Baker, but I'm gonna be grateful to you for the rest of my damn life. I'm never going to forget this, what you did for me and for—"

Michelle's voice shakes, and she can't hold back the tears anymore. They wrap their arms around each other, and Baker breathes in the scent of her friend, the rich, deep smell of this woman she's gotten to know so well. Out of the corner of her eyes, Baker sees

Freya, her illuminated face cocked to one side as she gazes up and watches their embrace. She waves again, a little gesture that says *come down here!* The breastfeeding woman looks up, too, and smiles.

Michelle takes Baker's face in her hands and leans in close. "If you're gonna stay, I think it would be good for you to get to know them. You can't—you don't need to do this by yourself. There's a guest today, a midwife from town." Michelle points to a woman coming down the dirt path toward the circle of women. She has braids streaked with gray, and she wears a long brown dress. Even from a distance, Baker can see the lines in her strong face. "That's her, the one who looks . . ."

"Like a midwife from town?" Baker finishes her sentence, and Michelle laughs.

"Exactly."

"I'll think about it, Michelle. You go join them."

Baker manages a confident-looking grin, but she knows she's not fooling Michelle. She can tell what her friend is thinking: that Baker is both stubborn and afraid. So damn smart, yet so naïve.

She *is* curious about the midwife, and wonders if she's come bearing important outside information that hasn't yet made its way in to this secretive space. Baker has so many questions, and it makes her feel panicky that there is still so much she doesn't know. She wants to ask if the midwife knows where the nearest hospital is. Things can go wrong, she knows that now. This place is beautiful, it's wild, it's natural. But Baker isn't sure that it feels safe. At least, not her kind of safe.

"I get it, B. You're done letting other people make decisions for you. And I think that's right-on."

Michelle kisses Baker on the cheek and heads down to the women, who wave to her with tan bare arms.

When Baker finally does come down, overcome with curiosity, Freya pulls another quilt from her bag and spreads it out, so Baker has a soft place to sit. The other women shift their bodies outward, creating space in the circle. The midwife uses her hands a lot as she talks, and the women sit transfixed and fascinated as she speaks. The babies are transfixed, too, and Baker sees how they lie peacefully on the blanket now, tracking the woman's slender, weathered fingers as she points and waves and creates shapes in the air in an effort to convey the unknowable.

"When the baby is ready, she will move into position *like this*," says the midwife, using the whole of both arms to pantomime a body turning upside down. "Sometimes the body will be twisted around, like *this*." She holds her fists up to her face and turns her body away. "A head *this big* will be preparing to enter a canal *this size*." Her hands make a big circle, then shrink dramatically. Baker shivers.

"When the cervix is dilated, it looks like *this*." The midwife holds the circle up to her eyes and peers at the group. "Now I'm going to show you some positions that your bodies might enjoy." She crawls into the middle of the circle and lies down next to the babies. "It can help to pull your knees up toward your shoulders like *this*. Or you can try *this*," she says, climbing onto all fours and arching her back like an angry cat. "Or *this*. Your body will tell you. Your body will know what it needs." This is both a surprise and a relief to Baker. *Will it?*

Then the midwife rears up into a wide squat and throws her head back. She closes her eyes and exhales with a surprising amount of force, fluttering her lips loudly like a horse on a hot day. Then she looks around, taking stock of their reactions. "That's a good release. Let's all do some big breathing."

They all close their eyes and take deep breaths. Then *whoooosh*, they exhale. Then they do it again. "Feel free to make some noise if that feels right for you," the midwife calls out, and then someone is moaning. Another woman releases her breath with a guttural shudder.

"Yes, yes, that's it!"

Baker feels the crisp air filling up her lungs, then rushing out of her. She does it again, gulping in air and feeling her lungs, her ribs, her heart—then *haaaaaaaaaaa*, she lets it go. She flutters her lips like the midwife; she tries humming like the woman next to her. It feels silly, but she's not embarrassed. She's curious. The positions the midwife just demonstrated, the terms she uses, the size of the cervix—what *is* a cervix? Where is this canal? Did the two babies on the blankets know exactly how to emerge from the bodies of their mothers? Baker's ears fill with the coos and cries of the babies, the heavy breaths of the women, the gusts of air being released, the moans and groans and grunts and gasps. She sucks in more air until she feels dizzy, so dizzy, and she grips the ground in front of her, and then the body of whoever is next to her, and then her head is floating, spinning. And everything goes dark.

When she opens her eyes, she is on her back, on the quilt, and May is there, hovering above her, running a rough damp cloth across her sweating forehead. The midwife comes into focus; then Michelle. Freya and the other women are blurry in the periphery, and Baker hears the squawks of the babies, who are unconcerned with the woman who just passed out. She blinks a few times, and then notices the tree above them. The fruit she didn't see before. So many ripe figs, hundreds perhaps, hanging, drooping, just waiting to be picked.

They help her sit up, and the midwife looks around. "She's very close." Then she turns to Baker and repeats herself. "You're very close, dear."

Baker looks to Michelle, then May, then back to the midwife. The women in the periphery are listening. "My due date isn't supposed to be until October. The *middle* of October. Isn't it still August?"

"It's September now, but that really doesn't matter. Due dates are just guesses. Your body is in charge. And when it's ready, it's ready." The midwife places her hands on Baker's body, running the slender fingers along her sides, pressing near her navel, and on the top, just below her braline, making a low *hmm* sound. Then she takes the hem of Baker's blouse between her fingertips and begins to lift.

"May I?"

"Okay." Baker's voice is weak, shaky.

The midwife runs a finger along the dark line that begins above her pubic bone and travels up toward her sternum, like a prime meridian. A path. An arrow pointing toward her heart. Baker noticed it a few months ago, and as she looks down now, she sees that it's darker than it was before. May and Michelle peer at it, too, their eyes wide, their faces serious.

"*Linea nigra,*" the midwife says. "Yours is lovely. And very telling. You've got a nice big baby in there." She lets the blouse fall back down. "And it's coming any day now."

May and Michelle take Baker to rest in the dress shop, a room in the barn that May's been fixing up. It's her big project: she figured out how to repair an old sewing machine, and she's built a few tables out of apple crates and old doors. The vision is a workshop where she can make clothes that will be functional and natural, yet still cool and stylish. Anyone can come in and pick out what they want to wear, leave what they're done with, get holes patched and mended. She'll do custom designs and take requests, and she's sketched out some simple patterns for smock shirts, long skirts, wrap dresses, even hooded robes and aprons.

May sits Baker down on an old sagging couch, and Michelle brings her a mug of tea. May's hands are stained red from dipping strips of cloth in beet juice. She whispers something to Michelle, who seems to agree. Baker's face is pale, and she shivers a bit. May grabs a length of thick flannel from a pile of fabric and wraps it around her. Then she stands with her arms crossed, looking at the two pregnant women.

"We need to figure out our plan, here."

Baker sips her tea and looks at the floor. She avoids May's eyes. She wishes she could disappear.

"A plan for your birth," Michelle adds. "And, like, *the baby.*"

"And, I don't know, your parents showing up here with a SWAT team trying to track you down!" May says.

"They won't do that."

"Don't you think they've called the police?"

"You know my mother. This is all a huge secret to begin with—you think she'd want the police involved?"

"Fine. But you know that *she* must be searching for you!"

"I sent them a postcard when I got here."

Michelle speaks up. "Baker, we've come this far. You've been so brave. Now it's time to get real about what comes next."

"We heard the midwife. She said it's happening soon."

Baker looks at them, her two most trusted friends. They're acting concerned, but Baker feels like they're ganging up on her. She feels trapped, an animal caught in the corner. Terrified. *Any day now.*

"She doesn't even know me. And that's not what the doctor said. I was told mid-October."

Michelle's voice gets delicate. It's a tone Baker hasn't heard before. "It's okay if you're scared, but we gotta just talk about it a little. Especially since I'm leaving."

May looks shocked, and opens her mouth to protest, but Michelle holds up a hand.

"Barry and I are so grateful to you all, May. But we gotta get back. It's any day now for me, too, and we've . . . we've got our own plan now."

The room is quiet for a moment. Outside, someone chops wood. *Thwak thwak* as the axe hits the stump.

Baker looks into her tea, as if there might be answers floating in there with the chamomile flowers. "I'm really happy for you both, Michelle. I really am." She's not lying. This is what she'd wished for Michelle; this is what she knows Michelle deserves. But Michelle's been her close companion, the person right by her side. And now she's got her guy. Baker feels sad, and a little left out.

"Me, too," says May. "But shit. Okay, it's you and me, kid."

"I'll always be there for you, Baker. You, too, May. Me and Barry. You've got our number." Michelle takes Baker's hand. "We're all gonna be alright."

There's a basket of apples on the floor next to the couch, and Baker bends down and picks one up. It looks perfect, its skin a shiny green, but when she turns it over, a black worm wiggles out of a hole. She screams and drops it. May laughs.

"I'm really amazed by both of you. What you've done is wild. It all takes some real guts. I'm proud of you, kid!"

"Thanks, May."

"You're like a *fugitive*. Pregnant girl on the lam!"

Baker and Michelle burst into laughter.

May shakes her head. "But Baker, Rose must be losing her damn mind. I honestly feel for her. Don't you?"

They all go quiet again, and Baker tries to push down the waves of guilt that threaten to crash over her heart. The thought of Rose's heartbreak is too much to bear. She remembers the closeness she'd felt when they sat in the car in Sausalito. When Rose opened up to her, shared her deepest secret. When she'd leaned into her mother and felt held, and safe. Rose loves her, she really does. And this is such a betrayal. Is Rose worried she's lost her, the way her own mother lost Rose?

May is still talking. "Was it really just less than a year ago that it was such a big deal for you to sneak out and go to *a concert* with me? You've come a long way, baby."

Baker chokes back the bitter pangs of regret and swallows a sudden urge to vomit. "I feel like an entirely different person."

"You're still *you*. Just more experienced. You've done *a lot* of living this year."

Baker remembers standing in the kitchen on New Year's Eve, staring at that calendar, so full of potential and the desire for more.

More life, more feelings, more of the real world. It feels like a million years ago, on another planet, in an entirely different galaxy. "I knew I was ready for something to change, but this wasn't what I had in mind." And it's true. She wanted a big life of adventure and excitement, love and passion, success and freedom. She just didn't realize how much can come with all that. The cost and the consequences. How difficult it is to actually *live*. Especially when you're a woman.

May pulls a clean, worm-free apple from the basket and hands it to Baker.

"Are you scared?"

"Of course."

May proceeds slowly. "What do you think you're going to do?"

Baker chews on her lower lip and then sips her tea. She used to be so good with making decisions, with having clear plans. And she did come up with a brilliant escape plan that worked, that destroyed the files, that set her and Michelle and Kitty free. She just hasn't quite gotten to the final step. "I need to think a little more."

May and Michelle share a knowing look. "Classic Baker," May mutters, and Michelle chuckles.

Baker lifts her chin and sets her jaw. "I'm going to figure it out."

"You know," May drags the words out in the way she does when she's not sure whether Baker will go for her idea. "We're having an encounter session tonight. You might want to join."

"What's an encounter session?"

May puts her hands on her hips and cocks her head. She looks at Michelle. "How can she be so damn smart and so totally not with it?"

Michelle shrugs. Baker scowls.

"I'm joking, but seriously. I'm *sure* they have encounter sessions at *Stahn-ford*."

Baker's heart skips at the mention of the school. It hits her: it's September now. Back-to-school. She's supposed to be starting college. That plan seems so far away, from the same distant universe as the calendar, the concert, the whirlwind of Wiley. Does she even want to go still? Is that who she is? She considers it, and the answer feels like *yes*.

May is still explaining the encounter sessions. "It's a big part of what we do here. It's . . . a group conversation."

"So it's talking."

"It's more than that. We open up, we move through blockages. It's really helped me. Maybe it could help you. With the think-ing."

"I'm in!" Michelle's in a great mood now.

"I don't know, May. I passed out from listening to a midwife today. I don't know what will happen if I listen to everyone here tell their deepest secrets." It felt so good to do that with the girls in the home, with the latch-hook rugs. Baker misses them all so much. How they grew closer with each class, how it felt to receive their stories, and how those stories sit safely in the pages of her journal. Waiting for her, whenever she's ready. No matter what, those girls exist. She could trust them. She still can. But she doesn't have that same feeling here at the Grove. It's cool that May does, but they're two different people—they always have been.

Dov is the first leader for the evening, but he makes it clear the position will rotate. "No hierarchy here," he says, "no kings. No queens, either." He winks at several of the women, who slouch to-gether against a stack of quilts.

"We're gathered here to tell it like it is. I'm just getting us going." He wears olive green army pants and a thick wool sweater with what look like small llamas running around the bottom. "I want to wel-come our newcomers. Michelle and Barry and Baker, please stand up."

Barry stands and looks around the room. Michelle and Baker, who sit on big round cushions, look at each other and shake their heads. "Nope," says Michelle. "Hello from our comfy seated positions." Baker offers an awkward wave. She feels like her body is the size of the earth.

The group murmurs *hello, hi, welcome, welcome.*

"Thank you, and yeah, I totally get not wanting to stand. Stay rooted to that earth." Dov clears his throat. "Everyone, please turn to the person next to you."

Baker immediately turns to Michelle, who sits to her right, but then Dov continues. "Remember, if you know the person real well, turn to the person on the *other* side."

Baker gives Michelle a nervous look—*What's about to happen?*—and Michelle smiles and shrugs, then turns to face Freya, who's sitting beside her with a beatific grin. She sees Barry on the other side of the circle, turning to face a man with a thin blond beard.

Baker feels a tap on her shoulder. It's one of the women from the circle with the midwife. One of the ones who doesn't look pregnant. "I'm Golden."

"I'm Baker."

"I love that name."

"Everyone ready? Now close your eyes and take each other's hands. Be with that for a moment, and then . . ." Dov draws out his instructions with a kind of glee. The group buzzes with anticipation, eyes closed, hands holding. "Reach out and get to know each other's bodies. You know what we say here: Be open. Be free. Let yourselves explore. One minute each. Go."

Baker's eyes fly open, but Golden's remain shut, as do everyone else's. Baker watches tentative hands traveling up from hands to arms to shoulders to faces.

Golden whispers, "I've never touched a woman who's this pregnant before. Can you believe that? Is it cool if I feel it?"

First the midwife, and now this. It's the most she's been touched in months. "Sure." Baker closes her eyes and takes Golden's slim hand. Her sterling and turquoise rings clink against each other as Baker lays her fingers at the top of her bump, up where the Bun tends to be most active. Baker and Golden sit still, breathing deep, and Baker allows the warmth from Golden's palm to feel good, and soothing. Finally, a little pop. The Bun kicks, then kicks again. Golden gasps.

"Was that . . . ?"

"Yes."

"Oh my god." Another kick, and then what is likely a foot protrudes just enough, lifting Golden's hand and traveling across Baker's body in a small arc. Golden's mouth gapes. "It's like . . . a serpent." She opens her eyes and gazes at Baker. "You're so lucky."

Baker's face tenses up and her eyebrows knit together. She wants to scoff and tell Golden that she has no idea what she's been through, what this is like. But then it occurs to her—maybe, in some strange ways that she doesn't fully understand yet, she is lucky? "Thank you."

Golden leans in and lowers her voice. "I got knocked up last year, right before I moved here. I wasn't ready for all this, though." She gestures broadly to Baker. "The abortion wasn't so bad, to be honest. I don't regret it."

It's stunning to hear a stranger share this so casually. The word alone was so charged in the home, even among the girls who agreed. It felt profane, dangerous, just to say it. Yet here's Golden, open and honest. "Really?"

"What good is regret?" Golden says, as if she's reflecting on a bad grade or an honest mistake. "I did what I had to do. It all happened pretty quick, and I felt okay after."

"That's good to hear."

"Lots of girls do it these days. And come on, let's be real, we've been doing it for *centuries*."

And now Baker knows how true that is.

"It's true. I just wish I'd known that." She'd thought she was so alone, had felt like a criminal risking it all. Why would she think otherwise? No one ever talked about it; no one told her anything. Including her mother.

"Seeing you and the other mamas here is cool, though. Makes me think I can do it again someday."

"You can," Baker says quickly, thinking of Rose, and how she didn't ruin her chances forever. "I mean, if you want to."

"We'll see. I'm really questioning a lot these days, Baker."

"Me, too."

Golden looks around the room. "Like, do I even *want* to make it with men? Look at them." She leans in even closer, her full lips brushing Baker's cheek as she whispers. Her breath is warm and sweet. "They say they're tuned in, but when it comes down to it, they're all *sex sex sex* and *war war war* and *me me me*. Women *see* each other. We create *life*. We're *beautiful*." She leans back and grins. "I mean, *look at you!*"

Baker looks down, at the moon that rises above her carefully crossed legs. Her expansive chest, her swollen hands, the thick locks of long dark hair that hang down. It does look kind of beautiful. She can see it.

Then the Bun shifts again, big time, and she gets a sharp shooting sensation way deep down. It's not exactly pain, but it's intense, and urgent, a new kind of pressure that's not like anything she's felt so far. She puts her hands where her waist used to be and pushes in, trying to contain the sensation.

Golden looks alarmed. "Are you okay?"

"I think I just need to use the restroom," Baker manages, trying to seem calm. She doesn't want to alarm the group. "Maybe partner with someone else. I might be awhile." She takes Golden's hand and presses it to her face. "And thank you. You're beautiful, too." Then she uncrosses her legs and pushes her heavy, cramping body off the ground.

"Bathroom is just past the kitchen. Watch out—these guys never remember to put the seat down."

*   *   *

In the bathroom, she splashes cool water on her face, then tries to pee, but nothing comes out, despite all the pressure. She lets the water run until it's hot, then puts her face as close to the stream as she can stand. She breathes in the steam the way she did when she was a girl and felt sick. No matter what it was—sore throat, runny nose, tummy ache—Rose's go-to home remedy was to close the bathroom door and fill the room with steam. Drops of hot water fleck her cheeks, her forehead, her eyelids. It burns, but in a good way.

When she's had enough and the steam dissipates, she can see herself in the mirror. She looks tired and worn out, but somehow also radiant. *Golden was right,* she thinks. Her face is rounder and fuller; her cheeks are rosy, warm, and glowing. Her eyes look deep, and alive. Now that her hair has been washed and brushed, it looks thick and shiny. Her shoulders are broad. Her chin is square. She looks like a woman who has been through a war, and that's why she's fatigued—but it's also why she's strong. It's why she's powerful. She wipes her face on a hand towel and smiles at herself. She is terrified, and she is determined.

She blows a kiss.

You can do this.

Then she leaves the bathroom and walks outside.

It's not dark yet, but it's close. The sun is setting behind the main house, orange and red and yellow. As she walks to her little make-shift room, she can hear the people still encountering one another, some voices rising, passionate and argumentative. She hears the sounds of dinner prep in the kitchen: plates and spoons and glasses clinking, water running, someone singing. It's working for them, this life. But not for Baker. She's been waiting to decide what to do next, convinced that the correct next step would become obvious, that the answer would appear in some clear, bright way. But that hasn't happened yet. There's no study guide, Michelle had joked so long ago, and Baker hates how true that is.

When she gets to her room, she grabs her journal and a pen, and puts them both in her bag. She adds a sweater, then steps outside. She sees the first star, twinkling in the dusky blue. She makes a wish and thinks about the midwife: *Your body will tell you. Your body will know what to do.* Could that actually be true? She begins to walk, and her feet find the path to the woods beyond the house. The massive trees loom large and dark, but they don't feel frightening. They feel safe. Welcoming.

She has studied the map that hangs in the kitchen and has a rough enough sense of where the trails lead. Her pace is fast at first, an awkward, stumbling trot, but soon she slows, a bit out of breath and afraid of tripping over a downed log or thick root as the sky quickly darkens. The ground beneath her is soft with the debris of redwood, the dry brown oak leaves, the bark, the tiny round cones, and eventually, as the Grove gets farther behind, the only sounds she can hear are the crunches beneath her feet and the heavy rhythm of her breath.

She squints and tries to focus on each plant around her, trying to make out the different branches, leaves, flowers, and thorns. The feathery ferns, prickly blackberry vines, poison oak. Tall bay laurels, so sophisticated with their glossy slender leaves and sweet sharp scent. Big, gnarled oaks, their sprawling branches dried up and twisted, the bark gray and rough and spotted with pale green lichen, the leaves shiny and jagged.

And of course, the redwoods. So upright and confident, with branches that extend in even horizontal rings, taking turns, circling the steady trunks. The soft dark exterior, almost furry, protecting a hard core. The roots, she knows, extend out rather than down, sending up new shoots all around it, so its babies grow up right there, within view. Not scattered on the wind by birds and weather, growing anywhere they're dropped. Just right there, close to home.

The ground slopes down as the path drops into the cool of the canyon. The trail switches back and forth, sharp and steep, and shadows start to fill the corners. She doesn't stop until the pressure on her bladder is too much, and the urine threatens to drip down her leg. She leans against an oak and does her best to squat, her dress bunched up in one hand, the other gripping the bottom of her heavy belly.

As she stands and pulls down her dress, she hears the high-pitched whir of a mosquito in her ear. She wonders how she tastes—sweet and full? Bitter and strange? Her first thought is to swat it away, but instead she holds out her arm, an offering. She remembers a lesson in her biology class, junior year, where Mr. Carter explained that female mosquitoes need blood to make their eggs. They need the iron, the protein. *Try it*, she whispers. *Go ahead.* There's just enough light still that she can see the insect as it lands on her arm. Baker stares, mesmerized, allowing this tiny thing to get what she needs.

She keeps going, and the trail takes her down farther into the canyon, then begins to wind up toward the ridge. She remembers from the map in the kitchen that the trail ends at what looks like a cliff, and the top of the hill she could see from the property. It's a long way up, and her feet hurt, her knees throb, her thighs burn, but she wants to get there. She has to. She will.

The ridge glows in the moonlight, and she goes right to the edge. She has lugged herself this far; she is pretty sure her feet are bleeding, and she feels dizzy and disoriented. It is dark now, truly dark, but the moon lets her see how far the drop is below. In the distance, she can make out the expanse of the ridgeline, the outlines of trees all around her, each one busy with its own ecosystem, alive and ancient and unconcerned with one singular human.

She looks down into the depths of the wild and remembers being on that overpass. The rush of traffic below her, the potential and the certainty, the way her body swayed as she imagined, briefly, giving in and letting go. Letting the wind decide, letting gravity choose, surrendering to forces beyond her body.

Baker throws her arms out and her head back, and she screams as loud as she can. It is a wild howl, a wolf's wail, a deep primal sound that can't be contained in a journal, or an article, or in any bound book. She releases it again, and again, letting it echo into the trees, the gulches, the canyons, the sky. She screams to the Grove, all the way back to Ms. White and the home, to Lizzie and Anna and Janey and Helen and Ida and Debra and Viv. To Marcy and Lydia, to Linda Moore. She cries out to Kitty, and she calls for her mother. *I am here,* she tells them all. *Help me!*

No one answers. No one is coming to save her. An owl hoots, the wind whips, and she drops to the ground, spent, her arms wrapped around her transformed body. Same soft skin, same arms. Same shoulders, same bones. Her breasts are huge, her hair is thick, she has no more waist and she can no longer see her toes, but she is still there. Inside her, the Bun rolls, stretches out a limb to see if the edges of its world are still there. Baker lies down on the cool earth, flushed and hot and so tired. And despite the rough terrain, the hard surface, the night sounds, the unknown rustling in the bushes, she falls deep asleep.

*S*he wakes, hours later, to a deep, pulsing cramp. Like two hands gripping her lower back, wringing her like a washcloth. It originates at the base of her spine and then radiates, wrapping around her hips, a low-slung belt made of fire. She doubles over. She clenches her fists. When it finally subsides, she looks around in a daze. It's still dark. The moon is gone. Her sweater is balled up beneath her. Her bag is still hanging across her chest; she checks and feels the journal still there. The right side of her face is cold and caked with dirt; there are dried leaves in her hair, and her arm is asleep.

Like severe menstrual cramps, they'd described.

But it's too early, she tells herself.

Any day now, the midwife had said, her gray braids swinging.

Your body will tell you.

Your body will know what to do.

The cramp comes again. *Oh,* she gasps. *Oh!* Something is happening. Something new. The pain is intense, but as she stands and braces her body against a thick tree, she feels a new and ferocious power. The fear remains, but it shifts, giving way to purpose and strength. That midwife *knew.* Kitty *knew.* And now, in this moment, Baker clearly, absolutely *knows.*

She has the answer to her own question.

It is time.

Time to leave the woods.

Time to go home.

*   *   *

"*May!* Wake up."

"Baker?"

She is crouched on May's floor, her mouth inches from her cousin's ear. She has figured out the plan. She knows what to do. She just needs May's help.

"May, it's time."

May doesn't respond. A male body in the bed next to her grunts, rolls over beneath the tattered quilt.

"May! We have to leave *now.*"

"What?" May reaches out in the dark, finds Baker's face.

"I need you to drive me home."

"Why?" The sun is just rising, and when May switches on her bedside light and sees her cousin, with dirt on her face and leaves in her hair, she gasps. "Are you okay?"

"Home. *Now.*" It's all she can think about: the driveway, the mailbox, the window boxes, the front door. The piano and the bathroom and her bedroom and the kitchen. Her mother. *Now.*

"Oh, shit. The baby?"

Baker moans and grabs May's shoulders as another contraction takes hold. May leaps from her bed, naked, and grabs a silk robe from the floor.

"Stay here. I'll get the others."

When Baker can speak again, she is firm. "No! I want to go home."

"What do you mean?"

"My house! I want my mother!"

"But Rose will kill us both if we show up!"

"*Home!*"

"It'll take us two hours—"

"*NOW.*" She is in pain, but she is still powerful. She heaves herself up out of her squat and fumbles for May's keys in the pile of jewelry and candles and junk on her dresser.

"But what if—I mean, are you gonna have it *now*? Shouldn't we just stay here?"

Baker's eyes squeeze shut again. May stands there and watches, stunned and frozen, until Baker exhales. "May. Listen to me. Michelle told me that when she had her first baby—"

"Her *first* baby? But—"

"Shut up! She told me she had a very clear sense of what she needed. I have that right now. I need you to drive me home. *Now.*"

And then May gets moving, throwing on a dress and her tan cowboy boots. She pulls the quilt over the bare shoulders of the still-sleeping man in her bed and takes the keys from Baker. "I'll get some towels and some blankets. Meet me at the car. I love you."

As Baker heads out to May's little yellow Karmann Ghia, she thinks about Michelle and Barry, asleep in the barn, planning to leave today as well. She wants so badly to go to Michelle, to tell her what's happening, to give her a hug and tell her she loves her. But it's like she's barreling down a steep hill at full speed. She can't do anything except what she's already doing. She climbs into the too-small passenger seat, and another spasm hits her, hard. She takes the journal from her bag and bites down on it to keep from screaming. Saliva pools around her tongue. She tastes the leather cover, the edges of the paper; she swears she can taste all the stories inside. May runs down toward her, arms overflowing with old towels, a white sheet flapping behind her in the night.

"Why are you eating a book?"

"Just DRIVE," Baker howls, and her voice echoes through the trees.

The drive feels like it takes forever, though May speeds like crazy and makes record time. She flies up the highway, taking the curves like a pro. Baker grips the seat, the dashboard, the door, the journal, her thighs. She huffs and puffs, moans and squirms, pants and begs

May to hurry up. At one point she squeezes May's hand so tightly that May cries out in pain.

"Ow! I need that hand to shift gears!"

"I'm sorry—I just—it hurts!"

"Grab my leg, then," May offers, and Baker grips her cousin's right thigh with her left hand as she braces for another spasm. May turns on the radio, thinking it will help distract her, but Baker yells "No music!" so May turns it off and speeds in silence.

It's 9:30 A.M. on a Saturday morning in September when they pull into the driveway. The neighborhood is quiet, peaceful, just as it was when Baker last saw it, four long months ago. But she doesn't look closely—she can't. She doesn't notice the new begonias that Rose has placed in decorative pots. She doesn't notice the fresh coat of paint on the shutters, or the new house numbers on the mailbox. And she doesn't notice the extra cars parked in front of the house.

May doesn't wait for Baker to get out of the car. She sprints to the front door and doesn't bother knocking, just flings it open and runs on in. Baker climbs out of the car slowly, grips the doorframe, and pauses, lets the blood circulate and her body adjust to standing. Another dull ache comes over her, so she waits in the driveway for it to pass. Across the street, Mrs. Thorp is watering her flowers: thirsty late-summer daisies, last-gasp hydrangeas. She waves, and Baker sees her eyes go wide when she takes in the full body of her neighbor's nice girl.

Baker watches from the doorway as May barrels into the house, like a ragged hippie tumbleweed. Her cowboy boots are dirt-caked; her paisley tunic is a shapeless sack. Rose is in the kitchen with a group of ladies from one of her committees. It's a breakfast meeting to prepare for their annual fundraiser. The luncheon is next week, and they're planning to spend the morning making centerpieces, place cards, and plans for floral arrangements. Gerald is golfing, his standing Saturday morning routine. Rose is sipping her coffee and chatting with her guests when May bursts in, calling her name.

"Aunt Rose, it's Baker! She's with me!" All the women stare, teacups half-raised to their lips. May stands in the kitchen doorway, breathless. "It's time."

Rose's eyes bulge, wide and alarmed, but she doesn't miss a beat—it's as if she's been waiting for this. She sets her cup on its saucer and turns to face her guests.

"Ladies. If you'll excuse me." And then she runs to the front door, with May just behind her. The women follow, whispering, *Oh my dear Lord* and *What on earth?*

"Mama." Baker is doubled over and panting on the doorstep. "It's happening."

Rose wraps her arms around her daughter, who hangs on with an ancient fury as she hunches over with another strong wave of pain. Rose kisses her head and brushes clumps of hair—still specked with leaves and debris from the forest floor—from her dirt-smudged, sunburned face. Tears stream down Baker's cheeks, into her mouth and down her chin, and when she finally opens her eyes and looks up, she sees that Rose is crying, too. A silent chorus of women stand behind her, speechless, their faces as round and stunned as last night's moon.

"It's okay, it's okay," Rose whispers, her voice shaky but firm. "Keep breathing. Let's get you to the hospital." She turns and begins to issue orders. "May, please get my purse from the hall closet, as well as my gray coat. Alice, please phone the clubhouse and have them tell Gerald to meet us at the hospital. Eleanor, if you could be so kind as to cover the cinnamon rolls and put them in the cupboard. Janis, the supplies for the table arrangements are on the dining table—you may take them with you and work on them at home this weekend. Everyone else: my apologies, but we'll have to meet another day. My daughter is having a baby."

*   *   *

"Keep breathing."

The smell of Rose's perfume

The way she leans so close to the steering wheel as she drives

"I'm sorry, Mother"

"I will call Ms. White from the hospital"

The cramping, the pressure, coming faster, lasting longer

Dirty hands, dusty feet, a twig pulled from the matted hair

"Keep breathing"

The sound of that midnight mountain scream, still echoing

"I didn't know what else to do"

"Where have you *been*"

Power lines overhead, flashing past

"You could have died"

Another searing cramp

Rose's clenched jaw, the tight tendon along her throat

"What were you thinking"

"I've been so scared"

The way she bites her upper lip when she is mad or scared

"How much farther"

Damp brow, curled toes, hands gripping the wide blue dashboard

"Breathe, breathe, breathe"

"I can't"

The big gray hospital building in the distance

Another red light

"I don't think I can do it"

"We're almost there"

Rose doesn't tell the doctor what the situation is. She doesn't mention the home, the paperwork, the good family waiting somewhere. Once they arrive, it all happens too fast, Baker howling, May shouting and waving down an orderly, who comes rushing with a wheelchair, the receptionist at the front desk handing Rose a clipboard and asking her to please sit down and fill out the information.

She writes down the basics—Baker's name, birthday, their home address—and then hands it to May, tells her to finish the rest if she can. Rose can explain the whole thing later, if at all. How her daughter wasn't supposed to deliver at this particular hospital, how it was all arranged to happen differently, you see, there was a particular doctor and a social worker and a lovely family. Her daughter is a good girl, very smart, headed to Stanford, in fact, these things happen, yes, yes. The paperwork, nearly all of it signed, and everything has been put in order to ensure a very smooth transition. That can happen later. For now, it's just Rose and May and Baker, the way it maybe was meant to be.

In the waiting room, Baker's pain is relentless, earthshaking, white-knuckle wild.

"It *hurts*," Baker leans into May's shaking arms. "Make it *stop*."

"Just breathe, kid, just *breathe*." May attempts to demonstrate, exhaling forcefully into Baker's face.

"Stop breathing on me!"

"Sorry!"

A nurse finally arrives with a bright white stretcher, and Rose and May help Baker onto it between contractions. Baker squeezes May's hand as hard as she can, once more, and May grits her teeth and lets her. Rose looks at the nurse expectantly.

"My daughter is in *pain*. Help her!"

"We'll give her something," the nurse assures her. "She's gonna need it."

And then Baker is wheeled away, down a hallway, toward a pair of swinging doors. Rose calls out "I love you!" and then the doors are shut and the hallway is quiet.

Alone on the stretcher, Baker looks up at the faces above her. Just the eyes of the nurses, the doctor—everything else covered by blue masks, white caps covering hair. The ceiling is white, the lights too bright. She turns her head and sees rooms, people, closed doors with numbers and charts, open doors with drawn curtains, beeping machines.

One door has a mirror on it, and Baker catches a fast and shocking glimpse. She's an absolute mess, and it occurs to her that everyone must know. They saw her come in with just her mother and May; there's clearly no nice young father-to-be, no tight wedding ring on her swollen finger, no overnight bag packed with a new nightgown from Macy's. She's been wearing the same dress for days—it's soaked now—and she smells like woodsmoke and dirt and sweat. She looks like someone who's been sleeping in a forest, or a hippie commune. And that must be why none of the nurses will look her in the eyes.

"We call it twilight sleep," a man's voice says, and suddenly, there is the doctor. Suddenly they're in a room. Suddenly she's being moved onto a bed.

"This will help you out, young lady." A large syringe in his right hand.

"What is it," she manages to ask.

"Just a little cocktail. Morphine and scopolamine," he says in a singsong voice. "Calms you right down. Better than what they used in the old days. Chloroform—can you believe it!" He signals to the nurse, and in

10

9

8

7

6

5

4

3

She becomes just the body, the vessel, the vehicle. She is swirling blue, hazy gray, lavender and pink and purple. She is entering the portal, she is slipping down the hole, she is trying to call out to May and her mother but the words won't come, she is getting smaller and smaller until she is floating in the blackness, in universes far beyond.

And she doesn't feel a thing.

These drugs come with fever dreams.

She is in Paris, laughing with strangers on a damp sidewalk, when fire begins to fall from the sky.

She is in a rocking chair, in the middle of the night, singing to a small, swaddled demon.

She's inside of a television, ash raining on her hair, bombs bursting in air. Who knew they could be so beautiful, so bright? A police line behind her.

She is in a bloody hallway, trying to wake Kitty, and the sounds of heavy boots on the stairs get louder and louder.

She is Bertha in the attic, burning down the mansion.

She is Alice, flooding the world with her tears.

She is Sylvia, climbing out of the oven.

She is a doctor in a mask, performing abortions on an endless stream of beautiful, terrified girls.

She is a tangled cluster of cells, a dark whirlpool, a latch-hook rug, a ponderous house.

She is on the overpass, dropping a child off the edge.

She is down below, on the road, trying to catch it, traffic whizzing by. The center of the road is white and broken, cracking and breaking and spreading apart beneath her legs that pull and pull as she is split apart.

She doesn't feel a thing.

Not the blazing contortion of every muscle in her body,

the fire in her inner thighs as her legs are wrenched apart,

the deep prodding,

pushing, probing,

the gloved hands reaching in,

the cold metal forceps,

the pushing and the pulling

the stretching and the tearing

the pulling

the pulling

She doesn't feel the incision, the extra cut to make room for the large head, the shoulders so wide just like the father's.

When they pull the baby out, it doesn't cry or scream.

A nurse records the details: the length, the weight, the sex, the circumference of the head.

The baby is normal

The baby is healthy

The baby is wrapped in a blanket and wheeled out of the room.

The doctor pulls the curtain, and steps back to Baker to sew up her bleeding body.

*S*he wakes the way one does from a nightmare: sudden, yanked back, still afraid. An ache that fades in and out like a radio signal, a throbbing between her legs but no real sensation yet. The blurred figure of a nurse comes closer, wipes her face with a damp cloth, then brings a cup of water and a tray of pills to her lips.

"Take these. Yellow ones to stop the milk, green to stop the tears."

When she wakes again, Rose is there, holding her hand, whispering hello. There are other figures in the room—Ms. White? Gerald? The doctor? She can't tell. Her eyes still blur.

She tries to speak. "Where is my . . . ?" but the drugs are strong, and she is out again before she can finish the sentence that no one wants to hear anyway.

The next time she wakes, she is alone in the room. No Rose, no nurses, no blurred figures. She scans the walls for a clock. A calendar. A window. She knows nothing of time, whether it's day or night, how long she's been here or where the Bun is. The baby. She musters great strength to prop herself up on her elbows—*everything* hurts—and she looks down. Her big round middle is *gone*. No longer a great balloon, rising. It is deflated, flopped over. Empty. She touches her chest and feels the bandage, wrapped tight over her hospital gown. She fumbles until it unties, and the release is sweet.

Her breasts swell, and she can breathe. She falls back against the pillow and waits.

When the drugs fully wear off, and she wakes for good, a new nurse is there.

"Just starting my shift." She seems nicer than the others. "How you doing?"

Baker blinks. "Where is my baby?"

The nurse glances over at the door, then speaks softly. "In the nursery. Legally it's still yours, so you *can* go see it. But I gotta be honest with you, I don't recommend it. I've seen what that does for girls. It's not pretty. Better to just take these meds, get some rest, get out of here. But that's just my opinion."

"Thank you. But where . . . ?"

"Out the door and to the right. End of the hall." She hands Baker a clothespin. "Don't forget to close the back of your gown. Your body's been through a lot. Best to keep it covered up for a while."

The hallway is long and glaring bright white. Baker creeps along slow, dizzy, nauseous, bare feet on cold floor, thighs on fire with every step. The lights above buzz; the floor is waxed to a brilliant shine. It is a hallway from a dream, endless and echoing, with identical doors on either side. But it does have an end: up ahead, she sees a big wide window. A room full of babies.

Will I recognize mine?

The word *mine* makes her stop. The nurse's words in her head: *Legally, it's still yours.*

She touches the wall to keep herself steady. Her feet are heavy. She wants to move faster, but she can't. She has to get there before someone sees her, before Rose comes, or Ms. White.

When she finally reaches the big window, she gasps. So many white bassinets lined up neat, adorned with blue or pink bows, labeled with little signs: BABY GIRL PETERS; BABY BOY SMITH. And inside each bassinette are all these little faces, round and new and clean, bodies bound in blankets. Some sleep, a few cry, some stare out into the new world, their tiny mouths opening and closing like the mouths of goldfish, waiting for it all to begin.

She looks and looks until she sees it: back row, on the left, the sign that just says BABY GIRL.

No last name.

Baby Girl.

It's a girl.

A girl, a girl, another girl in the world, an actual human *girl*. Her heart shudders in the cage of her aching chest. Baby Girl is red-faced, wailing. Baby Girl is angry; she is lonely. Baby Girl wants to be picked up. And every inch of Baker's body, every bit of skin and blood and tissue and bone and marrow, every microscopic cell and speck, wants desperately to reach through the glass and hold her. She could smash the window. It's what she's supposed to do.

A nurse approaches. She bends over and picks up Baby Girl, cradles the bundle close, and begins to sway and sing. Then she looks up at Baker. Their eyes lock, and Baker can tell she knows who Baker is. She *knows*. The nurse coos to Baby Girl again, then looks around, as if checking to see if she's being watched by anyone but the unwed mother on the other side of the glass. Then she begins to walk Baby Girl to the window, still singing, bouncing gently.

There she is: the Bun, the Baby Girl. Baker's daughter's face, right there, clear and pink and soft and real. She has stopped crying. She is no longer alone. She is so beautiful.

And then another sound: the door at the far end of the hallway opens, slow, and Rose is there, face mottled and puffy, fresh lipstick applied, escorted by another nurse. She begins to call out, to walk toward her daughter, but Baker holds up her hand and shakes her head. *Stop*, she is saying. *This is for me.*

Baker turns back to the window, to Baby Girl, and the same trembling hand that told her mother *no* now reaches out and waves.

Hello, she whispers, *hello Baby Girl.*

She looks at the nurse and leans in closer, her fingers and face against the cold glass, her breath making a fog circle, Rose and the nurse still stopped at the end of the hospital hallway, unable to see what's taking place.

I love you.

It's a deep rush, a full tingling swell, a dam breaking, as Baker's breasts grow hard and full and the front of her gown becomes soaked with the milk that drips, then gushes, as if her heart were cracking open. It runs a warm river down her aching belly, to her thighs, in thin lines down her shins, all the way to her feet, the sterile linoleum floor. It pools there, a lake of sustenance, an ocean of everything.

It's okay, mouths the nurse, and Baker whispers *Thank you.* Then she turns and walks back toward her room. She smiles at her mother.

She knows what she is going to do.

Author's Note

One Christmas Eve, when I was in my early twenties, my mother burst into tears and told me she had something to confess: ten years before I was born, when she was eighteen, she'd been pregnant. Twice. Back-to-back, with different men, but the story was the same each time: my grandparents had sent her away to private homes, where she lived in secret until giving birth. She'd surrendered both babies in closed adoptions, and her family never spoke of it again. Like the many other young, mostly white, middle-class women who got pregnant and "went away" in the decades before *Roe v. Wade,* she was told to put it behind her and move on. But she never stopped thinking about those two children. And she didn't tell anyone else, aside from my father, until she shared her story with me.

I was blindsided. I was heartbroken for my mother and couldn't comprehend how she'd been living with such an enormous secret all this time. I was also fascinated. As a feminist, a history lover, and a recent recipient of an undergraduate degree in Women's Studies, I was stunned that I'd never heard of any stories like this before. I had marched for abortion rights; I had done volunteer clinic defense at my local Planned Parenthood. I'd read feminist oral histories in college seminars and pored over my mother's first-edition copy of *Our Bodies, Ourselves.* I knew the phrase "back-alley abortion" and I understood the significance of the coat hanger image. And yet I had never heard of pregnant girls being disappeared, sent away from their parents and friends and schools, to give birth, surrender their babies, and then return to their former lives like nothing had happened. I couldn't believe that this was the experience of more than 1.5 million young American women in the 1950s and '60s—including my very own mother.

I was raised in the San Francisco Bay Area, in the tie-dyed shadows of the hippie era, so I was struck by how this hidden history contrasted with the assumptions I'd had about my free-spirited parents and the era I'd idealized as so progressive and liberatory. My conception of the women's movement and the sexual revolution came from the images I'd seen in magazines and movies: young women wearing bell-bottoms at rock concerts and marching on college campuses, rejecting the homogeny of their parents' generation. I thought of the photos I'd seen of my own mother from those years: a free-spirited woman wearing beads and fringe, with long dark hair and a toothy smile that masked the sense of failure and loss that plagued her. These women had access to so much more than their mothers did—what could it have been like if they'd had even more? If they'd been trusted to know their own bodies, to make their own choices? And what other secrets were these women hiding?

And then *I* became a mother, and my desire to understand my mother's story, and the stories of all these young women, intensified. I began to work on early iterations of this book, and my mom began to share more details with me, slowly unburdening herself of the silent shame she'd been carrying for decades. How she feared that she'd "ruined everything"; how little she knew about her own body, about sex, about abortion; how she thought of those babies so often and felt sad every year on their birthdays. I knew I wanted to create a fictional world inspired by, but not based on, my mother's experiences, so I began doing research. I conducted interviews, read books and blogs and online forums, and had countless conversations with friends, colleagues, community members. As I learned about people's sisters, neighbors, cousins, best friends, classmates, I realized how many women had similar experiences. I also saw how therapeutic it was for my mom to hear about them as I brought those stories back to her, each one a tiny light that seemed to fill the dark space where the secrets had lived.

One evening, we went to a theater in San Francisco to see a screening of *A Girl Like Her,* a short documentary based on Ann Fessler's groundbreaking collection of oral histories, *The Girls Who Went Away.* As multiple women recounted their experiences with maternity homes and secret adoptions onscreen, the audience— mostly women in their sixties and seventies, my mother's peers— reacted audibly, crying, cheering, gasping, and *hmm*ing in agreement and recognition throughout the film. As we walked outside after it ended, we saw a group of women standing under the marquee, hugging and crying. I watched as my mom made eye contact with these total strangers, paused for a moment, then walked right into their arms for a collective embrace. They didn't need to say a word: for possibly the first time in their lives, their secret was understood, their grief was validated. Finally, they were not alone.

Where the Girls Were is a historical novel, set in the past, when America was on the brink of so much change—including the legalization of abortion. I wish this book was being published in a different present. I wish these stories didn't feel like such essential cautionary tales, that the idea of young women not having access to birth control, safe abortion, and shame-free reproductive experiences wasn't so . . . relevant. So dire. The liberated legal future that Baker and the other girls dreamed of did come—and now it's gone, stripped away by the patriarchal desire to control our bodies, and our families. But that can—that must!—remain our vision, our goal. And to reclaim that future, we have to know our histories— especially the ones that have been hidden.

Through Baker's story—and my mother's, and the women who embraced her, and the thousands of women like them—I hope to show what can happen, and what can change, when we are allowed to make our own decisions, and tell our own stories. When we resist being silenced, and when we insist on agency and empowerment, instead of obedience and shame. My hope is that you come away from this book inspired to speak up, to tell your truths, and to be lovingly, respectfully curious of the stories of those around you—especially the women who came before you. I hope you feel moved to question the versions of history that you think you already know, and to challenge the forces that seek to control us. And I hope that you consider what it might look like for you to take a stand, in the name of all mothers, and the choice, freedom, and love they deserve.

Acknowledgments

It has taken many years, drafts, and conversations to get this book here, in your hands.

My deepest and most heartfelt gratitude to everyone who has offered their time, edits, feedback, curiosity, guidance, and care, including Kelli Auerbach, Jessica Blank, Amra Brooks, Caro de Robertis, Ariel Gore, Micah Perks, Jenn Phillips, Jason Pontius, Leslie van Every, Shoshana Von Blanckensee, and the members of the Secret Conversation who knew Baker during her most formative years.

Thank you for the quiet spaces to write and think: the Sullivan and Mayer-Stewart families, Western Hills Garden, and the Wellstone Center in the Redwoods. Thank you to my collaborators who worked on other books with me but always asked about this one, too: W. Kamau Bell, Dr. Kelly Rafferty, and Miriam Klein Stahl. Chiara Barzini, you're my forever writing partner.

Thank you to Ann Fessler, Leslie J. Reagan, and Rickie Solinger, for your invaluable work and critical scholarship on the history of women's bodies and reproductive rights in America.

Clio Seraphim, you are an incredible editor. Thank you for seeing Baker, and for parenting this book as you became a mother yourself. To Whitney Frick, Leila Tejani, Peter Dyer, Corina Diez, and the entire Dial team—I'm thrilled to be with you all. As always, I'm forever indebted to my agents: Jesseca Salky and the legendary Charlotte Sheedy.

To Nancy Murray, Jerry Murray, and Doug Schatz: my family, yes, but also my favorite hippies. Thank you for your wild stories and historically accurate fact-checking. Aubrey Schatz/Auntie, you're the absolute best. Dave and Greg: How amazing to know you. This story is yours, too.

To my beloved, inspiring, hilarious children: How incredibly lucky am I to get to be your mom?

To my wife Lauren: thank you for your wild patience. There's no one I would rather spend my one precious life with.

Most of all: to my mother, Barbara Schatz—thank you for telling and trusting us.

And to the girls who went through it, who grew up to become the women who will never forget. I'm so grateful to all of you who have bravely found ways to share your stories. To those who still hold your secrets close: you are not alone.

About the Author

KATE SCHATZ is the *New York Times* bestselling author of the "Rad Women" book series, including *Rad American Women A–Z, Rad Women Worldwide, Rad Girls Can,* and *Rad American History A–Z,* as well as *Do the Work!: An Antiracist Activity Book,* with W. Kamau Bell. Her novella, *Rid of Me: A Story,* was published as part of the cult favorite 33⅓ series. She lives with her wife and children in California.

kateschatz.com
Instagram: @k8shots
kateschatz.substack.com

About the Type

This book was set in Fairfield, the first typeface from the hand of the distinguished American artist and engraver Rudolph Ruzicka (1883–1978). Ruzicka was born in Bohemia (in the present-day Czech Republic) and came to America in 1894. He set up his own shop, devoted to wood engraving and printing, in New York in 1913 after a varied career working as a wood engraver, in photoengraving and banknote printing plants, and as an art director and freelance artist. He designed and illustrated many books, and was the creator of a considerable list of individual prints—wood engravings, line engravings on copper, and aquatints.

Books Driven by the Heart

Sign up for our newsletter
and find more you'll love:

thedialpress.com

⊙ @THEDIALPRESS

▶ @THEDIALPRESS